Of Time and the River

Of Time and the River

BOOKS I-III

A LEGEND OF MAN'S HUNGER
IN HIS YOUTH

by

Thomas Wolfe

"Who knoweth the spirit of man that goeth upward, and the spirit of the beast that goeth downward to the earth?"

CHARLES SCRIBNER'S SONS

NEW YORK

To

MAXWELL EVARTS PERKINS

A GREAT EDITOR AND A BRAVE AND HONEST MAN, WHO STUCK TO
THE WRITER OF THIS BOOK THROUGH TIMES OF BITTER HOPELESS-
NESS AND DOUBT AND WOULD NOT LET HIM GIVE IN TO HIS OWN
DESPAIR, A WORK TO BE KNOWN AS "OF TIME AND THE RIVER" IS
DEDICATED WITH THE HOPE THAT ALL OF IT MAY BE IN SOME WAY
WORTHY OF THE LOYAL DEVOTION AND THE PATIENT CARE WHICH
A DAUNTLESS AND UNSHAKEN FRIEND HAS GIVEN TO EACH PART OF
IT, AND WITHOUT WHICH NONE OF IT COULD HAVE BEEN WRITTEN

*"Crito, my dear friend Crito, that, be-
lieve me, that is what I seem to hear, as
the Corybants hear flutes in the air, and
the sourd of those words rings and
echoes in my ears and I can listen to
nothing else."*

Contents

BOOK ONE

PAGE

ORESTES: FLIGHT BEFORE FURY   I

BOOK TWO

YOUNG FAUSTUS   87

BOOK THREE

TELEMACHUS   325

Of Time and the River

"Kennst du das Land, wo die Zitronen blühn,
Im dunkeln Laub die Gold-Orangen glühn,
Ein sanfter Wind vom blauen Himmel weht,
Die Myrte still und hoch der Lorbeer steht,
Kennst du es wohl?
          Dahin! Dahin
Möcht' ich mit dir, O mein Geliebter, ziehn!

Kennst du das Haus, auf Säulen ruht sein Dach,
Es glänzt der Saal, es schimmert das Gemach,
Und Marmorbilder stehn und sehn mich an:
Was hat man dir, du armes Kind, getan?
Kennst du es wohl?
          Dahin! Dahin
Möcht' ich mit dir, O mein Beschützer, ziehn!

Kennst du den Berg und seinen Wolkensteg?
Das Maultier sucht im Nebel seinen Weg,
In Höhlen wohnt der Drachen alte Brut,
Es stürzt der Fels und über ihn die Flut:
Kennst du ihn wohl?
          Dahin! Dahin
Geht unser Weg; *O Vater, lass uns ziehn!*"

BOOK I

ORESTES: FLIGHT BEFORE FURY

. . . of wandering forever and the earth again . . . of seed-time, bloom, and the mellow-dropping harvest. And of the big flowers, the rich flowers, the strange unknown flowers.

Where shall the weary rest? When shall the lonely of heart come home? What doors are open for the wanderer? And which of us shall find his father, know his face, and in what place, and in what time, and in what land? Where? Where the weary of heart can abide forever, where the weary of wandering can find peace, where the tumult, the fever, and the fret shall be forever stilled.

Who owns the earth? Did we want the earth that we should wander on it? Did we need the earth that we were never still upon it? Whoever needs the earth shall have the earth: he shall be still upon it, he shall rest within a little place, he shall dwell in one small room forever.

Did he feel the need of a thousand tongues that he sought thus through the moil and horror of a thousand furious streets? He shall need a tongue no longer, he shall need no tongue for silence and the earth: he shall speak no word through the rooted lips, the snake's cold eye will peer for him through sockets of the brain, there will be no cry out of the heart where wells the vine.

The tarantula is crawling through the rotted oak, the adder lisps against the breast, cups fall: but the earth will endure forever. The flower of love is living in the wilderness, and the elmroot threads the bones of buried lovers.

The dead tongue withers and the dead heart rots, blind mouths crawl tunnels through the buried flesh, but the earth will endure forever; hair grows like April on the buried breast and from the sockets of the brain the death flowers grow and will not perish.

O flower of love whose strong lips drink us downward into death, in all things far and fleeting, enchantress of our twenty thousand days, the brain will madden and the heart be twisted, broken by her kiss, but glory, glory, glory, she remains: Immortal love, alone and aching in the wilderness, we cried to you: You were not absent from our loneliness.

I

About fifteen years ago, at the end of the second decade of this century, four people were standing together on the platform of the railway station of a town in the hills of western Catawba. This little station, really just a suburban adjunct of the larger town which, behind the concealing barrier of a rising ground, swept away a mile or two to the west and north, had become in recent years the popular point of arrival and departure for travellers to and from the cities of the east, and now, in fact, accommodated a much larger traffic than did the central station of the town, which was situated two miles westward around the powerful bend of the rails. For this reason a considerable number of people were now assembled here, and from their words and gestures, a quietly suppressed excitement that somehow seemed to infuse the drowsy mid-October afternoon with an electric vitality, it was possible to feel the thrill and menace of the coming train.

An observer would have felt in the complexion of this gathering a somewhat mixed quality—a quality that was at once strange and familiar, alien and native, cosmopolitan and provincial. It was not the single native quality of the usual crowd that one saw on the station platforms of the typical Catawba town as the trains passed through. This crowd was more mixed and varied, and it had a strong coloring of worldly smartness, the element of fashionable sophistication that one sometimes finds in a place where a native and alien population have come together. And such an inference was here warranted: the town of Altamont a mile or so away was a well-known resort and the mixed gathering on the station platform was fairly representative of its population. But all of these people, both strange and native, had been drawn here by a common experience, an event which has always been of first interest in the lives of all Americans. This event is the coming of the train.

It would have been evident to an observer that of the four people who were standing together at one end of the platform three—the two women and the boy—were connected by the relationship of blood. A stranger would have known instantly that the boy and the young woman were brother and sister and that the woman was their mother. The relation-

3

ship was somehow one of tone, texture, time, and energy, and of the grain and temper of the spirit. The mother was a woman of small but strong and solid figure. Although she was near her sixtieth year, her hair was jet black and her face, full of energy and power, was almost as smooth and unlined as the face of a girl. Her hair was brushed back from a forehead which was high, white, full, and naked-looking, and which, together with the expression of her eyes, which were brown, and rather worn and weak, but constantly thoughtful, constantly reflective, gave her face the expression of straight grave innocence that children have, and also of strong native intelligence and integrity. Her skin was milk white, soft of texture, completely colorless save for the nose, which was red, broad and fleshy at the base, and curiously masculine.

A stranger seeing her for the first time would have known somehow that the woman was a member of a numerous family, and that her face had the tribal look. He would somehow have felt certain that the woman had brothers and that if he could see them, they would look like her. Yet, this masculine quality was not a quality of sex, for the woman, save for the broad manlike nose, was as thoroughly female as a woman could be. It was rather a quality of tribe and character—a tribe and character that was decisively masculine.

The final impression of the woman might have been this:—that her life was somehow above and beyond a moral judgment, that no matter what the course or chronicle of her life may have been, no matter what crimes of error, avarice, ignorance, or thoughtlessness might be charged to her, no matter what suffering or evil consequences may have resulted to other people through any act of hers, her life was somehow beyond these accidents of time, training, and occasion, and the woman was as guiltless as a child, a river, an avalanche, or any force of nature whatsoever.

The younger of the two women was about thirty years old. She was a big woman, nearly six feet tall, large, and loose of bone and limb, almost gaunt. Both women were evidently creatures of tremendous energy, but where the mother suggested a constant, calm, and almost tireless force, the daughter was plainly one of those big, impulsive creatures of the earth who possess a terrific but undisciplined vitality, which they are ready to expend with a whole-souled and almost frenzied prodigality on any person, enterprise, or object which appeals to their grand affections.

This difference between the two women was also reflected in their faces. The face of the mother, for all its amazing flexibility, the startled animal-like intentness with which her glance darted from one object to another, and the mobility of her powerful and delicate mouth, which she pursed and convolved with astonishing flexibility in such a way as to show the constant reflective effort of her mind, was nevertheless the face of a woman whose spirit had an almost elemental quality of patience, fortitude and calm.

The face of the younger woman was large, high-boned, and generous and already marked by the frenzy and unrest of her own life. At moments it bore legibly and terribly the tortured stain of hysteria, of nerves stretched to the breaking point, of the furious impatience, unrest and dissonance of her own tormented spirit, and of impending exhaustion and collapse for her overwrought vitality. Yet, in an instant, this gaunt, strained, tortured, and almost hysterical face could be transformed by an expression of serenity, wisdom, and repose that would work unbelievably a miracle of calm and radiant beauty on the nervous, gaunt, and tortured features.

Now, each in her own way, the two women were surveying the other people on the platform and the new arrivals with a ravenous and absorptive interest, bestowing on each a wealth of information, comment, and speculation which suggested an encyclopædic knowledge of the history of every one in the community.

"—Why, yes, child," the mother was saying impatiently, as she turned her quick glance from a group of people who at the moment were the subject of discussion—"that's what I'm telling you!—Don't I know? . . . Didn't I grow up with all those people? . . . Wasn't Emma Smathers one of my girlhood friends? . . . That boy's not this woman's child at all. He's Emma Smathers' child by that first marriage."

"Well, that's news to me," the younger woman answered. "That's certainly news to me. I never knew Steve Randolph had been married more than once. I'd always thought that all that bunch were Mrs. Randolph's children."

"Why, of course not!" the mother cried impatiently. "She never had any of them except Lucille. All the rest of them were Emma's children. Steve Randolph was a man of forty-five when he married her. He'd been a widower for years—poor Emma died in childbirth when Bernice was born—nobody ever thought he'd marry again and nobody ever expected this woman to have any children of her own for she was almost as old as he was—why, yes!—hadn't she been married before, a widow, you know, when she met him, came here after her first husband's death from some place way out West—oh, Wyoming, or Nevada or Idaho, one of those States, you know—and had never had chick nor child, as the saying goes—till she married Steve. And that woman was every day of forty-four years old when Lucille was born."

"Uh-huh! . . . Ah-hah!" the younger woman muttered absently, in a tone of rapt and fascinated interest, as she looked distantly at the people in the other group, and reflectively stroked her large chin with a big, bony hand. "So Lucille, then, is really John's half-sister?"

"Why, of course!" the mother cried. "I thought every one knew that. Lucille's the only one that this woman can lay claim to. The rest of them were Emma's."

"—Well, that's certainly news to me," the younger woman said slowly as before. "It's the first *I* ever heard of it. . . . And you say she was forty-four when Lucille was born?"

"Now, she was all of *that,*" the mother said. "I know. And she may have been even older."

"Well," the younger woman said, and now she turned to her silent husband, Barton, with a hoarse snigger, "it just goes to show that while there's life there's hope, doesn't it? So cheer up, honey," she said to him, "we may have a chance yet." But despite her air of rough banter her clear eyes for a moment had a look of deep pain and sadness in them.

"Chance!" the mother cried strongly, with a little scornful pucker of the lips—"why, of course there is! If I was your age again I'd have a dozen—and never think a thing of it." For a moment she was silent, pursing her reflective lips. Suddenly a faint sly smile began to flicker at the edges of her lips, and turning to the boy, she addressed him with an air of sly and bantering mystery:

"Now, boy," she said—"there's lots of things that you don't know . . . you always thought you were the last—the youngest—didn't you?"

"Well, wasn't I?" he said.

"H'm!" she said with a little scornful smile and an air of great mystery — "There's lots that I could tell you——"

"Oh, my God!" he groaned, turning towards his sister with an imploring face. "More mysteries! . . . The next thing I'll find that there were five sets of triplets after I was born— Well, come on, Mama," he cried impatiently. "Don't hint around all day about it. . . . What's the secret now—how many were there?"

"H'm!" she said with a little bantering, scornful, and significant smile.

"O Lord!" he groaned again— "Did she ever tell you what it was?" Again he turned imploringly to his sister.

She snickered hoarsely, a strange high-husky and derisive falsetto laugh, at the same time prodding him stiffly in the ribs with her big fingers:

"Hi, hi, hi, hi, hi," she laughed. "More spooky business, hey? You don't know the half of it. She'll be telling you next you were only the fourteenth."

"H'm!" the older woman said, with a little scornful smile of her pursed lips. "Now I could tell him more than that! The fourteenth! Pshaw!" she said contemptuously—"I could tell him——"

"O God!" he groaned miserably. "I knew it! . . . I don't want to hear it."

"K, k, k, k, k," the younger woman snickered derisively, prodding him in the ribs again.

"No, sir," the older woman went on strongly—"and that's not all either!— Now, boy, I want to tell you something that you didn't know," and as she spoke she turned the strange and worn stare of her serious brown eyes on him, and levelled a half-clasped hand, fingers pointing, a gesture loose, casual, and instinctive and powerful as a man's.— "There's a lot I could tell you that you never heard. Long years after you were born, child—why, at the time I took you children to the Saint Louis Fair—" here her face grew stern and sad, she pursed her lips strongly and shook her head with a short convulsive movement—"oh, when I think of it—to think what I went through—oh, awful, awful, you know," she whispered ominously.

"Now, Mama, for God's sake, I don't want to hear it!" he fairly shouted, beside himself with exasperation and foreboding. "God-damn it, can we have no peace—even when I go away!" he cried bitterly and illogically. "Always these damned gloomy hints and revelations—this Pentland spooky stuff," he yelled—"this damned I-could-if-I-wanted-to-tell-you air of mystery, horror, and damnation!" he shouted incoherently. "Who cares? What does it matter?" he cried, adding desperately, "I don't want to hear about it— No one cares."

"Why, child, now, I was only saying—" she began hastily and diplomatically.

"All right, all right, all right," he muttered. "I don't care——"

"But, as I say, now," she resumed.

"I don't care!" he shouted. "Peace, peace, peace, peace, peace," he muttered in a crazy tone as he turned to his sister. "A moment's peace for all of us before we die. A moment of peace, peace, peace."

"Why, boy, I'll vow," the mother said in a vexed tone, fixing her reproving glance on him, "what on earth's come over you? You act like a regular crazy man. I'll vow you do."

"A moment's peace!" he muttered again, thrusting one hand wildly through his hair. "I beg and beseech you for a moment's peace before we perish!"

"K, k, k, k, k," the younger woman snickered derisively, as she poked him stiffly in the ribs— "There's no peace for the weary. It's like that river that goes on forever," she said with a faint loose curving of lewd humor around the edges of her generous big mouth— "Now you see, don't you?" she said, looking at him with this lewd and challenging look. "You see what it's like now, don't you? . . . *You're* the lucky one! *You* got away! You're smart enough to go way off somewhere to college—to Boston—Harvard—anywhere—but *you're* away from it. You get it for a short time when you come home. How do you think *I* stand it?" she said challengingly. "I have to hear it *all* the time. . . . Oh, *all* the time, and *all* the time, and *all* the time!" she said with a kind of weary desperation. "If they'd only leave me *alone* for five minutes some time I think I'd be able to pull myself together, but it's this way *all* the time and *all* the time and *all* the time. You see, don't you?"

But now, having finished, in a tone of hoarse and panting exasperation, her frenzied protest, she relapsed immediately into a state of marked, weary, and dejected resignation.

"Well, I know, I know," she said in a weary and indifferent voice. ". . . Forget about it. . . . Talking does no good. . . . Just try to make the best of it the little time you're here. . . . I used to think something could be done about it . . . but I know different now," she muttered, although she would have been unable to explain the logical meaning of these incoherent and disjointed phrases.

"Hah? . . . What say?" the mother now cried sharply, darting her glances from one to another with the quick, startled, curiously puzzled intentness of an animal or a bird. "What say?" she cried sharply again, as no one answered. "I thought——"

But fortunately, at this moment, this strange and disturbing flash in which had been revealed the blind and tangled purposes, the powerful and obscure impulses, the tormented nerves, the whole tragic perplexity of soul which was of the very fabric of their lives, was interrupted by a

commotion in one of the groups upon the platform, and by a great guffaw of laughter which instantly roused these three people from this
painful and perplexing scene, and directed their startled attention to the
place from which the laughter came.

And now again they heard the great guffaw—a solid "Haw! Haw!
Haw!" which was full of such an infectious exuberance of animal good-
nature that other people on the platform began to smile instinctively,
and to look affectionately towards the owner of the laugh.

Already, at the sound of the laugh, the young woman had forgotten
the weary and dejected resignation of the moment before, and with
an absent and yet eager look of curiosity in her eyes, she was staring
towards the group from which the laugh had come, and herself now
laughing absently, she was stroking her big chin in a gesture of meditative curiosity, saying:

"Hah! Hah! Hah! . . . That's George Pentland. . . . You can tell
him anywhere by his laugh."

"Why, yes," the mother was saying briskly, with satisfaction. "That's
George all right. I'd know him in the dark the minute that I heard that
laugh.— And say, what about it? He's always had it—why, ever since he
was a kid-boy—and was going around with Steve. . . . Oh, he'd come
right out with it anywhere, you know, in Sunday school, church, or
while the preacher was sayin' prayers before collection that big, loud
laugh, you know, that you could hear, from here to yonder, as the sayin'
goes. . . . Now I don't know where it comes from—none of the others
ever had it in our family; now we all liked to laugh well enough, but I
never heard no such laugh as that from any of 'em—there's one thing
sure, Will Pentland never laughed like that in his life— Oh, Pett, you
know! Pett!"—a scornful and somewhat malicious look appeared on the
woman's face as she referred to her brother's wife in that whining and
affected tone with which women imitate the speech of other women
whom they do not like—"Pett got so mad at him one time when he
laughed right out in church that she was goin' to take the child right
home an' whip him.—Told me, says to me, you know—'Oh, I could
wring his neck! He'll disgrace us all,' she says, 'unless I cure him of it,'
says, 'He burst right out in that great roar of his while Doctor Baines
was sayin' his prayers this morning until you couldn't hear a word the
preacher said.' Said, 'I was so mortified to think he could do a thing like
that that I'd a-beat the blood right out of him if I'd had my buggy whip,'
says, 'I don't know where it comes from'—oh, sneerin'-like, you know,"

the woman said, imitating the other woman's voice with a sneering and viperous dislike—" 'I don't know where it comes from unless it's some of that common Pentland blood comin' out in him'—'Now you listen to me,' I says; oh, I looked her in the eye, you know"—here the woman looked at her daughter with the straight steady stare of her worn brown eyes, illustrating her speech with the loose and powerful gesture of the half-clasped finger-pointing hand—" 'you listen to me. I don't know where that child gets his laugh,' I says, 'but you can bet your bottom dollar that he never got it from his father—or any other Pentland that I ever heard of—for none of them ever laughed that way—Will, or Jim, or Sam, or George, or Ed, or Father, or even Uncle Bacchus,' I said—'no, nor old Bill Pentland either, who was that child's great-grandfather—for I've seen an' heard 'em all,' I says. 'And as for this common Pentland blood you speak of, Pett'—oh, I guess I talked to her pretty straight, you know," she said with a little bitter smile, and the short, powerful, and convulsive tremor of her strong pursed lips—" 'as for that common Pentland blood you speak of, Pett,' I says, 'I never heard of that either—for we stood high in the community' I says, 'and we all felt that Will was lowerin' himself when he married a Creasman!' "

"Oh, you didn't say that, Mama, surely not," the young woman said with a hoarse, protesting, and yet abstracted laugh, continuing to survey the people on the platform with a bemused and meditative curiosity, and stroking her big chin thoughtfully as she looked at them, pausing from time to time to grin in a comical and rather formal manner, bow graciously, and murmur:

"How-do-you-do? ah-hah? How-do-you-do, Mrs. Willis?"

"Haw! Haw! Haw!" Again the great laugh of empty animal good nature burst out across the station platform, and this time George Pentland turned from the group of which he was a member and looked vacantly around him, his teeth bared with savage joy, as, with two brown fingers of his strong left hand, he dug vigorously into the muscular surface of his hard thigh. It was an animal reflex, instinctive and unconscious, habitual to him in moments of strong mirth.

He was a powerful and handsome young man in his early thirties, with coal-black hair, a strong thick neck, powerful shoulders, and the bull vitality of the athlete. He had a red, sensual, curiously animal and passionate face, and when he laughed his great guffaw, his red lips were bared over two rows of teeth that were white and regular and solid as ivory.

—But now, the paroxysm of that savage and mindless laughter having left him, George Pentland had suddenly espied the mother and her children, waved to them in genial greeting, and excusing himself from his companions—a group of young men and women who wore the sporting look and costume of "the country club crowd"—he was walking towards his kinsmen at an indolent swinging stride, pausing to acknowledge heartily the greetings of people on every side, with whom he was obviously a great favorite.

As he approached, he bared his strong white teeth again in greeting, and in a drawling, rich-fibred voice, which had unmistakably the Pentland quality of sensual fulness, humor, and assurance, and a subtle but gloating note of pleased self-satisfaction, he said:

"Hello, Aunt Eliza, how are you? Hello, Helen—how are you, Hugh?" he said in his high, somewhat accusing, but very strong and masculine voice, putting his big hand in an easy affectionate way on Barton's arm. "Where the hell you been keepin' yourself anyway?" he said accusingly. "Why don't some of you folks come over to see us sometime? Ella was askin' about you all the other day—wanted to know why Helen didn't come around more often."

"Well, George, I tell you how it is," the young woman said with an air of great sincerity and earnestness. "Hugh and I have intended to come over a hundred times, but life has been just one damned thing after another all summer long. If I could only have a moment's peace— if I could only get away by myself for a moment—if *they* would only leave me *alone* for an hour at a time, I think I could get myself together again—do you know what I mean, George?" she said hoarsely and eagerly, trying to enlist him in her sympathetic confidence—"If they'd only do something for *themselves* once in a while—but they *all* come to me when anything goes wrong—they never let me have a moment's peace—until at times I think I'm going crazy—I get *queer*—funny, you know," she said vaguely and incoherently. "I don't know whether something happened Tuesday or last week or if I just imagined it." And for a moment her big gaunt face had the dull strained look of hysteria.

"The strain on her has been very great this summer," said Barton in a deep and grave tone. "It's—it's," he paused carefully, deeply, searching for a word, and looked down as he flicked an ash from his long cigar, "it's—been too much for her. Everything's on her shoulders," he concluded in his deep grave voice.

"My God, George, what is it?" she said quietly and simply, in the tone of one begging for enlightenment. "Is it going to be this way all our lives? Is there never going to be any peace or happiness for us? Does it always have to be this way? Now I want to ask you—is there nothing in the world but trouble?"

"Trouble!" he said derisively. "Why, I've had more trouble than any one of you ever heard of. . . . I've had enough to kill a dozen people . . . but when I saw it wasn't goin' to kill me, I quit worryin'. . . . So you do the same thing," he advised heartily. "Hell, don't *worry*, Helen! . . . It never got you anywhere. . . . You'll be all right," he said. "You got nothin' to worry over. You don't know what trouble is."

"Oh, I'd be all right, George—I think I could stand anything—all the rest of it—if it wasn't for Papa. . . . I'm almost crazy from worrying about him this summer. There were three times there when I knew he was gone. . . . And I honestly believe I pulled him back each time by main strength and determination—do you know what I mean?" she said hoarsely and eagerly—"I was just determined not to let him go. If his heart had stopped beating I believe I could have done something to make it start again—I'd have stood over him and blown my breath into him—got my blood into him—shook him," she said with a powerful, nervous movement of her big hands—"anything just to keep him alive."

"She's—she's—saved his life—time after time," said Barton slowly, flicking his cigar ash carefully away, and looking down deeply, searching for a word.

"He'd—he'd—have been a dead man long ago—if it hadn't been for her."

"Yeah—I know she has," George Pentland drawled agreeably. "I know you've sure stuck by Uncle Will—I guess he knows it, too."

"It's not that I mind it, George—you know what I mean?" she said eagerly. "Good heavens! I believe I could give away a dozen lives if I thought it was going to save his life! . . . But it's the *strain* of it. . . . Month after month . . . year after year . . . lying awake at night wondering if he's all right over there in that back room in Mama's house—wondering if he's keeping warm in that old cold house——"

"Why, no, child," the older woman said hastily. "I kept a good fire burnin' in that room all last winter—that was the warmest room in the whole place—there wasn't a warmer——"

But immediately she was engulfed, swept aside, obliterated in the flood-tide of the other's speech.

"—Wondering if he's sick or needs me—if he's begun to bleed again—

oh! George, it makes me sick to think about it—that poor old man left there all alone, rotting away with that awful cancer, with that horrible smell about him all the time—everything he wears gets simply *stiff* with that rotten corrupt matter— Do you know what it is to wait, wait, wait, year after year, and year after year, never knowing when he's going to die, to have him hang on by a thread until it seems you've lived forever—that there'll never be an end—that you'll never have a chance to live your own life—to have a moment's peace or rest or happiness yourself? My God, does it always have to be this way? . . . Can I never have a moment's happiness? . . . Must they *always* come to me? Does *everything* have to be put on my shoulders? . . . Will you tell me that?" Her voice had risen to a note of frenzied despair. She was glaring at her cousin with a look of desperate and frantic entreaty, her whole gaunt figure tense and strained with the stress of her hysteria.

"That's—that's the trouble now," said Barton, looking down and searching for the word. "She's . . . She's . . . made the goat for every one. . . . She . . . she has to do it all. . . . That's . . . that's the thing that's got her down."

"Not that I mind—if it will do any good. . . . Good heavens, Papa's life means more to me than anything on earth. . . . I'd keep him alive at any cost as long as there was a breath left in him. . . . But it's the strain of it, the *strain* of it—to wait, to wait year after year, to feel it hanging over you all the time, never to know when he will die—always the *strain,* the strain—do you see what I mean, George?" she said hoarsely, eagerly, and pleadingly. "You see, don't you?"

"I sure do, Helen," he said sympathetically, digging at his thigh, and with a swift, cat-like grimace of his features. "I know it's been mighty tough on you. . . . How is Uncle Will now?" he said. "Is he any better?"

"Why, yes," the mother was saying, "he seemed to improve—" but she was cut off immediately.

"Oh, yes," the daughter said in a tone of weary dejection. "He pulled out of this last spell and got well enough to make the trip to Baltimore— we sent him back a week ago to take another course of treatments. . . . But it does no real good, George. . . . They can't cure him. . . . We know that now. . . . They've told us that. . . . It only prolongs the agony. . . . They help him for a little while and then it all begins again. . . . Poor old man!" she said, and her eyes were wet. "I'd give everything I have—my own blood, my own life—if it would do him any good—but,

George, he's gone!" she said desperately. "Can't you understand that? . . . They can't save him! . . . Nothing can save him! . . . Papa's a dead man now!"

George looked gravely sympathetic for a moment, winced swiftly, dug hard fingers in his thigh, and then said:

"Who went to Baltimore with him?"

"Why, Luke's up there," the mother said. "We had a letter from him yesterday—said Mr. Gant looks much better already—eats well, you know, has a good appetite—and Luke says he's in good spirits. Now——"

"Oh, Mama, for heaven's sake!" the daughter cried. "What's the use of talking that way? . . . He's not getting any better. . . . Papa's a sick man—dying—good God! Can no one ever get that into their heads!" she burst out furiously. "Am I the only one that realizes how sick he is?"

"No, now I was only sayin'," the mother began hastily— "Well, as I say, then," she went on, "Luke's up there with him—and Gene's on his way there now—he's goin' to stop off there tomorrow on his way up north to school."

"Gene!" cried George Pentland in a high, hearty, bantering tone, turning to address the boy directly for the first time. "What's all this I hear about you, son?" He clasped his muscular hand around the boy's arm in a friendly but powerful grip. "Ain't one college enough for you, boy?" he drawled, becoming deliberately ungrammatical and speaking good-naturedly but with a trace of the mockery which the wastrel and ne'er-do-well sometimes feels towards people who have had the energy and application required for steady or concentrated effort. "Are you one of those fellers who needs two or three colleges to hold him down?"

The boy flushed, grinned uncertainly, and said nothing.

"Why, son," drawled George in his hearty, friendly and yet bantering tone, in which a note of malice was evident, "you'll be gettin' so educated an' high brow here before long that you won't be able to talk to the rest of us at all. . . . You'll be floatin' around there so far up in the clouds that you won't even see a roughneck like me, much less talk to him"— As he went on with this kind of sarcasm, his speech had become almost deliberately illiterate, as if trying to emphasize the superior virtue of the rough, hearty, home-grown fellow in comparison with the bookish scholar.

"—Where's he goin' to this time, Aunt Eliza?" he said, turning to her questioningly, but still holding the boy's arm in his strong grip. "Where's he headin' for now?"

"Why," she said, stroking her pursed serious mouth with a slightly puzzled movement, "he says he's goin' to Harvard. I reckon," she said, in the same puzzled tone, "it's all right—I guess he knows what he's about. Says he's made up his mind to go—I told him," she said, and shook her head again, "that I'd send him for a year if he wanted to try it—an' then he'll have to get out an' shift for himself. We'll see," she said. "I reckon it's all right."

"Harvard, eh?" said George Pentland. "Boy, you *are* flyin' high! . . . What you goin' to do up there?"

The boy, furiously red of face, squirmed, and finally stammered: "Why . . . I . . . guess . . . I guess I'll do some studying!"

"You *guess* you will!" roared George. "You'd damn well *better* do some studying—I bet your mother'll take it out of your hide if she finds you loafin' on her money."

"Why, yes," the mother said, nodding seriously, "I told him it was up to him to make the most of this——"

"Harvard, eh!" George Pentland said again, slowly looking his cousin over from head to foot. "Son, you're flyin' high, you are! . . . Now don't fly so high you never get back to earth again! . . . You know the rest of us who didn't go to Harvard still have to walk around upon the ground down here," he said. "So don't fly too high or we may not even be able to see you!"

"George! George!" said the young woman in a low tone, holding one hand to her mouth, and bending over to whisper loudly as she looked at her young brother. "Do you think any one could fly very high with a pair of feet like that?"

George Pentland looked at the boy's big feet for a moment, shaking his head slowly in much wonderment.

"Hell, no!" he said at length. "He'd never get off the ground! . . . But if you cut 'em off," he said, "he'd go right up like a balloon, wouldn't he? Haw! Haw! Haw! Haw!" The great guffaw burst from him, and grinning with his solid teeth, he dug blindly at his thigh.

"Hi, hi, hi, hi, hi," the sister jeered, seeing the boy's flushed and angry face and prodding him derisively in the ribs— "This is our Harvard boy! k, k, k, k!"

"Don't let 'em kid you, son," said George now in an amiable and friendly manner. "Good luck to you! Give 'em hell when you get up there! . . . You're the only one of us who ever had guts enough to go through college, and we're proud of you! . . . Tell Uncle Bascom and

Aunt Louise and all the rest of 'em hello for me when you get to Boston. . . . And remember me to your father and Luke when you get to Baltimore. . . . Good-bye, 'Gene—I've got to leave you now. Good luck, son," and with a friendly grip of his powerful hand he turned to go. "You folks come over sometime—all of you," he said in parting. "We'd like to see you." And he went away.

At this moment, all up and down the platform, people had turned to listen to the deep excited voice of a young man who was saying in a staccato tone of astounded discovery:

"You *don't* mean it! . . . You *swear* she did! . . . And *you* were there and saw it with your *own* eyes! . . . Well, if that don't beat all I ever heard of! . . . I'll be *damned!*" after which ejaculation, with an astounded falsetto laugh, he looked about him in an abstracted and unseeing manner, thrust one hand quickly and nervously into his trouser's pocket in such a way that his fine brown coat came back, and the large diamond-shaped pin of the Delta Kappa Epsilon fraternity was revealed, and at the same time passing one thin nervous hand repeatedly over the lank brown hair that covered his small and well-shaped head, and still muttering in tones of stupefied disbelief—"Lord! Lord! . . . What do you know about that?" suddenly espied the woman and her two children at the other end of the platform, and without a moment's pause, turned on his heel, and walked towards them, at the same time muttering to his astonished friends:

"Wait a minute! . . . Some one over here I've got to speak to! . . . Back in a minute!"

He approached the mother and her children rapidly, at his stiff, prim and somewhat lunging stride, his thin face fixed eagerly upon them, bearing towards them with a driving intensity of purpose as if the whole interest and energy of his life was focussed on them, as if some matter of the most vital consequence depended on his reaching them as soon as possible. Arrived, he immediately began to address the other youth without a word of greeting or explanation, bursting out with the sudden fragmentary explosiveness that was part of him:

"Are you taking this train, too? . . . Are you going today? . . . Well, what did you decide to do?" he demanded mysteriously in an accusing and challenging fashion. "Have you made up your mind yet? . . ."

"Pett Barnes says you've decided on Harvard. Is that it?"

"Yes, it is."

"Lord, Lord!" said the youth, laughing his falsetto laugh again. "I don't see how you can! . . . You'd better come on with me. . . . What ever got into your head to do a thing like that?" he said in a challenging tone. "Why do you want to go to a place like that?"

"Hah? What say?" The mother who had been looking from one to the other of the two boys with the quick and startled attentiveness of an animal, now broke in:

"You know each other. . . . Hah? . . . You're taking this train, too, you say?" she said sharply.

"Ah-hah-hah!" the young man laughed abruptly, nervously; grinned, made a quick stiff little bow, and said with nervous engaging respectfulness: "Yes, Ma'am! . . . Ah-hah-hah! . . . How d'ye do! . . . How d'ye do, Mrs. Gant?" He shook hands with her quickly, still laughing his broken and nervous "ah-hah-hah"—"How d'ye do," he said, grinning nervously at the younger woman and at Barton. "Ah-hah-hah! How d'ye do!"

The older woman still holding his hand in her rough worn clasp looked up at him a moment calmly, her lips puckered in tranquil meditation:

"Now," she said quietly, in the tone of a person who refuses to admit failure, "I know you. I know your face. Just give me a moment and I'll call you by your name."

The young man grinned quickly, nervously, and then said respectfully in his staccato speech:

"Yes, Ma'am. . . . Ah-hah-hah. . . . Robert Weaver."

"*Ah-h,* that's *so!*" she cried, and shook his hand with sudden warmth. "You're Robert Weaver's boy, of course."

"Ah-hah-hah!" said Robert, with his quick nervous laugh. "Yes, Ma'am. . . . That's right. . . . Ah-hah-hah. . . . Gene and I went to school together. We were in the same class at the University."

"Why, of course!" she cried in a tone of complete enlightenment, and then went on in a rather vexed manner, "I'll *vow!* I knew you all along! I knew that I'd seen you just as soon as I saw your face! Your name just slipped my mind a moment—and then, of course, it all flashed over me. . . . You're Robert Weaver's boy! . . . And you *are,*" she still held his hand in her strong, motherly and friendly clasp, and looking at him with a little sly smile hovering about the corners of her mouth, she was silent a moment, regarding him quizzically—"now, boy," she said quietly, "you may think I've got a pretty poor memory for names and faces—but I want to tell you something that may surprise you. . . . I know more about you than you think I do. Now," she said, "I'm going to tell you something and you can tell me if I'm right."

"Ah-hah-hah!" said Robert respectfully. "Yes, Ma'am."

"You were born," she went on slowly and deliberately, "on September 2nd, 1898, and you are just two years and one month and one day older than this boy here—" she nodded to her own son. "Now you can tell me if I'm right or wrong."

"Ah-hah-hah!" said Robert. "Yes, Ma'am. . . . That's right. . . . You're absolutely right," he cried, and then in an astounded and admiring tone, he said: "Well, I'll declare. . . . If that don't beat all! . . . How on earth did you ever remember it!" he cried in an astonished tone that obviously was very gratifying to her vanity.

"Well, now, I'll tell you," she said with a little complacent smile— "I'll tell you how I *know*. . . . I remember the day you were born, boy— because it was on that very day that one of my own children—my son, Luke—was allowed to get up out of bed after havin' typhoid fever. . . . That very day, sir, when Mr. Gant came home to dinner, he said—'Well, I was just talking to Robert Weaver on the street and everything's all right. His wife gave birth to a baby boy this morning and he says she's out of danger.' And I know I said to him, 'Well, then, it's been a lucky day for both of us. McGuire was here this morning and he said Luke is now well enough to be up and about. He's out of danger.'—And I reckon," she went on quietly, "that's why the date made such an impression on me—of course, Luke had been awfully sick," she said gravely, and shook her head, "we thought he was goin' to die more than once—so when the doctor came and told me he was out of danger— well, it was a day of rejoicin' for me, sure enough. But that's how I know—September 2nd, 1898—that's when it was, all right, the very day when you were born."

"Ah-hah-hah!" said Robert. "That is certainly right. . . . Well, if that don't beat all!" he cried with his astounded and engaging air of surprise. "The most remarkable thing I ever heard of!" he said solemnly.

"So the next time you see your father," the woman said, with the tranquil satisfaction of omniscience, "you tell him that you met Eliza Pentland—he'll know who *I* am, boy—I can assure you—for we were born and brought up within five miles from each other and you can tell him that she knew you right away, and even told you to the hour and minute the day when you were born! . . . You tell him that," she said.

"Yes, Ma'am!" said Robert respectfully, "I certainly will! . . . I'll tell him! . . . That is certainly a remarkable thing. . . . Ah-hah-hah! . . . Beats all I ever heard of! . . . Ah-hah-hah," he kept bowing and smiling to the young woman and her husband, and muttering "ah-hah-hah! . . . Pleased to have met you. . . . Got to go now: some one over here I've got to see . . . but I'll certainly tell him . . . ah-hah-hah. . . . Gene, I'll see you on the train. . . . Good-bye. . . . Good-bye. . . . Glad to have met you all. . . . Ah-hah-hah. . . . Certainly a remarkable thing. . . . Good-bye!" and turning abruptly, he left them, walking rapidly along at his stiff, prim, curiously lunging stride.

The younger woman looked after the boy's tall form as he departed, stroking her chin in a reflective and abstracted manner:

"So that's Judge Robert Weaver's son, is it? . . . Well," she went on, nodding her head vigorously in a movement of affirmation. "He's all right. . . . He's got good manners. . . . He looks and acts like a gentleman. . . . You can see he's had a good bringing up. . . . I like him!" she declared positively again.

"Why, yes," said the mother, who had been following the tall retreating form with a reflective look, her hands loose-folded at her waist—"Why, yes," she continued, nodding her head in a thoughtful and conceding manner that was a little comical in its implications— "He's a good-looking all-right sort of a boy. . . . And he certainly seems to be intelligent enough." She was silent for a moment, pursing her lips thoughtfully and then concluded with a little nod—"Well, now, the boy may be all right. . . . I'm not saying that he isn't. . . . He may turn out all right, after all."

"All right?" her daughter said, frowning a little and showing a little annoyance, but with a faint lewd grin around the corners of her mouth —"what do you mean by all right, Mama? Why, of course he's all right. . . . What makes you think he's not?"

The other woman was silent for another moment: when she spoke again, her manner was tinged with portent, and she turned and looked at her daughter a moment in a sudden, straight and deadly fashion before she spoke:

"Now, child," she said, "I'm going to tell you: perhaps everything will turn out all right for that boy—I hope it does—but——"

"Oh, my God!" the younger woman laughed hoarsely but with a shade of anger, and turning, prodded her brother stiffly in the ribs. "Now we'll get it!" she sniggered, prodding him, "k-k-k-k-k! What do you call it?" she said with a lewd frowning grin that was indescribably comic in its evocations of coarse humor—"the low down?—the dirt?— Did you ever know it to fail?—The moment that you meet any one, and up comes the family corpse."

"—Well, now, child, I'm not saying anything against the boy—perhaps it won't touch him—maybe he'll be the one to escape—to turn out all right—but——"

"Oh, my God!" the younger woman groaned, rolling her eyes around in a comical and imploring fashion. "Here it comes."

"You are too young to know about it yourself," the other went on gravely—"you belong to another generation—you don't know about it— but I *do*." She paused again, shook her pursed lips with a convulsive pucker of distaste, and then looking at her daughter again in her straight and deadly fashion, said slowly, with a powerful movement of the hand:

"There's been insanity in that boy's family for generations back!"

"Oh, my God! I knew it!" the other groaned.

"Yes, sir!" the mother said implacably—"and two of his aunts—Robert Weaver's own sisters died raving maniacs—and Robert Weaver's mother herself was insane for the last twenty years of her life up to the hour of her death—and I've heard tell that it went back——"

"Well, deliver me," the younger woman checked her, frowning, speaking almost sullenly. "I don't want to hear any more about it. . . . It's a mighty funny thing that they all seem to get along now—better than we do . . . so let's let bygones be bygones . . . don't dig up the past."

Turning to her brother with a little frowning smile, she said wearily: "Did you ever know it to fail? . . . They know it all, don't they?" she said mysteriously. "The minute you meet any one you like, they spill the dirt. . . . Well, I don't care," she muttered. "You stick to people like that. . . . He looks like a nice boy and—" with an impressed look over towards Robert's friends, she concluded, "he goes with a nice crowd. . . . You stick to that kind of people. I'm all for him."

Now the mother was talking again: the boy could see her powerful and delicate mouth convolving with astonishing rapidity in a series of pursed thoughtful lips, tremulous smiles, bantering and quizzical jocosities, old sorrow and memory, quiet gravity, the swift easy fluency of tears that the coming of a train always induced in her, thoughtful seriousness, and sudden hopeful speculation.

"Well, boy," she was now saying gravely, "you are going—as the sayin' goes—" here she shook her head slightly, strongly, rapidly with powerful puckered lips, and instantly her weak worn eyes of brown were wet with tears "—as the sayin' goes—to a strange land—a stranger among strange people.—It may be a long long time," she whispered in an old husky tone, her eyes tear-wet as she shook her head mysteriously with a brave pathetic smile that suddenly filled the boy with rending pity, anguish of the soul, and a choking sense of exasperation and of woman's unfairness "—I hope we are all here when you come back again. . . . I hope you find us all alive. . . ." She smiled bravely, mysteriously, tearfully. "You never know," she whispered, "you never know."

"Mama," he could hear his voice sound hoarsely and remotely in his throat, choked with anguish and exasperation at her easy fluency of sorrow, "—Mama—in Christ's name! Why do you have to act like this every time some one goes away! . . . I beg of you, for God's sake, not to do it!"

"Oh, stop it! Stop it!" his sister said in a rough, peremptory and yet kindly tone to the mother, her eyes grave and troubled, but with a faint rough smile about the edges of her generous mouth. "He's not going away forever! Why, good heavens, you act as if some one is dead! Boston's not so far away you'll never see him again! The trains are running every day, you know. . . . Besides," she said abruptly and with an assurance that infuriated the boy, "he's not going today, anyway. Why, you haven't any intention of going today, you know you haven't," she said to him. "He's been fooling you all along," she now said, turning to the mother with an air of maddening assurance. "He has no idea of taking that train. He's going to wait over until tomorrow. I've known it all along."

The boy went stamping away from them up the platform, and then came stamping back at them while the other people on the platform grinned and stared.

"Helen, in God's name!" he croaked frantically. "Why do you start that when I'm all packed up and waiting here at the God-damned station for the train! You *know* I'm going away today!" he yelled, with a sudden sick desperate terror in his heart as he thought that something might now come in the way of going. "You *know* I am! Why did we come here? What in Christ's name are we waiting for if you don't think I'm going?"

The young woman laughed her high, husky laugh which was almost deliberately irritating and derisive—"Hi! Hi! Hi! Hi! Hi!"—and prodded him in the ribs with her large stiff fingers. Then, almost wearily, she turned away, plucking at her large chin absently, and said: "Well, have it your own way! It's your own funeral! If you're determined to go today, no one can stop you. But I don't see why you can't just as well wait over till tomorrow."

"Why, yes!" the mother now said briskly and confidently. "That's exactly what I'd do if I were you! . . . Now, it's not going to do a bit of harm to any one if you're a day or so late in gettin' there. . . . Now I've never been there myself," she went on in her tone of tranquil sarcasm, "but I've always heard that Harvard University was a good big sort of place—and I'll bet you'll find," the mother now said gravely, with a strong slow nod of conviction—"I'll bet you'll find that it's right there where it always was when you get there. I'll bet you find they haven't moved a foot," she said, "and let me tell you something, boy," she now continued, looking at him almost sternly, but with the ghost of a smile about her powerful and delicate mouth "—now I haven't had your education and I reckon I don't know as much about universities as you do— but I've never heard of one yet that would run a feller away for bein' a day late as long as he's got money enough to pay his tuition. . . . Now you'll find 'em waitin' for you when you get there—and *you'll get in,*" she said slowly and powerfully. "You don't have to worry about that— they'll be glad to see you, and they'll take you in a hurry when they see you've got the price."

"Now, Mama," he said in a quiet frenzied tone, "I beg of you, for God's sake, please, not to——"

"All right, all right," the mother answered hastily in a placating tone, "I was only sayin'——"

"If you will kindly, please, for God's sake——"

"K-k-k-k-k!" his sister snickered, poking him in the ribs.

But now the train was coming. Down the powerful shining tracks a half mile away, the huge black snout of the locomotive swung slowly round the magnificent bend and flare of the rails that went into the railway yards of Altamont two miles away, and with short explosive thunders of its squat funnel came barging slowly forward. Across the golden pollenated haze of the warm autumnal afternoon they watched it with numb lips and an empty hollowness of fear, delight, and sorrow in their hearts.

And from the sensual terror, the ecstatic tension of that train's approach, all things before, around, about the boy came to instant life, to such sensuous and intolerable poignancy of life as a doomed man might feel who looks upon the world for the last time from the platform of the scaffold where he is to die. He could feel, taste, smell, and see everything with an instant still intensity, the animate fixation of a vision seen instantly, fixed forever in the mind of him who sees it, and sense the clumped dusty autumn masses of the trees that bordered the tracks upon the left, and smell the thick exciting hot tarred caulking of the tracks, the dry warmth and good worn wooden smell of the powerful railway ties, and see the dull rusty red, the gaping emptiness and joy of a freight car, its rough floor whitened with soft siltings of thick flour, drawn in upon a spur of rusty track behind a warehouse of raw concrete blocks, and see with sudden desolation, the warehouse flung down rawly, newly, there among the hot, humid, spermy, nameless, thick-leaved field-growth of the South.

Then the locomotive drew in upon them, loomed enormously above them, and slowly swept by them with a terrific drive of eight-locked pistoned wheels, all higher than their heads, a savage furnace-flare of heat, a hard hose-thick hiss of steam, a moment's vision of a lean old head, an old gloved hand of cunning on the throttle, a glint of demon hawk-eyes fixed forever on the rails, a huge tangle of gauges, levers, valves, and throttles, and the goggled blackened face of the fireman, lit by an intermittent hell of flame, as he bent and swayed with rhythmic swing of laden shovel at his furnace doors.

The locomotive passed above them, darkening the sunlight from their faces, engulfing them at once and filling them with terror, drawing the souls out through their mouths with the God-head of its instant absoluteness, and leaving them there, emptied, frightened, fixed forever, a cluster of huddled figures, a bough of small white staring faces, upturned, silent, and submissive, small, lonely, and afraid.

Then as the heavy rust-black coaches rumbled past, and the wheels ground slowly to a halt, the boy could see his mother's white stunned face beside him, the naked startled innocence of her eyes, and feel her rough worn clasp upon his arm, and hear her startled voice, full of apprehension, terror, and surprise, as she said sharply:

"Hah? What say? Is this his train? I thought——"

It was his train and it had come to take him to the strange and secret heart of the great North that he had never known, but whose austere and lonely image, whose frozen heat and glacial fire, and dark stern beauty had blazed in his vision since he was a child. For he had dreamed and hungered for the proud unknown North with that wild ecstasy, that intolerable and wordless joy of longing and desire, which only a Southerner can feel. With a heart of fire, a brain possessed, a spirit haunted by the strange, secret and unvisited magic of the proud North, he had always known that some day he should find it—his heart's hope and his father's country, the lost but unforgotten half of his own soul,—and take it for his own.

And now that day had come, and these two images—call them rather lights and weathers of man's soul—of the world-far, lost and lonely South, and the fierce, the splendid, strange and secret North were swarming like a madness through his blood. And just as he had seen a thousand images of the buried and silent South which he had known all his life, so now he had a vision of the proud fierce North with all its shining cities, and its tides of life. He saw the rocky sweetness of its soil and its green loveliness, and he knew its numb soft prescience, its entrail-stirring ecstasy of coming snow, its smell of harbors and its traffic of proud ships.

He could not utter what he wished to say and yet the wild and powerful music of those two images kept swelling in him and it seemed that the passion of their song must burst his heart, explode the tenement of bright blood and agony in which they surged, and tear the sinews of his life asunder unless he found some means to utter them.

But no words came. He only knew the image of man's loneliness, a feeling of sorrow, desolation, and wild mournful secret joy, longing and desire, as sultry, moveless and mysterious in its slow lust as the great rivers of the South themselves. And at the same moment that he felt this wild and mournful sorrow, the slow, hot, secret pulsings of desire, and breathed the heavy and mysterious fragrance of the lost South again, he felt suddenly and terribly, its wild strange pull, the fatal absoluteness of its world-lost resignation.

Then, with a sudden feeling of release, a realization of the incredible escape that now impended for him, he knew that he was waiting for the train, and that the great life of the North, the road to freedom, solitude and the enchanted promise of the golden cities was now before him. Like a dream made real, a magic come to life, he knew that in another hour he would be speeding world-ward, life-ward, North-ward out of the enchanted, time-far hills, out of the dark heart and mournful mystery of the South forever.

And as that overwhelming knowledge came to him, a song of triumph, joy, and victory so savage and unutterable, that he could no longer hold it in his heart was torn from his lips in a bestial cry of fury, pain, and ecstasy. He struck his arms out in the shining air for loss, for agony, for joy. The whole earth reeled about him in a kaleidoscopic blur of shining rail, massed heavy greens, and white empetalled faces of the staring people.

And suddenly he was standing there among his people on the platform of the little station. All things and shapes on earth swam back into their proper shape again, and he could hear his mother's voice, the broken clatter of the telegraph, and see, there on the tracks, the blunt black snout, the short hard blasts of steam from its squat funnel, the imminent presence, the enormous bigness of the train.

II

The journey from the mountain town of Altamont to the tower-masted island of Manhattan is not, as journeys are conceived in America, a long one. The distance is somewhat more than 700 miles, the time required to make the journey a little more than twenty hours. But so relative are the qualities of space and time, and so complex and multiple their shifting images, that in the brief passage of this journey one may live a life, share instantly in 10,000,000 other ones, and see pass before his eyes the infinite panorama of shifting images that make a nation's history.

First of all, the physical changes and transitions of the journey are strange and wonderful enough. In the afternoon one gets on the train and with a sense of disbelief and wonder sees the familiar faces, shapes, and structures of his native town recede out of the last fierce clasp of life and vision. Then, all through the waning afternoon, the train is toiling down around the mountain curves and passes. The great shapes of the hills, embrowned and glowing with the molten hues of autumn, are all about him: the towering summits, wild and lonely, full of joy and strangeness and their haunting premonitions of oncoming winter soar above him, the gulches, gorges, gaps, and wild ravines, fall sheer and suddenly away with a dizzy terrifying steepness, and all the time the great train toils slowly down from the mountain summits with the sinuous turnings of an enormous snake. And from the very toiling slowness of the train, together with the terrific stillness and nearness of the marvellous hills, a relation is established, an emotion evoked, which it is impossible to define, but which, in all its strange and poignant mingling of wild sorrow and joy, grief for the world that one is losing, swelling triumph at the thought of the strange new world that one will find, is instantly familiar, and has been felt by every one.

The train toils slowly round the mountain grades, the short and power-ful blasts of its squat funnel sound harsh and metallic against the sides of rocky cuts. One looks out the window and sees cut, bank, and gorge slide slowly past, the old rock wet and gleaming with the water of some buried mountain spring. The train goes slowly over the perilous and dizzy height of a wooden trestle; far below, the traveller can see and hear the clean foaming clamors of rock-bright mountain water; beside the track, before his little hut, a switchman stands looking at the train with the slow wondering gaze of the mountaineer. The little shack in which he lives is stuck to the very edge of the track above the steep and perilous ravine. His wife, a slattern with a hank of tight drawn hair, a snuff-stick in her mouth, and the same gaunt, slow wondering stare her husband has, stands in the doorway of the shack, holding a dirty little baby in her arms.

It is all so strange, so near, so far, so terrible, beautiful, and instantly familiar, that it seems to the traveller that he must have known these people forever, that he must now stretch forth his hand to them from the windows and the rich and sumptuous luxury of the pullman car, that he must speak to them. And it seems to him that all the strange and bitter miracle of life—how, why, or in what way, he does not know—is in that instant greeting and farewell; for once seen, and lost the moment that he sees it, it is his forever and he can never forget it. And then the slow toiling train has passed these lives and faces and is gone, and there is something in his heart he cannot say.

At length the train has breached the last great wall of the soaring ranges, has made its slow and sinuous descent around the powerful bends and cork-screws of the shining rails (which now he sees above him seven times) and towards dark, the lowland country has been reached. The sun goes down behind the train a tremendous globe of orange and pollen, the soaring ranges melt swiftly into shapes of smoky and enchanted purple, night comes—great-starred and velvet-breasted night—and now the train takes up its level pounding rhythm across the piedmont swell and convolution of the mighty State.

Towards nine o'clock at night there is a pause to switch cars and change engines at a junction town. The traveller, with the same feeling of wild unrest, wonder, nameless excitement and wordless expectancy, leaves the train, walks back and forth upon the platform, rushes into the little station lunch room or out into the streets to buy cigarettes, a sandwich—really just to feel this moment's contact with another town. He sees vast flares and steamings of gigantic locomotives on the rails, the seamed, blackened, lonely faces of the engineers in the cabs of their great engines, and a little later he is rushing again across the rude, mysterious visage of the powerful, dark, and lonely earth of old Catawba.

Toward midnight there is another pause at a larger town—the last stop in Catawba—again the feeling of wild unrest and nameless joy and sorrow. The traveller gets out, walks up and down the platform. sees the vast slow flare and steaming of the mighty engine, rushes into the station, and looks into the faces of all the people passing with the same sense of instant familiarity, greeting, and farewell,—that lonely, strange, and poignantly wordless feeling that Americans know so well. Then he is in the pullman again, the last outposts of the town have slipped away from him and the great train which all through the afternoon has travelled eastward from the mountains half across the mighty State, is now for the first time pointed northward, worldward, towards the secret borders of Virginia, towards the great world cities of his hope, the fable of his childhood legendry, and the wild and secret hunger of his heart, his spirit and his life.

Already the little town from which he came in the great hills, the faces of his kinsmen and his friends, their most familiar voices, the shapes of things he knew seem far and strange as dreams, lost at the bottom of the million-visaged sea-depth of dark time, the strange and bitter miracle of life. He cannot think that he has ever lived there in the far lost hills, or ever left them, and all his life seems stranger than the dream of time, and the great train moves on across the immense and lonely visage of America, making its great monotone that is the sound of silence and forever. And in the train, and in ten thousand little towns, the sleepers sleep upon the earth.

Then bitter sorrow, loneliness and joy come swelling to his throat—quenchless hunger rises from the adyts of his life and conquers him, and with wild wordless fury horsed upon his life, he comes at length, in dark mid-watches of the night, up to the borders of the old earth of Virginia.

Who has seen fury riding in the mountains? Who has known fury striding in the storm? Who has been mad with fury in his youth, given no rest or peace or certitude by fury, driven on across the earth by fury, until the great vine of the heart was broke, the sinews wrenched, the little tenement of bone, blood, marrow, brain, and feeling in which great fury raged, was twisted, wrung, depleted, worn out, and exhausted by the fury which it could not lose or put away? Who has known fury, how it came?

How have we breathed him, drunk him, eaten fury to the core, until we have him in us now and cannot lose him anywhere we go? It is a strange and subtle worm that will be forever feeding at our heart. It is a madness working in our brain, a hunger growing from the food it feeds upon, a devil moving in the conduits of our blood, it is a spirit wild and dark and uncontrollable forever swelling in our soul, and it is in the saddle now, horsed upon our lives, rowelling the spurs of its insatiate desire into our naked and defenseless sides, our owner, master, and the mad and cruel tyrant who goads us on forever down the blind and brutal tunnel of kaleidoscopic days at the end of which is nothing but the blind mouth of the pit and darkness and no more.

Then, then, will fury leave us, he will cease from those red channels of our life he has so often run, another sort of worm will work at that great vine, whereat he fed. Then, then, indeed, he must give over, fold his camp, retreat; there is no place for madness in a dead man's brain, no place for hunger in a dead man's flesh, and in a dead man's heart there is a place for no desire.

At what place of velvet-breasted night long long ago, and in what leafy darkened street of mountain summer, hearing the footsteps of approaching lovers in the night, the man's voice, low, hushed, casual, confiding, suddenly the low rich welling of a woman's laughter, tender and sensual in the dark, going, receding, fading, and then the million-noted silence of the night again? In what ancient light of fading day in a late summer; what wordless passion then of sorrow, joy, and ecstasy—was he betrayed to fury when it came?

Or in the black dark of some forgotten winter's morning, child of the storm and brother to the dark, alone and wild and secret in the night as he leaned down against the wind's strong wall towards Niggertown, blocking his folded papers as he went, and shooting them terrifically in the wind's wild blast against the shack-walls of the jungle-sleeping blacks, himself alone awake, wild, secret, free and stormy as the wild wind's blast, giving it howl for howl and yell for yell, with madness, and a demon's savage and exultant joy, up-welling in his throat! Oh, was he then, on such a night, betrayed to fury—was it then, on such a night, that fury came?

He never knew; it may have been a rock, a stone, a leaf, the moths of golden light as warm and moving in a place of magic green, it may have been the storm-wind howling in the barren trees, the ancient fading light of day in some forgotten summer, the huge unfolding mystery of undulant, on-coming night.

Oh, it might have been all this in the April and moist lilac darkness of some forgotten morning as he saw the clean line of the East cleave into morning at the mountain's ridge. It may have been the first light, bird-song, an end to labor and the sweet ache and pure fatigue of the lightened shoulder as he came home at morning hearing the single lonely hoof, the jinking bottles, and the wheel upon the street again, and smelled the early morning breakfast smells, the smoking wheat-cakes, and the pungent sausages, the steaks, biscuits, grits, and fried green apples, and the brains and eggs. It may have been the coil of pungent smoke upcurling from his father's chimney, the clean sweet gardens and the peach-bloom, apples, crinkled lettuce wet with dew, bloom and cherry bloom down drifting in their magic snow within his father's orchard, and his father's giant figure awake now and astir, and moving in his house!

Oh, ever to wake at morning knowing he was there! To feel the fire-full chimney-throat roar up a-tremble with the blast of his terrific fires, to hear the first fire crackling in the kitchen range, to hear the sounds of morning in the house, the smells of breakfast and the feeling of security never to be changed! Oh, to hear him prowling like a wakened lion below, the stertorous hoarse frenzy of his furious breath; to hear the ominous muttering mounting to faint howls as with infuriated relish he prepared the roaring invective of the morning's tirade, to hear him muttering as the coal went rattling out upon the fire, to hear him growling as savagely the flame shot up the trembling chimney-throat, to hear him muttering back and forth now like a raging beast, finally to hear his giant stride racing through the house prepared now, storming to the charge, and the well-remembered howl of his awakened fury as springing to the door-way of the back-room stairs he flung it open, yelling at them to awake.

Was it in such a way, one time as he awoke, and heard below his father's lion-ramp of morning that fury came? He never knew, no more than one could weave the great web of his life back through the brutal chaos of ten thousand furious days, unwind the great vexed pattern of his life to silence, peace, and certitude in the magic land of new beginnings, no return.

He never knew if fury had lain dormant all those years, had worked secret, silent, like a madness in the blood. But later it would seem to him that fury had first filled his life, exploded, conquered, and possessed him, that he first felt it, saw it, knew the dark illimitable madness of its power, one night years later on a train across Virginia.

III

It was a little before midnight when the youth entered the smoking room of the pullman where, despite the lateness of the hour, several men still sat. At just this moment the train had entered the State of Virginia although, of course, none of the men who sat there talking knew this.

It is true that some of them might have known had their interest and attention been directed toward this geographic fact, had they been looking for it. Just at this moment, indeed, as the train, scarcely slackening its speed, was running through the last of the Catawba towns, one of the men glanced up suddenly from the conversation in which he and the others were earnestly engaged, which was exclusively concerned with the fascinating, ever mounting prices of their property and the tempting profits undoubtedly to be derived from real-estate speculation in their native town. He had looked up quickly, casually, and absently, with that staggering indifference of prosperous men who have been so far, so often, on such splendid trains, that a trip across the continent at night toward the terrific city is no longer a grand adventure of their lives, but just a thing of custom, need, and even weariness, and who, therefore, rarely look out windows any more:

"What is this?" he said quickly. "Oh, Maysville, probably. Yes, I guess this must be Maysville," and had then returned vigorously from his brief inspection of the continent of night, a few lights, and a little town, to the enticing topic which had for several hours absorbed the interests of the group.

Nor was there any good reason why this traveller who had glanced so swiftly and indifferently from the window of the train should feel any greater interest than he showed. Certainly the briefest and most casual

inspection would have convinced the observer that, in Baedeker's celebrated phrase, there was "little here that need detain the tourist."
What the man saw in the few seconds of his observation was the quiet,
dusty and sparsely lighted street of a little town in the upper South. The
street was shaded by large trees and there were some level lawns, more
trees, and some white frame houses with spacious porches, gables, occasionally the wooden magnificence of Georgian columns.

On everything—trees, houses, foliage, yards, and street there was a
curious loneliness of departure and October, an attentive almost mournful waiting. And yet this dark and dusty street of the tall trees left
a haunting, curiously pleasant feeling of strangeness and familiarity.
One viewed it with a queer sudden ache in the heart, a feeling of friendship and farewell, and this feeling was probably intensified by the swift
and powerful movement of the train which seemed to slide past the town
almost noiselessly, its wheels turning without friction, sound, or vibrance
on the pressed steel ribbons of the rails, giving to a traveller, and particularly to a youth who was going into the secret North for the first time, a
feeling of illimitable and exultant power, evoking for him the huge
mystery of the night and darkness, and the image of ten thousand lonely
little towns like this across the continent.

Then the train slides by the darkened vacant-looking little station and
for a moment one has a glimpse of the town's chief square and business
centre. And as he sees it he is filled again with the same feeling of loneliness, instant familiarity, and departure. The square is one of those
anomalous, shabby-ornate, inept, and pitifully pretentious places that
one finds in little towns like these. But once seen, if only for this frac-
tion of a moment, from the windows of a train, the memory of it will
haunt one forever after.

And this haunting and lonely memory is due probably to the combina-
tion of two things: the ghastly imitation of swarming life and metropolitan gaiety in the scene, and the almost total absence of life itself. The
impression one gets, in fact, from that brief vision is one of frozen cataleptic silence in a world from which all life has recently been extinguished by some appalling catastrophe. The lights burn, the electric
signs wink and flash, the place is still horribly intact in all its bleak
prognathous newness, but all the people are dead, gone, vanished. The
place is a tomb of frozen silence, as terrifying in its empty bleakness as
those advertising backdrops one saw formerly in theatres, where the
splendid buildings, stores, and shops of a great street are painted in the

richest and most flattering colors, and where there is no sign of life whatever.

So was it here, save that here the illusion of the dead world gained a hideous physical reality by its stark, staring, nakedly concrete dimensions.

All this the boy had seen, or rather sensed, in the wink of an eye, a moment's vision of a dusty little street, a fleeting glimpse of a silent little square, a few hard lights, and then the darkness of the earth again —these half-splintered glimpses were all the boy could really see in the eye-wink that it took the train to pass the town. And yet, all these fragmentary things belonged so completely to all the life of little towns which he had known, that it was not as if he had seen only a few splintered images, but rather as if the whole nocturnal picture of the town was instantly whole and living in his mind.

Beyond the station, parked in a line against the curb is a row of empty motor cars, and he knows instantly that they have been left there by the patrons of the little moving-picture theatre which explodes out of the cataleptic silence of the left-hand side of the square into a blaze of hard white and flaming posters which seem to cover the entire façade. Even here, no movement of life is visible, but one who has lived and known towns like these feels for the first time an emotion of warmth and life as he looks at the gaudy, blazing bill-beplastered silence of that front.

For suddenly he seems to see the bluish blaze of carbon light that comes from the small slit-like vent-hole cut into the wall and can hear again—one of the loneliest and most haunting of all sounds—the rapid shuttering sound of the projection camera late at night, a sound lonely, hurried, unforgettable, coming out into those cataleptic squares of silence in the little towns—as if the operator is fairly racing through the last performance of the night like a weary and exhausted creature whose stale, over-driven life can find no joy in what is giving so much joy to others, and who is pressing desperately ahead toward the merciful rewards of food, sleep, and oblivion which are already almost in his grasp.

And as he remembers this, he also suddenly sees and knows the people in the theatre, and in that instant greets them, feels his lonely kinship with them, with the whole family of the earth, and says farewell. Small, dark, lonely, silent, thirsty, and insatiate, the people of the little town are gathered there in that one small cell of radiance, warmth, and joy. There for a little space they are united by the magic spell the theatre casts upon them. They are all dark and silent leaning forward like a single mind and congeries of life, and yet they are all separate too.

Yes, lonely, silent, for a moment beautiful, he knows the people of the town are there, lifting the small white petals of their faces, thirsty and insatiate, to that magic screen: now they laugh exultantly as their hero triumphs, weep quietly as the mother dies, the little boys cheer wildly as the rascal gets his due—they are all there in darkness, under immense immortal skies of time, small nameless creatures in a lost town on the mighty continent, and for an instant we have seen them, known them, said farewell.

Around the four sides of the square at even intervals, the new standards of the five-bulbed lamps cast down implacably upon those cataleptic pavements the cataleptic silence of their hard white light. And this, he knows, is called "the Great White Way," of which the town is proud. Somehow the ghastly, lifeless silence of that little square is imaged nowhere else so cruelly as in the harsh, white silence of these lights. For they evoke terribly, as nothing else can do, the ghastly vacancy of light without life. And poignantly, pitifully, and unutterably their harsh, white silence evokes the moth-like hunger of the American for hard, brilliant, blazing incandescence.

It is as if there may be in his soul the horror of the ancient darkness, the terror of the old immortal silences, which will not down and must be heard. It is as if he feels again the ancient fear of—what? Of the wilderness, the wet and lidless eye of shame and desolation feeding always on unhoused and naked sides. It is as if he fears the brutal revelation of his loss and loneliness, the furious, irremediable confusion of his huge unrest, his desperate and unceasing flight from the immense and timeless skies that bend above him, the huge, doorless and unmeasured vacancies of distance, on which he lives, on which, as helpless as a leaf upon a hurricane, he is driven on forever, and on which he cannot pause, which he cannot fence, wall, conquer, make his own.

Then the train, running always with its smooth, powerful, almost noiseless movement, has left the station and the square behind it. The last outposts of the town appear and vanish in patterns of small, lonely light, and there is nothing but huge and secret night before us, the lonely, everlasting earth, and presently Virginia.

And surely, now, there is little more to be seen. Surely, now, there is almost nothing that by day would be worthy of more than a glance from those great travellers who have ranged the earth, and known all its wild and stormy seas, and seen its rarest glories. And by night, now, there is nothing, nothing by night but darkness and a space we call Virginia through which the huge projectile of the train is hurtling onward in the dark.

Field and fold and gulch and hill and hollow, forest and stream and bridge and bank and cut, the huge earth, the rude earth, the wild, form-less, infinitely various, most familiar, ever haunting earth, the grand and casual earth that is so brown, so harsh, so dusty, so familiar, the strange and homely earth wrought in our blood, our brain, our heart, the earth that can never be forgotten or described, is flowing by us, by us, by us in the night.

What is it that we know so well and cannot speak? What is it that we want to say and cannot tell? What is it that keeps swelling in our hearts its grand and solemn music, that is aching in our throats, that is pulsing like a strange wild grape through all the conduits of our blood, that maddens us with its exultant and intolerable joy and that leaves us tongueless, wordless, maddened by our fury to the end?

We do not know. All that we know is that we lack a tongue that could reveal, a language that could perfectly express the wild joy swelling to a music in our heart, the wild pain welling to a strong ache in our throat, the wild cry mounting to a madness in our brain, the thing, the word, the joy we know so well, and cannot speak! All that we know is that the little stations whip by in the night, the straggling little towns whip by with all that is casual, rude, familiar, ugly, and unutterable. All that we know is that the earth is flowing by us in the darkness, and that this is the way the world goes—with a field and a wood and a field! And of the huge and secret earth all we know is that we feel with all our life its texture with our foot upon it.

All that we know is that having everything we yet hold nothing, that feeling the wild song of this great earth upwelling in us we have no words to give it utterance. All that we know is that here the passionate enigma of our lives is so bitterly expressed, the furious hunger that so haunts and hurts Americans so desperately felt—that being rich, we all are yet so poor, that having an incalculable wealth we have no way of spending it, that feeling an illimitable power we yet have found no way of using it.

Therefore we hurtle onward in the dark across Virginia, we hurtle onward in the darkness down a million roads, we hurtle onward driven by our hunger down the blind and brutal tunnel of ten thousand furious and kaleidoscopic days, the victims of the cruel impulse of a million chance and fleeting moments, without a wall at which to thrust the shoulder of our strength, a roof to hide us in our nakedness, a place to build on, or a door.

IV

As the boy entered the smoking compartment, the men who were talking together paused, and looked up at him briefly with the intent, curious, momentary stare of men interrupted in a conversation. The boy, a leggy creature racing into unfledged lengths of shank and arm and shoulder, fumbled nervously in his coat pocket for a package of cigarettes and then sat down abruptly on the upholstered leather seat beside one of the men.

The boy's manner betrayed that mixture of defiance and diffidence which a young man going out into the world for the first time feels in the presence of older and more experienced men. And this was the way he felt. And for this reason in the sharp and casual stare which the men fixed briefly on him there may have been unconsciously something affectionate and tender as each one recalled a moment of his own lost youth.

The boy felt the powerful movement of the train beneath him and the lonely austerity and mystery of the dark earth outside that swept past forever with a fanlike stroke, an immortal and imperturbable stillness. It seemed to him that these two terrific negatives of speed and stillness, the hurtling and projectile movement of the train and the calm silence of the everlasting earth, were poles of a single unity—a unity coherent with his destiny, whose source was somehow in himself.

It seemed to him that this incredible and fortunate miracle of his own life and fate had ordered all these accidental facts into coherent and related meanings. He felt that everything—the powerful movement of the train, the infinite mystery and lonely wildness of the earth, the feeling of luxury, abundance, and unlimited wealth that was stimulated by the rich furnishings of the pullman, and the general air of affluence of these prosperous men—belonged to him, had come out of his own life, and were ready to serve him at his own behest and control.

It seemed to him that the glorious moment for which his whole life had been shaped, and toward which every energy and desire in his spirit had been turned, was now here.

As that incredible knowledge came to him, a fury, wild, savage, wordless, pulsed through his blood and filled him with such a swelling and exultant joy as he had never known before. He felt the savage tongueless cry of pain and joy swell up and thicken in his throat, he felt a rending and illimitable power in him as if he could twist steel between his fingers, and he felt an almost uncontrollable impulse to yell into the faces of the men with a demonic glee.

Instead he just sat down quickly with an abrupt, half-defiant movement, lit his cigarette, and spoke to one of the men quickly and diffidently, saying:

"Hello, Mr. Flood."

For a moment, the man thus addressed said nothing, but sat staring at the boy stupidly with an expression of heavy surprise. He was a well-dressed but bloated-looking man in his fifties whose gross figure even in repose betrayed a gouty tenderness. His face, which had the satiny rosy texture, veinous and tender, that alcoholism and a daily massage can give, was brutally coarse and sensual, but was given a disturbing and decisive character by his bulging yellow eyeballs and the gross lewd mouth which, because of several large buck teeth whose discolored surfaces protruded under the upper lip, seemed always to be half opened and half smiling. And it was not a pleasant smile. It was a smile, faint, unmistakably sensual, and rather sly. It seemed to come from some huge choking secret glee and there was in it a quality that was jubilantly obscene.

For a moment more Mr. Flood stared through his bulging eyes at the boy who had just spoken to him, with an air of comical and stupid surprise. Then amiably, but with a puzzled undertone, he said gruffly:

"Hello. Oh, hello, son! How are you?"

And after looking at the boy a moment longer, he turned his attention to the other men again.

It was at just that season of the year when two events which are dear to the speculations of the American had absorbed the public interest. These events were baseball and politics, and at that moment both were thrillingly imminent. The annual baseball contests for "the championship of the world" were to begin within another day or two, and the national campaign for the election of the American president, which would be held in another month, was moving daily to its furious apogee of speeches, accusations, dire predictions, and impassioned promises. Both events gave the average American a thrill of pleasurable anticipation: his approach to both was essentially the same. It was the desire of

a man to see a good show, to "take sides" vigorously in an exciting contest—to be amused, involved as an interested spectator is involved, but
not to be too deeply troubled or concerned by the result.

It was just natural, therefore, that at the moment when the boy entered the smoking compartment of the train, the conversation of the men
assembled there should be chiefly concerned with these twin sports. As he
came in, there was a hum of voices, a sound of argument, and then he
could see the hearty red-faced man—the politician—shaking his head
dubiously and heard him say, with a protesting laugh:

"Ah-h, I don't know about that. From what I hear it's just the other
way. I was talking to a man from Tennessee the other day, and from
what he says, Cox is gaining everywhere. He said that a month ago he
wouldn't have given two cents for his chances, but now he thinks
he's going to carry the State."

"It's going to be close," another conceded. "He may win yet—but it
looks to me as if he's got a hard uphill fight on his hands. Tennessee always polls a big Republican vote—in some of those mountain districts
they vote two to one Republican—and this year it looks as if they're all
set for a change. . . . What do you think about it, Emmet?" he said,
appealing to the small, swarthy and important-looking little man, who
sat there, swinging his short little legs and chewing on a fat cigar with
an air of wise reflection.

"Well," that person answered slowly after a thoughtful moment, taking his cigar in his pudgy fingers and looking at it studiously—"it may
be—it may be—that the country's ready for a change—now don't mis-
understand me," he went on hastily, as if eager to set their perturbed
minds at rest— "I'm not saying that I want to see Harding elected—that
I'm going to cast my vote for him—as you know, I'm a party man and
have voted the Democratic ticket ever since I came of age—but," again
he paused, frowned importantly at his cigar, and spoke with careful
deliberation—"it may just be that we are due for a change this year—
that the country is ready for it—that we need it. . . . Now, I supported
Wilson twice, in 1912, when he got elected to his first term of office, and
again in 1916——"

"The time he kept us out of war," some one said ironically.

"And," the little man said deliberately—"if he was running again—if
he was well enough to run—if he wanted a third term—(although I'm
against the third term in principle)," he amended hastily again—"why,
I believe I'd go ahead and vote for him. That's how much I think of

him. But," again he paused, and meditated his chewed cigar profoundly—"it may be we're due now for a change. Wilson was a great
president—in my opinion, the greatest man we've had since Lincoln—I
don't believe any other man could have done the job he did as well as
he—*but*," the word came out impressively, "the job is done! The war is
over——"

"Yes, thank God!" some one murmured softly but fervently.

"The people want to forget about the war—they want to forget all
their sacrifices and suffering—" said this little man who had sacrificed
and suffered nothing—"they are looking forward to better times. . . .
And in my opinion," he spoke again with his air of slow deliberation,
important carefulness—"in my opinion, better times are before us. I
think that after this election, we are going to witness one of the greatest
periods of national development and expansion that the world has ever
known. . . . Why, we haven't begun yet! We haven't even started!" he
cried suddenly, with a note of passionate conviction in his voice— "Do
you realize that this country is only a little more than a hundred years
old? Why, we haven't even begun to show what we can do yet! We've
spent all that time in getting started—in building cities—settling the
country—building railroads and factories—developing the means of
production—making the tools with which to work. . . . The resources
of this country are scarcely tapped as yet. And in my opinion we are on
the eve of the greatest period of prosperity and growth the world has
ever known. . . . Look at Altamont, for example," he went on cogently.
"Ten years ago, in 1910, the census gave us a population of 18,000. . . .
Now, we have thirty, according to government figures, and that doesn't
begin to take the whole thing in: it doesn't take in Biltburn, Lunn's
Cove, Beaver Hills, Sunset Parkway—a dozen other places I can mention, all really part of the town but not included in the census figures.
. . . If all the suburbs were included we'd have a population of at least
40,000 inhabitants——"

"I'd call it nearer fifty," said another patriot.

"And within another ten years we'll go to seventy-five, perhaps a
hundred. . . . Why, that town hasn't begun to grow yet!" he said, bending his short body forward in his enthusiasm and tapping his fat knee—
"It has been less than eight years since we established the Citizen's Bank
and Trust Company with a capital of $25,000 and capital stock at $100 a
share. . . . Now," he paused a moment, and looked around him, his
swarthy face packed with strong conviction—"*now,* we have a capital of

$2,000,000—deposits totalling more than $18,000,000—and as for the stock
—" for a moment the little man's swarthy face was touched with a faint
complacent smile, he said smugly, "I don't know exactly how much stock
you gentlemen may hold among you, but if any of you wants to sell what
he has, I will pay you $1000 a share—here and now," he slapped a fat
small hand down upon a fat small knee—"here and now! for every share
you own."

And he looked at them steadily for a moment with an air of challenge.

"Not for mine!" the florid heavy man cried heartily. "No sir! I've
only got ten shares, Emmet, but you can't buy it from me at any price! I
won't sell!"

And the swarthy little man, pleased by the answer, smiled complacently about him before he spoke again.

"Yes, sir!" he said. "That's the way it is. And the thing that's begun
to happen at home already is going to happen everywhere—all over the
country. From now on you're going to see a period of rising prices and
high wages—increased production, a boom in real estate, stocks, invest-
ments, business of all kinds—rising values everywhere such as you never
saw before and never hoped to see."

"And where is it going to stop?"

"Stop!" the swarthy little man spoke almost curtly, and then barked,
"It's not going to stop! Not during *our* lifetime, anyway! I tell you,
man, we're just beginning! How can there be any talk of stopping
when we haven't *started* yet! . . . There's been nothing like it before,"
he cried with passionate earnestness—"nothing to match it in the history
of the world. We've had wars, booms, good times, hard times, slumps,
periods of prosperity—but, I tell you, gentlemen!" and here he smote
himself sharply on the knee and his voice rose with the strength of an
unshakable conviction—"this thing is different! We have reached a
stage in our development that no other country in the world has ever
known—that was never dreamed of before—a stage that is beyond
booms, depressions, good times, hard times—anything——"

"You mean that after this we shall never be affected by those things?"

"Yes, sir!" he cried emphatically. "I mean just that! I mean that we
have learned the causes for each of those conditions. I mean that we
have learned how to check them, how to control them. I mean that so
far as we are concerned they don't *exist* any more!" His voice had become almost shrill with the force of his persuasive argument, and sud-

denly whipping a sheaf of envelopes, tied with a rubber band, out of his
inner pocket, and gripping a stub of pencil in his stubby hand, he crossed
his short fat legs with an energetic movement, bent forward poised above
the envelopes, and said quietly but urgently:

"See here, now!— I'd like to show you a few figures! My business,
as you know, is to look after other people's money—your money, the
town's money, everybody's money—I've got to keep my fingers on the
pulse of business at every moment of the day—my business is to *know*
—to *know*—and let me tell you something," he said quietly, looking
directly in their eyes, "I *do* know—so pay attention just a moment while
I show these figures to you."

And for some moments he spoke quietly, persuasively, his dark
features packed with an energy of powerful conviction, while he rapidly
jotted figures down upon the backs of the soiled envelopes, and they
bent around him—their medicine-man of magic numerals—in an
attitude of awed and rapt attentiveness. And when he had finished,
there was silence for a moment, save for the rhythmic clack of wheels,
the rocketing sound of the great train. Then one of the men, stroking
his chin thoughtfully, and with an impressed air, said:

"I see. . . . And you think, then, that in view of these conditions it
would be better for the country if Harding is elected."

The little man's manner became instantly cautious, non-committal,
"conservative":

"I don't say that," he said, shaking his head in a movement of denial—
"I only say that whoever gets elected we're in for a period of unparalleled
development. . . . Now both of them are good men—as I say, I shall
probably vote for Cox—but you can rest assured," he spoke deliberately
and looked around him in his compelling way—"you can rest assured
that no matter which one gets elected the country will be in good hands.
There's no question about that."

"Yes, sir," said the florid-faced politician in his amiable and hearty way.
"I agree with you. . . . I'm a Democrat myself, both in practice and in
principle. I'm going to vote for Cox, but if Harding gets elected I won't
shed any tears over his election. We'll have to give the Republicans
credit for a good deed this time—they couldn't have made a wiser or a
better decision. He has a long and honorable career in the service of his
country,"—as he spoke his voice unconsciously took on the sententious
ring and lilt of the professional politician—"no breath of scandal has ever
touched his name: in public and in private life he has remained as he

began—a statesman loyal to the institutions of his country, a husband devoted to his family life, a plain American of simple tastes who loves his neighbors as himself, and prefers the quiet life of a little town, the democracy of the front porch, to the marble arches of the capitol—so, whatever the result may be," the orator concluded, "this nation need fear nothing: it has chosen well and wisely in both cases, its future is secure."

Mr. Flood, during the course of this impassioned flight, had remained ponderously unmoved. In the pause that followed, he sat impassively, his coarse jowled face and bulging yellowed eyes fixed on the orator in their customary expression of comic stupefaction. Now, breathing hoarsely and stertorously, he coughed chokingly and with an alarming rattling noise into his handkerchief, peered intently at his wadded handkerchief for a moment, and then said coarsely:

"Hell! What all of you are saying is that you are goin' to vote for Cox but that you hope that Harding wins."

"No, now, Jim—" the politician, Mr. Candler, said in a protesting tone— "I never said——"

"Yes, you did!" Mr. Flood wheezed bluntly. "You meant it, anyhow, every one of you is sayin' how he always was a Democrat and what a great man Wilson is, and how he's goin' to vote for Cox—and every God-damn one of you is praying that the other feller gets elected. . . . Why? I'll tell you why," he wheezed coarsely, "—it's because we're sick an' tired of Woodrow, all of us—we want to put the rollers under him an' see the last of him! Oh, yes, we are," he went on brutally as some one started to protest—"we're tired of Woodrow's flowery speeches, an' we're tired of hearin' about wars an' ideals an' democracy an' how fine an' noble we all are an' 'Mister won't you please subscribe.' We're tired of hearin' bunk that doesn't pay an' we want to hear some bunk that does— an' we're goin' to vote for the crook that gives it to us. . . . Do you know what we all want—what we're lookin' for?" he demanded, glowering brutally around at them. "We want a piece of the breast with lots of gravy—an' the boy that promises us the most is the one we're for! . . . Cox! Hell! All of you know Cox has no more chance of getting in than a snowball has in hell. When they get through with him he won't know whether he was run over by a five-ton truck or chewed up in a sausage mill. . . . Nothing has changed, the world's no different, we're just the same as we always were—and I've watched 'em come an' go for forty years—Blaine, Cleveland, Taft, McKinley, Roosevelt—the whole damned lot of 'em—an' what we want from them is just the same: all we can get for ourselves, a free grab with no holts barred, and to hell with the other fellow."

"So who are you going to vote for, Jim?" said Mr. Candler smiling.

"Who? Me?" said Mr. Flood with a coarse grin. "Why, hell, you ought to know that without asking. Me—I'm a Democrat, ain't I?—don't I publish a Democratic newspaper? I'm going to vote for Cox, of course."

And, in the burst of laughter that followed, some one could be heard, saying jestingly:

"And who's going to win the Series, Jim? Some one told me you're for Brooklyn!"

"Brooklyn!" Mr. Flood jeered wheezingly. "Brooklyn has just the same kind of chance Cox has—the chance a snowball has in hell! Brooklyn! They're in just the same fix the Democrats are in—they've got nothing on the ball. When Speaker and that Cleveland gang get through with them, Brooklyn is going to look just like Cox the day after the election. Brooklyn," he concluded with brutal conviction, "hasn't got a chance."

And again the debate between the men grew eager, animated and vociferous: they shouted, laughed, denied, debated, jeered good-naturedly, and the great train hurtled onward in the darkness, and the everlasting earth was still.

And other men, and other voices, words, and moments such as these would come, would pass, would vanish and would be forgotten in the huge record and abyss of time. And the great trains of America would hurtle on through darkness over the lonely, everlasting earth—the earth which only was eternal—and on which our fathers and our brothers had wandered, their lives so brief, so lonely, and so strange—into whose substance at length they all would be compacted. And the great trains would hurtle on forever over the silent and eternal earth—fixed in that design of everlasting stillness and unceasing change. The trains would hurtle onward bearing other lives like these, all brought together for an instant between two points of time—and then all lost, all vanished, broken and forgotten. The trains would bear them onward to their million destinations—each to the fortune, fame, or happiness he wished, whatever it was that he was looking for—but whether any to a sure success, a certain purpose, or the thing he sought—what man could say? All that he knew was that these men, these words, this moment would vanish, be forgotten—and that great wheels would hurtle on forever. And the earth be still.

Mr. Flood shifted his gouty weight carefully with a movement of his fat arm, grunting painfully as he did so. This delicate operation completed, he stared sharply and intently at the boy again and at length said bluntly:

"You're one of those Gant boys, ain't you? Ain't you Ben's brother?"

"Yes, sir," the boy answered. "That's right."

"Which one are you?" Mr. Flood said with this same brutal directness. "You ain't the one that stutters, are you?"

"No," one of the other men interrupted with a laugh, but in a decided tone. "He's not the one. You're thinking of Luke."

"Oh," said Mr. Flood stupidly. "Is Luke the one that stutters?"

"Yes," the boy said, "that's Luke. I'm Eugene."

"Oh," Mr. Flood said heavily. "I reckon you're the youngest one."

"Yes, sir," the boy answered.

"Well," said Mr. Flood with an air of finality, "I didn't know which one you were but I knew you were one of them. I knew I'd seen you somewhere."

"Yes, sir," the boy answered. He was about to go on, hesitated for a moment, and suddenly blurted out: "I used to carry a route on *The Courier* when you owned it. I guess that's how you remembered me."

"Oh," said Mr. Flood stupidly, "you did? Yes, that's it, all right. I remember now." And he continued to look at the boy with his bulging stare of comic stupefaction and for a moment there was silence save for the pounding of the wheels upon the rail.

"How many of you boys are there?" The swarthy and important-looking man who had previously been addressed as Emmet now spoke curiously: "There must be five or six in all."

"No," the boy said, "there's only three now. There's Luke and Steve and me."

"Oh, Steve, Steve," the little man said with an air of crisp finality, as if this was the name that had been at the tip of his tongue all the time. "Steve was the oldest, wasn't he?"

"Yes, sir," said the boy.

"Whatever became of Steve, anyway?" the man said. "I don't believe I've seen him in ten or fifteen years. He doesn't live at home any more, does he?"

"No, sir," the boy said. "He lives in Indiana."

"Does he for a fact?" said the little man, as if this was a rare and curious bit of information. "What's Steve doing out there? Is he in business?"

For a moment the boy was going to say, "No, he runs a pool room and lives up over it with his wife and children," but feeling ashamed to say this, he said:

"I think he runs some kind of cigar store out there."

"Is that so?" the man answered with an air of great interest. "Well," he went on in a moment in a conciliatory tone, "Steve was always smart enough. He had brains enough to do almost anything if he tried."

Emmet Wade, the man who had asked the boy all these questions, was a quick, pompous little figure, corpulently built, but so short in stature as to be almost dwarfish-looking. His skin was curiously and unpleasantly swarthy, and save for a fringe of thin black hair at either side, his head was completely bald. In that squat figure, the suggestion of pompous authority and mountainous conceit was so pronounced that even in repose, as now, the whole man seemed to strut. He was, by virtue of that fortuitous chance and opportunity which has put so many small men in great positions, the president of the leading bank of the community. Even as he sat there in the smoking compartment, with his short fat legs crossed, the boy could see him sitting at his desk in the bank, swinging back and forth in his swivel chair thoughtfully, his pudgy hands folded behind his head as he dictated a letter to his obsequious secretary.

"Where's old Luke? What's he doing, anyway?" another of the men demanded suddenly, beginning to chuckle even as he spoke. The speaker was the florid-faced, somewhat countrified-looking man already noted, who wore the string neck-tie and spoke with the rhetorical severity of the small-town politician. He was one of the town commissioners and in his hearty voice and easy manner there was a more genial quality than any of the others had. "I haven't seen that boy in years," he continued. "Some one was asking me just the other day what had become of him."

"He's got a job selling farm machinery and lighting equipment," the boy answered.

"Is that so?" the man replied with this same air of friendly interest. "Where is he located? He doesn't get home very often, does he?"

"No, sir," the boy said, "not very often. He comes in every two or three weeks, but he doesn't stay home long at a time. His territory is down through South Carolina and Georgia—all through there."

"What did you say he was selling?" said Mr. Flood, who had been staring at the boy fixedly during all this conversation with his heavy expression of a slow, intent and brutal stupefaction.

"He sells lighting systems and pumps and farm equipment and machinery—for farms," the boy said awkwardly.

"That's Luke—who does that?" said Mr. Flood after a moment, when this information had had time to penetrate.

"Yes, sir. That's Luke."

"And he's the one that stutters?"

"Yes, sir."

"The one that used to have the agency for *The Saturday Evening Post* and did all that talking when he sold 'em to you?"

"Yes, sir. That's Luke."

"And what d'you say he's doing now?" said Mr. Flood heavily. "Selling farm machinery?"

"Yes, sir. That's what he's doing."

"Then, by God," said Mr. Flood, with a sudden and explosive emphasis which, after his former attitude of heavy, brutal stupefaction, was startling, "he'll do it!" The other men laughed and Mr. Flood shook his ponderous, crimson head slowly from side to side to emphasize his conviction in the matter.

"If any one can sell 'em, he'll do it," he said positively. "That boy could sell Palm Beach suits to the Esquimaux. They'd have to buy 'em just to keep him from talking them to death."

"I'll tell you what I saw him do one time," said the politician, shifting his weight a little in order to accommodate himself more comfortably to the motion of the train. "I was standing in front of the post office one day talking to Dave Redmond about some property he owned out on the Haw Creek Road—oh, it must have been almost fifteen years ago—when here he comes hustling along, you know, with a big bundle of his papers under his arm. Well, he sails right into us, talking about a mile a minute and going so fast neither of us had a chance to get a word in edgeways. 'Here you are, gentlemen,' he says, 'hot off the press, just the thing you've been waiting for, this week's edition of *The Saturday Evening Post,* five cents, only a nickel, the twentieth part of a dollar.' By that time," said Mr. Candler, "he had the thing all opened up and shoved up right under Dave Redmond's nose, and he was turning the pages and telling him all about the different pieces it had in it and who wrote them and what was in them, and what a bargain it was for five cents. 'W-w-w-why,' he says, 'if you b-b-b-bought it in a book, why it'd cost you a d-d-d-dollar and a half and then,' he says, 'it wouldn't be half as good.' Well, Dave was getting sort of red in the face by that time," Mr. Candler said, "and I could see he was sort of annoyed at being interrupted, but the boy kept right on with his spiel and wouldn't give up. 'I don't want it,' says Dave, 'I'm busy' and he tries to turn away from him, but Luke moves right around to the other side and goes after him about twice as hard as before. 'Go on, go on,' says Dave. 'We're busy! I don't want it! I can't read!' he says. 'All right,' says Luke, 'then you can look at the p-p-p-pictures. Why, the pictures alone,' he says, 'are w-w-w-worth a half a dollar. It's the b-b-b-bargain of a life time,' he says. Well, the boy was pressing him pretty hard and I guess Dave lost his temper. He sort of knocked the magazine away from him and shouted, 'Damn it, I told you that I didn't want it, and I mean it! Now go on! We're busy.' Well," said Mr. Candler, "Luke didn't say a word for a moment. He took his magazine and put it under his arm again, and he just stood there looking at Dave Redmond for a moment, and then he said, just as quiet as you please, 'All right, sir. You're the doctor. But I think you're going to regret it!' And then he turned and walked away from us. Well, sir," said Mr. Candler, laughing, "Dave Redmond's face was a study. You could see he felt pretty small to think he had shouted at the boy like that, and acted as he did. And Luke hadn't gone twenty feet before Dave Redmond called him back. 'Here, son,' he says, diving his hand down into his pocket, 'give me one of those things! I may never read it but it's worth a dollar just to hear you talk.' And he gave him a dollar, too, and made him take it," Mr. Candler said, "and from that day on Dave Redmond was one of the biggest boosters that Luke had. . . . 'I think you're going to regret it,'" said Mr. Candler again, laughing at the memory. "That's the thing that did it—that's what got him—the way the boy just looked at him and said, 'All right, sir, but I think you're going to regret it.' That did the trick, all right." And pleased with his story and the memory it evoked, Mr. Candler looked mildly out the window for a moment, smiling.

"That was Luke that done that?" Mr. Flood demanded hoarsely after a moment, with his air of brutal and rather stunned surprise. "The one that stutters?"

"Yes, that's the one all right," said Mr. Candler. "That's who it was."

Mr. Flood pondered this information for a moment with his bulging eyes still fastened on Mr. Candler in their look of stupefied curiosity. Then, as the full import of what he had heard at length soaked into his intelligence, he shook his great coarse head once, slowly, in a movement of ponderous but emphatic satisfaction, and said with hoarse conviction:

"Well, he's a good 'un! If any one can sell 'em, he's the one."

This judgment was followed by a brief but heavy pause, which was broken in a moment by the voice of the pompous, swarthy little man who, in a tone of detached curiosity, said:

"Whatever became of that other boy—the one who used to work there in *The Courier* office when you owned it? What was his name, anyway?"

"Ben," said Mr. Flood heavily, but without hesitation. "That was Ben." Here he coughed in an alarming, phlegmy sort of way, cleared his throat and spat chokingly into the spittoon at his feet, wiped his mouth with his wadded handkerchief and in a moment, panting for breath, wheezed:

"Ben was the one that worked for me."

"Oh, yes, yes, yes!" the swarthy little man said rapidly, as if now it all came back to him. "Ben! That was the one! What ever became of him? I haven't seen him recently."

"He's dead," said Mr. Flood, still wheezing rapidly for breath and gazing at the spittoon. "That's the reason you haven't seen him," he said seriously. And suddenly, as if the long-awaited moment had come, he bent over, torn by a fit of choking and phlegmy sounds of really astounding proportions. When it was over, he raised himself, settled back slowly and painfully in his seat, and for a moment with closed eyes, did nothing but wheeze rapidly. In a moment, still with closed eyes, he gasped almost inaudibly:

"Ben was the one that died."

"Oh, yes! I do remember now," the pompous little man declared, nodding his head sharply with an air of conviction. "That's been some time ago, hasn't it?" he said to the boy.

"He died two years ago," the boy replied, "during the war."

"Oh, that's so, he did! I remember now!" the man cried instantly, with an air of recollection that somehow said that he remembered nothing. "He was overseas at the time, wasn't he?" he asked smoothly.

"No, sir," the boy answered. "He was at home. He died of pneumonia —during that big epidemic."

"I know," the man said regretfully. "That got a lot of the boys. Ben was in service at the time, wasn't he?"

"No," the boy answered. "He never got in. Luke was the one who was in service. Ben tried to get in twice but he couldn't pass the examinations."

"Is that so?" the man said vaguely. "Well, I was mighty sorry to hear about his death. Old Ben was one fine boy!"

Nothing was said for a moment.

"I'll tell you how fine he was," Mr. Flood, who had been wheezing with closed eyes, now grunted suddenly, glaring solemnly about him with an air of brutal earnestness. "Now I think I knew that boy about as well as any man alive—he worked for me for almost fifteen years—started out when he was ten years old as a route-boy on *The Courier* and kept right on working for my paper until just a year or two before he died! And I'm here to tell you," he wheezed solemnly, "that they don't come any better than Ben!" Here he glowered around him pugnaciously as if the character of a dead saint had been called in question. "Now he wasn't one of your big talkers who'd promise everything and do nothing. Ben was a do-er, not a talker. You could depend on him," said Mr. Flood, hoarsely and impressively. "When he told you he'd do a thing, you'd know it was going to get done! As regular as a clock and as steady as the day is long! And as quiet a fellow as you ever saw," said Mr. Flood. "That was Ben for you! Am I right?" he demanded, suddenly turning to the boy. "Was that Ben?"

"Yes, sir," the boy answered. "That was Ben."

"And until you asked him something he'd go for days at a time without speaking to you, but I knew he didn't mean anything by it, it was just his way. He believed in tending to his own business and he expected every one else to do the same." And for a moment, exhausted by these eulogies, he wheezed rapidly.

"Well, the world would be a lot better off if there were more like him," the pompous, swarthy little man now said virtuously, as if this sentiment expressed his own pious belief and practice. "There are too many people sticking their noses in other people's business, as it is."

"Well, they didn't stick their noses in Ben's business," said Mr. Flood with grim emphasis, "not after the first time, anyway. But they didn't come any better than that boy. I couldn't have thought more of him if he'd been my own son," he concluded piously and then gasped stertorously, lifted his cigar slowly to his lips with the thick, gouty tenderness that characterized all his movements and for a moment puffed slowly, wheezing reflectively over it.

"Not that he was ever much like a boy," he grunted suddenly, with a surprising flash of insight. "He was always more like an old man—didn't ever seem to be a kid like the others. Why," suddenly he chuckled with a phlegmy hoarseness, "I remember when he first began to come down there in the morning as a carrier, the other kids all called him 'Pop.' That was Ben for you. Always had that scowl on his face, even when he was laughing—as serious and earnest as an old man. But he was one of the best—as good as they come." Again he coughed chokingly, bent over with a painful grunt, and cleared his throat phlegmily into the polished brass spittoon beside him. Then, wheezing a little, he drew the wadded silk handkerchief from a side-pocket, wiped his mouth with it, raised himself up in his seat a little, and settled back slowly, tenderly, wheezing, with a sigh! Then for a moment he labored painfully, eyes closed, with his rapid wheezing breath and finally, when it seemed he must be exhausted by his efforts and done with conversation for the evening, he wheezed faintly and unexpectedly:

"That was Ben."

"Oh, I remember that boy now," the swarthy pompous-looking man suddenly broke in with a flash of recollective inspiration—"Wasn't Ben the boy who used to stand in the windows of *The Courier* offices when the World Series was being played, and post the score up on the scoreboard as they phoned it in to him?"

"Yes," wheezed Mr. Flood, nodding heavily, "You got him now, all right. That was Ben."

"I remember now," the swarthy little man said thoughtfully, with a far-away look in his eye. "I was thinking about him the other day when I went by *The Courier* office. They were playing the Series then. They had another fellow in the window and I wondered what had become of him. So that was Ben?"

"Yes," Mr. Flood wheezed hoarsely again. "That was Ben."

For a moment as the gouty old rake had spoken of the boy's dead brother, the boy had felt within him a sense of warmth: a wakening of dead time, a stir of grateful affection for the gross old man as if there might have been in this bloated carcass some trace of understanding for the dead boy of whom he spoke—an understanding faint and groping as a dog who bays the moon might have of the sidereal universe, and yet genuine and recognizable.

And for a moment present time fades out and the boy sits there staring blindly out at the dark earth that strokes forever past the train, and now he has the watch out and feels it in his hands. . . . And suddenly Ben is standing there before his vision, smoking, and scowls down through the window of the office at the boy.

He jerks his head in a peremptory gesture: the boy, obedient to his brother's command, enters the office and stands there waiting at the counter. Ben steps down from the platform in the window, puts the ear-phones on a table and walks over to the place where the boy is standing. For a moment, scowling fiercely, he stands there looking at the boy across the counter. The scowl deepens, he makes a sudden threatening gesture of his hard white hand as if to strike the boy, but instead he reaches across the counter quickly, seizes the boy by the shoulders, pulls him closer, and with rough but skillful fingers tugs, pulls and jerks the frayed string of neck-tie which the boy is wearing into a more orderly and presentable shape.

The boy starts to go.

"Wait!" says Ben, quietly, in a deliberately off-hand kind of tone. He opens a drawer below the counter, takes out a small square package, and scowling irritably, and without looking at the boy, he thrusts it at him. "Here's something for you," he says, and walks away.

"What is it?" The boy takes the package and examines it with a queer numb sense of expectancy and growing joy.

"Why don't you open it and see?" Ben says, his back still turned, and scowling down into a paper on the desk.

"Open it?" the boy says, staring at him stupidly.

"Yes, open it, fool!" Ben snarls. "It's not going to bite you!"

While the boy fumbles with the cords that tie the package, Ben prowls over toward the counter with his curious, loping, pigeon-toed stride, leans on it with his elbows and, scowling, begins to look up and down the want-ad columns, while blue, pungent smoke coils slowly from his nostrils. By this time, the boy has taken off the outer wrapping of the package, and is holding a small case, beautifully heavy, of sumptuous blue velvet, in his hands.

"Well, did you look at it?" Ben says, still scowling up and down the want-ads of the paper, without looking at the boy.

The boy finds the spring and presses it, the top opens, inside upon its rich cushion of white satin is a gold watch, and a fine gold chain. It is a miracle of design, almost as thin and delicate as a wafer. The boy stares at it with bulging eyes and in a moment stammers:

"It's—it's a watch!"

"Does it look like an alarm clock?" Ben jeers quietly, as he turns a page and begins to scowl up and down the advertisements of another column.

"It's—for me?" the boy says thickly, slowly, as he stares at it.

"No," Ben says, "it's for Napoleon Bonaparte, of course! . . . You little idiot! Don't you know what day this is? Have I got to do all the thinking for you? Don't you ever use your head for anything except a hat-rack? . . . Well," he goes on quietly in a moment, still looking at his paper, "what do you think of it? . . . There's a spring in the back that opens up," he goes on casually. "Why don't you look at it?"

The boy turns the watch over, feels the smooth golden surface of that shining wafer, finds the spring, and opens it. The back of the watch springs out, upon the inner surface is engraved, in delicate small words, this inscription:

"To Eugene Gant
Presented To Him On His Twelfth Birthday
By His Brother
B. H. Gant
October 3, 1912"

"Well," Ben says quietly in a moment. "Did you read what it says?"

"I'd just like to say—" the boy begins in a thick, strange voice, staring blindly down at the still open watch.

"Oh, for God's sake!" Ben says, lifting his scowling head in the direction of his unknown demon, and jerking his head derisively towards the boy. "Listen to this, won't you? . . . Now, for God's sake, try to take good care of it and don't abuse it!" he says quickly and irritably. "You've got to look after a watch the same as anything else. Old man Enderby" —this is the name of the jeweller from whom he has bought the watch—"told me that a watch like that was good for fifty years, if you take care of it. . . . You know," he goes on quietly, insultingly, "you're not supposed to drive nails with it or use it for a hammer. You know that, don't you?" he says, and for the first time turns and looks quietly at the boy. "Do you know what a watch is for?"

"Yes."

"What is it for?"

"To keep time with," says the boy.

Ben says nothing for a moment, but looks at him.

"Yes," he says quietly at length, with all the bitter weariness of a fathomless resignation and despair, the infinite revulsion, scorn, disgust which life has caused in him. "That's it. That's what it's for. To keep time with." The weary irony in his voice has deepened to a note of passionate despair. "And I hope to God you keep it better than the rest of us! Better than Mama or the old man—better than me! God help you if you don't! . . . Now go on home," he says quietly in a moment, "before I kill you."

"To keep time with!"

What is this dream of time, this strange and bitter miracle of living? Is it the wind that drives the leaves down the bare path fleeing? Is it the storm-wild flight of furious days, the storm-swift passing of the million faces, all lost, forgotten, vanished as a dream? Is it the wind that howls above the earth, is it the wind that drives all things before its lash, is it the wind that drives all men like dead ghosts fleeing? Is it the one red leaf that strains there on the bough and that forever will be fleeing? All things are lost and broken in the wind: the dry leaves scamper down the path before us, in their swift-winged dance of death the dead souls flee along before us driven with rusty scuffle before the fury of the demented wind. And October has come again, has come again.

What is this strange and bitter miracle of life? Is it to feel, when furious day is done, the evening hush, the sorrow of lost, fading light, far sounds and broken cries, and footsteps, voices, music, and all lost—and something murmurous, immense and mighty in the air?

And we have walked the pavements of a little town and known the passages of barren night, and heard the wheel, the whistle and the tolling bell, and lain in the darkness waiting, giving to silence the huge prayer of our intolerable desire. And we have heard the sorrowful silence of the river in October—and what is there to say? October has come again, has come again, and this world, this life, this time are stranger than a dream.

May it not be that some day from this dream of time, this chronicle of smoke, this strange and bitter miracle of life in which we are the moving and phantasmal figures, we shall wake? Knowing our father's voice upon the porch again, the flowers, the grapevines, the low rich moons of waning August, and the tolling bell—and instantly to know we live, that we have dreamed and have awakened, and find then in our hands some object, like this real and palpable, some gift out of the lost land and the unknown world as token that it was no dream—that we have really been there? And there is no more to say.

For now October has come back again, the strange and lonely month comes back again, and you will not return.

Up on the mountain, down in the valley, deep, deep, in the hill, Ben—cold, cold, cold.

"To keep time with!"

And suddenly the scene, the shapes, the voices of the men about him swam back into their focus, and he could hear the rhythmed pounding of the wheels below him, and in his palm the frail-numbered visage of the watch stared blank and plain at him its legend. It was one min-ute after twelve o'clock, Sunday morning, October the third, 1920, and he was hurtling across Virginia, and this world, this life, this time were stranger than a dream.

The train had halted for a moment at one of the Virginia towns, and for a moment the people were conscious of the strange yet casual famil-iarity of all those sounds which suddenly will intercept the rhythmic spell of time and memory which a journey in a train can cast upon its passengers. Suddenly this spell was broken by the intrusion of peculiar things—of sounds and voices—the sense of instant recognition, union to a town, a life which they had never known, but with which they now felt immediately familiar. A trainman was coming swiftly down the station platform beneath the windows of the train, pausing from time to time to hammer on the car-wheels of each truck. A negro toiled past below them with a heavy rattling truck in tow, piled high with baggage.

And elsewhere there were the casual voices of the train men—con-ductors, porters, baggage masters, station men—greeting each other with friendly words, without surprise, speaking of weather, work, plans for the future, saying farewell in the same way. Then the bell tolled, the whistle blew, the slow panting of the engine came back to them, the train was again in motion; the station, and the station lights, a glimpse of streets, the thrilling, haunting, white-glazed incandescence of a cotton mill at night, the hard last lights of town, slid past the windows of the train. The train was in full speed now, and they were rushing on across the dark and lonely earth again.

Then one of the men in the compartment, the politician, who had been looking curiously out the window at this town and station scene, turned and spoke with a casual interest to the boy:

"Your father's in Baltimore now, isn't he, son?" he said.

"Yes, sir. He's at Hopkins. Luke's up there with him?"

"Well, I thought I read something in the paper a week or two back about his being there," said the man with the florid face.

"What's wrong with him?" Mr. Flood demanded coarsely in a moment, after he had absorbed this information. "Ain't he feeling good?"

The boy shifted nervously in his seat before he answered. His father was dying of cancer, but for some reason it did not seem possible or proper for him to say this to these men. He said:

"He's got some kind of kidney trouble, I think. He goes up there for radium treatments."

"It's the same thing John Rankin had," the florid-faced man glibly interposed at this moment. "Some sort of prostate trouble, isn't it?" he said.

"Yes, sir, that's it," the boy said. For some reason he felt a sense of relief and gratefulness towards the man with the florid face. The easy, glib and false assurance that his father's "trouble" was "the same thing John Rankin had" seemed to give the disease a respectable standing and to divest the cancer of its fatal, shameful and putrescent horror.

"I know what it is," the florid-faced man was saying, nodding his head in a confident manner. "It's the same thing John Rankin had. A lot of men get it after they're fifty. John told me he went through agony with it for ten years. Said he used to be up with it a dozen times a night. It got so he couldn't sleep, he couldn't rest, he couldn't do anything but walk the floor with it. It got him down so that he was nothing but skin and bones, he was walking around like a dead man. Then he went up there and had that operation and he's been a new man ever since. He looks better than he's looked in twenty years. I was talking to him the other day and he told me he didn't have an ache or a pain in the world. He said he was going to live to be a hundred and he looked it—the picture of health."

"Well," he said in a friendly tone, now turning to the boy, "remember me to your father when you see him. Tell him Frank Candler asked to be remembered to him."

"Are you and him good friends?" Mr. Flood demanded heavily, after another staring pause, with the brutal, patient, and somehow formidable curiosity which belonged to him. "You know him well?"

"Who? Mr. Gant?" Mr. Candler cried with the hearty geniality of the politician, which seemed to suggest he knew the man so well that the very question was amusing to him. "Why, I've known him all my life— I've known him ever since he first came to Altamont—let's see, that's all of forty years ago when he first came there?" Mr. Candler went on reflectively, "or no, maybe a little less than that. Wait a minute." He considered seriously for a moment. "The first time I ever saw your father," said Mr. Candler very slowly and impressively, with a frown on his face and not looking at any one, but staring straight before him, "was in October, 1882—and I believe—I believe," he said strongly, "that was the very year he came to town—yes, sir! I'm positive of it!" he cried. "For Altamont was nothing but a cross-roads village in those days—I don't believe we had 2000 people there—why, that's all in the world it was." Mr. Candler now interrupted himself heartily. "The courthouse up there on the square and a few stores around it—when you got two blocks away you were right out in the country. Didn't Captain Bob Porter offer me three lots he owned down there on Pisgah Avenue, not a block from the square, for a thousand dollars, and didn't I laugh at him to think he was fool enough to ask such a price as that and expect to get it! Why!" Mr. Candler declared, with a full countrified laugh, "it was nothing but a mud-hole down in the holler. I've seen old Captain Porter's hawgs wallerin' around in it many's the time. 'And you,' I said to him, 'you—do you think I'd pay you a price like that for a mud-hole? Why, you must think I'm crazy, sure enough.' 'All right,' he says, 'have it your own way, but you'll live to see the day you'll regret not buying it. You'll live to see the day when you can't buy *one* of those lots for a thousand dollars!' *One* of them!" Mr. Candler now cried in hearty self-derision. "Why, if I owned one of those lots today, I'd be a rich man! I don't believe you could buy a foot of that land today for less than a thousand dollars, could you, Bruce?" he said, addressing himself to the swarthy, pompous-looking man who sat beside the boy.

"Five thousand a front foot would come closer to it, I should think," the pompous little man replied, with the crisp, brisk and almost strutting assurance that characterized all his words and gestures. He crossed and uncrossed his fat little legs briskly as he uttered these words and then sat there "all reared back" as the saying goes, unable even to reach the floor with his fat little legs, but smiling a complacent smile and simply exud-

ing conceit and strutting self-satisfaction from every pore. "Yes, sir!"
the swarthy little man continued, pompously, "I should doubt very
much if you could buy a foot of that property for less than $5000 today!"

"Well," said Mr. Candler with a satisfied air. "That's what I thought!
I knew it would be way up there somewheres. But I could have had the
whole thing once for a thousand dollars. I've kicked myself in the seat
of the pants a thousand times since to think what a fool I was for not
taking it when I had the chance! I'd be a rich man today if I had! It
just goes to show you, doesn't it?" he concluded indefinitely.

"Yes, sir," the pompous, swarthy little man replied, in his dry, briskly
assured tones, "it goes to show that our hindsight is usually a great deal
better than our foresight!" And he glanced about him complacently,
obviously pleased with his wit and convinced that he had said something
remarkably pungent and original.

"It was about that time when I first met your father," said Mr. Candler, turning to the boy again. "Along there in the fall of '82—that's
when it was all right—and I don't think he'd been in town then more
than a month, for in a town that size, I'd have known if he'd been there
longer. And, yes, of course!" he cried sharply, struck by sudden recollection, "that very first day I saw him he was standing there in front
of his shop with two nigger men, unloading some blocks of marble and
granite and tombstones, I reckon, and moving them back into his shop.
I guess he was just moving in at the time. He'd rented an old shack over
there at the northeast corner of the square where the Sluder building is
now. That's where it was, all right. I was working for old man Weaver at
the time—he had a grocery and general-goods store there opposite the
old courthouse about where the Blue Ridge Coal and Ice Company is
now. I was going back to work after dinner and had just turned the
corner at the Square there from Academy Street when I saw your father.
I remember stopping to watch him for a moment because there was
something about his appearance—I don't know what it was, but if you
saw him once you'd never forget him—there was something about the
way he looked and talked and worked that was different from any one
I'd ever seen. Of course, he was an awful tall, big-boned, powerful-look-
ing sort of man—how tall is your father, son?"

"He was about six feet five," the boy answered, "but I guess he's not
that much now—he's stooped over some since he got old."

"Well, he didn't stoop in those days," said Mr. Candler. "He always
carried himself as straight as an arrow. I noticed that. He was an awful

big man—not that he had much weight on him—he was always lean and *skinny* like—but he *looked* big—he had big bones—his *frame* was big!" cried Mr. Candler. "You'll make a big man too when you fill out," he continued, giving the boy an appraising look. "Of course, you look like your mother's people, you're a Pentland and they're fleshy people, but you've got the old man's frame. You may make a bigger man than he is when you put on weight and widen out—but it wasn't that your father was so big—I think he looked bigger than he really was—it was something else about him—about the way he gave orders to the niggers and went about his work," said Mr. Candler, in a rather puzzled tone. "I don't know what it was, but I'd never seen any one like him before. For one thing he was dressed so good!" he said suddenly. "He always wore his good clothes when he worked—I'd never seen a man who did hard labor with his hands who dressed that way. Here he was, you know, sweating over those big blocks of stone with those two niggers and wearing better clothes than you and me would go to church in. Of course, he had his coat off, and his cuffs rolled back, and he was wearing one of those big striped aprons that go the whole way up across the shoulders—but you could see his clothes was *good*," said Mr. Candler. "Looked like black broadcloth that had been made by a tailor and wearing a *boiled* shirt, mind you, and one of those wing collars with a black silk neck-tie—and not afraid to work, either! Why, the first thing I saw him do," said Mr. Candler, laughing, "he let out a string of words at those niggers you could have heard from here to yonder because they were sweating and straining to get a big hunk of marble up on the rollers, that they hadn't been able to budge an inch. 'Merciful God,' he says, that's just the way he talked, you know—'Merciful God! Has it come to this that I must do everything for myself while you stand there gloating at my agony? I could as soon look for help from a couple of God-damned wooden Indians! In the name of God, stand back. I'll do it myself, sick and feeble as I am!' Well," said Mr. Candler, chuckling with the recollection, "with that he reaches down and gets a grip on that big hunk of stone and gives a heave and up she comes on to the rolling pins as nice and easy as anything you ever saw. Well, sir, you should have seen the look upon those niggers' faces—I thought their eyes were going to pop out of their heads. And that's the first time I ever spoke to him, you know. I can remember the very words I said. I said to him, 'Well, if you call that being sick and feeble, most of the folks up in this part of the country are already dead and in their graves.'"

The man's story had stirred in the boy's mind a thousand living memories of his father. For a moment it seems to him that the lost world which these words evoked has never died, lives yet in all the radiant and enchanted color of his childhood, in all its proud, dense, and single fabric of passion, fury, certitude and joy. Every memory that the story brought to life is part of him. There are a thousand buried, nameless and forgotten lives, ten thousand strange and secret tongues alive now, urgent, swarming in his blood, and thronging at the gateways of his memory. They are the lives of the lost wilderness, his mother's people; they are the tongues, the faces of the secret land, the dark half of his heart's desire, the fertile golden earth from which his father came.

He knows the farmer boy who stood beside the road and watched the dusty rebels marching past towards Gettysburg. He smells the sweet fragrance of that lavish countryside, he hears the oaths, the jests, the laughter of the marching soldiers, he hears the cricketing stitch of noon in drowsy fields, the myriad woodnotes, secret, green, and cool, the thrumming noises. He feels the brooding wait and murmur of hot afternoon, the trembling of the distant guns in the hot air, and the vast, oncoming hush and peace and silence of the dusk.

And then he is lying beside his father in the little gabled room upstairs. He is there beside his father and his father's brothers in the darkness—waiting, silent, waiting—with an unspoken single question in their hearts. They are thinking of an older brother who that night is lying twelve miles away, shot through the lungs. He sees his father's gaunt, long form in darkness, the big-boned hands, the gaunt, long face, the cold, green-gray, restless and weary eyes, so deep and untelling, so strangely lonely, and the slanting, almost reptilian large formation of the skull that has, somehow, its own strange dignity—as of some one lost. And the great stars of America blaze over them, the vast and lonely earth broods round them, then as now, with its secret and mysterious presences, and then as now the million-noted ululation of the night throngs up from silence the song of all its savage, dark and measureless fecundity. And he lies there in the darkness with his father and the brothers—silent, waiting—their cold, gray eyes turned upward to the loneliness of night, the blazing stars, having no words to say the thing they feel, the dream of time and the dark wonder of man's destiny which has drenched with blood the old earth, the familiar wheat, and fused that day the image of immortal history in a sleepy country town twelve miles away.

He sees the gaunt figure of the stonecutter coming across the square at his earth-devouring stride. He hears him muttering underneath his breath the mounting preludes of his huge invective. He sees him striding on forever, bent forward in his haste, wetting his thumb and clearing his throat with an infuriated and anticipatory relish as he comes. He sees him striding round the corner, racing up-hill towards the house, bearing huge packages of meat beneath his arm. He sees him take the high front steps four at a time, hasten like a hurricane into the house, lay down the meat upon the kitchen table, and then without a pause or introduction, comes the storm—fire, frenzy, curses, woes and lamentations, and then news out of the streets, the morning's joy, the smoking and abundant dinner.

A thousand memories of that life of constant and unresting fury brim in the boy's mind in an instant. At this moment, with telescopic force, all of these memories of his father's life become fused and blurred to one terrific image, in which it seems that the whole packed chronicle, from first to last, is perfectly comprised.

At the same moment the boy became conscious that the men were getting up around him, preparatory to departure, and that the florid-faced man, who had been speaking of his father, had laid his hand upon his shoulder in a friendly gesture, and was speaking to him.

"Good-night, son," the man was saying. "I'm getting off at Washington. If I don't see you again, good-luck to you. I suppose you'll be getting off at Baltimore to see your father before you go on, won't you?"

"Yes. Yes, sir," the boy stammered confusedly, getting to his feet.

"Remember me to him, won't you? Tell him you saw Frank Candler on the train and he sent his best regards."

"Yes, sir—thank you— I will," the boy said.

"All right. And good luck to you, boy," the politician said, giving him his broad, fleshy and rather tender hand. "Give 'em hell when you get up there," he said quietly, with a firm, friendly clasp and a good-natured wink.

"Yes—I certainly will—thank you—" the boy stammered, flaming in the face, with a feeling of proud hope, and with affection for the man who had spoken to him.

Then the man had gone, but his words had brought back to the boy suddenly the knowledge that in the morning he was to see his father. And that knowledge instantly destroyed all the exultancy of flight and

darkness, the incredible realization of his escape, the image of new
lands, the new life, and the shining city that had been swelling in his
spirit all night long. It had interposed its leaden face between him and
this image of wild joy towards which he was rushing onward in the
darkness, and its gray oppressive cloud weighed down upon him suddenly a measureless weight of dull weariness, horror and disgust.

He knew that next day he must meet his brother and his father, he
knew that the dreaded pause and interruption of his flight would last but
two short days, and that in this brief time he might see and know for
the last time all that was living of his father, and yet the knowledge of
this hated meeting filled him with loathing, a terrible desire to get away
from it as quickly as possible, to forget it, to escape from it forever.

He knew in his heart that for the wretched, feeble, whining old man
whom he must meet next day, he felt no love whatever. He knew, indeed, that he felt instead a kind of hate—the wretched kind of hatred
that comes from intolerable pity without love, from suffering and disgust,
from the agony of heart and brain and nerves, the poisonous and morbid
infection of our own lives, which a man dying of a loathsome disease
awakes in us, and from the self-hate, the self-loathing that it makes us
feel because of our terrible desire to escape him, to desert him, to blot
out the horrible memory we have for him, utterly to forget him.

Now the three men remaining in the compartment were rising to depart. Old Flood got up with a painful grunt, carefully dropped the
chewed butt of his cigar into the brass spittoon, and walked tenderly
with a gouty and flat-footed shuffle across the little room to the mirrored
door of the latrine. He opened it, entered, and closed it behind him.
The pompous swarthy little man got up, stretched his short fat arms out
stiffly, and said, "Well, I'll be turning in. I'll see you in the morning,
won't I, Jim?"

The man with the thin, tight, palely freckled face, to whom these
words had been addressed, looked up quickly from the magazine he
was reading, and said sharply, in a rather cold, surprised and distant
tone:

"What? . . . Oh! Yes. Good-night, Wade."

He got up then, carefully detached the horn-rimmed spectacles from
his long, pointed nose, folded them carefully and put them in the breast
pocket of his coat, and then took up the brief-case at his side. At this
moment, a man, accompanied by Robert Weaver and by another youth
who was about the same age as the boy, entered the smoking-room.

The man, who was in his middle thirties, was a tall lean Englishman, already bald, with bitten and incisive features, a cropped mustache, and the high hard flush of the steady drinker.

His name was John Hugh William Macpherson Marriott. He was the youngest son of an ancient family of the English nobility and just a year or two before he had married the great heiress, Virginia Willets. To the boy, and to all the other men in the train, except the man with the cold thin face and pointed nose, the Englishman was known only by sight and rumor, and his sudden entrance into the smoking-room had much the same effect as would the appearance of a figure from some legendary world of which they had often heard, but which they had never seen.

The reason for this feeling was that the Englishman and his wife lived on the great estate near town which her father had built and left to her. All the people in the town had seen this immense estate, had driven over some of its 90,000 acres, had seen its farms, its fields, its pastures, and its forests, its dairies, buildings, and its ranges of wild, smoke-blue mountains. And finally they had all seen from a distance its great mansion house, the gables, roof, and spires of a huge stone structure modelled on one of the great châteaux of France. But few of them had ever been inside the place or known the wonderful people who lived there.

All the lives of these fortunate people had become, therefore, as strange and wonderful to the people of the town as the lives of legendary heroes. And in a curious way that great estate had shaped the whole life of the town. To be a part of that life, to be admitted there, to know the people who belonged to it would have been the highest success, the greatest triumph that most of the people in the town could imagine. They could not admit it, but it was the truth. At the heart of the town's desire was the life of that great house.

The Englishman had entered the smoking compartment with the driving movement of a man who has been drinking hard, but is used to it. The moment that he entered, however, and saw the other people there he stopped short, with a kind of stunned abruptness. In a moment, after an astounded silence, he spoke to them, greeting them with the rough, brief, blurted-out friendliness of a shy and reticent man:

"Hello! . . . Oh, hello! . . . How do!" He grinned formally and suddenly began to stare with an astounded expression at the gouty figure of old Flood who at just this moment had opened the door of the latrine

and was shuffling painfully out into the compartment. Mr. Flood
stopped and returned his look in kind, with his bulging and bejowled
stare of comic stupefaction.

In a moment more the Englishman recovered himself, grimaced with
his shy, quick, toothy grin, and blurted out at Flood, as to the other men:
"Oh, hello! Hello! How d'ye do!"

"I'm pretty good, thank you!" old Flood said hoarsely and slowly,
after a heavy pause. "How are you?" and continued to stare heavily and
stupidly at him.

But already the Englishman had turned abruptly from him, his face
and lean neck reddening instantly and fiercely with the angry embarrassment of a shy man. And with the same air of astonished discovery
he now addressed himself to the man with the long thin nose and palely
freckled face, blurting his words out rapidly and by rushes as before,
but somehow conveying to the others the sense of his intimacy and
friendship with this man and of their own exclusion.

"Oh! . . . There you are, Jim!" he was saying in his astounded and
explosive fashion. "Where the devil have you been all night? . . . I
say!" he went on rapidly without waiting for an answer, "won't you
come in and have a spot with me before you turn in?"

Every suggestion of the disdain and cold aloofness which had characterized the other man's manner towards his fellow passengers, had now
vanished at the Englishman's words. Indeed, in the way he now came
forward, smiling, and put his hand in a friendly manner on the Englishman's arm, there was something almost scrambling in its effusive eagerness. "Why yes, Hugh," he said hastily. "I'd be delighted, of course!
. . . Just a minute," he said in an almost confused tone of voice, "till I
get my brief-case. . . . Where did I leave it? Oh, here it is!" he cried,
picking it up, and making for the door with his companion, "I'm all
ready now! Let's go!"

"Hugh! Hugh!" cried Robert who had accompanied the Englishman
when he entered the compartment, and whom the Englishman now
seemed to have forgotten entirely, "will I see you tomorrow before you
get off? The words were spoken in a deep, rapid, eager tone of voice,
and in the tone and manner of the youth who spoke them there was
the same suggestion of almost fawning eagerness that had characterized
the older man.

"Eh! What's that?" the Englishman cried in a startled tone, turning
abruptly and staring at the young man who had addressed him. "Oh!

Yes, Robert! I'm stopping at Washington! Look in for a moment, won't you, if you're up!"

Something in his tone and manner plainly and definitely said that the young man's company was no longer wanted for the evening, but the youth immediately nodded his head energetically and decisively, saying in a satisfied manner:

"Good! Good! I'll do that! I'll be in to say good-bye tomorrow morning."

"Right!" the Englishman said curtly. "Good-night! . . . Good-night! . . . Good-night!" he blurted out, turning around and addressing every one, yet seeing no one, in a series of toothy grimaces. "Oh—good-night!" he said suddenly, before going out, grinning and shaking hands briefly, in a gesture of permanent dismissal, with the other young man, who was a blond insignificant-looking youth, obviously a "hanger-on," with whom the Englishman evidently cared to have no further acquaintance. Then, pushing his companion before him through the green curtain, he went out suddenly with the same desperate shy abruptness, and in a moment the other men, saying good-night all around, had followed him, and the three young men were left alone in the compartment. It was now after one o'clock. Outside, the moon was up, flooding the dark earth of Virginia with a haunting light. That grand, moon-haunted earth stroked calmly past and, through the media of its changeless and unceasing change, the recession and recurrent movement of the enchanted scene, the train made on forever its tremendous monotone that was itself the rhythm of suspended time, the sound of silence and forever.

For a moment, after the men had gone, Robert stared down sternly and quizzically at the boy, with an expression of mock gravity, and then, in his rapid, eager, deep-toned and rather engaging voice, said:

"Well, Colonel? . . . What have you to say for yourself? . . . Was there grass on the back of her back, or was the foul deed perpetrated in your Hudson Super Six? . . . Come, sir! Explain yourself! Were you drunk or sober?" And suddenly lifting his thin, young, yet almost tortured-looking face and his restless eyes, which were inflamed with drink, and in whose haggard depths the incipient flashes of the madness which later would destroy him were already visible, he laughed suddenly, a strange, small, hoarsely falsetto kind of laugh, jerking his head towards the boy, and saying in an annoying and indefinite way:

"Crazy! Crazy! Crazy! . . . The craziest man I ever saw!" He stopped suddenly and, looking down at the boy for a moment with this same expression of haggard, over-driven restlessness, demanded impatiently:

"What have you been doing by yourself all night? Just sitting there all alone and doing nothing? . . . I'll swear, I don't see how you do it! . . . I'd go crazy sitting in one place like that without any one to talk to!" he said in an accusing and impatient tone of voice, as if the other youth had really done some extraordinary and unreasonable thing. He thrust one hand quickly and impatiently into the trousers' pocket of his well-cut clothes in such a way that his Delta Kappa Epsilon pin was for a moment visible. Then he stood there, jingling some coins about in his pocket and looking at the boy with his inflamed, restless, furiously desperate eyes. Turning away suddenly, with a movement of impatience, he shook his head in a gesture of astounded disbelief, laughed his little hoarse falsetto laugh again, and said:

"It beats me! . . . Don't see how he does it! . . . Damnedest man I ever saw! . . . It'd drive me crazy to be alone like that!"

He turned abruptly again, thrust both hands into his pockets, and for a moment stood looking at the boy with the old expression of mock gravity, and with a faintly malicious smile hovering about the edges of his thin, nervous, strongly modelled mouth.

"Do you know what they're saying about you at home? . . . Do you know what those people think of you? . . . Do you know what all those old women up there are doing now?" he said hoarsely and accusingly, in his deep, sonorous, and rapid tone.

"Now, Robert!" the boy suddenly shouted, in a choking and furious tone, getting to his feet. "Don't you start that stuff! I'm not going to listen to it! You can't fool me! They're not saying anything!"

Robert lifted his thin, finely drawn face and laughed again, his little annoying hoarse-falsetto laugh, in which a note of malice and triumph was audible.

"Why, they *are!*" he said solemnly. "It's the truth! . . . I think you ought to know about it! . . . I heard it everywhere, all over town!"

"Oh, Robert, you're a liar!" the boy cried furiously. *"What* did you hear all over town? You heard nothing!"

"Why, I *did!*" said Robert solemnly, as before. "I'll swear it to you. . . . Do you know what I heard the other day?" he went on in a blunt, accusing tone. "I heard that one of those women up there—some old sister in the Baptist Church—said she grew up with your mother and has known her all her life—well, she's praying for you!" said Robert solemnly. "I'll swear she is!"

"Praying for me!" the boy cried in an exasperated tone, but at the same time, feeling the numb white nauseous sickness of the heart which the intolerable thought that people are talking in a disparaging manner about him, his talents, or the success or failure of his life, can always bring to a young man. "Praying for me!" he fiercely shouted. "Why the hell should any one pray for me?"

"I know! I know!" said Robert, nodding his head vigorously, and speaking with grave agreement. "That's what I told them. That's just the way I felt about it! . . . But some of those people down there think you've gone to hell for good. . . . Do you know what I heard a woman say the other day? She said that Eugene Gant had gone straight to the devil since he went away to the State University——"

"Robert, I don't believe you!" the boy shouted. "You're making all this up!"

"Why, she did! So help me God, I heard her say it, as sure as I'm standing here," swore Robert solemnly. "She said you'd gone down there and taken Vergil Weldon's courses in philosophy and that you were ruined for life! She said you had turned into a regular infidel—didn't believe in God or anything any more. . . . Said she certainly did feel sorry for your mother," said Robert maliciously.

"Feel sorry for my mother!" the boy fairly howled, dancing around now like a maniac. "Why the hell should the old bitch feel sorry for my mother! My mother can take care of herself; she doesn't need any one to feel sorry for her! . . . All right, then!" he cried bitterly, with sudden acceptation of the other's story. "Let 'em pray! If that's the way they feel, let 'em pray till they wear corns on their God-damned knees! The dirty hypocrites!" he cried bitterly. "I'll show them! Sneaking around behind your back to tell their rotten lies about you—and their talk of praying for your soul! I'm glad I'm out of that damned town! The two-faced bastards! I wouldn't trust any of them as far as I could throw an elephant by his tail!"

"I know! I know!" said Robert, wagging his head in solemn agreement. "I agree with you absolutely. It's awful—that's what it is."

It was extraordinary that this absurd story, whether true or not, should have had such a violent effect on the emotions of the boy. Yet now that he had been told of some unknown woman's concern for the salvation of his soul, and that certain people of the praying sort already thought that he was "lost" the words were fastened in his flesh like rankling and envenomed barbs. And instantly, the moment that he heard this story and had cursed it, he thought that it was true. Now his mind could no longer remember the time just a moment before when Robert's words had seemed only an idle and malicious fabrication, probably designed to goad him, or, even if true, of no great importance.

But now, as if the idle gossip of the other youth had really pronounced some fatal and inexorable judgment against his whole life, the boy's spirit was set against "them" blindly, as against a nameless and hostile antagonist. Plunged suddenly into a dark weather of fatality and grim resolution, something in him was saying grimly and desperately:

"All right, then. If that's the way they feel about me, I'll show them." And seeing the lonely earth outside that went stroking past the windows of the train, he suddenly felt the dark and brooding joy of desperation and escape, and thought again: "Thank God, I've got away at last. Now there's a new land, a new life, new people like myself who will see and know me as I am and value me—and, by God, I'll show them! I'll show *them*, all right."

And at just this moment of his gloomy thoughts, he muttered sombrely, aloud, with sullen face:

"All right! To hell with them! I'll show them!"

—And was instantly aware that Robert was looking at him, laughing his little, malicious, hoarse, falsetto laugh, and that the other youth, who was a fair-haired, red-cheeked and pleasant-featured boy named Creasman, obviously somewhat inflamed by drink and by his social triumphs of the evening, was now, with an eager excessiveness of good-fellowship, slapping him on the back and saying boisterously:

"Don't let him kid you, Gene! To hell with them! What do you care what they say, anyway?"

With these words, he produced from his pocket a flask of the raw, colorless, savagely instant corn whiskey, of which both of them apparently had been partaking pretty freely, and tendering it to the boy, said:

"Here, take a drink!"

The boy took the flask, pulled out the cork, and putting the bottle to his lips, instantly gulped down two or three powerful swallows of the fiery stuff. For a moment, he stood there blind and choking, instantly robbed of breath, his throat muscles swelling, working, swallowing convulsively in an aching struggle to keep down the revolting and nauseous tasting stuff, and on no account to show the effort it was costing him.

"Is that the kick of the mule, or not?" said the Creasman boy, grinning and taking back his flask. "How is it?"

"Good!" the boy said hoarsely, gasping. "Fine! Best I ever tasted!" And he blinked his eyes rapidly to keep the tears from coming.

"Well, there's lots more where that came from, boy," said Creasman. "I've got two pint jars of it in my berth. Let me know when you want some more." And putting the bottle to his lips with a smile, he tilted his head, and drank in long easy swallows which showed he was no novice to the act.

"Damn!" cried Robert, staring at him, in his familiar tone of astounded disbelief. "Do you mean to tell me you can stand there drinking that stuff straight! Phew!" he said, shuddering, and making a face. "That old pukey stuff! Why, it'd rot the guts of a brass monkey! . . . I don't see how you people do it!" he cried protestingly, as he took the bottle. In three gulps he had drained it to the last drop, and even as he was looking around for a place to throw the empty flask, he shuddered convulsively again, made a contracted grimace of disgust, and said to the others accusingly, with his small falsetto laugh of astounded protest:

"Why, you'll kill yourself drinking that stuff raw! Don't you know that? You must be crazy! . . . Wait a minute," he muttered suddenly, comically, dropping the bottle deftly into his pocket, as the swarthy, pompous little man named Wade entered, attired in blue pajamas and a dressing gown, and holding a tooth-brush and a tube of tooth paste in his hand:

"Good-evening, sir! . . . Ah-hah! . . . How d'ye do!" said Robert, bowing slightly and stiffly, and speaking in his grave, staccato, curiously engaging tone.

"Still up, are you, boys?" the pompous little man remarked, with his usual telling aptness.

"Ah-hah-hah!" said Robert appreciatively. "Yes, sir! . . . Just fixin' to go! . . . Come on," he muttered to the others, jerking his head towards the little man warningly. "Not here! . . . Well, good-night, sir! . . . Goin' now."

"Good-night, boys," said the little man, who now had his back turned to them, and was standing at the silvery basin with his toothbrush held in readiness. "See you in the morning."

"Ah-hah-hah!" said Robert. "Yes, sir. That's right. Good-night."

And frowning in a meaningful way at his companions, he jerked his head toward the corridor, and, with an air of great severity, led them out.

"Didn't want him to see us with that bottle," he muttered when they were outside in the corridor. "Hell! He's got the biggest bank in town! Where'd you be if Emmet Wade ever got the idea you're a liquor-head! . . . Wait a minute!" he said, with the dissonant abruptness that characterized so much of his speech and action. "Come outside here—on the platform: nobody to see you there!"

"I'll meet you out there. I'll go and get another bottle," whispered Creasman, and disappeared along the darkened corridor in the direction of his berth. In a moment he returned, and the three of them went out upon the platform at the car-end, closed the door behind them and there, among the rocking and galloping noises of the pounding wheels, they took another long drink of the savage liquor. By this time the fiery stuff was leaping, pulsing, pounding the mounting and exuberant illusions of its power and strength through every tissue of their blood and life.

And outside, floating past their vision the huge pageant of its enchanted and immortal stillness, the old earth of Virginia now lay dreaming in the moon's white light.

So here they are now, three atoms on the huge breast of the indifferent earth, three youths out of a little town walled far away within the great rim of the silent mountains, already a distant, lonely dot upon the immense and sleeping visage of the continent. Here they are—three youths bound for the first time towards their image of the distant and enchanted city, sure that even though so many of their comrades had found there only dust and bitterness, the shining victory will be theirs. Here they are hurled onward in the great projectile of the train across the lonely visage of the everlasting earth. Here they are—three nameless grains of life among the manswarm ciphers of the earth, three faces of the million faces, three drops in the unceasing flood—and each of them a flame, a light, a glory, sure that his destiny is written in the blazing stars, his life shone over by the fortunate watches of the moon, his fame nourished and sustained by the huge earth, whose single darling charge he is, on whose immortal stillness he is flung onward in the night, his glorious fate set in the very brain and forehead of the fabulous, the unceasing city, of whose million-footed life he will tomorrow be a part.

Therefore they stand upon the rocking platform of the train, wild and dark and jubilant from the fierce liquor they have drunk, but more wild and dark and jubilant from the fury swelling in their hearts, the mad fury pounding in their veins, the savage, exultant and unutterable fury working like a madness in the adyts of their soul. And the great wheels smash and pound beneath their feet, the great wheels pound and smash and give a rhyme to madness, a tongue to hunger and desire, a certitude to all the savage, drunken, and exultant fury that keeps mounting, rising, swelling in them all the time!

Click, clack, clackety-clack; click, clack, clackety-clack; click, clack, clackety-clack; clackety-clackety-clack!

Hip, hop, hackety-hack; stip, step, rackety-rack; come and fetch it, come and fetch it, hickety hickety hack!

Rock, reel, smash, and swerve; hit it, hit it, on the curve; steady, steady, does the trick, keep her steady as a stick; eat the earth, eat the earth, slam and slug and beat the earth, and let her whir-r, and let her pur-r, at eighty per-r!

—Whew-w!

—Wow!

—God-dam!

—Put 'er there, boy!

—Put 'er there—whah!—*whah-h!* you ole long-legged frowsle-headed son-of-a-bitch!

—Whoop-ee! Whah—*whah-h!* Why, Go-d-d-dam!

—Whee! Vealer rog?

—Wadja say? Gant hearya!

—I say 'ja vealer rog? Wow! Pour it to her, son! Give 'er the gas! We're out to see the world! Run her off the god-damn track, boy! We don't need no rail, do we?

—Hell no! Which way does this damn train go, anyway, after it leaves Virginia?

—Maryland.

—Maryland my—! I don't want to go to Maryland! To hell with Mary's land! Also to hell with Mary's lamb and Mary's calf and Mary's blue silk underdrawers! Good old Lucy's the girl for me—the loosier the better! Give me Lucy any day! Good old Lucy Bowles, God bless her—she's the pick of the crowd, boys! Here's to Lucy!

Robert! Art there, boy?

—Aye, aye, sir! Present!

—Hast seen the damsel down in Lower Seven?

—I' sooth, sir, that I have! A comely wench, I trow!

—Peace, fool! Don't think, proud Princocke, thou canst snare this dove of innocence into the nets of infamous desire with stale reversions of thy wit! Out, out, vile lendings! An but thou carried'st at thy shrunken waist that monstrous tun of guts thou takest for a brain 'twould so beslubber this receiving earth with lard as was not seen twixt here and Nottingham since butter shrove! Out, out upon you, scrapings of the pot! A dove, a doe, it is a faultless swan, I say, a pretty thing!

Now Virginia lay dreaming in the moonlight. In Louisiana bayous the broken moonlight shivers the broken moonlight quivers the light of many rivers lay dreaming in the moonlight beaming in the moonlight dreaming in the moonlight moonlight moonlight seeming in the moonlight moonlight moonlight to be gleaming to be streaming in the moonlight moonlight moonlight moonlight moonlight moonlight moonlight moonlight

—Mo-hoo-oonlight-oonlight oonlight oonlight oonlight oonlight oonlight oonlight oonlight oonlight

—To be seeming to be dreaming in the moonlight!

WHAM!
SMASH!

—Now! God-dam, let her have it! Wow-w!

With slamming roar, hoarse waugh, and thunderbolted light, the southbound train is gone in one projectile smash of wind-like fury, and the open empty silence of its passing fills us, thrills us, stills us with the vision of Virginia in the moonlight, with the dream-still magic of Virginia in the moon.

And now, as if with recollected force, the train gains power from the train it passed, leaps, gathers, springs beneath them, smashes on with recollected demon's fury in the dark . . .

With slam-bang of devil's racket and God-dam of curse—give us the bottle, drink, boys, drink!—the power of Virginia lies compacted in the moon. To you, God-dam of devil's magic and slam-bang of drive, fire-flame of the terrific furnace, slam of rod, storm-stroke of pistoned wheel and thunderbolt of speed, great earth-devourer, city-bringer—hail!

To you, also, old glint of demon hawkeyes on the rail and the dark

gloved hand of cunning—you, there, old bristle-crops!—Tom Wilson,
H. F. Cline, or T. J. Johnson—whatever the hell your name is——
    CASEY JONES! Open the throttle, boy, and let her rip! Boys, I'm a
belly-busting bastard from the State of old Catawba—a rootin' tootin'
shootin' son-of-a-bitch from Saw Tooth Gap in Buncombe—why, God
help this lovely bastard of a train—it is the best damned train that ever
turned a wheel since Casey Jones's father was a pup—why, you sweet
bastard, run! Eat up Virginia!—Give her the throttle, you old goggle-
eyed son-of-a-bitch up there!—Pour it to her! Let 'er have it, you nigger-
Baptist bastard of a shovelling fireman—let 'er rip!—Wow! By God,
we'll be in Washington for breakfast!
    —Why, God bless this lovely bastard of a train! It is the best damned
train that ever pulled a car since Grant took Richmond!—Which way
does the damn thing go?—Pennsylvania?—Well, that's all right! Don't
you say a word against Pennsylvania! My father came from Pennsylvania, boys, he was the best damned man that ever lived—He was
a stonecutter and he's better than any son-of-a-bitch of a plumber you
ever saw—He's got a cancer and six doctors and they can't kill him!—
But to hell with going where we go!—We're out to see the world, boy!
—To hell with Baltimore, New York, Boston! Run her off the God-
damn rails! We're going West! Run her through the woods—cross
fields—rivers, through the hills! Hell's pecker! But I'll shove her up the
grade and through the gap, no double-header needed!—Let's see the
world now! Through Nebraska, boy! Let's shove her through, now,
you can do it!—Let's run her through Ohio, Kansas, and the unknown
plains! Come on, you hogger, let's see the great plains and the fields of
wheat—Stop off in Dakota, Minnesota, and the fertile places—Give us a
minute while you breathe to put our foot upon it, to feel it spring back
with the deep elastic feeling, 8000 miles below, unrolled and lavish,
depthless, different from the East.

    Now Virginia lay dreaming in the moonlight! And on Florida's
bright waters the fair and lovely daughters of the Wilsons and the Potters; the Cabots and the Lowells; the Weisbergs and O'Hares; the Astors
and the Goulds; the Ransoms and the Rands; the Westalls and the Pat-
tons and the Webbs; the Reynolds and McRaes; the Spanglers and the
Beams; the Gudgers and the Blakes; the Pedersons and Craigs—all the
lovely daughters, the Robinsons and Waters, the millionaires' sweet
daughters, the Boston maids, the Beacon Slades, the Back Bay Wades,

all of the merchant, lawyer, railroad and well-monied grades of Hudson River daughters in the moon's bright living waters—lay dreaming in the moonlight, beaming in the moonlight, seeming in the moonlight, to be dreaming to be gleaming in the moon.

—Give 'em hell, son!

—Here, give him another drink!—Attaboy! Drink her down!

—Drink her down—drink her down—drink her down—damn your soul—drink her down!

—By God, I'll drink her down and flood the whole end of Virginia, I'll drown out Maryland, make a flood in Pennsylvania—I tell you boys I'll float 'em, I'll raise 'em up, I'll bring 'em down stream, now—I mean the Potters and the Waters, the rich men's lovely daughters, the city's tender daughters, the Hudson river daughters——

Lay dreaming in the moonlight, beaming in the moonlight, to be seeming to be beaming in the moonlight moonlight moonlight oonlight oonlight oonlight oonlight oonlight.

And Virginia lay dreaming in the moon.

Then the moon blazed down upon the vast desolation of the American coasts, and on all the glut and hiss of tides, on all the surge and foaming slide of waters on lone beaches. The moon blazed down on 18,000 miles of coast, on the million sucks and scoops and hollows of the shore, and on the great wink of the sea, that ate the earth minutely and eternally. The moon blazed down upon the wilderness, it fell on sleeping woods, it dripped through moving leaves, it swarmed in weaving patterns on the earth, and it filled the cat's still eye with blazing yellow. The moon slept over mountains and lay like silence in the desert, and it carved the shadows of great rocks like time. The moon was mixed with flowing rivers, and it was buried in the heart of lakes, and it trembled on the water like bright fish. The moon steeped all the earth in its living and unearthly substance, it had a thousand visages, it painted continental space with ghostly light; and its light was proper to the nature of all the things it touched: it came in with the sea, it flowed with the rivers, and it was still and living on clear spaces in the forest where no men watched.

And in woodland darkness great birds fluttered to their sleep—in sleeping woodlands strange and secret birds, the teal, the nightjar, and the flying rail went to their sleep with flutterings dark as hearts of sleeping men. In fronded beds and on the leaves of unfamiliar plants where the tarantula, the adder, and the asp had fed themselves asleep on their

own poisons, and on lush jungle depths where green-golden, bitter red
and glossy blue proud tufted birds cried out with brainless scream, the
moonlight slept.

The moonlight slept above dark herds moving with slow grazings in
the night, it covered lonely little villages; but most of all it fell upon the
unbroken undulation of the wilderness, and it blazed on windows, and
moved across the face of sleeping men.

Sleep lay upon the wilderness, it lay across the faces of the nations, it
lay like silence on the hearts of sleeping men; and low upon lowlands,
and high upon hills, flowed gently sleep, smooth-sliding sleep—sleep—
sleep.

—Robert—

—Go on to bed, Gene, go to bed now, go to bed.

—There's shump'n I mush shay t'you——

—Damn fool! Go to bed!

—Go to bed, my balls! I'll go to bed when I'm God-damn good and
ready! I'll not go to bed when there's shump'n I mush shay t'you——

—Go on to bed now, Gene. You've had enough.

— Creasman, you're a good fellow maybe but I don't know you. . . .
You keep out of this. . . . Robert . . . I'm gonna tell y' shump'n. . . .
You made a remark t'night I didn' like—Prayin' for me, are they,
Robert?

—You damn fool!—You don't know what you're talkin' 'bout! Go on
to bed!——

—I'll go to bed, you bastard—I got shump'n to shay t'you!—Prayin'
for me, are yuh?—Pray for yourself, y' bloody little Deke!

—Damn fool's crazy! Go on to bed now——

—I'll bed yuh, you son-of-a-bitch! What was it that y' said that
day?——

—What day? You damned fool, you don't know what you're saying!

—I'll tell yuh what day!—Coming along Chestnut Street that day after
school with you and me and Sunny Jim Curtis and Ed Petrie and Bob
Pegram and Carl Hartshorn and Monk Paul—and the rest of those
boys——

—You damn fool! Chestnut Street! I don't know what you're talking
about!

—Yes, you do!— You and me and Bob and Carl and Irwin and Jim
Homes and some other boys— 'Member what y' said, yuh son-of-a-bitch?

Old man English was in his yard there burning up some leaves and it was October and we were comin' along there after school and you could smell the leaves and it was after school and you said, "Here's Mr. Gant the tomb-stone cutter's son."

—You damn fool! I don't know what you're talking about!——

—Yes, you do, you cheap Deke son-of-a-bitch— Too good to talk to us on the street when you were sucking around after Bruce Martin or Steve Patton or Jack Marriott—but a life-long brother—oh! couldn't see enough of us, could you, when you were alone?

—The damn fool's crazy!

—Crazy, am I?—Well, we never had any old gummy grannies tied down and hidden in the attic—which is more than some people that I know can say!—you son-of-a-bitch—who do you think you are with your big airs and big Deke pin!—My people were better people than your crowd ever hoped to be—we've been here longer and we're better people —and as for the tombstone cutter's son, my father was the best damned stonecutter that ever lived—he's dying of cancer and all the doctors in the world can't kill him—he's a better man than any little ex-police court magistrate who calls himself a judge will ever be—and that goes for you too—you——

Why, you crazy fool! I never said anything about your father——

To hell with you, you damn little bootlicking——

Come on Gene come on you've had enough you're drunk now come on.

Why God-damn you to hell, I hate your guts you——

All right, all right—He's drunk! He's crazy—Come on, Bill! Leave him alone!—He don't know what he's doing——

All right. Good night, Gene. . . . Be careful now—See you in the morning, boy.

All right, Robert, I mean nothing against you—you——

All right!—All right!—Come on, Bill. Let him alone! Good night, Gene—Come on—let's go to bed!——

To bed to bed to bed to bed to bed! So, so, so, so, so! Make no noise, make no noise, draw the curtains; so, so, so. We'll go to supper i' the morning: so so, so.

And Ile goe to bedde at noone.

Alone, alone now, down the dark, the green, the jungle aisle between the dark drugged snorings of the sleepers. The pause, the stir, the sigh, the sudden shift, the train that now rumbles on through the dark forests of the dream-charged moon-enchanted mind its monotone of silence and forever: Out of these prison bands of clothes, now, rip, tear, toss, and haul while the green-curtained sleepers move from jungle depths and the even-pounding silence of eternity—into the stiff white sheets, the close, hot air, his long body crookedly athwart, lights out, to see it shining faintly in the coffined under-surface of the berth above—and sleepless, Virginia floating, dreamlike, in the still white haunting of the moon——

—At night, great trains will pass us in the timeless spell of an unsleeping hypnosis, an endless, and unfathomable stupefaction. Then suddenly in the unwaking never sleeping century of the night, the sensual limbs of carnal whited nakedness that stir with drowsy silken warmth in the green secrecies of Lower Seven, the slow swelling and lonely and swarmhaunted land—and suddenly, suddenly, silence and thick hardening lust of dark exultant joy, the dreamlike passage of Virginia!— Then in the watches of the night a pause, the sudden silence of up-welling night, and unseen faces, voices, laughter, and farewells upon a lonely little night-time station—the lost and lonely voices of Americans:—"Good-bye! Good-bye, now! Write us when you get there, Helen! Tell Bob he's got to write! Give my love to Emily!—Good-bye, good-bye now—write us, soon!"— And then the secret, silken and subdued rustling past the thick green curtains and the sleepers, the low respectful negroid tones of the black porter—and then the whistle cry, the tolling bell, the great train mounting to its classic monotone again, and presently the last lights of a little town, the floating void and loneliness of moon-haunted earth—Virginia!

Also, in the dream—thickets of eternal night—there will be huge steamings on the rail, the sudden smash, the wall of light, the sudden flarings of wild, roaring light upon the moon-haunted and dream-tortured faces of the sleepers!

—And finally, in that dark jungle of the night, through all the visions, memories, and enchanted weavings of the timeless and eternal spell of time, the moment of forever—there are two horsemen, riding, riding, riding in the night.

Who are they? Oh, we know them with our life and they will ride across the land, the moon-haunted passage of our lives forever. Their names are Death and Pity, and we know their face: our brother and our father ride ever beside us in the dream-enchanted spell and vista of the night; the hooves keep level time beside the rhythms of the train.

Horsed on the black and moon-maned steeds of fury, cloaked in the dark of night, the spell of time, dream-pale, eternal, they are rushing on across the haunted land, the moon-enchanted wilderness, and their hooves make level thunder with the train.

Pale Pity and Lean Death their names are, and they will ride forevermore the moon-plantations of Virginia keeping time time time to the level thunder of the train pounding time time time as with four-hooved thunder of phantasmal hooves they pound forever level with the train across the moon-plantations of Virginia.

Quadrupedante putrem sonitu quatit ungula campum as with storm-phantasmal hooves Lean Death and Pale Pity will quadrupedante putrem sonitu quatit ungula campum . . . campum . . . quadrupedante . . . putrem . . . putrem . . . putrem putrem putrem as with sonitu quatit ungula campum quadrupedante putrem . . . putrem . . . putrem putrem putrem . . . putrem . . . putrem . . . putrem putrem putrem quadrupedante quadrupedante quadrupedante putrem putrem as with sonitu quatit ungula campum quadrupedante putrem . . . putrem . . . putrem putrem putrem . . . as with sonitu quatit ungula campum quadrupedante putrem . . . ungula campum . . . campum . . . ungula .   ungula campum . . .

V

At day-break suddenly, he awoke. The first light of the day, faint, gray-white, shone through the windows of his berth. The faint gray light fell on the stiff white linen, feverishly scuffed and rumpled in the distressful visions of the night, on the hot pillows and on the long cramped figure of the boy, where dim reflection already could be seen on the polished surface of the berth above his head. Outside, that smoke-gray light had stolen almost imperceptibly through the darkness. The air now shone gray-blue and faintly luminous with day, and the old brown earth was just beginning to emerge in that faint light. Slowly, the old brown earth was coming from the darkness with that strange and awful stillness which the first light of the day has always brought.

The earth emerged with all its ancient and eternal quality: stately and solemn and lonely-looking in that first light, it filled men's hearts with all its ancient wonder. It seemed to have been there forever, and, though they had never seen it before, to be more familiar to them than their mother's face. And at the same time it seemed they had discovered it once more, and if they had been the first men who ever saw the earth, the solemn joy of this discovery could not have seemed more strange or more familiar. Seeing it, they felt nothing but silence and wonder in their hearts, and were naked and alone and stripped down to their bare selves, as near to truth as men can ever come. They knew that they would die and that the earth would last forever. And with that feeling of joy, wonder, and sorrow in their hearts, they knew that another day had gone, another day had come, and they knew how brief and lonely are man's days.

The old earth went floating past then in that first gaunt light of the morning, and it seemed to be the face of time itself, and the noise the train made was the noise of silence. They were fixed there in that classic design of time and silence. The engine smoke went striding out upon the air, the old earth—field and wood and hill and stream and wood and field and hill—went stroking, floating past with a kind of everlasting repetitiveness, and the train kept making on its steady noise that was like silence and forever—until it almost seemed that they were poised there in that image of eternity forever—in moveless movement, unsilent silence, spaceless flight.

All of the noises, rhythms, sounds and variations of the train seemed to belong to all the visions, images, wild cries and oaths and songs and haunting memories of the night before, and now the train itself seemed united to this infinite monotone of silence, and the boy felt that this land now possessed his life, that he had known it forever, and could now think only with a feeling of unbelief and wonder that yesterday—just yesterday—he had left his home in the far mountains and now was stroking eastward, northward towards the sea.

And against the borders of the East, pure, radiant, for the first time seen in the unbelievable wonder of its new discovery, bringing to all of us, as it had always done, the first life that was ever known on this earth, the golden banner of the day appeared.

VI

IN morning sunlight on a hospital porch, five flights above the ground, an old dying spectre of a man was sitting, looking mournfully out across the sun-hazed sweep of the city he had known in his youth. He sat there, a rusty, creaking hinge, an almost severed thread of life, a shockingly wasted integument of skin and bone, of which every fibre and sinew was almost utterly rotted out, consumed and honey-combed by the great plant of the cancer which flowered from his entrails and had now spread its fibrous roots to every tissue of his life. Everything was gone: everything was wasted from him: the face was drawn tight and boney as a beak, the skin was clean, tinged with a fatal cancerous yellow, and almost delicately transparent. The great thin blade of nose cut down across the face with knife-like sharpness and in the bony, slant-ing, almost reptilian cage-formation of the skull, the smallish cold-gray-green eyes were set wearily, with a wretched and enfeebled dullness, out across the great space of the city which swept away and melted at length into the sun-hazed vistas of October.

Nothing was left but his hands. The rest of the man was dead. But the great hands of the stonecutter, on whose sinewy and bony substance there was so little that disease or death could waste, looked as power-ful and living as ever. Although one of his hands—the right one—had been stiffened years before by an attack of rheumatism, they had lost none of their character of power and massive shapeliness.

In the huge shapely knuckles, in the length and sinewy thickness of the great fingers—which were twice the size of an ordinary man's—and in the whole length and sinewy contour of the hand, there was a quality of sculptural design which was as solid and proportionate as any of the marble hands of love and grace which the stonecutter had so often carved upon the surface of a grave-yard monument.

Thus, as he sat there now, staring dully out across the city, an emaciated and phantasmal shadow of a man, there was, in the appear-ance of these great living hands of power (one of which lay with an enormous passive grace and dignity across the arm of his chair and the other extended and clasped down upon the handle of a walking stick), something weirdly incongruous, as if the great strong hands had been unnaturally attached to the puny lifeless figure of a scarecrow.

Now, wearily, desperately, the old enfeebled mind was trying to grope with the strange and bitter miracle of life, to get some meaning out of that black, senseless fusion of pain and joy and agony, that web that had known all the hope and joy and wonder of a boy, the fury, passion, drunkenness, and wild desire of youth, the rich adventure and fulfilment of a man, and that had led him to this fatal and abominable end.

But that fading, pain-sick mind, that darkened memory could draw no meaning and no comfort from its tragic meditation.

The old man's land of youth was far away in time, yet now only the

magic lonely hills of his life's journey, his wife's people, seemed sorrowful, lonely, lost, and strange to him. Now he remembered all places,
things, and people in his land of youth as if he had known them instantly
and forever!

Oh, what a land, a life, a time was that—that world of youth and no
return. What colors of green-gold, magic, rich plantations, and shining cities were in it! For now when this dying man thought about
this vanished life that tragic quality of sorrow and loneliness had vanished instantly. All that he had read in books about old wars seemed far
and lost and in another time, but when he thought about these things
that he had known as a boy, he saw them instantly, knew them, breathed
them, heard them, felt them, was there beside them, living them with
his own life. He remembered now his wife's people!—tramping in along
the Carlisle Pike on that hot first morning in July, as they marched in
towards Gettysburg. He had been standing there with his next older
brother Gil, beside the dusty road, as they came by.

And he could see them now, not as shadowy, lost, phantasmal figures
of dark time, the way they were in books; he saw them, heard them,
knew them again as they had been in their shapeless rags of uniforms,
their bare feet wound in rags, their lank disordered hair, sometimes
topped by stove-pipe hats which they had looted out of stores.

"God!" the old man thought, wetting his great thumb briefly, grinning thinly, as he shook his head, "What a scare-crow crew that was!
In all my days I never saw the like of it! A bum-looking lot, if ever there
was one!—And the bravest of the brave, the finest troops that ever lived!"
—his mind swung upward to its tide of rhetoric—"Veterans all of them,
who had been through the bloodiest battles of the war, they did not
know the meaning of the word 'fear,' and they would have gone into
the valley of death, the jaws of hell, at a word from their Commander!"
His mind was alive again, in full swing now, the old voice rose and
muttered on the tides of rhetoric, the great hand gestured, the cold-gray,
restless eyes glared feverishly about—and all of it began to live for him
again.

He remembered how he and Gil had been standing there beside the
road, two barefoot farmer boys, aged thirteen and fifteen, and he remembered how the rebels would halt upon their march, and shout jesting remarks at the two boys standing at the road. One shouted out to Gil:

"Hi, there, Yank! You'd better hide! Jeb Stuart's on the way an'
he's been lookin' fer you!"

And Gil, older, bolder, more assured than he, quick-tempered, stubborn, fiercely partisan, had come back like a flash:

"He'll be lookin' fer *you* when we get through with you!" said Gil and the rebels had slapped their ragged thighs and howled with laughter, shouting at their crestfallen, grinning comrade:

" 'Y, God! I reckon you'll be quiet now! He shore God put it on ye that time!"

And he was there beside his brother, seeing, hearing, living it again, as he remembered his strange first meeting with the Pentland tribe, the haunting miracle of that chance meeting. For among that ragged crew he had first seen his wife's uncle, the prophet, Bacchus Pentland, and he had seen him, heard him that hot morning, and had never been able to forget him, although it would be twenty years, after many strange turnings of the roads of destiny and wandering, before he was to see the man again, and know his name, and join together the two halves of fated meeting.

Yes, there had been one among the drawling and terrible mountaineers that day who passed there on that dusty road, and paused, and talked, and waited in the heat, one whose face he had never been able to forget—one whose full, ruddy face and tranquil eyes were lighted always by a smile of idiot and beatific saintliness, whose powerful fleshy body gave off a stench that would have put a goat to shame, and who on this account was called by his jesting comrades, "Stinking Jesus." Yes, he had been there that morning, Bacchus Pentland, the fated and chosen of God, the supernatural appearer on roads at nightfall, the harbinger of death, the prophet, chanting even then his promises of Armageddon and the Coming of the Lord, speaking for the first time to the fascinated ears of those two boys, the full, drawling, unctuous accents of the fated, time-triumphant Pentlands.

They came, they halted in the dust before the two young brothers, the lewd tongues mocked and jested, but that man of God, the prophet Bacchus Pentland, was beautifully unmoved by their unfaith, and chanted, with a smile of idiot beatitude, his glorious assurances of an end of death and battle, everlasting peace:

"Hit's a comin'!" cried the prophet with the sweet purity of his saintly smile. "Hit's a comin'! Accordin' to my figgers the Great Day is almost here! Oh, hit's a comin', boys!" he sweetly, cheerfully intoned, "Christ's kingdom on this airth's at hand! We're marchin' in to Armageddon now!"

"Hell, Back!" drawled one, with a slow grin of disbelief. "You said the same thing afore Chancellorsville, an' all I got from it was a slug of canister in my tail!"—and the others slapped their ragged thighs and shouted.

"Hit's a comin'!" Bacchus cried, with a brisk wink, and his seraphic smile, unmoved, untouched, by their derision. "He'll be here a-judgin' an' decreein' afore the week is over, settin' up His Kingdom, an' sortin' us all out the way it was foretold—the sheep upon His right hand an' the goats upon His left."

"An' which side are you goin' to be on, Back, when all this sortin' starts?" one drawled with evil innocence. "Are you goin' to be upon the sheep-side or the goat-side?" he demanded.

"Oh," cried Bacchus cheerfully, with his seraphic smile, "I'll be upon the sheep-side, brother, with the Chosen of the Lord."

"Then, Back," the other slowly answered, "you'd shore God better begin to smell a whole lot better than you do right now, for if the Lord starts sortin' in the dark, Back, He's goin' to put you where you don't belong—He'll have you over thar among the goats!"—and the hot brooding air had rung then with their roars of laughter. Then a word was spoken, an order given, the ragged files trudged on again, and they were gone.

Now this was lost, a fume of smoke, the moment's image of a fading memory, and he could not say it, speak it, find a word for it—but he could see that boy of his lost youth as he sat round the kitchen table with the rest of them. He could see his cold-gray, restless, unhappy eyes, the strange, gaunt, almost reptilian conformation of his staring face, his incredibly thin, blade-like nose, as he waited there in silence, looking uneasily at the others with his cold-gray, shallow, most unhappy eyes. And the old man seemed to be the spy of destiny, to look at once below the roofs of a million little houses everywhere and on the star-shone, death-flung mystery of the silent battlefield.

He seemed to be a witness of the secret weavings of dark chance that threads our million lives into strange purposes that we do not know. He thought of those dead and wounded men upon the battlefield whose lives would touch his own so nearly, the wounded brother that he knew, the wounded stranger he had seen that day by magic chance, whom he could not forget, and whose life, whose tribe, in the huge abyss and secret purpose of dark time would one day interweave into his own.

Oh, he could not find a word, a phrase to utter it, but he seemed to have the lives not only of those people in him, but the lives of millions of others whose dark fate is thus determined, interwove, and beyond their vision or their knowledge, foredone and made inevitable in the dark destiny of unfathomed time. And suddenly it seemed to him that all of it was his, even as his father's blood and earth was his, the lives and deaths and destinies of all his people. He had been a nameless atom in the great family of earth, a single, unknown thread in the huge warp of fate and chance that weaves our lives together and because of this he had been the richest man that ever lived; the power, grandeur, glory of this earth and all its lives of men were his.

And for a moment he forgot that he was old and dying, and pride, joy, pain, triumphant ecstasy that had no tongue to utter it rose like a wordless swelling pæan in his throat, because it seemed to him that this great familiar earth on which his people lived and wrought was his, that all the mystery, grandeur and beauty in the lives of men were his, and that he must find a word, a tongue, a door to utter what was his, or die!

How could he say it! How could he ever find a word to speak the joy, the pain, the grandeur bursting in the great vine of his heart, swelling like a huge grape in his throat—mad, sweet, wild, intolerable with all the mystery, loneliness, wild secret joy, and death, the ever-returning and renewing fruitfulness of the earth!

A cloud-shadow passed and left no light but loneliness on the massed green of the wilderness! A bird was calling in a secret wood! And there was something going, coming, fading there across the sun—oh, there was something lonely and most sorrowful, his mother's voice, the voices of lost men long, long ago, the flowing of a little river in the month of April—and all, all of it was his!

A man had passed at sunset on a lonely road and vanished unknown years ago! A soldier had toiled up a hill at evening and was gone! A man was lying dead that day upon a bloody field!—and all, all, all of it was his!

He had stood beside a dusty road, feet bare, his gaunt boy's face cold-eyed, staring, restless, and afraid. The ragged jesting rebels passed before him in the dusty heat, the huge drowse and cricketing stitch of noon was rising from the sweet woods and nobly swelling, fertile fields of Pennsylvania and all, all, all of it was his!

A prophet passed before him in the road that day with the familiar haunting unction of an unmet, unheard tribe; a wounded prophet lay that night below the stars and chanted glory, peace, and Armageddon; the boy's brother lay beside the prophet bleeding from the lungs; the boy's people grimly waited all night long in a little house not fourteen miles away; and all, all, all of it was his!

Over the wild and secret earth, the lonely, everlasting, and unchanging earth, under the huge tent of the all-engulfing night, amid the fury, chaos, blind confusions of a hundred million lives, something wild and secret had been weaving through the generations, a dark terrific weaving of the threads of time and destiny.

But it had come to this: an old man dying on a porch, staring through the sun-hazed vistas of October towards the lost country of his youth.

This was the end of man, then, end of life, of fury, hope, and passion, glory, all the strange and bitter miracle of chance, of history, fate, and destiny which even a stonecutter's life could include. This was the end, then:—an old man, feeble, foul, complaining and disease-consumed who sat looking from the high porch of a hospital at the city of his youth. This was the sickening and abominable end of flesh, which infected time and all man's living memory of morning, youth, and magic with the death-putrescence of its cancerous taint, and made us doubt that we had ever lived, or had a father, known joy: this was the end, and the end was horrible in ugliness. At the end it was not well.

On the last morning when his sons came, Gant was there on the high porch of the hospital, among the other old men who were sitting there. All of the old men looked very feeble, shrunk, and wasted, their skins had the clear and frail transparency that men get in hospitals, and in the bright tremendous light of morning and October, the old men looked forlorn.

Some looked out wearily and vacantly across the sun-hazed vistas of the city, with the dull and apathetic expression of men who are tired of pain and suffering and disease, and who wish to die. Others, who were in a state of convalescence after operations, looked out upon the sun-lit city with pleased, feeble smiles, awkwardly holding cigars in their frail fingers, putting them in their mouths with the uncertain and unaccustomed manner which a convalescent has, and looking up slowly, questioningly, with a feeble and uncertain smile into the faces of their relatives, wives, or children, as if to ask if it could really be true that they were going to live instead of die.

Their smiles and looks were pitiful in their sense of childish trust, of growing hopefulness, of wondering disbelief, but there was something shameful in them, too. In these feeble smiles of the old men there was something pleased and impotent, as if they had been adroitly castrated in the hospital, and shorn of their manhood. And for some reason, one felt suddenly a choking anger and resentment against some force in life which had betrayed these old men and made them impotent—something unspeakably ruthless, cruel, and savage in the world which had made these old and useless capons. And this anger against this unknown force suddenly took personal form in a blind resentment against doctors, nurses, internes, and the whole sinister and suave perfection of the hospital which, under glozing words and cynical assurances, could painlessly and deftly mutilate a living man.

The great engine of the hospital, with all its secret, sinister, and inhuman perfections, together with its clean and sterile smells which seemed to blot out the smell of rotting death around one, became a hateful presage of man's destined end. Suddenly, one got an image of his own death in such a place as this—of all that death had come to be—and the image of that death was somehow shameful. It was an image of a death without man's ancient pains and old gaunt aging—an image of death drugged and stupefied out of its ancient terror and stern dignities —of a shameful death that went out softly, dully in anesthetized oblivion, with the fading smell of chemicals on man's final breath. And the image of that death was hateful.

Thus, as Gant sat there, his great figure wasted to the bone, his skin yellow and transparent, his eyes old and dead, his chin hanging loose and petulant, as he stared dully and unseeingly out across the great city of his youth, his life seemed already to have been consumed and wasted, emptied out into the void of this cruel and inhuman space. Nothing was left, now, to suggest his life of fury, strength and passion except his hands. And the hands were still the great hands of the stone-cutter, powerful, sinewy, and hairy as they had always been, attached now with a shocking incongruity to the wasted figure of a scarecrow.

Then, as he sat there staring dully and feebly out upon the city, his great hairy hands quietly at rest upon the sides of his chair, the door opened and his two sons came out upon the porch.

"W-w-w-well, Papa," Luke sang out in his rich stammering tones. "Wy- wy, wy, wy, I f'ought we'd just c-c-c-come by for a m-m-m-moment to let Gene say g-g-good-bye to you." In a low tone to his younger brother he added nervously, "Wy, I f'ink, I f'ink I'd m-m-make it short and snappy if I were you. D-d-don't say anyf'ing to excite him, wy, wy, wy, I'd just say good-bye."

"Hello, son," said Gant quietly and dully, looking up at him. For a moment his great hand closed over the boy's, and he said quietly:

"Where are you going?"

"Wy, wy, wy, he's on his way up Norf . . . wy . . . he's g-g-going to Harvard, Papa."

"Be a good boy, son," Gant said gently. "Do the best you can. If you need anything let your mother know," he said wearily and indifferently, and turned his dead eyes away across the city.

"Wy . . . wy . . wy he'd like to tell you——"

"Oh, Jesus. . . . I don't want to hear about it," Gant began to sniffle in a whining tone. . . . "Why must it all be put on me . . . sick and old as I am? . . . If he wants anything let him ask his mother for it . . . it's fearful, it's awful, and it's cruel that you should afflict a sick man in this way." He was sniffling petulantly and his chin, on which a wiry stubble of beard was growing, trembled and shook like that of a whining child.

"I . . . I . . . I f'ink I'd just say g-g-good-bye now, Gene . . . m-m-make it, wy make it quick if you can: he's not f-f-feeling good today."

"Good-bye, Papa," the boy said, and bending, took his father's great right hand.

"Good-bye, son," Gant now said quietly as before, looking up at him. He presented his grizzled mustache, and the boy kissed him briefly, feeling the wiry bristles of the mustache brush his cheek as they had always done.

"Take care of yourself, son," said Gant kindly. "Do the best you can." And for a moment he covered the boy's hand with one great palm, and gestured briefly across the city: "I was a boy here," Gant said quietly, "over fifty years ago . . . old Jeff Streeter's hotel where I lived was there," he pointed briefly with his great forefinger. ". . . I was alone in this great city like the city you are going to—a poor friendless country boy who had come here to learn his trade as apprentice to a stonecutter . . . and I had come from . . . *there!*" as he spoke these words, a flash of the old power and life had come into Gant's voice, and now he was pointing his great finger strongly towards the sun-hazed vistas of the North and West.

"There!" cried Gant strongly now, his eye bright and shining as he followed the direction of his pointing finger. "Do you see, son? . . .

Pennsylvania . . . Gettysburg . . . Brant's Mill . . . the country that I came from is *there!* . . . Now I shall never see it any more," he said. "I'm an old man and I'm dying. . . . The big farms . . . the orchards . . . the great barns bigger than houses. . . . You must go back, son, someday to see the country that your father came from. . . . I was a boy here," the old man muttered. "Now I'm an old man. . . . I'll come back no more. . . . No more . . . it's pretty strange when you come to think of it," he muttered, "by God it is!"

"Wy, wy, P-p-p-papa," Luke said nervously, "I . . . I f'ink if he's g-g-going to get his train wy we'd better——"

"Good-bye, son," Gant said quietly again, giving the boy the pressure of his great right hand. "Be a good boy, now."

But already all the fires of life, so briefly kindled by this memory of the past, had died away: he was an old sick man again, and he had turned his dead eyes away from his son and was staring dully out across the city.

"Good-bye, Papa," the boy said, and then paused uncertainly, not knowing further what to say. From the old man there had come suddenly the loathesome stench of rotting death, corrupt mortality, and he turned swiftly away with a feeling of horror in his heart, remembering the good male smell of childhood and his father's prime—the smell of the old worn sofa, the chairs, the sitting room, the roaring fires, the plug tobacco on the mantelpiece.

At the screen door he paused again and looked back down the porch. His father was sitting there as he had left him, among the other old dying men, his long chin loose, mouth half open, his dead dull eye fixed vacantly across the sun-hazed city of his youth, his great hand of power quietly dropped upon his cane.

Down in the city's central web, the boy could distinguish faintly the line of the rails, and see the engine smoke above the railroad yards, and as he looked, he heard far off that haunting sound and prophecy of youth and of his life—the bell, the wheel, the wailing whistle—and the train.

Then he turned swiftly and went to meet it—and all the new lands, morning, and the shining city. Upon the porch his father had not moved or stirred. He knew that he should never see him again.

BOOK II

YOUNG FAUSTUS

VII

THE train rushed on across the brown autumnal land, by wink of water and the rocky coasts, the small white towns and flaming colors and the lonely, tragic and elemental beauty of New England. It was the country of his heart's desire, the dark Helen in his blood forever burning —and now the fast approach across October land, the engine smoke that streaked back on the sharp gray air that day!

The coming on of the great earth, the new lands, the enchanted city, the approach, so smoky, blind and stifled, to the ancient web, the old grimed thrilling barricades of Boston. The streets and buildings that slid past that day with such a haunting strange familiarity, the mighty engine steaming to its halt, and the great train-shed dense with smoke and acrid with its smell and full of the slow pantings of a dozen engines, now passive as great cats, the mighty station with the ceaseless throngings of its illimitable life, and all of the numerous, remote and mighty sounds of time forever held there in the station, together with a tart and nasal voice, a hand'sbreadth off that said: "There's hahdly time, but try it if you want."

He saw the narrow, twisted age-browned streets of Boston, then, with their sultry fragrance of fresh-roasted coffee, the sight of the man-swarm passing in its million-footed weft, the distant drone and murmur of the great mysterious city all about him, the shining water of the Basin, and the murmur of the harbor and its ships, the promise of glory and of a thousand secret, lovely and mysterious women that were waiting somewhere in the city's web.

He saw the furious streets of life with their unending flood-tide of a million faces, the enormous library with its million books; or was it just one moment in the flood-tide of the city, at five o'clock, a voice, a face, a brawny lusty girl with smiling mouth who passed him in an instant at the Park Street station, stood printed in the strong October wind a moment—breast, belly, arm, and thigh, and all her brawny lustihood—and then had gone into the man-swarm, lost forever, never found.

Was it at such a moment—engine-smoke, a station, a street, the sound of time, a face that came and passed and vanished, could not be forgot—

here or *here* or *here,* at such a moment of man's unrecorded memory, that he breathed fury from the air, that fury came?

He never knew; but now mad fury gripped his life, and he was haunted by the dream of time. Ten years must come and go without a moment's rest from fury, ten years of fury, hunger, all of the wandering in a young man's life. And for what? For what?

What is the fury which this youth will feel, which will lash him on against the great earth forever? It is the brain that maddens with its own excess, the heart that breaks from the anguish of its own frustration. It is the hunger that grows from everything it feeds upon, the thirst that gulps down rivers and remains insatiate. It is to see a million men, a million faces and to be a stranger and an alien to them always. It is to prowl the stacks of an enormous library at night, to tear the books out of a thousand shelves, to read in them with the mad hunger of the youth of man.

It is to have the old unquiet mind, the famished heart, the restless soul; it is to lose hope, heart, and all joy utterly, and then to have them wake again, to have the old feeling return with overwhelming force that he is about to find the thing for which his life obscurely and desperately is groping—for which all men on this earth have sought— one face out of the million faces, a wall, a door, a place of certitude and peace and wandering no more. For what is it that we Americans are seeking always on this earth? Why is it we have crossed the stormy seas so many times alone, lain in a thousand alien rooms at night hearing the sounds of time, dark time, and thought until heart, brain, flesh and spirit were sick and weary with the thought of it; "Where shall I go now? What shall I do?"

He did not know the moment that it came, but it came instantly, at once. And from that moment on mad fury seized him, from that moment on, his life, more than the life of any one that he would ever know, was to be spent in solitude and wandering. Why this was true, or how it happened, he would never know; yet it was so. From this time on—save for two intervals in his life—he was to live about as solitary a life as a modern man can have. And it is meant by this that the number of hours, days, months, and years—the actual time he spent alone— would be immense and extraordinary.

And this fact was all the more astonishing because he never seemed to seek out solitude, nor did he shrink from life, or seek to build himself into a wall away from all the fury and the turmoil of the earth. Rather, he loved life so dearly that he was driven mad by the thirst and hunger which he felt for it. Of this fury, which was to lash and drive him on for fifteen years, the thousandth part could not be told, and what is told may seem unbelievable, but it is true. He was driven by a hunger so literal, cruel and physical that it wanted to devour the earth and all the things and people in it, and when it failed in this attempt, his spirit would drown in an ocean of horror and desolation, smothered below the overwhelming tides of this great earth, sickened and made sterile, hopeless, dead by the stupefying weight of men and objects in the world, the everlasting flock and flooding of the crowd.

Now he would prowl the stacks of the library at night, pulling books out of a thousand shelves and reading in them like a madman. The thought of these vast stacks of books would drive him mad: the more he read, the less he seemed to know—the greater the number of the books he read, the greater the immense uncountable number of those which he could never read would seem to be. Within a period of ten years he read at least 20,000 volumes—deliberately the number is set low—and opened the pages and looked through many times that number. This may seem unbelievable, but it happened. Dryden said this about Ben Jonson: "Other men read books but he read libraries"—and so now was it with this boy. Yet this terrific orgy of the books brought him no comfort, peace, or wisdom of the mind and heart. Instead, his fury and despair increased from what they fed upon, his hunger mounted with the food it ate.

He read insanely, by the hundreds, the thousands, the ten thousands, yet he had no desire to be bookish; no one could describe this mad assault upon print as scholarly: a ravening appetite in him demanded that he read everything that had ever been written about human experience. He read no more from pleasure—the thought that other books were waiting for him tore at his heart forever. He pictured himself as tearing the entrails from a book as from a fowl. At first, hovering over book stalls, or walking at night among the vast piled shelves of the library, he would read, watch in hand, muttering to himself in triumph or anger at the timing of each page: "Fifty seconds to do that one. Damn you, we'll see! You will, will you?"—and he would tear through the next page in twenty seconds.

This fury which drove him on to read so many books had nothing to do with scholarship, nothing to do with academic honors, nothing to do with formal learning. He was not in any way a scholar and did not want to be one. He simply wanted to know about everything on earth; he wanted to devour the earth, and it drove him mad when he saw he could not do this. And it was the same with everything he did. In the midst of a furious burst of reading in the enormous library, the thought of the streets outside and the great city all around him would drive through his body like a sword. It would now seem to him that every second that he passed among the books was being wasted—that at this moment something priceless, irrecoverable was happening in the streets, and that if he could only get to it in time and see it, he would somehow get the knowledge of the whole thing in him—the source, the well, the spring from which all men and words and actions, and every design upon this earth proceeds.

And he would rush out in the streets to find it, be hurled through the tunnel into Boston and then spend hours in driving himself savagely through a hundred streets, looking into the faces of a million people, trying to get an instant and conclusive picture of all they did and said and were, of all their million destinies, and of the great city and the everlasting earth, and the immense and lonely skies that bent above them. And he would search the furious streets until bone and brain and blood could stand no more—until every sinew of his life and spirit was wrung, trembling, and exhausted, and his heart sank down beneath its weight of desolation and despair.

Yet a furious hope, a wild extravagant belief, was burning in him all the time. He would write down enormous charts and plans and projects of all that he proposed to do in life—a program of work and living which would have exhausted the energies of 10,000 men. He would get up in the middle of the night to scrawl down insane catalogs of all that he had seen and done:—the number of books he had read, the number of miles he had travelled, the number of people he had known, the number of women he had slept with, the number of meals he had eaten, the number of towns he had visited, the number of states he had been in.

And at one moment he would gloat and chuckle over these stupendous lists like a miser gloating over his board, only to groan bitterly with despair the next moment, and to beat his head against the wall, as he remembered the overwhelming amount of all he had not seen or done, or known. Then he would begin another list filled with enormous catalogs of all the books he had not read, all the food he had not eaten, all the women that he had not slept with, all the states he had not been in, all the towns he had not visited. Then he would write down plans and programs whereby all these things must be accomplished, how many years it would take to do it all, and how old he would be when he had finished. An enormous wave of hope and joy would surge up in him, because it now looked easy, and he had no doubt at all that he could do it.

He never asked himself in any practical way how he was going to live while this was going on, where he was going to get the money for this gigantic adventure, and what he was going to do to make it possible. If he thought about it, it seemed to have no importance or reality whatever—he just dismissed it impatiently, or with a conviction that some old man would die and leave him a fortune, that he was going to pick up a purse containing hundreds of thousands of dollars while walking in the Fenway, and that the reward would be enough to keep him going, or that a beautiful and rich young widow, true-hearted, tender, loving, and voluptuous, who had carrot-colored hair, little freckles on her face, a snub nose and luminous gray-green eyes with something wicked, yet loving and faithful in them, and one gold filling in her solid little teeth, was going to fall in love with him, marry him, and be forever true and faithful to him while he went reading, eating, drinking, whoring, and devouring his way around the world; or finally that he would write a book or play every year or so, which would be a great success, and yield him fifteen or twenty thousand dollars at a crack. Thus, he went storming away at the whole earth about him, sometimes mad with despair, weariness, and bewilderment; and sometimes wild with a jubilant and exultant joy and certitude as the conviction came to him that everything would happen as he wished. Then at night he would hear the vast sounds and silence of the earth and of the city, he would begin to think of the dark sleeping earth and of the continent of night, until it seemed to him it all was spread before him like a map—rivers, plains, and mountains and 10,000 sleeping towns; it seemed to him that he saw everything at once.

VIII

One morning, a few days after his arrival in Cambridge, he had received a letter, written on plain but costly paper in a fine but almost feminine hand. The letter read as follows:

"Dear Sir: I should be pleased to have your company for dinner

Wednesday evening at eight-thirty at The Cock Horse Tavern on Brattle
Street. In case of your acceptance will you kindly call at my rooms in
Holyoke House, opposite the Widener Library, at seven-fifteen?

Sincerely yours,

FRANCIS STARWICK."

He read that curt and cryptic note over and over with feelings mixed
of astonishment and excitement. Who was Francis Starwick? Why
should Francis Starwick, a stranger of whom he had never heard, invite
him to dinner? And why was that laconic note not accompanied by a
word of explanation?

It is likely he would have gone anyway, from sheer curiosity, and because of the desperate eagerness with which a young man, alone in a
strange world for the first time, welcomes any hope of friendship. But
before the day was over, he had learned from another student in Professor
Hatcher's celebrated course for dramatists, of which he himself was
now a member, that Francis Starwick was Professor Hatcher's assistant;
and correctly inferring that the invitation had some connection with this
circumstance, he resolved to go.

In this way, his acquaintance began with that rare and tragically gifted
creature who was one of most extraordinary figures of his generation
and who, possessing almost every talent that an artist needs, was lacking
in that one small grain of common earth that could have saved him, and
brought his work to life.

No fatality rested on that casual meeting. He could not have foreseen
in what strange and sorrowful ways his life would weave and interweave
with this other one, nor could he have known from any circumstance of
that first meeting that this other youth was destined to be that triune
figure in his life, of which each man knows one and only one, in youth,
and which belongs to the weather of man's life, and to the fabric of his
destiny: his friend, his brother—and his mortal enemy. Nor was there,
in the boy he met that night, any prefigurement of the tragic fatality with
which that brilliant life was starred, the horrible end toward which,
perhaps, it even then was directed.

They were both young men, and both filled with all the vanity, anguish
and hot pride of youth, and with its devotion and humility; they were
both strong in their proud hope and faith and untried confidence; they
both had shining gifts and powers and they were sure the world was
theirs; they were splendid and fierce and weak and strong and foolish;

the prescience of wild swelling joy was in them; and the goat cry was still torn from their wild young throats. They knew that the most fortunate, good and happy life that any man had ever known was theirs, if they would only take it; they knew that it impended instantly—the fortune, fame, and love for which their souls were panting; neither had yet turned the dark column, they knew that they were twenty, and that they could never die.

Francis Starwick, on first sight, was a youth of medium height and average weight, verging perhaps toward slenderness, with a pleasant ruddy face, brown eyes, a mass of curly auburn-reddish hair, and a cleft chin. The face in its pleasant cast and healthy tone, and spacious, quiet intelligence was strikingly like those faces of young Englishmen which were painted by Hoppner and Sir Henry Raeburn towards the beginning of the nineteenth century. It was an attractive, pleasant immensely sensitive and intelligent face, but when Starwick spoke this impression of warmth and friendliness was instantly destroyed.

He spoke in a strange and rather disturbing tone, the pitch and timbre of which it would be almost impossible to define, but which would haunt one who had heard it forever after. His voice was neither very high nor low, it was a man's voice and yet one felt it might almost have been a woman's; but there was nothing at all effeminate about it. It was simply a strange voice compared to most American voices, which are rasping, nasal, brutally coarse or metallic. Starwick's voice had a disturbing lurking resonance, an exotic, sensuous, and almost voluptuous quality. Moreover, the peculiar mannered affectation of his speech was so studied that it hardly escaped extravagance. If it had not been for the dignity, grace, and intelligence of his person, the affectation of his speech might have been ridiculous. As it was, the other youth felt the moment's swift resentment and hostility that is instinctive with the American when he thinks some one is speaking in an affected manner.

As Starwick welcomed his guest his ruddy face flushed brick-red with the agonizing embarrassment of a shy and sensitive person to whom every new meeting is an ordeal; his greeting was almost repellently cold and formal, but this, too, with the studied affectation of his speech, was protective armor for his shyness.

"A-d'ye-do," he said, shaking hands, the greeting coming from his throat through lips that scarcely seemed to move. "It was good of you to come."

"It was good of you to ask me," the other boy said awkwardly, fumbled desperately for a moment, and then blurted out—"I didn't know who you were at first—when I got your note—but then somebody told me:—you're Professor Hatcher's assistant, aren't you?"

"Ace," said Starwick, this strange sound which was intended for "yes" coming through his lips in the same curious and almost motionless fashion. The brick-red hue of his ruddy face deepened painfully, and for a moment he was silent—"Look!" he said suddenly, yet with a casualness that was very warm and welcome after the stilted formality of his greeting, "would you like a drink? I have some whiskey."

"Why, yes—sure—certainly," the other stammered, almost feverishly grateful for the diversion—"I'd like it."

Starwick opened the doors of a small cupboard, took out a bottle, a siphon, and some glasses on a tray, and placed them on a table.

"Help yourself," he said. "Do you like it with soda—or plain water— or how?"

"Why—any way you do," the other youth stammered. "Aren't you going to drink? I don't want to, unless you do."

"Ace," said Starwick again, "I'll drink with you. I like the soda," he added, and poured a drink for himself and filled it with the siphon. "Go on. Pour your own. . . . Look," he said abruptly again, as the other youth was awkwardly manipulating the unaccustomed siphon. "Do you mind if I drink mine while I'm shaving? I just came in. I'd like to shave and change my shirt before we go out. Do you mind?"

"No, of course not," the other said, grateful for the respite thus afforded. "Go ahead. Take all the time you like. I'll drink my drink and have a look at your books, if you don't mind."

"Please do," said Starwick, "if you find anything you like. I think this is the best chair." He pushed a big chair up beneath a reading lamp and switched the light on. "There are cigarettes on the table," he said in his strange mannered tone, and went into the bathroom, where, after a moment's inspection of his ruddy face, he immediately began to lather himself and to prepare for shaving.

"This is a nice place you have here," the visitor said presently, after another awkward pause, during which the only sound was the minute scrape of the razor blade on Starwick's face.

"Quite," he answered concisely, in his mannered tone, and with that blurred sound of people who try to talk while they are shaving. For a few moments the razor scraped on. "I'm glad you like it," Starwick said presently, as he put the razor down and began to inspect his work in the mirror. "And what kind of place did you find for yourself? Do you like it?"

"Well, it will do, I guess," the other boy said dubiously. "Of course, it's nothing like this—it's not an apartment; it's just a room I rented."

"Ace," said Starwick from the bathroom. "And where is that?"

"It's on a street called Buckingham Road. Do you know where that is?"

"Oh," said Starwick coldly, and he craned carefully with his neck, and was silent a moment as he did a little delicate razor-work around the Adam's apple. "Ace," he said at length as he put the razor down again. "I think I do. . . . And how did you happen to go out there?" he inquired coldly as he began to dry his face on a towel. "Did some one tell you about the place?"

"Well—yes. I knew about it before I came. It's a room in a house that some people I know have rented."

"Oh," said Starwick coldly, formally again, as he thrust his arms into a fresh shirt. "Then you do know people here in Cambridge?"

"Well, no: they are really people from home."

"Home?"

"Yes—from my own state, the place I came from, where I went to school before I came here."

"Oh," said Starwick, buttoning his shirt, "I see. And where was that? What state are you from?"

"Catawba."

"Oh. . . . And you went to school down there?"

"Yes. To the State University."

"I see. . . . And these people who have the house where you are living now—what are they doing here?"

"Well, the man—he's a professor at the State University down there—he's up here getting some sort of degree in education."

"In what?"

"In education."

"Oh. I see. . . . And what does his wife do; has he got a wife?"

"Yes; and three children. . . . Well," the other youth said uncertainly, and then laughed suddenly, "I haven't seen her do anything yet but sit on her tail and talk."

"Ace?" said Starwick, knotting his tie very carefully. "And what does she talk about?"

"Of people back home, mostly—the professors at the University, and their wives and families."

"Oh," said Starwick gravely, but there was now lurking in his voice an indefinable drollery of humor. "And does she say nice things about them?" He looked out towards his guest with a grave face, but a sly burble in his voice now escaped him and broke out in an infectious chuckling laugh. "Or is she—" for a moment he was silent, trembling a little with secret merriment, and his pleasant face reddened with laughter—"or is she," he said with sly insinuation—"bitter?"

The other, somehow conquered by the sly yet broad and vulgar humor in Starwick's tone, broke out into a loud guffaw, and said:

"God! she's bitter—and nothing but! That's just the word for it."

"Has any one escaped yet?" said Starwick slyly.

"Not a damned one of them," the other roared. "She's worked her way from the President and his family all the way down to the instructors. Now she's started on the people of the town. I've heard about every miscarriage and every dirty pair of drawers that ever happened there. We've got a bet on a friend of mine from home who's also staying there—he's in the Law School—whether she's going to say anything good about any one before the year is over."

"And which side have you?" said Starwick.

"I say she won't—but Billy Ingram says she will. He says that the last time she said anything good about any one was when some one died during the influenza epidemic in 1917; and he claims she's due again."

"And what is the lady's name?" said Starwick. He had now come out into the living room and was putting on his coat.

"Trotter," the other said, feeling a strange convulsive humor swelling in him. "Mrs. Trotter."

"What?" said Starwick, his face reddening and the sly burble appearing in his voice again. "Mrs.—who?"

"Mrs. Trotter!" the other choked, and the room rang suddenly with their wild laughter. When it had subsided, Starwick blew his nose vigorously, and his pleasant face still reddened with laughter, he asked smoothly:

"And what does Professor Trotter say while this is going on?"

"He doesn't say anything," the other laughed. "He can't say anything. He just sits there and listens. . . . The man's all right. Billy and I feel sorry for him. He's got this damned old shrew of a wife who sits there talking ninety to the minute, and three of the meanest, dirtiest, noisiest little devils you ever saw falling over his feet and raising hell from morning to night, and this sloppy nigger wench they brought up with them from the South—the place looks like an earthquake hit it, and the poor devil is up here trying to study for a degree—it's pretty hard on him. He's a nice fellow, and he doesn't deserve it."

"God!" said Starwick frankly and gravely, "but it sounds dreary! Why did you ever go to such a place?"

"Well, you see, I didn't know any one in Cambridge—and I had known these people back home."

"I should think that would have made you anxious to avoid them," Starwick answered. "And it's most important that you have a pleasant place to work in. It really is, you know," he said earnestly and with a note of reproof in his mannered tone. "You really should be more careful about that," he said.

"Yes, I suppose it is. You certainly have a good place here."

"Ace," said Starwick. "It is very pleasant. I'm glad you like it."

He came out, with his drink in his hand, put the drink down on a table and sat down beside it, crossing his legs and reaching for one of the straw-tipped cigarettes in a small and curiously carved wooden box. The impression he made on the other youth was one of magnificence and luxury. The boy's rooms seemed to fit his sensuous and elegant personality like a glove: he was only twenty-two years old but his distinctive and incomparable quality was everywhere about him in these two rooms.

To the unaccustomed eyes of the younger boy, these modest rooms seemed to be the most magnificent apartment he had seen. For a moment he thought that Starwick must be an immensely wealthy person to live in such a way. The fact that a man so young should live in such splendid and luxurious independence—that he should "have his own place," an apartment of his own, instead of a rented room, the thrilling solitudes of midnight privacy to himself, the freedom to come and go as he pleased, to do as he wished, to invite to his place whoever he chose, "to bring a girl there" whenever he wanted, without fear or the need for stealth—all these simple things which are just part of the grand and hopeful joy of youth, which the younger boy had never known, but to which he had aspired, as every youth aspires, in many a thrilling fantasy —now made Starwick's life seem almost impossibly fortunate, happy and exciting.

And yet it was not merely his own inexperience that made Starwick seem so wealthy. Starwick, although he had no regular income save a thousand dollars a year which he received for his work as Professor

Hatcher's assistant, and small sums he got from time to time from his family—he was, incredibly enough, the youngest of a middle-western family of nine children, small business and farming people in modest circumstances—gave the impression of wealth because he really was a wealthy person: he had been born wealthy, endowed with wealth by nature. In everything he did and said and was, in all he touched, in the whole quality of his rare and sensuous personality there was an opulence of wealth and luxury such as could not be found in a hundred million-aires. He had that rare and priceless quality that is seldom found in any one, and almost never in Americans, of being able to give to any simple act or incident a glamour of luxury, pleasure, excitement. Thus, when he smoked a cigarette, or drank a drink, or invited some one to go with him to the theatre, or ordered a meal in a shabby Italian restaurant, or made coffee in his rooms, or talked of something he had read in a book, or tied his neck-tie—all these things had a rare, wonderful and thrilling quality in them that the richest millionaire in the world could not have bought for money. And for this reason, people were instantly captivated by the infinite grace and persuasiveness of Starwick's personality: he had the power, as few people in the world have ever had the power, instantly to conquer and command the devotion of people because, while they were with him, everything in the world took on a freshness, wonder, joy and opulence it had never had before, and for this reason people wanted to be near him, to live in this thrilling enhancement that he gave to everything.

Even as he sat there smoking, drinking and talking with his guest, he did a simple and characteristic thing that yet seemed wonderful and thrilling to the other boy.

"Look," said Starwick suddenly, getting up, going over to one of his bookshelves and switching on a light. "Look," he said again, in his strangely fibred voice, "did you ever read this?"

As he uttered these words he took a book from one of the shelves and put on his spectacles. There was something strange and wonderful about the spectacles, and in the way he put them on, quietly, severely, plainly; the spectacles had thick old-fashioned silver rims, and silver handles. Their plain, honest and old-fashioned sobriety was somehow remarkable, and as he put them on, with a patient and quiet movement, and turned his attention to the pages of the book, the gravity and maturity of quiet and lonely thought in the boy's face and head was remarkably evident.

"Did you ever read this?" he said quietly, turning to the other youth, and handing him the book. It was a copy of George Moore's *Confessions of a Young Man:* the other replied he had not read it.

"Then," said Starwick, "why don't you take it along with you? It's really quite amusing." He switched off the light above the book shelves, took off his glasses with a quiet tired movement, and folding them and putting them in his breast pocket, came back to the table and sat down.

"I think it may interest you," he said.

Alhough the other boy had always felt an instinctive repulsion towards books which some one else urged him to read, something in Starwick's simple act had suddenly given the book a strange rare value: he felt a strange and pleasurable excitement when he thought about it, and was instantly eager and curious to read it. Moreover, in an indefinable way, he had understood the moment that Starwick turned to him, that he was *giving,* and not *lending* him the book; and this act, too, instantly was invested with a princely and generous opulence. It was this way with everything that Starwick did: everything he touched would come instantly to life with grace and joy; his was an incomparable, an enslaving power—a Midas-gift of life and joy almost too fortunate and effortless for one man to possess and in the end like all his other gifts of life and joy, a power that would serve death, not life, that would spread corruption instead of health, and that finally would turn upon its owner and destroy him.

Later, when they left his rooms and went out on the street, the sensuous quickening of life, the vital excitement and anticipation which Starwick was somehow able to convey to everything he did and give to every one he knew and liked, was constantly apparent. It was a fine clear night in early October, crispness and an indefinable smell of smoke were in the air, students were coming briskly along the street, singly or in groups of two or three, light glowed warmly in the windows of the book-shops, pharmacies, and tobacco stores near Harvard Square, and from the enormous library and the old buildings in the Harvard Yard there came a glow of lights, soft, rich, densely golden, embedded in old red brick.

All of these things, vital, exciting, strangely, pleasurably stirring as they were, gained a curious enhancement from Starwick's presence until they gave to the younger boy not only a feeling of sharp, mounting, strangely indefinable excitement, but a feeling of power and wealth—a sense of being triumphant and having before him the whole golden and unvisited plantation of the world to explore, possess and do with as he would—the most fortunate and happy life that any man had ever known.

Starwick went into a tobacco shop to cash a check and the whole place, with its pungent smells of good tobacco, its idling students, its atmosphere of leisure and enjoyment, became incomparably wealthy, rich, exciting as it had never been before.

And later, when the two young men had gone into the Cock House Tavern on Brattle Street, the prim and clean little rooms of the old house, the clean starched waitresses and snowy table cloth, the good food, and several healthy and attractive-looking girls of the New England type all gained an increased value. He felt a thrill of pleasurable anticipation and a feeling of unlimited wealth, simply because Starwick was there ordering the meal, conferring on everything around him the sense of wealth and ease and nameless joy which his wonderful personality with its magic touch instantly gave to anything on earth.

Yet during the meal the feeling of hostile constraint between the two young men was not diminished, but grew constantly. Starwick's impeccable cold courtesy—really the armor of a desperately shy person—his mannered tone, with its strange and disturbing accent, the surgical precision of his cross-examination into the origin, experience, and training of the other youth sharpened a growing antagonism in the other's spirit, and put him on his guard. Moreover, failure to give any information about himself—above all his complete reticence concerning his association with Professor Hatcher and the reason for his curt and brusquely-worded invitation to dinner—all this began to bear now with oppressive weight upon the other's spirit. It seemed to him there was a deliberate arrogance in this cold reticence. He began to feel a sullen resentment because of this secretive and mysterious conduct. And later that evening when the two young men parted, the manner of each of them was cold and formal. They bowed stiffly, shook hands with each other coldly, and marched away. It was several months before the younger would again talk to Starwick, and during that period he thought of him with a feeling of resentment, almost of dislike.

IX

THAT first impact of the city had stunned him with its huge and instant shock, and now, like a swimmer whelmed in a raging storm, he sought desperately among that unceasing flood of faces for one that he knew, one that he could call his own, and suddenly he thought of

Uncle Bascom. When his mother had told him he should go to see his uncle and his family as soon as he could he had nodded his head mechanically and muttered a few words of perfunctory assent, but so busy were his mind and heart with his shining vision of the city and all the magic he was sure to find there that it had never seriously occurred to him that he would turn eagerly to the old man for companionship and help.

But now, the day after his arrival in the city, he found himself pawing eagerly through the pages of the phone book for his uncle's business address: he found it the familiar words, "Bascom Pentland" stared up out of the crowded page with a kind of unreal shocking incandescence, and in another moment he heard himself speaking across the wire to a puzzled voice that came to him with its curious and unearthly remoteness as if from some planetary distance and suddenly the howling recognition of the words—words whose unearthly quality now came back to him in a searing flash of memory, although he had not heard his uncle's voice for eight years, when he was twelve years old:

"Oh, hello! hello! hello!" that unearthly voice howled faintly at him. "How are you, my boy, how are you, how are you, how are you! . . . And say!" the voice yelled with a sudden comical transition to matter-of-factness—"I had a letter from your mother just this morning. She told me you were on your way. . . . I've been expecting you."

"Can I come over to see you now, Uncle Bascom?"

"Oh, by all means, by all means, by all means!" that unearthly and passionate voice howled back at once enthusiastically. "Come over at once, my boy, at once! Oh, by all means, by all means, by all means! . . . And now, my boy!" the voice became faintly and comically precise, and he could hear his uncle smacking his large rubbery lips with pedantical relish as he pronounced the words: "Know-ing you are a young man alone in this great city for the first time, I shall give you a few brief—and, I trust, reasonably clear, di-rections," again Bascom smacked his lips with audible relish as he pronounced this lovely word—"concerning your i-tin-er-ary"—his joy as he smacked his lips over this last word was almost indecently evident, and he went on with meticulous elaboration through a bewildering labyrinth of instructions until even he was satisfied at the confusion he had caused. Then he said goodbye, upon the assurance of his nephew that he would come at once. And it was in this way, after eight years of absence, that the boy again met his uncle.

He found the old man hardly changed at all. He was, indeed, a member of that race of men who scarcely vary by a jot from one decade to another; he was a trifle grayer, the stringy gauntness of his tall stooped frame was perhaps a little more pronounced, his eccentric tricks of speech and manner a little more emphatic—but this was all. In dress, speech, manner and appearance he was to an amazing degree the same as he had been the last time that his nephew saw him.

It is doubtful, in fact, if he had changed appreciably in thirty years. And certainly during the first twenty-five years of this century, business people who had their offices in or near State Street, Boston, and who had grown very familiar with that cadaverous and extraordinary figure, could have testified that he had not changed at all. His daily appearances, indeed, had become so much a part of the established process of events in that crowded street, that they had attained a kind of ritualistic dignity, and any serious alteration in their pattern would have seemed to hundreds of people to whom his gaunt bowed figure had become familiar, almost to constitute a serious disruption of the natural order.

Shortly before nine o'clock of every working-day he would emerge from a subway exit near the head of the street and pause vaguely for a moment, making a craggy eddy in the tide of issuing workers that foamed swiftly about him while he stood with his enormous bony hands clutched comically before him at the waist, as if holding himself in, at the same time making the most horrible grimaces with his lean and amazingly flexible features. These grimaces were made by squinting his small sharp eyes together, widening his mouth in a ghastly travesty of a grin, and convolving his chin and cheek in a rapid series of pursed lips and horrible squints as he swiftly pressed his rubbery underlip against a few enormous horse teeth that decorated his upper jaw. Having completed these facial evolutions, he glanced quickly and, it must be supposed, blindly, in every direction; for he then plunged heedlessly across the street, sometimes choosing the moment when traffic had been halted, and pedestrians were hurrying across, sometimes diving into the midst of a roaring chaos of motor cars, trucks, and wagons, through which he sometimes made his way in safety, accompanied only by a scream of brake bands, a startled barking of horns, and the hearty curses of frightened drivers, or from which, howling with terror in the centre of a web of traffic which he had snarled hopelessly and brought to a complete standstill, he was sometimes rescued by a red-faced and cursing young Irishman who was on point duty at that corner.

But Bascom was a fated man and he escaped. Once, it is true, a bright mindless beetle of machinery, which had no thought for fated men, had knocked him down and skinned and bruised him; again, an uninstructed wheel had passed across the soft toe-end of his shoe and held him prisoner, as if he were merely some average son of destiny—but he escaped. He escaped because he was a fated man and because the providence which guides the steps of children and the blind was kind to him; and because this same policeman whose simian upper lip had once been thick and twisted with its curses had long since run the scale from anger to wild fury, and thence to madness and despair and resignation, and had now come to have a motherly affection for this stray sheep, kept his eye peeled for its appearance every morning or, failing this, at once shrilled hard upon his whistle when he heard the well-known howl of terror and surprise, plunged to the centre of the stalled traffic snarl, plucked Bascom out to safety under curse and shout and scream of brake, and marched him tenderly to the curb, gripping his brawny hand around the old man's arm, feeling his joints, testing his bones, massaging anxiously his sinewy carcass, and calling him "bud"—although Bascom was old enough to be his grandfather. "Are you all right, bud? You're not hurt, are you, bud? Are you O. K.?"—to which Bascom, if his shock and terror had been great, could make no answer for a moment save to pant hoarsely and to howl loudly and huskily from time to time "Ow! Ow! Ow! Ow!"

At length, becoming more coherent, if not more calm, he would launch into an ecclesiastical indictment of motor cars and their drivers delivered in a high, howling, and husky voice that suggested the pronouncements of a prophet from a mountain. This voice had a quality of strange remoteness and, once heard, would never be forgotten. It actually had a howling note in it, and carried to great distances, and yet it was not loud: it was very much as if Mr. Bascom Pentland were standing on a mountain and shouting to some one in a quiet valley below—the sounds came to one plainly but as if from a great distance, and it was full of a husky, unearthly passion. It was really an ecclesiastical voice, the voice of a great preacher; one felt that it should be heard in churches, which was exactly where it once was heard, for Bascom had at various times and with great conviction, in the course of his long and remarkable life, professed and preached the faith of the Episcopalians, the Presbyterians, the Methodists, the Baptists, and the Unitarians.

Quite often, in fact, as now, when he had narrowly escaped disaster in the streets, Bascom still preached from the corner: as soon as he recovered somewhat from his shock, he would launch forth into a sermon of eloquent invective against any driver of motor cars within hearing, and if any of them entered the fray, as sometimes happened, a very interesting performance occurred.

"What happened to *you?*" the motorist might bitterly remark. "Do the keepers know you're out?"

Mr. Pentland would thereupon retort with an eloquent harangue, beginning with a few well-chosen quotations from the more violent prophets of the Old Testament, a few predictions of death, destruction and damnation for the owners of motor cars, and a few apt references to Days of Judgment and Reckoning, Chariots of Moloch, and Beasts of the Apocalypse.

"Oh, for God's sake!" the exasperated motorist might reply. "Are you *blind?* Where do you think you are? In a cow-pasture? Can't you read the signals? Didn't you see the cop put his hand up? Don't you know when it says to 'Stop' or 'Go'? Did you ever hear of the traffic law?"

"The *traffic* law!" Bascom sneeringly exclaimed, as if the mere use of the word by the motorist evoked his profoundest contempt. His voice now had a precise and meticulous way of speech, there was something sneering and pedantical in the way he pronounced each word, biting it off with a prim, nasal and heavily accented enunciation in the manner of certain pedants and purists who suggest by their pronunciation that language in the mouths of most people is vilely and carelessly treated, that each word has a precise, subtle, and careful meaning of its own, and that they— *they* alone—understand these matters. "The *traffic* law!" he repeated again: then he squinted his eyes together, pursed his rubbery lip against the big horsey upper teeth, and laughed down his nose in a forced, sneering manner, "The *traffic* law!" he said. "Why, you pit-i-ful ig-no-*ram*-us! You il-*lit*-ter-ate ruffian! You dare to speak to me—to *me!*" he howled suddenly with an ecclesiastical lift of his voice, striking himself on his bony breast and glaring with a majestical fury as if the word of a mighty prophet had been contradicted by an upstart—"of the traffic law, when it is doubtful if you could *read* the law if you saw it,"—he sneered—"and it is obvious to any one with the perception of a school-boy that you would not have intelligence enough to understand it, and"—here his voice rose to a howling emphasis and he held one huge bony finger up to command attention—"*and* to interpret it, if you could read."

"Is *that* so!" the motorist heavily remarked. "A *wise* guy, eh? One of these guys who knows it all, eh? You're a *pretty* wise guy, aren't you?" the motorist continued bitterly, as if caught up in the circle of his refrain and unable to change it. "Well, let me tell *you* something. You think you're pretty smaht, don't you? Well, you're not. See? It's wise guys like you who go around looking for a good bust on the nose. See? That's how smaht you are. If you wasn't an old guy I'd give you one, too," he said, getting a moody satisfaction from the thought.

"Ow-w! Ow-w! Ow-w!" Bascom howled in sudden terror.

"If you know so much, if you're so smaht as you think you are, what is the traffic law?"

Then, assuredly, if there was a traffic law, the unfortunate motorist was lost, for Uncle Bascom would deliver it to him verbatim, licking his lips with joy over all the technicalities of legal phrasing and pronouncing each phrase with a meticulous and pedantical enunciation.

"And furthermore!" he howled, holding up his big bony finger, "the Commonwealth of Massachusetts has decreed, by a statute that has been on the books since 1856, by a statute that is irrevocably, inexorably, ineluctably plain that any driver, director, governor, commander, manager, agent or conductor, or any other person who shall conduct or cause to be conducted any vehicular instrument, whether it be of two, four, six, eight or any number of wheels whatsoever, whether it be in the public service, or in the possession of a private individual, whether it be " but by this time, the motorist, if he was wise, had had enough, and had escaped.

If, however, it had been one of his more fortunate mornings, if he had blindly but successfully threaded the peril of roaring traffic, Uncle Bascom proceeded rapidly down State Street, still clutching his raw bony hands across his meagre waist, still contorting his remarkable face in its endless series of pursed grimaces, and presently turned in to the entrance of a large somewhat dingy-looking building of blackened stone, one of those solid, unpretentious, but very valuable properties which smell and look like the early 1900's, and which belong to that ancient and enormously wealthy corporation across the river known as Harvard University.

Here, Uncle Bascom, still clutching himself together across the waist, mounted a flight of indented marble entry steps, lunged through revolving doors into a large marble corridor that was redolent with vibrating waves of hot steamy air, wet rubbers and galoshes, sanitary disinfectant, and serviceable but somewhat old-fashioned elevators and, entering one of the cars which had just plunged down abruptly, banged open its door, belched out two or three people and swallowed a dozen more, he was finally deposited with the same abruptness on the seventh floor, where he stepped out into a wide dark corridor, squinted and grimaced uncertainly to right and left as he had done for twenty-five years, and then went left along the corridor, past rows of lighted offices in which one could hear the preliminary clicking of typewriters, the rattling of crisp papers, and the sounds of people beginning their day's work. At the end of the corridor Bascom Pentland turned right along another corridor and at length paused before a door which bore this inscription across the familiar glazed glass of American business offices: The John T. Brill Realty Co.—Houses For Rent or Sale. Below this bold legend in much smaller letters was printed: Bascom Pentland— Att'y at Law—Conveyancer and Title Expert.

The appearance of this strange figure in State Street, or anywhere else, had always been sufficient to attract attention and to draw comment. Bascom Pentland, if he had straightened to his full height, would have been six feet and three or four inches tall, but he had always walked with a stoop and as he grew older, the stoop had become confirmed: he presented a tall, gnarled, bony figure, cadaverous and stringy, but tough as hickory. He was of that race of men who seem never to wear out, or to grow old, or to die: they live with almost undiminished vitality to great ages, and when they die they die suddenly. There is no slow wastage and decay because there is so little to waste or decay: their mummied and stringy flesh has the durability of granite.

Bascom Pentland clothed his angular figure with an assortment of odd garments which seemed to have the same durability: they were immensely old and worn, but they also gave no signs of ever wearing out, for by their cut and general appearance of age, it seemed that his frugal soul had selected in the 'nineties materials which it hoped would last forever. His coat, which was originally of a dark dull pepper-and-salt gray, had gone green at the seams and pockets, and moreover it was a ridiculously short skimpy coat for a gaunt big-boned man like this: it was hardly more than a jacket, his great wristy hands burst out of it like lengths of cordwood, and the mark of his high humped narrow shoulders cut into it with a knife-like sharpness. His trousers were also tight and skimpy, of a lighter gray and of a rough woolly texture from which all fuzz and fluff had long ago been rubbed; he wore rough country brogans with raw-hide laces, and a funny little flat hat of ancient black felt, which had also gone green along the band. One understands now why the policeman called him "Bud": this great bony figure seemed ruthlessly to have been crammed into garments in which a country fledgling of the 'eighties might have gone to see his girl, clutching a bag of gumdrops in his large red hand. A stringy little necktie, a clean but dilapidated collar which by its bluish and softly mottled look Bascom Pentland must have laundered himself (a presumption which is quite correct since the old man did all his own laundry work, as well as his mending, repairing, and cobbling)—this was his costume, winter and summer, and it never changed, save that in winter he supplemented it with an ancient blue sweater which he wore buttoned to the chin and whose frayed ends and cuffs projected inches below the scanty little jacket. He had never been known to wear an overcoat, not even on the coldest days of those long, raw, and formidable winters which Boston suffers.

The mark of his madness was plain upon him: intuitively men knew he was not a poor man, and the people who had seen him so many times in State Street would nudge one another, saying: "You see that old guy? You'd think he was waitin' for a handout from the Salvation Army, wouldn't you? Well, he's not. He's *got* it, brother. Believe me, he's *got* it good and plenty: he's *got* it salted away where no one ain't goin' to touch it. That guy's got a sock full of dough!"

"Jesus!" another remarks. "What good's it goin' to do an old guy like that? He can't take any of it with him, can he?"

"You said it, brother," and the conversation would become philosophical.

Bascom Pentland was himself conscious of his parsimony, and although he sometimes asserted that he was "only a poor man" he realized that his exaggerated economies could not be justified to his business associates on account of poverty: they taunted him slyly, saying, "Come on, Pentland, let's go to lunch. You can get a good meal at the Pahkeh House for a couple of bucks." Or "Say, Pentland, I know a place where they're havin' a sale of winter overcoats: I saw one there that would just suit you—you can get it for sixty dollars." Or "Do you need a good laundry, Reverend? I know a couple of Chinks who do good work."

To which Bascom, with the characteristic evasiveness of parsimony, would reply, snuffling derisively down his nose: "No, sir! You won't catch me in any of their stinking restaurants. You never know what you're getting: if you could see the dirty, nasty, filthy kitchens where your food is prepared you'd lose your appetite quick enough." His parsimony had resulted in a compensating food mania: he declared that "in his young days" he "ruined his digestion by eating in restaurants," he painted the most revolting pictures of the filth of these establishments, laughing scornfully down his nose as he declared: "I suppose you think it tastes better after some dirty, nasty, stinking *nigger* has wiped his old hands all over it" (phuh-phuh-phuh-phuh-phuh!)—here he would contort his face and snuffle scornfully down his nose; and he was bitter in his denunciation of "rich foods," declaring they had "destroyed more lives than all the wars and all the armies since the beginning of time."

As he had grown older he had become more and more convinced of the healthy purity of "raw foods," and he prepared for himself at home raw revolting messes of chopped-up carrots, onions, turnips, even raw potatoes, which he devoured at table, smacking his lips with an air of keen relish, and declaring to his wife: "You may poison *yourself* on your old roasts and oysters and turkeys if you please: you wouldn't catch *me* eating that stuff. No, sir! Not on your life! I think too much of my stomach!" But his use of the pronoun "you" was here universal rather than particular because if that lady's longevity had depended on her abstinence from "roasts and oysters and turkeys" there was no reason why she should not have lived forever.

Or again, if it were a matter of clothing, a matter of fencing in his bones and tallows against the frozen nail of Boston winter, he would howl derisively: "An overcoat! Not on your life! I wouldn't give two cents for all the old overcoats in the world! The only thing they're good for is to gather up germs and give you colds and pneumonia. I haven't worn an overcoat in thirty years, and I've never had the *vestige*—no! not the *semblance*—of a cold during all that time!"—an assertion that was not strictly accurate since he always complained bitterly of at least two or three during the course of a single winter, declaring at those times that no more hateful, treacherous, damnable climate than that of Boston had ever been known.

Similarly, if it were a question of laundries he would scornfully declare that he would not send "*his* shirts and collars to let some dirty old Chinaman spit and *hock* upon them—*yes!*" he would gleefully howl, as some new abomination of nastiness suggested itself to his teeming brain— "*yes!* and iron it *in,* too, so you can walk around done up in old Chinaman's spit!"—(Phuh-phuh-phuh-phuh-phuh!)—here he would grimace, contort his rubbery lip, and laugh down his nose in forced snarls of gratification and triumph.

This was the old man who, even now, as his nephew sped to meet him, stood in his dusty little office clutching his raw and bony hands across his waist.

In spite of the bewildering elaboration of his uncle's direction, the boy found his offices without much trouble. He went in and a moment later, his hand was being vigorously pumped by his uncle's great stiff paw, and he heard that instant howling voice of welcome—the voice of a prophet calling from the mountain tops—coming to him without preliminary or introduction, as he had heard it last eight years before.

"Oh, hello, hello, hello. . . . How are you, how are you, how are you . . . say!" his uncle turned abruptly and in a high howling tone addressed several people who were staring at the young man curiously, "I want you all to meet my sister's youngest son—my nephew, Mr. Eugene Gant . . . and say!" he bawled again, but in remoter tone, in a strangely confiding and insinuating tone— "would you know he was a Pentland by the look of him? . . . Can you see the family resemblance?" He smacked his rubbery lips together with an air of relish, and suddenly threw his great gaunt arms up and let them fall with an air of ecstatic jubilation, squinted his small sharp eyes together, contorted his rubbery lips in their amazing and grotesque grimace, and stamping ecstatically at the floor with one long stringy leg, taking random ecstatic kicks at any object that was within reach, he began to snuffle with his strange forced laughter, and howled deliriously, "Oh, *my* yes! . . . The thing is evident. . . . He is a Pentland beyond the shadow of a vestige of a doubt! . . . Oh, by all means, by all means, by all means!" and he went on snuffling, stamping, howling, and kicking at random objects in this way until the strange seizure of his mirth had somewhat subsided. Then, more quietly, he introduced his nephew to his associates in the curious business of which he was a partner.

And it was in this way that the boy first met the people in his uncle's office—an office and people who were, during the years that followed, and in the course of hundreds of visits, to become a part of the fabric of his life—so hauntingly real, so strangely familiar that in the years that followed he could forget none of them, remember everything just as it was.

These offices, which he saw for the first time that day, were composed of two rooms, one in front and one behind, L-shaped, and set in the elbow of the building, so that one might look out at the two projecting wings of the building, and see lighted layers of offices, in which the actors of a dozen enterprises "took" dictation, clattered at typewriters, walked back and forth importantly, talked into telephones or, what they did with amazing frequency, folded their palms behind their skulls, placed their feet restfully on the nearest solid object, and gazed for long periods dreamily and tenderly at the ceilings.

Through the broad and usually very dirty panes of the window in the front office one could catch a glimpse of Faneuil Hall and the magnificent and exultant activity of the markets.

These dingy offices, however, from which a corner of this rich movement might be seen and felt, were merely the unlovely counterpart of millions of others throughout the country and, in the telling phrase of Baedeker, offered "little that need detain the tourist": a few chairs, two scarred roll-top desks, a typist's table, a battered safe with a pile of thumb-worn ledgers on top of it, a set of green filing cases, an enormous green, greasy water-jar always half filled with a rusty liquid that no one drank, and two spittoons, put there because Brill was a man who chewed and spat widely in all directions—this, save for placards, each bearing several photographs of houses with their prices written below them—8 rooms, Dorchester, $6500; 5 rooms and garage, Melrose, $4500, etc.—completed the furniture of the room, and the second room, save for the disposition of objects, was similarly adorned.

Such then was the scene in which the old man and his nephew met again after a separation of eight years.

X

THE youth was drowned in the deepest sea—an atom bombarded, ignorant of all defense in a tumultuous world. The shell of custom, the easy thoughtless life which had sucked pleasure from the world about, these four years past, crumbled like caked mud. He was nothing, nobody—there was no heart or bravery left in him; he was conscious of unfathomable ignorance—the beginning, as Socrates suggested, of wisdom—he was lost.

He had wanted to cut a figure in the world—he had simply never imagined the number of people that were in it. And like most people who hug loneliness to them like a lover, the need of occasional companionship, forever tender and forever true, which might be summoned or dismissed at will, cut through him like a sword.

There was, of course, among the members of the play-writing class an energetic and calculated sociability. The supposed advantages of discussion with one another, the interplay of wit, and so on, above all what was called "the exchange of ideas," but what most often was merely the exchange of other people's ideas,—all these were mentioned often; they were held in the highest esteem as one of the chief benefits to be derived from the course.

Manifestly, one could write anywhere. But where else could one write with around one the constant stimulus of other people who also wrote? Where could one learn one's faults so well as before a critical and serious congress of artists? They were content with it—they got what they wanted. But the lack of warmth, the absence of inner radial heat which, not being fundamental in the structure of their lives, had never been wanted, filled him with horror and impotent fury.

The critical sense had stirred in him hardly at all, the idea of questioning authority and position had not occurred to him.

He was facing one of the oldest—what, for the creative mind, must be one of the most painful—problems of the spirit—the search for a standard of taste. He had, at seventeen, as a sophomore, triumphantly denied God, but he was unable now to deny Robert Browning. It had never occurred to him that there was a single authoritatively beautiful thing in the world that might not be agreed on, by a community of all the enlightened spirits of the universe, as beautiful. *Every one,* of course, *knew* that *King Lear* was one of the greatest plays that had ever been written. Only, he was beginning to find, every one didn't.

And now for the first time he began to worry about being "modern." He had the great fear young people have that they will not be a part of the most advanced literary and artistic movements of the time. Several of the young men he knew had contributed stories, poems, and criticisms to little reviews, published by and for small groups of literary adepts. They disposed of most of the established figures with a few well-chosen words of contempt, and they replaced these figures with obscure names of their own who, they assured him, were the important people of the future.

For the first time, he heard the word "Mid-Victorian" applied as a term of opprobrium. What its implications were he had no idea. Stevenson, too, to him hardly more than a writer of books for boys, books that he had read as a child with interest and delight, was a symbol of some vague, but monstrously pernicious influence.

But he discovered at once that to voice any of these questionings was to brand oneself in the esteem of the group; intuitively he saw that their jargon formed a pattern by which they might be placed and recognized; that, to young men most of all, to be placed in a previous discarded pattern was unendurable disgrace. It represented to them the mark of intellectual development, just as in a sophomore's philosophy, the belief that God is an old man with a long beard brings ridicule and odium upon the believer, but the belief that God is an ocean without limit, or an all-pervasive and inclusive substance, or some other equally naive and extraordinary idea, is regarded as a certain sign of bold enlightenment. Thus, it often happens, when one thinks he has extended the limits of his life, broken the bonds, and liberated himself in the wider ether, he has done no more than to exchange a new superstition for an old one, to forsake a beautiful myth for an ugly one.

The young men in Professor Hatcher's class were sorry for many things and many people.

"Barrie?" began Mr. Scoville, an elegant and wealthy young dawdler from Philadelphia, who, by his own confession, had spent most of his life in France, "Barrie?" he continued regretfully, in answer to a question. For a moment, he drew deeply on his cigarette, then raised sad, languid eyes. "I'm sorry," he said gently, with a slight regretful movement of his head—"I can't read him. I've tried it—but it simply can't be done." They laughed, greatly pleased.

"But it is a pity, you know, a *great* pity," Francis Starwick remarked languidly, using effectively his trick of giving a tired emphasis to certain words which conveyed a kind of sad finality, a weary earnestness to what he said. He turned to go.

"But—but—but—how—how—how very interesting! Why *is* it, Frank?" Hugh Dodd demanded with his earnest stammering eagerness. He was profoundly respectful of Starwick's critical ability.

"Why is what?" said Starwick in his curiously mannered voice, his air of languid weariness.

"Why is it a great pity about Barrie?" knitting his bushy brows together, and scowling with an air of intense concentration over his words as he spoke. "Because," said the appraiser of Values, as he prepared to depart, arranging with feminine luxuriousness the voluptuous folds of his blue silk scarf, "the man really had something one time. He really did. Something strange and haunting—the genius of the Kelt." Swinging his cane slowly, acutely and painfully conscious that he was being watched, with the agonizing stiffness that was at the bottom of his character, he strolled off across the Yard, stark and lovely with the harsh white snow and wintry branches of bleak winter.

"You know—you know—you know—that's very interesting," said Dodd, intent upon his words. "I'd—I'd—I'd never thought of it in *just* that way."

"Barrie," drawled Wood, the maker of epigrams, "is a stick of taffy, floating upon a sea of molasses."

There was laughter.

He was forever making these epigrams; his face had a somewhat saturnine cast, his lips twisted ironically, his eyes shot splintered promises of satiric wisdom. He looked like a very caustically humorous person; but unhappily he had no humor. But they thought he had. No one with a face like that could be less than keen.

So he had something to say for every occasion. He had discovered that the manner counted for wit. If the talk was of Shaw's deficiencies as a dramatist, he might say:

"But, after all, if one is going in for all that sort of thing, why not have lantern slides and a course of lectures."

Thus he was known, not merely as a subtle-souled and elusive psychologist but also as a biting wit.

"Galsworthy wrote something that looked like a play once," some one remarked. "There were parts of *Justice* that weren't bad."

"Yes. Yes," said Dodd, peering intently at his language. *"Justice*— there were some interesting things in that. It's—it's—it's rather a *pity* about him, isn't it?" And as he said these words he frowned earnestly and intently. There was genuine pity in his voice, for the man's spirit had great charity and sweetness in it.

As they dispersed, some one remarked that Shaw might have made a dramatist if he had ever known anything about writing a play.

"But he *dates* so—how he *dates!*" Scoville remarked.

"Those earlier plays——"

"Yes, I agree"—thus Wood again. "Almost Mid-Victorian. Shaw:—a prophet with his face turned backwards." Then they went away in small groups.

XI

To reach his own "office," as Bascom Pentland called the tiny cubicle in which he worked and received his clients, the old man had to traverse the inner room and open a door in a flimsy partition of varnished wood and glazed glass at the other end. This was his office: it was really a very narrow slice cut off from the larger room, and in it there was barely space for one large dirty window, an ancient dilapidated desk and swivel chair, a very small battered safe buried under stacks of yellowed newspapers, and a small bookcase with glass doors and two small shelves on which there were a few worn volumes. An inspection of these books would have revealed four or five tattered and musty law books in their ponderous calf-skin bindings—one on *Contracts,* one on *Real Property,* one on *Titles*—a two-volume edition of the poems of Matthew Arnold, very dog-eared and thumbed over; a copy of *Sartor Resartus,* also much used; a volume of the essays of Ralph Waldo Emerson; the Iliad in Greek with minute yellowed notations in the margins; a volume of the *World Almanac* several years old; and a very worn volume of the Holy Bible, greatly used and annotated in Bascom's small, stiffly laborious, and meticulous hand.

If the old man was a little late, as sometimes happened, he might find his colleagues there before him. Miss Muriel Brill, the typist, and the eldest daughter of Mr. John T. Brill, would be seated in her typist's chair, her heavy legs crossed as she bent over to undo the metal latches of the thick galoshes she wore during the winter season. It is true there were also other seasons when Miss Brill did not wear galoshes, but so sharply and strongly do our memories connect people with certain gestures which, often for an inscrutable reason, seem characteristic of them, that any frequent visitor to these offices at this time of day would doubtless have remembered Miss Brill as always unfastening her galoshes. But the probable reason is that some people inevitably belong to seasons, and this girl's season was winter—not blizzards or howling winds, or the blind skirl and sweep of snow, but gray, grim, raw, thick, implacable winter: the endless successions of gray days and gray monotony. There was no spark of color in her, her body was somewhat thick and heavy, her face was white, dull, and thick-featured and instead of tapering downwards, it tapered up: it was small above, and thick and heavy below, and even in her speech, the words she uttered seemed to have been chosen by an automaton, and could only be remembered later by their desolate banality. One always remembered her as saying as one entered: ". . . Hello! . . . You're becoming quite a strangeh! . . . It's been some time since you was around, hasn't it? . . . I was thinkin' the otheh day it had been some time since you was around. . . . I'd begun to think you had forgotten us. . . . Well, how've you been? Lookin' the same as usual, I see. . . . Me? . . . Oh, can't complain. . Keepin' busy? *I'll* say! I manage to keep goin'. . . . Who you lookin' for? Father? He's in *there*. . . . Why, yeah! Go right on in."

This was Miss Brill, and at the moment that she bent to unfasten her galoshes, it is likely that Mr. Samuel Friedman would also be there in the act of rubbing his small dry hands briskly together, or of rubbing the back of one hand with the palm of the other in order to induce circulation. He was a small youngish man, a pale somewhat meagre-looking little Jew with a sharp ferret face: he, too, was a person who goes to "fill in" those vast swarming masses of people along the pavements and in the subway—the mind cannot remember them or absorb the details of their individual appearance but they people the earth, they make up life. Mr. Friedman had none of the richness, color, and humor that some members of his race so abundantly possess; the succession of gray days, the grim weather seemed to have entered his soul as it enters the souls of many different races there—the Irish, the older New England stock, even the Jews—and it gives them a common touch that is prim, drab, careful, tight and sour. Mr. Friedman also wore galoshes, his clothes were neat, drab, a little worn and shiny, there was an odor of thawing dampness and warm rubber about him as he rubbed his dry little hands saying: "Chee! How I hated to leave that good wahm bed this morning! When I got up I said, '*Holy* Chee!' My wife says, 'Whatsa mattah?' I says, 'Holy Chee! You step out heah a moment where I am an' you'll see whatsa mattah.' 'Is it cold?' she says. 'Is it cold! I'll tell the cock-eyed wuhld!' I says. Chee! You could have cut the frost with an axe: the wateh in the pitchehs was frozen hahd; an' she has the nuhve to ask me if it's cold! 'Is it cold!' I says. 'Do you know any more funny stories?' I says. Oh, how I do love my bed! Chee! I kept thinkin' of that guy in Braintree I got to go see today an' the more I thought about him, the less I liked him! I thought my feet would tu'n into two blocks of ice before I got the funniss stahted! 'Chee! I hope the ole bus is still workin',' I says. 'If I've got to go thaw that damned thing out,' I says, 'I'm ready to quit.' Chee! Well, suh, I neveh had a bit of trouble: she stahted right up an' the way that ole moteh was workin' is nobody's business."

During the course of this monologue Miss Brill would give ear and assent from time to time by the simple interjection: "Uh!" It was a sound she uttered frequently, it had somewhat the same meaning as "Yes," but it was more non-committal than "Yes." It seemed to render assent to the speaker, to let him know that he was being heard and understood, but it did not commit the auditor to any opinion, or to any real agreement.

The third member of this office staff, who was likely to be present at this time, was a gentleman named Stanley P. Ward. Mr. Stanley P. Ward was a neat middling figure of a man, aged fifty or thereabouts; he was plump and had a pink tender skin, a trim Vandyke, and a nice comfortable little pot of a belly which slipped snugly into the well-pressed and well-brushed garments that always fitted him so tidily. He was a bit of a fop, and it was at once evident that he was quietly but enormously pleased with himself. He carried himself very sprucely, he took short rapid steps and his neat little paunch gave his figure a movement not unlike that of a pouter pigeon. He was usually in quiet but excellent spirits, he laughed frequently and a smile—rather a subtly amused look—was generally playing about the edges of his mouth. That smile and his laugh made some people vaguely uncomfortable: there was a kind of deliberate falseness in them, as if what he really thought and felt was not to be shared with other men. He seemed, in fact, to have discovered some vital and secret power, some superior knowledge and wisdom, from which the rest of mankind was excluded, a sense that he was "chosen" above other men, and this impression of Mr. Stanley Ward would have been correct, for he was a Christian Scientist, he was a pillar of the church, and a very big church at that—for Mr. Ward, dressed in fashionable striped trousers, rubber soles, and a cut-away coat, might be found somewhere under the mighty dome of the Mother Church on Huntington Avenue every Sunday suavely, noiselessly, and expertly ushering the faithful to their pews.

This completes the personnel of the first office of the John T. Brill Realty Company, and if Bascom Pentland arrived late, if these three people were already present, if Mr. Bascom Pentland had not been defrauded of any part of his worldly goods by some contriving rascal of whom the world has many, if his life had not been imperilled by some speed maniac, if the damnable New England weather was not too damnable, if, in short, Bascom Pentland was in fairly good spirits he would on entering immediately howl in a high, rapid, remote and perfectly monotonous tone: "Hello, Hello, Hello! Good-morning, Good-morning, Good-morning!"—after which he would close his eyes, grimace horribly, press his rubbery lip against his big horse teeth, and snuffle with laughter through his nose, as if pleased by a tremendous stroke of wit. At this demonstration the other members of the group would glance at one another with those knowing, subtly supercilious nods and winks, that look of common self-congratulation and humor with which the more "normal" members of society greet the conduct of an eccentric, and Mr. Samuel Friedman would say: "What's the mattah with you, Pop? You look happy. Some one musta give you a shot in the ahm."

At which, a coarse powerful voice, deliberate and rich with its intimation of immense and earthy vulgarity, might roar out of the depth of the inner office: "No, I'll tell you what it is." Here the great figure of Mr. John T. Brill, the head of the business, would darken the doorway. "Don't you know what's wrong with the Reverend? It's that widder he's been takin' around." Here, the phlegmy burble that prefaced all of Mr. Brill's obscenities would appear in his voice, the shadow of a lewd smile would play around the corner of his mouth: "It's the widder. She's let him have a little of it."

At this delicate stroke of humor, the burble would burst open in Mr. Brill's great red throat, and he would roar with that high, choking, phlegmy laughter that is frequent among big red-faced men. Mr. Friedman would laugh drily ("Heh, heh, heh, heh, heh!"), Mr. Stanley Ward would laugh more heartily, but complacently, and Miss Brill would snicker in a coy and subdued manner as became a modest young girl. As for Bascom Pentland, if he was really in a good humor, he might snuffle with nosey laughter, bend double at his meagre waist, clutching his big hands together, and stamp at the floor violently several times with one stringy leg; he might even go so far as to take a random ecstatic kick at objects, still stamping and snuffling with laughter, and prod Miss Brill stiffly with two enormous bony fingers, as if he did not wish the full point and flavor of the jest to be lost on her.

Bascom Pentland, however, was a very complicated person with many moods, and if Mr. Brill's fooling did not catch him in a receptive one, he might contort his face in a pucker of refined disgust, and mutter his disapproval, as he shook his head rapidly from side to side. Or he might rise to great heights of moral denunciation, beginning at first in a grave low voice that showed the seriousness of the words he had to utter: "The lady to whom you refer," he would begin, "the very charming and cultivated lady whose name, sir," here his voice would rise on its howling note and he would wag his great bony forefinger, "whose name, sir, you have so foully traduced and blackened——"

"No, I wasn't, Reverend. I was only tryin' to whiten it," said Mr. Brill, beginning to burble with laughter.

"—Whose name, sir, you have so foully traduced and blackened with your smutty suggestions," Bascom continued implacably, "—that lady is known to me, as you very well know, sir," he howled, wagging his great finger again, "solely and simply in a professional capacity."

"Why, hell, Reverend," said Mr. Brill innocently, "I never knew she was a perfessional. I thought she was an amatoor."

At this conclusive stroke, Mr. Brill would make the whole place tremble with his laughter, Mr. Friedman would laugh almost noiselessly, holding himself weakly at the stomach and bending across a desk, Mr. Ward would have short bursts and fits of laughter, as he gazed out the window, shaking his head deprecatingly from time to time, as if his more serious nature disapproved, and Miss Brill would snicker, and turn to her machine, remarking: "This conversation is getting too rough for me!"

And Bascom, if this jesting touched his complex soul at one of those moments when such profanity shocked him, would walk away, confiding into vacancy, it seemed, with his powerful and mobile features contorted in the most eloquent expression of disgust and loathing ever seen on any face, the while he muttered, in a resonant whisper that shuddered with passionate revulsion: "Oh, *bad!* Oh, *bad!* Oh, *bad, bad, bad!*"— shaking his head slightly from side to side with each word.

Yet there were other times, when Brill's swingeing vulgarity, the vast coarse sweep of his profanity not only found Uncle Bascom in a completely receptive mood, but evoked from him gleeful responses, counter essays in swearing which he made slyly, craftily, snickering with pleasure and squinting around at his listeners at the sound of the words, and getting such stimulus from them as might a renegade clergyman exulting in a feeling of depravity and abandonment for the first time.

To the other people in this office—that is, to Friedman, Ward, and Muriel, the stenographer—the old man was always an enigma; at first they had observed his peculiarities of speech and dress, his eccentricity of manner, and the sudden, violent, and complicated fluctuation of his temperament, with astonishment and wonder, then with laughter and ridicule, and now, with dull, uncomprehending acceptance. Nothing he did or said surprised them any more, they had no understanding and little curiosity, they accepted him as a fact in the gray schedule of their lives. Their relation to him was habitually touched by a kind of patronizing banter—"kidding the old boy along" they would have called it—by the communication of smug superior winks and the conspiracy of feeble jests. And in this there was something base and ignoble, for Bascom was a better man than any of them.

He did not notice any of this, it is not likely he would have cared if he had, for, like most eccentrics, his thoughts were usually buried in a world of his own creating to whose every fact and feeling and motion he was the central actor. Again, as much as any of his extraordinary family, he had carried with him throughout his life the sense that he was "fated" —a sense that was strong in all of them—that his life was pivotal to all the actions of providence, that, in short, the time might be out of joint, but not himself. Nothing but death could shake his powerful egotism, and his occasional storms of fury, his railing at the world, his tirades of invective at some motorist, pedestrian, or laborer occurred only when he discovered that these people were moving in a world at cross-purposes to his own and that some action of theirs had disturbed or shaken the logic of his universe.

It was curious that, of all the people in the office, the person who had the deepest understanding and respect for him was John T. Brill. Mr. Brill was a huge creature of elemental desires and passions: a river of profanity rushed from his mouth with the relentless sweep and surge of the Mississippi, he could no more have spoken without swearing than a whale could swim in a frog-pond—he swore at everything, at every one, and with every breath, casually and unconsciously, and yet when he addressed Bascom his oath was always impersonal, and tinged subtly by a feeling of respect.

Thus, he would speak to Uncle Bascom somewhat in this fashion: "God-damn it, Pentland, did you ever look up the title for that stuff in Malden? That feller's been callin' up every day to find out about it."

"Which fellow?" Bascom asked precisely. "The man from Cambridge?"

"No," said Mr. Brill, "not him, the other son of a bitch, the Dorchester feller. How the hell am I goin' to tell him anything if there's no goddamn title for the stuff?"

Profane and typical as this speech was, it was always shaded nicely with impersonality toward Bascom—conscious to the full of the distinction between "damn *it*" and "damn *you*." Toward his other colleagues, however, Mr. Brill was neither nice nor delicate.

Brill was an enormous man physically: he was six feet two or three inches tall, and his weight was close to three hundred pounds. He was totally bald, his skull was a gleaming satiny pink; above his great red moon of face, with its ponderous and pendulous jowls, it looked almost egg-shaped. And in the heavy, deliberate, and powerful timbre of his voice there was always lurking this burble of exultant, gargantuan obscenity: it was so obviously part of the structure of his life, so obviously his only and natural means of expression, that it was impossible to condemn him. His epithet was limited and repetitive—but so, too, was Homer's, and, like Homer, he saw no reason for changing what had already been used and found good.

He was a lewd and innocent man. Like Bascom, by comparison with these other people, he seemed to belong to some earlier, richer and grander period of the earth, and perhaps this was why there was more actual kinship and understanding between them than between any of the other members of the office. These other people—Friedman, Brill's daughter Muriel, and Ward—belonged to the myriads of the earth, to those numberless swarms that with ceaseless pullulation fill the streets of life with their gray immemorable tides. But Brill and Bascom were men in a thousand, a million: if one had seen them in a crowd he would have looked after them, if one had talked with them, he could never have forgotten them.

It is rare in modern life that one sees a man who can express himself with such complete and abundant certainty as Brill did—completely, and without doubt or confusion. It is true that his life expressed itself chiefly by three gestures—by profanity, by his great roar of full-throated, earth-shaking laughter, and by flatulence, an explosive comment on existence which usually concluded and summarized his other means of expression.

Although the other people in the office laughed heartily at this soaring rhetoric of obscenity, it sometimes proved too much for Uncle Bascom. When this happened he would either leave the office immediately, or stump furiously into his own little cupboard that seemed silted over with the dust of twenty years, slamming the door behind him so violently that the thin partition rattled, and then stand for a moment pursing his lips, and convolving his features with incredible speed, and shaking his gaunt head slightly from side to side, until at length he whispered in a tone of passionate disgust and revulsion: "Oh, *bad! Bad! Bad!* By every *gesture,* by every *act,* he betrays the *boor,* the *vulgarian!* Can you imagine"—here his voice sunk even lower in its scale of passionate whispering repugnance—"can you for one *moment* imagine a man of *breeding* and the social graces breaking wind publicly?—And before his own daughter. Oh, *bad! Bad! Bad! Bad!*"

And in the silence, while Uncle Bascom stood shaking his head in its movement of downcast and convulsive distaste, they could hear, suddenly, the ripping noise Brill would make as his pungent answer to all the world—and his great bellow of throaty laughter. Later on, if Bascom had to consult him on any business, he would open his door abruptly, walk out into Brill's office clutching his hands together at his waist, and with disgust still carved upon his face, say: "Well, sir, . . . If you have concluded your morning devotions," here his voice sank to a bitter snarl, "we might get down to the transaction of some of the day's business."

"Why, Reverend!" Brill roared. "You ain't heard nothin' yet!"

And the great choking bellow of laughter would burst from him again, rattling the windows with its power as he hurled his great weight backward, with complete abandon, in his creaking swivel-chair.

It was obvious that he liked to tease the old man, and never lost an opportunity of doing so: for example, if any one gave Uncle Bascom a cigar, Brill would exclaim with an air of innocent surprise: "Why, *Reverend,* you're not going to smoke that, are you?"

"Why, certainly," Bascom said tartly. "That is the purpose for which it was intended, isn't it?"

"Why, yes," said Brill, "but you know how they make 'em, don't you? I didn't think you'd touch it after some dirty old Spaniard has wiped his old hands all over it—yes! an' *spit* upon it, too, because that's what they do!"

"Ah!" Bascom snarled contemptuously. "You don't know what you're talking about! There is nothing cleaner than good tobacco! Finest and healthiest plant on earth! No question about it!"

"Well," said Brill, "I've learned something. We live and learn, Reverend. You've taught me somethin' worth knowing: when it's free it's clean; when you have to pay for it it stinks like hell!" He pondered heavily for a moment, and the burble began to play about in his great throat: "And by God!" he concluded, "tobacco's not the only thing that applies to, either. Not by a damned sight!"

Again, one morning when his nephew was there, Bascom cleared his throat portentously, coughed, and suddenly said to him: "Now, Eugene, my boy, you are going to have lunch with me today. There's no question about it whatever!" This was astonishing news, for he had never before invited the youth to eat with him when he came to his office, although the boy had been to his house for dinner many times. "Yes, sir!" said Bascom, with an air of conviction and satisfaction. "I have thought it all over. There is a splendid establishment in the base-ment of this building—small, of course, but everything clean and of the highest order! It is conducted by an Irish gentleman whom I have known for many years. Finest people on earth: no question about it!"

It was an astonishing and momentous occasion; the boy knew how infrequently he went to a restaurant. Having made his decision, Uncle Bascom immediately stepped into the outer offices, and began to dis-cuss and publish his intentions with the greatest satisfaction.

"Yes, sir!" he said in a precise tone, smacking his lips in a ruminant fashion, and addressing himself to every one rather than to a particular person. "We shall go in and take our seats in the regular way, and I shall then give appropriate instructions, to one of the attendants—" again he smacked his lips as he pronounced this word with such an in-describable air of relish that immediately the boy's mouth began to water, and the delicious pangs of appetite and hunger began to gnaw his vitals—"I shall say: 'This is my nephew, a young man now enrolled at Harvard Un-i-ver-sit-tee!' "—here Bascom smacked his lips together again with that same maddening air of relish—" 'Yes, sir' (I shall say!) —'You are to fulfil his order without *stint,* without *delay,* and without *question,* and to the *utmost* of your ability' "—he howled, wagging his great bony forefinger through the air— "As for myself," he declared abruptly, "I shall take nothing. Good Lord, no!" he said with a scornful laugh. "I wouldn't touch a thing they had to offer. You couldn't pay me to: I shouldn't sleep for a month if I did. But you, my boy!" he howled, turning suddenly upon his nephew, "—are to have everything your heart desires! Everything, everything, everything!" He made an in-clusive gesture with his long arms; then closed his eyes, stamped at the floor, and began to snuffle with laughter.

Mr. Brill had listened to all this with his great-jowled face slack-jawed and agape with astonishment. Now, he said, heavily: "He's goin' to have everything, is he? Where are you goin' to take him to git it?"

"Why, sir!" Bascom said in an annoyed tone, "I have told you all along—we are going to the modest but excellent establishment in the basement of this very building."

"Why, Reverend," Brill said in a protesting tone, "you ain't goin' to take your nephew *there*, are you? I thought you said you was goin' to git somethin' to *eat*."

"I had supposed," Bascom said with bitter sarcasm, "that one went there for that purpose. I had not supposed that one went there to get shaved."

"Well," said Brill, "if you go there you'll git shaved, all right. You'll not only git *shaved*, you'll git *skinned* alive. But you won't git anything to eat." And he hurled himself back again, roaring with laughter.

"Pay no attention to him!" Bascom said to the boy in a tone of bitter repugnance. "I have long known that his low and vulgar mind attempts to make a joke of everything, even the most sacred matters. I assure you, my boy, the place is excellent in every way:—do you suppose," he said now, addressing Brill and all the others, with a howl of fury—"do you suppose, if it were not, that I should for a single moment *dream* of taking him there? Do you suppose that I would for an instant *contemplate* taking my own nephew, my sister's son, to any place in which I did not repose the fullest confidence? Not on your life!" he howled. "Not on your life!"

And they departed, followed by Brill's great bellow, and a farewell invitation which he shouted after the young man. "Don't worry, son! When you git through with that cockroach stew, come back an' I'll take you out to lunch with *me!*"

Although Brill delighted in teasing and baiting his partner in this fashion, there was, at the bottom of his heart, a feeling of deep humility, of genuine respect and admiration for him: he respected Uncle Bascom's intelligence, he was secretly and profoundly impressed by the fact that the old man had been a minister of the gospel and had preached in many churches.

Moreover, in the respect and awe with which Brill greeted these evidences of Bascom's superior education, in the eagerness he showed when he boasted to visitors, as he often did, of his partner's learning, there was a quality of pride that was profoundly touching and paternal: it was as if Bascom had been his son, and as if he wanted at every opportunity to display his talents to the world. And this, in fact, was exactly what he did want to do. Much to Bascom's annoyance, Brill was constantly speaking of his erudition to strangers who had come into the office for the first time, and constantly urging him to perform for them, to "say some of them big words, Reverend." And even when the old man answered him, as he frequently did, in terms of scorn, anger, and contempt, Brill was completely satisfied, if Uncle Bascom would only use a few of the "big words" in doing it. Thus, one day, when one of his boyhood friends, a New Hampshire man whom he had not seen in thirty-five years, had come in to renew their acquaintance Brill, in describing the accomplishments of his partner, said with an air of solemn affirmation: "Why, hell yes, Jim! It'd take a college perfesser to know what the Reverend is talkin' about half the time! No ordinary son-of-a-bitch is able to understand him! So help me God, it's true!" he swore solemnly, as Jim looked incredulous. "The Reverend knows words the average man ain't never heard. He knows words that ain't even in the dictionary. Yes, sir!—an' uses 'em, too—all the time!" he concluded triumphantly.

"Why, my dear sir!" Bascom answered in a tone of exacerbated contempt, "What on earth are you talking about? Such a man as you describe would be a monstrosity, a heinous perversion of natural law! A man so wise that no one could understand him:—so literate that he could not communicate with his fellow creatures:—so erudite that he led the inarticulate and incoherent life of a beast or a savage!"—here Uncle Bascom squinted his eyes tightly shut, and laughted sneeringly down his nose: "Phuh! phuh! phuh! phuh! phuh!— Why, you con-sum-mate fool!" he sneered, "I have long known that your ignorance was bottomless—but I had never hoped to see it equalled—Nay, surpassed!" he howled, "by your asininity."

"There you are!" said Brill exultantly to his visitor, "What did I tell you? There's one of them words, Jim: 'asserninity,' why, damn it, the Reverend's the only one who knows what that word means—you won't even find it in the dictionary!"

"Not find it in the dictionary!" Bascom yelled. "Almighty God, come down and give this ass a tongue as Thou did'st once before in Balaam's time!"

Again, Brill was seated at his desk one day engaged with a client in those intimate, cautious, and confidential preliminaries that mark the consummation of a "deal" in real estate. On this occasion the prospective buyer was an Italian: the man sat awkwardly and nervously in a chair beside Brill's desk while the great man bent his huge weight ponderously and persuasively toward him. From time to time the Italian's voice, sullen, cautious, disparaging, interrupted Brill's ponderous and coaxing drone. The Italian sat stiffly, his thick, clumsy body awkwardly clad in his "good" clothes of heavy black, his thick, hairy, blunt-nailed hands cupped nervously upon his knees, his black eyes glittering with suspicion under his knitted inch of brow. At length, he shifted nervously, rubbed his paws tentatively across his knees and then, with a smile mixed of ingratiation and mistrust, said: "How mucha you want, eh?"

"How mucha we want?" Brill repeated vulgarly as the burble began to play about within his throat. "Why, how mucha you got? . . . You know we'll take every damn thing you got! It's not how mucha we want, it's how mucha you got!" And he hurled himself backward, bellowing with laughter. "By God, Reverend," he yelled as Uncle Bascom entered, "ain't that right? It's not how mucha we want, it's how mucha you got! 'od damn! We ought to take that as our motter. I've got a good mind to git it printed on our letterheads. What do you think, Reverend?"

"Hey?" howled Uncle Bascom absently, as he prepared to enter his own office.

"I say we ought to use it for our motter."

"Your what?" said Uncle Bascom scornfully, pausing as if he did not understand.

"Our motter," Brill said.

"Not your *motter*," Bascom howled derisively. "The word is *not* motter," he said contemptuously. "Nobody of any refinement would say *motter*. *Motter* is *not* correct!" he howled finally. "Only an igno-*ram*-us would say *motter*. No!" he yelled with final conclusiveness. "That is *not* the way to pronounce it! That is ab-so-lute-ly and em-phat-ic-ally *not* the way to pronounce it!"

"All right, then, Reverend," said Brill, submissively. "You're the doctor. What is the word?"

"The word is *motto*," Uncle Bascom snarled. "Of course! Any fool knows that!"

"Why, hell," Mr. Brill protested in a hurt tone. "That's what I said, ain't it?"

"No-o!" Uncle Bascom howled derisively. "No-o! By no means, by no means, by no means! You said *motter*. The word is *not* motter. The word is motto: m-o-t-t-o! M-O-T-T-O does *not* spell motter," he remarked with vicious decision.

"What does it spell?" said Mr. Brill.

"It spells *motto*," Uncle Bascom howled. "It *has* always spelled motto! It *will* always spell motto! As it was in the beginning, is now, and ever shall be: A-a-men!" he howled huskily in his most evangelical fashion. Then, immensely pleased at his wit, he closed his eyes, stamped at the floor, and snarled and snuffled down his nose with laughter.

"Well, anyway," said Brill, "no matter how you spell it, it's not how mucha we want, it's how mucha you got! That's the way we feel about it!"

And this, in fact, without concealment, without pretense, without evasion, was just how Brill did feel about it. He wanted everything that was his and, in addition, he wanted as much as he could get. And this rapacity, this brutal and unadorned gluttony, so far from making men wary of him, attracted them to him, inspired them with unshakable confidence in his integrity, his business honesty. Perhaps the reason for this was that concealment did not abide in the man: he published his intentions to the world with an oath and a roar of laughter—and the world, having seen and judged, went away with the confidence of this Italian—that Brill was "one fine-a man!" Even Bascom, who had so often turned upon his colleague the weapons of scorn, contempt, and mockery, had a curious respect for him, an acrid sunken affection: often, when the old man and his nephew were alone, he would recall something Brill had said and his powerful and fluent features would suddenly be contorted in that familiar grimace, as he laughed his curious laugh which was forced out, with a deliberate and painful effort, through his powerful nose and his lips, barred with a few large teeth. "Phuh! phuh! phuh! phuh! phuh! . . . Of course!" he said, with a nasal rumination, as he stared over the apex of his great bony hands, clasped in meditation—"of course, he is just a poor ignorant fellow! I don't suppose—no, sir, I really do not suppose that Brill ever went to school over six months in his life!—Say!" Bascom paused suddenly, turned abruptly with his strange fixed grin, and fastened his sharp old eyes keenly on the boy: in this sudden and abrupt change, this transference of his vision from his own secret and personal world, in which his thought and feeling were sunken, and which seemed to be so far away from the actual world about him, there was something impressive and disconcerting. His eyes were gray, sharp, and old, and one eyelid had a heavy droop or ptosis which, although it did not obscure his vision, gave his expression at times a sinister glint, a malevolent humor. "—Say!" here his voice sank to a deliberate and confiding whisper, "(Phuh! phuh! phuh! phuh! phuh!) Say—a man who would—he told me—Oh, vile! vile! vile! my boy!" his uncle whispered, shutting his eyes in a kind of shuddering ecstasy as if at the memory of things too gloriously obscene to be repeated. "Can you *imagine,* can you even *dream* of such a state of affairs if he had possessed an atom, a *scintilla* of delicacy and good breeding! Yes, sir!" he said with decision. "I suppose there's no doubt about it! His beginnings were very lowly, very poor and humble, indeed! . . . Not that that is in any sense to his discredit!" Uncle Bascom said hastily, as if it had occurred to him that his words might bear some taint of snobbishness. "Oh, by no means, by no means, by no means!" he sang out, with a sweeping upward gesture of his long arm, as if he were clearing the air of wisps of smoke. "Some of our finest men—some of the nation's *leaders,* have come from just such surroundings as those. Beyond a doubt! Beyond a doubt! There's no question about it whatever! Say!"—here he turned suddenly upon the boy again with the ptotic and sinister intelligence of his eye. "Was *Lincoln* an aristocrat? Was he the issue of wealthy parents? Was he brought up with a silver spoon in his mouth? Was our *own* former governor, the Vice-President of the United States today, reared in the lap of luxury! Not on your life!" howled Uncle Bascom. "He came from frugal and thrifty Vermont farming stock, he has never deviated a *jot* from his early training, he remains today what he has always been—one of the simplest of men! Finest people on earth, no question about it whatever!"

Again, he meditated gravely with lost stare across the apex of his great joined hands, and the boy noticed again, as he had noticed so often, the great dignity of his head in thought—a head that was highbrowed, lean and lonely, a head that not only in its cast of thought but even in its physical contour, and in its profound and lonely earnestness, bore an astonishing resemblance to that of Emerson—it was, at times like these, as grand a head as the young man had ever seen, and on it was legible the history of man's loneliness, his dignity, his grandeur and despair.

"Yes, sir!" said Bascom, in a moment. "He is, of course, a vulgar fellow

and some of the things he says at times are Oh, vile! vile! vile!" cried Bascom, closing his eyes and laughing, "Oh, vile! *most* vile! . . . but (phuh!
phuh! phuh!) you can't help laughing at the fellow at times because he
is so . . . Oh, I could tell you things, my boy! . . . Oh, *vile! vile!*" he
cried, shaking his head downwards. "What coarseness! . . . What *in-
vect*-ive!" he whispered, in a kind of ecstasy.

XII

EUGENE was now a member of Professor Hatcher's celebrated course
for dramatists, and although he had come into this work by chance,
and would in the end discover that his heart and interest were not in it,
it had now become for him the rock to which his life was anchored, the
rudder of his destiny, the sole and all-sufficient reason for his being here.
It now seemed to him that there was only one work in life which he
could possibly do, and that this work was writing plays, and that if he
could not succeed in this work he had better die, since any other life
than the life of the playwright and the theatre was not to be endured.

Accordingly every interest and energy of his life was now fastened
on this work with a madman's passion; he thought, felt, breathed, ate,
drank, slept, and lived completely in terms of plays. He learned all the
jargon of the art-playwriting cult, read all the books, saw all the shows,
talked all the talk, and even became a kind of gigantic eavesdropper
upon life, prowling about the streets with his ears constantly straining to
hear all the words and phrases of the passing crowd, as if he might hear
something that would be rare and priceless in a play for Professor
Hatcher's celebrated course.

Professor James Graves Hatcher was a man whose professional career had been made difficult by two circumstances: all the professors
thought he looked like an actor and all the actors thought he looked
like a professor. In reality, he was wholly neither one, but in character
and temper, as well as in appearance, he possessed some of the attributes
of both.

His appearance was imposing: a well-set-up figure of a man of fifty-
five, somewhat above the middle height, strongly built and verging
toward stockiness, with an air of vital driving energy that was always
filled with authority and a sense of sure purpose, and that never de-
generated into the cheap exuberance of the professional hustler. His
voice, like his manner, was quiet, distinguished, and controlled, but al-

ways touched with the suggestions of great latent power, with reserves of passion, eloquence, and resonant sonority.

His head was really splendid: he had a strong but kindly-looking face touched keenly, quietly by humor; his eyes, beneath his glasses, were also keen, observant, sharply humorous, his mouth was wide and humorous but somewhat too tight, thin and spinsterly for a man's, his nose was large and strong, his forehead shapely and able-looking, and he had neat wings of hair cut short and sparse and lying flat against the skull.

He wore eye-glasses of the pince-nez variety, and they dangled in a fashionable manner from a black silk cord: it was better than going to a show to see him put them on, his manner was so urbane, casual, and distinguished when he did so. His humor, although suave, was also quick and rich and gave an engaging warmth and humanity to a personality that sometimes needed them. Even in his display of humor, however, he never lost his urbane distinguished manner—for example, when some one told him that one of his women students had referred to another woman in the course, an immensely tall angular creature who dressed in rusty brown right up to the ears, as "the queen of the angleworms," Professor Hatcher shook all over with sudden laughter, removed his glasses with a distinguished movement, and then in a rich but controlled voice, remarked:

"Ah, she has a very pretty wit. A very pretty wit, indeed!"

Thus, even in his agreeable uses of the rich, subtle and immensely pleasant humor with which he had been gifted, Professor Hatcher was something of an actor. He was one of those rare people who really "chuckle," and although there was no doubting the spontaneity and naturalness of his chuckle, it is also probably true that Professor Hatcher somewhat fancied himself as a chuckler.

The Hatcherian chuckle was just exactly what the word connotes: a movement of spontaneous mirth that shook his stocky shoulders and strong well-set torso with a sudden hearty tremor. And although he could utter rich and sonorous throat-sounds indicative of hearty mirth while this chuckling process was going on, an even more characteristic form was completely soundless, the tight lips firmly compressed, the edges turned up with the convulsive inclination to strong laughter, the fine distinguished head thrown back, while all the rest of him, throat, shoulders, torso, belly, arms—the whole man—shook in the silent tremors of the chuckle.

It could also be said with equal truth that Professor Hatcher was one of the few men whose eyes could really "twinkle," and it is likewise true that he probably fancied himself as somewhat of a twinkler.

Perhaps one fact that made him suspect to professors was his air of a distinguished and mature, but also a very worldly, urbanity. His manner, even in the class room, was never that of the scholar or the academician, but always that of the cultured man of the world, secure in his authority, touched by fine humor and fine understanding, able, knowing and assured. And one reason that he so impressed his students may have been that he made some of the most painful and difficult labors in the world seem delightfully easy.

For example, if there were to be a performance by a French club at the university of a French play, produced in the language of its birth, Professor Hatcher might speak to his class in his assured, yet casual and urbanely certain tones, as follows:

"I understand *Le Cercle Français* is putting on De Musset's *Il faut qu'une porte soit ouverte ou fermée* on Thursday night. If you are doing nothing else, I think it might be very well worth your while to brush up on your French a bit and look in on it. It is, of course, a trifle and perhaps without great significance in the development of the modern theatre, but it is De Musset in rather good form and De Musset in good form is charming. So it might repay you to have a look at it."

What was there in these simple words that could so impress and captivate these young people? The tone was quiet, pleasant and urbanely casual, the manner easy yet authoritative, what he said about the play was really true. But what was so seductive about it was the flattering unction which he laid so casually to their young souls—the easy off-hand suggestion that people "brush up on their French a bit" when most of them had no French at all to brush up on, that if they had "nothing else to do," they might "look in" upon De Musset's "charming trifle," the easy familiarity with De Musset's name and the casual assurance of the statement that it was "De Musset in rather good form."

It was impossible for a group of young men, eager for sophistication and emulous of these airs of urbane worldliness, not to be impressed by them. As Professor Hatcher talked they too became easy, casual and urbane in their manners, they had a feeling of being delightfully at ease in the world and sure of themselves, the words "brush up on your French a bit" gave them a beautifully comfortable feeling that they would really be able to perform this remarkable accomplishment in an hour or two of elegant light labor. And when he spoke of the play as being "De Musset in rather good form" they nodded slightly with little understanding smiles as if De Musset and his various states of form were matters of the most familiar knowledge to them.

What was the effect, then, of this and other such-like talk upon these young men eager for fame and athirst for glory in the great art-world of the city and the theatre? It gave them, first of all, a delightful sense of being in the know about rare and precious things, of rubbing shoulders with great actors and actresses and other celebrated people, of being expert in all the subtlest processes of the theatre, of being travelled, urbane, sophisticated and assured.

When Professor Hatcher casually suggested that they might "brush up on their French a bit" before going to a performance of a French play, they felt like cosmopolites who were at home in all the great cities of the world. True, "their French had grown a little rusty"—it had been some time since they were last in Paris—a member of the French Academy, no doubt, might detect a few slight flaws in their pronunciation—but all that would arrange itself by a little light and easy "polishing"—"tout s'arrange, hein?" as we say upon the boulevards.

Again, Professor Hatcher's pleasant and often delightfully gay anecdotes about the famous persons he had known and with whom he was on such familiar terms—told always casually, apropos of some topic of discussion, and never dragged in or labored by pretense— "The last time I was in London, Pinero and I were having lunch together one day at the Savoy"—or "I was spending the week-end with Henry Arthur Jones"—or "It's very curious you should mention that. You know, Barrie was saying the same thing to me the last time I saw him—" or—"Apropos of this discussion, I have a letter here from 'Gene O'Neill which bears on that very point. Perhaps you would be interested in knowing what he has to say about it."— All this, of course, was cakes and ale to these young people—it made them feel wonderfully near and intimate with all these celebrated people, and with the enchanted world of art and of the theatre in which they wished to cut a figure.

It gave them also a feeling of amused superiority at the posturings and antics of what, with a slight intonation of disdain, they called "the commercial producers"—the Shuberts, Belascos, and others of this kind. Thus, when Professor Hatcher told them how he had done some pioneer service in Boston for the Russian Players and had received a telegram from the Jewish producer in New York who was managing them, to this effect: "You are the real wonder boy"—they were instantly able to respond to the sudden Hatcherian chuckle with quiet laughter of their own.

Again, he once came back from New York with an amusing story of a visit he had paid to the famous producer, David Belasco. And he described drolly how he had followed a barefoot, snaky-looking female, clad in a long batik gown, through seven gothic chambers mystical with chimes and incense. And finally he told how he had been ushered into the presence of the great ecclesiastic who sat at the end of a cathedral-like room beneath windows of church glass, and how he was preceded all the time by Snaky Susy who swept low in obeisance as she approached, and said in a silky voice—"One is here to see you, Mahster," and how she had been dismissed with Christ-like tone and movement of the hand—"Rise, Rose, and leave us now." Professor Hatcher told this story with a quiet drollery that was irresistible, and was rewarded all along by their shouts of astounded laughter, and finally by their smiling and astonished faces, lifting disbelieving eyebrows at each other, saying, "Simply incredible! It doesn't seem possible! . . . *Marvellous!*"

Finally, when Professor Hatcher talked to them of how a Russian actress used her hands, of rhythm, tempo, pause, and timing, of lighting, setting, and design, he gave them a language they could use with a feeling of authority and knowledge, even when authority and knowledge was lacking to them. It was a dangerous and often very trivial language—a kind of jargonese of art that was coming into use in the world of those days, and that seemed to be coincident with another jargonese—that of science—"psychology," as they called it—which was also coming into its brief hour of idolatry at about the same period, and which bandied about its talk of "complexes," "fixations," "repressions," "inhibitions," and the like, upon the lips of any empty-headed little fool that came along.

But although this jargon was perhaps innocuous enough when rattled off the rattling tongue of some ignorant boy or rattle-pated girl, it could be a very dangerous thing when uttered seriously by men who were trying to achieve the best, the rarest, and the highest life on earth—the life which may be won only by bitter toil and knowledge and stern living—the life of the artist.

And the great danger of this glib and easy jargon of the arts was this: that instead of knowledge, the experience of hard work and patient living, they were given a formula for knowledge; a language that sounded very knowing, expert and assured, and yet that knew nothing, was experienced in nothing, was sure of nothing. It gave to people without talent and without sincerity of soul or integrity of purpose, with nothing, in fact, except a feeble incapacity for the shock and agony of life, and a desire to escape into a glamorous and unreal world of make believe—a justification for their pitiable and base existence. It gave to people who had no power in themselves to create anything of merit or of beauty—people who were the true Philistines and enemies of art and of the artist's living spirit—the language to talk with glib knowingness of things they knew nothing of—to prate of "settings," "tempo," "pace," and "rhythm," of "boldly stylized conventions," and the wonderful way some actress "used her hands." And in the end, it led to nothing but falseness and triviality, to the ghosts of passion, and the spectres of sincerity, to the shoddy appearances of conviction and belief in people who had no passion and sincerity, and who were convinced of nothing, believed in nothing, were just the disloyal apes of fashion and the arts.

"I think you ought to go," says one. "I really do. I really think you might be interested."

"Yes," says number two, in a tone of fine, puzzled, eyebrow-lifting protest, "but I hear the play is pretty bad. The reviews were rather awful —they really were, you know."

"Oh, the play!" the other says, with a slight start of surprise, as if it never occurred to him that any one might be interested in the play— "the play, the play *is* rather terrible. But my dear fellow, no one goes to see the *play* . . . the play is nothing," he dismisses it with a contemptuous gesture— "It's the *sets!*" he cries— "the *sets* are really quite remarkable. You ought to go, old boy, just to see the *sets!* They're very good—they really are."

"H'm!" the other says, stroking his chin in an impressed manner. "Interesting! In that case, I shall go!"

The *sets!* The *sets!* One should not go to see the play; the only thing that matters is the sets. And this is the theatre—the magic-maker and the world of dreams; and these the men that are to fashion for it—with their trivial ape's talk about "sets." Did any one ever hear such damned stuff as this since time began?

False, trivial, glib, dishonest, empty, without substance, lacking faith —is it any wonder that among Professor Hatcher's young men few birds sang?

XIII

THAT year the youth was twenty, it had been his first year in New England, and the winter had seemed very long. In the man-swarm he felt alone and lost, a desolate atom in the streets of life. That year he went to see his uncle many times.

Sometimes he would find him in his dusty little cubicle, bent over the intricacy of a legal form, painfully and carefully, with compressed lips, filling in the blank spaces with his stiff, angular and laborious hand. Bascom would speak quietly, without looking up, as he came in: "Hello, my boy. Sit down, won't you? I'll be with you in a moment." And for a time the silence would be broken only by the heavy rumble of Brill's voice outside, by the minute scratching of his uncle's pen, and by the immense and murmurous sound of time, which rose above the city, which caught up in the upper air all of the city's million noises, and yet seemed remote, essential, imperturbable and everlasting—fixed and unchanging, no matter what men lived or died.

Again, the boy would find his uncle staring straight before him, with his great hands folded in a bony arch, his powerful gaunt face composed in a rapt tranquillity of thought. At these times he seemed to have escaped from every particular and degrading thing in life—from the excess of absurd and eccentric speech and gesture, from all demeaning parsimonies, from niggling irascibilities, from everything that contorted his face and spirit away from its calmness and unity of thought. His face at such a time might well have been the mask of thought, the visage of contemplation. Sometimes he would not speak for several minutes, his mind seemed to brood upon the lip and edge of time, to be remote from every dusty moment of the earth.

One day the boy went there and found him thus: after a few moments he lowered his great hands and, without turning toward his nephew, sat for some time in an attitude of quiet relaxation. At length he said: "What is man that thou art mindful of him?"

It was one of the first days of spring: the spring had come late, with a magical northern suddenness. It seemed to have burst out of the earth overnight, the air was lyrical and sang with it.

Spring came that year like a triumph and like a prophecy—it sang and shifted like a moth of light before the youth, but he was sure that it would bring him a glory and fulfilment he had never known.

His hunger and thirst had been immense: he was caught up for the first time in the midst of the Faustian web—there was no food that could feed him, no drink that could quench his thirst. Like an insatiate and maddened animal he roamed the streets, trying to draw up mercy from the cobblestones, solace and wisdom from a million sights and faces, or he prowled through endless shelves of high-piled books, tortured by everything he could not see and could not know, and growing blind, weary, and desperate from what he read and saw. He wanted to know all, have all, be all—to be one and many, to have the whole riddle of this vast and swarming earth as legible, as tangible in his hand as a coin of minted gold.

Suddenly spring came, and he felt at once exultant certainty and joy. Outside his uncle's dirty window he could see the edge of Faneuil Hall, and hear the swarming and abundant activity of the markets. The deep roar of the markets reached them across the singing and lyrical air, and he drank into his lungs a thousand proud, potent, and mysterious odors which came to him like the breath of certainty, like the proof of magic, and like the revelation that all confusion had been banished—the world that he longed for won, the word that he sought for spoken, the hunger that devoured him fed and ended. And the markets, swarming with richness, joy, and abundance, thronged below him like a living evidence of fulfilment. For it seemed to him that nowhere more than here was the passionate enigma of New England felt: New England, with its harsh and stony soil, and its tragic and lonely beauty; its desolate rocky coasts and its swarming fisheries, the white, piled, frozen bleakness of its winters with the magnificent jewelry of stars, the dark firwoods, and the warm little white houses at which it is impossible to look without thinking of groaning bins, hung bacon, hard cider, succulent bastings and love's warm, white, and opulent flesh.

There was the rustle of gingham by day and sober glances; then, under low eaves and starlight, the stir of the satiny thighs in feather beds, the white small bite and tigerish clasp of secret women—always the buried heart, the sunken passion, the frozen heat. And then, after the long, unendurably hard-locked harshness of the frozen winter, the coming of spring as now, like a lyrical cry, like a flicker of rain across a window glass, like the sudden and delicate noises of a spinet—the coming of spring and ecstasy, and overnight the thrum of wings, the burst of the tender buds, the ripple and dance of the roughened water, the light of flowers, the sudden, fleeting, almost captured, and exultant spring.

And here, within eighty yards of the dusty little room where his uncle Bascom had his desk, there was living evidence that this intuition was not false: the secret people, it was evident, did not subsist alone on codfish and a jug full of baked beans—they ate meat, and large chunks of it, for all day long, within the market district, the drivers of big wagons were standing to their chins in meat, boys dragged great baskets of raw meat along the pavements, red-faced butchers, aproned with gouts of blood, and wearing the battered straw hats that butchers wear, toiled through the streets below with great loads of loin or haunch or rib, and in chill shops with sawdust floors the beeves were hung in frozen regimental rows.

Right and left, around the central market, the old buildings stretched down to the harbor and the smell of ships: this was built-on land, in old days ships were anchored where these cobbles were, but the warehouses were also old—they had the musty, mellow, blackened air and smell of the 'seventies, they looked like Victorian prints, they reeked of ancient ledgers, of "counting houses," of proud, monied merchants, and the soft-spoken rumble of victorias.

By day, this district was one snarled web of chaos: a *gewirr* of deep-bodied trucks, powerful dappled horses, cursing drivers, of loading, unloading, and shipping, of dispatch and order, of the million complicated weavings of life and business.

But if one came here at evening, after the work of the day was done, if one came here at evening on one of those delicate and sudden days of spring that New England knows, if one came here as many a lonely youth had come here in the past, some boy from the inland immensity of America, some homesick lad from the South, from the marvellous hills of Old Catawba, he might be pierced again by the bitter ecstasy of youth, the ecstasy that tears him apart with a cry that has no tongue, the ecstasy that is proud, lonely, and exultant, that is fierce with joy and blind with glory, but yet carries in it a knowledge, born in such a moment, that the intangible cannot be touched, the ungraspable cannot be grasped—the imperial and magnificent minute is gone forever which, with all its promises, its million intuitions, he wishes to clothe with the living substance of beauty. He wishes to flesh the moment with the thighs and breast and belly of a wonderful mistress, he wishes to be great and glorious and triumphant, to distill the ether of this ecstasy in a liquor, and to drink strong joy forever; and at the heart of all this is the bitter knowledge of death—death of the moment, death of the day, death of one more infrequent spring.

Perhaps the thing that really makes New England wonderful is this sense of joy, this intuition of brooding and magic fulfilment that hovers like a delicate presence in the air of one of these days. Perhaps the answer is simple: perhaps it is only that this soft and sudden spring, with its darts and flicks of evanescent joy, its sprite-like presence that is only half-believed, its sound that is the sound of something lost and elfin and half-dreamed, half-heard, seems wonderful after the grim frozen tenacity of the winter, the beautiful and terrible desolation, the assault of the frost and ice on living flesh which resists it finally as it would resist the cruel battering of a brute antagonist, so that the tart, stingy speech, the tight gestures, the withdrawn and suspicious air, the thin lips, red pointed noses and hard prying eyes of these people are really the actions of those who, having to defend themselves harshly against nature, harshly defend themselves against all the world.

At any rate, the thing the boy feels who comes here at the day's end is not completion, weariness, and sterility, but a sense of swelling ecstasy, a note of brooding fulfilment. The air will have in it the wonderful odors of the market and the smell of the sea, as he walks over the bare cobbled pavement under the corrugated tin awnings of the warehouses and produce stores a hundred smells of the rich fecundity of the earth will assail him: the clean sharp pungency of thin crated wood and the citric nostalgia of oranges, lemons, and grapefruit, the stench of a decayed cabbage and the mashed pulp of a rotten orange. There will be also the warm coarse limy smell of chickens, the strong coddy smell of cold fish and oysters; and the crisp moist cleanliness of the garden smells—of great lettuces, cabbages, new potatoes, with their delicate skins loamy with sweet earth, the wonderful sweet crispness of crated celery; and then the melons—the ripe golden melons bedded in fragrant straw—and all the warm infusions of the tropics: the bananas, the pineapples and the alligator pears.

The delicate and subtle air of spring touches all these odors with a new and delicious vitality; it draws the tar out of the pavements also, and it draws slowly, subtly, from ancient warehouses, the compacted perfumes of eighty years: the sweet thin piney scents of packing-boxes, the glutinous composts of half a century, that have thickly stained old warehouse plankings, the smells of twine, tar, turpentine and hemp, and of thick molasses, ginseng, pungent vines and roots and old piled sacking; the clean, ground strength of fresh coffee, brown, sultry, pungent, and exultantly fresh and clean; the smell of oats, baled hay and bran, of crated eggs and cheese and butter; and particularly the smell of meat, of frozen beeves, slick porks, and veals, of brains and livers and kidneys, of haunch, paunch, and jowl; of meat that is raw and of meat that is cooked, for upstairs in that richly dingy block of buildings there is a room where the butchers, side by side with the bakers, the bankers, the brokers and the Harvard boys, devour thick steaks of the best and tenderest meat, smoking-hot breads, and big, jacketed potatoes.

And then there is always the sea. In dingy blocks, memoried with time and money, the buildings stretch down to the docks, and there is always the feeling that the sea was here, that this is built-on earth. A single truck will rattle over the deserted stones, and then there is the street that runs along the harbor, the dingy little clothing shops and eating places, the powerful strings of freight cars, agape and empty, odorous with their warm fatigued planking and the smells of flanges and axles that have rolled great distances.

And finally, by the edges of the water, there are great piers and storehouses, calm and potent with their finished work: they lie there, immense, starkly ugly, yet touched with the powerful beauty of enormous works and movements; they are what they are, they have been built without a flourish for the work they do, their great sides rise in level cliffs of brick, they are pierced with tracks and can engulf great trains; and now that the day is done they breathe with the vitality of a tired but living creature. A single footfall will make remote and lonely echoes in their brooding depths, there will be the expiring clatter of a single truck, the sound of a worker's voice as he says "Good-night," and then the potent and magical silence.

And then there is the sea—the sea, beautiful and mysterious as it is only when it meets the earth in harbors, the sea that bears in swell and glut of tides the odorous savor of the earth, the sea that swings and slaps against encrusted piles, the sea that is braided with long ropes of scummy weed, the sea that brings the mast and marly scent of shelled decay. There is the sea, and there are the great ships—the freighters, the fishing schooners, the clean white one-night boats that make the New York run, now also potent and silent, a glitter of bright lights, of gleam-

ing brasses, of opulent saloons—a token of joy and splendor in dark
waters, a hint of love and the velvet belly upon dark tides—and the sight
of all these things, the fusion of all these odors by the sprite of May is
freighted with unspeakable memories, with unutterable intuitions for
the youth: he does not know what he would utter, but glory, love, power,
wealth, flight, and movement and the sight of new earth in the morning,
and the living corporeal fulfilment of all his ecstasy is in his wish and
his conviction.

Certainly, these things can be found in New England, but perhaps the
person who finds this buried joy the most is this lonely visitor—and
particularly the boy from the South, for in the heart of the Southerner
alone, perhaps, is this true and secret knowledge of the North: it is there
in his dreams and his childhood premonition, it is there like the dark
Helen, and no matter what he sees to cheat it, he will always believe in
it, he will always return to it. Certainly, this was true of the gnarled and
miserly old man who now sat not far from all this glory in his dingy
State Street office, for Bascom Pentland, although the stranger on seeing
him might have said, "There goes the very image of a hard-bitten
old Down-Easter," had come, as lonely and wretched a youth as ever
lived, from the earth of Old Catawba, he had known and felt these
things and, in spite of his frequent bitter attacks on the people, the
climate, the life, New England was the place to which he had returned
to live, and for which he felt the most affection.

Now, ruminant and lost, he stared across the archway of his hands.
In a moment, with what was only an apparent irrelevance, with what
was really a part of the coherent past, a light plucked from dark adyts
of the brain, he said: "Who knoweth the spirit of man that goeth upward, and the spirit of the beast that goeth downward to the earth?"

He was silent and thoughtful for a moment; then he added sadly: "I
am an old man. I have lived a long time. I have seen so many things.
Sometimes everything seems so long ago."

Then his eye went back into the wilderness, the lost earth, the buried
men.

Presently he said, "I hope you will come out on Sunday. O, by all
means! By all means! I believe your aunt is expecting you. Yes, sir, I
believe she said something to that effect. Or perhaps she intends to pay
a visit to one of her children. I do not know, I have not the *remotest*—
not the *faintest* idea of what she proposes to do," he howled. "Of course,"

he said impatiently and scornfully, "I never have any notion what she has in mind. No, sir, I really could not tell you. I no longer pay any attention to what she says—O! not the slightest!" he waved his great hand through the air— *"Say!"* stiffly and harshly he tapped the boy's knee, grinning at him with the combative glitter of his ptotic eye— *"Say!* did you ever find *one* of them with whom it was possible to carry on a coherent conversation? Did you ever find one of them who would respond to the processes of reason and ordered thought? My dear boy!" he cried, "you cannot talk to them. I assure you, you cannot talk to them. You might as well whistle into the wind or spit into the waters of the Nile, for all the good it will do you. In his youth man will bare the riches of his spirit to them, will exhaust the rich accumulations of his genius—his wisdom, his learning, his philosophy—in an effort to make them worthy of his companionship—and in the end, what does he *always* find? Why," said Uncle Bascom bitterly, "that he has spent his powers in talking to an imbecile"—and he snarled vengefully through his nose. In a moment more, he contorted his face, and nasally whined in a grotesque and mincing parody of a woman's voice, "O, I feel *so* sick! O, deary *me,* now! I think my *time* is coming on again! O, you don't *love* me any mo-o-ore! O, I *wish* I was dead! O, I can't get *up* to-day! O, I wish you'd bring me something *nice* from *ta-own!* O, if you loved me you'd buy me a *new* hat! O, I've got nothing to *we-e-ar!"* here his voice had an added snarl of bitterness—"I'm ashamed to go out on the street with all the other wim-men!"

Then he paused broodingly for a moment more, wheeled abruptly and tapped the boy on the knee again: "The proper study of mankind is —say!" he said with a horrible fixed grimace and in a kind of cunning whisper—"does the poet say—*woman?* I want to ask you: *does* he, now? Not on your life!" yelled Uncle Bascom. "The word is *man, man, man!* Nothing else but *man!"*

Again he was silent: then, with an accent of heavy sarcasm, he went on: "Your aunt likes music. You may have observed your aunt is fond of music——"

It was, in fact, the solace of her life: on a tiny gramophone which one of her daughters had given her, she played constantly the records of the great composers.

"—Your aunt is fond of music," Bascom said deliberately. "Perhaps you may have thought—perhaps it seemed to you that she discovered it—perhaps you thought it was your aunt's own patent and invention—

but there you would be wrong! O yes! my boy!" he howled remotely. "You may have thought so, but you would be wrong— Say!" he turned slowly with a malevolent glint of interrogation, a controlled ironic power —"was the Fifth Symphony written by a woman? Was the object of your aunt's worship, Richard Wagner, a *female?*" he snarled. "By no means! Where are their great works—their mighty symphonies, their great paintings, their epic poetry? Was it in a woman's skull that the *Critique of Pure Reason* was conceived? Is the gigantic work upon the ceiling of the Sistine Chapel the product of a woman's genius?—Say! did you ever hear of a lady by the name of William Shakespeare? Was it a female of that name who wrote *King Lear?* Are you familiar with the works of a nice young lady named John Milton? Or Fräulein Goethe, a sweet German girl?" he sneered. "Perhaps you have been edified by the writ-ings of Mademoiselle Voltaire or Miss Jonathan Swift? Phuh! Phuh! Phuh! Phuh! Phuh!"

He paused, stared deliberately across his hands, and in a moment re-peated, slowly and distinctly: "The woman gave me of the tree and I did eat. Ah! that's it! There, my boy, you have it! There, in a nut-shell, you have the work for which they are best fitted." And he turned upon his nephew suddenly with a blaze of passion, his voice husky and trem-ulous from the stress of emotion. "The tempter! The Bringer of Forbid-den Fruit! The devil's ambassador! Since the beginning of time that has been their office—to madden the brain, to turn man's spirit from its highest purposes, to corrupt, to seduce, and to destroy! To creep and crawl, to intrude into the lonely places of man's heart and brain, to wind herself into the core of his most secret life as a worm eats its way into a healthy fruit—to do all this with the guile of a serpent, the cunning of a fox—that, my boy, is what she's here for!—and she'll never change!" And, lowering his voice to an ominous and foreboding whisper, he said mysteriously, "Beware! Beware! Do not be deceived!"

In a moment more he had resumed his tone and manner of calm de-liberation and, with an air of irrelevance, somewhat grudgingly, as if throwing a bone to a dog, he said, "Your aunt, of course, was a woman of considerable mentality—considerable, that is, for a female. Of course, her mind is no longer what it used to be. I never talk to her any more," he said indifferently. "I do not listen to her. I think she said something to me about your coming out on Sunday! But I do not know. No, sir, I could not tell you what her plans are. I have my own interests, and I suppose she has hers. Of course, she has her music. . . . Yes, sir, she always has her music," he said indifferently and contemptuously, and, staring across the apex of his hands, he forgot her.

Yet, he had been young, and full of pain and madness. For a space he had known all the torments any lover ever knew. So much Louise had told her nephew, and so much Bascom had not troubled to deny. For bending toward the boy swiftly, fiercely, and abruptly, as if Bascom was not there, she whispered: "Oh, yes! he's indifferent enough to me now—but there was a time, there was a time, I tell you!—when he was mad about me! The old fool!" she cackled suddenly and bitterly with a seeming irrelevance. Then bending forward suddenly with a resumption of her former brooding intensity, she whispered: "Yes! he was mad, mad, mad! Oh, he can't deny it!" she cried. "He couldn't keep his eyes off me for a minute! He went cwazy if any other man so much as looked at me!"

"Quite true, my dear! Quite true!" said Uncle Bascom without a trace of anger or denial in his voice, with one of his sudden and astonishing changes to a mood of tender and tranquil agreement. "Oh, yes," he said again, staring reminiscently across the apex of his great folded hands, "it is all quite true—every word as she has spoken it—quite true, quite true. I had forgotten but it's all quite true." And he shook his gaunt head gently from side to side, turning his closed eyes downward, and snuffling gently, blindly, tenderly, with laughter, with a passive and indifferent memory.

For a year or two after his marriage, she had said, he had been maddened by a black insanity of jealousy. It descended on his spirit like a choking and pestilence-laden cloud, it entered his veins with blackened tongues of poison, it crept along the conduits of his blood, sweltered venomously in his heart, it soaked into the convolutions of his brain until his brain was fanged with hatred, soaked in poison, stricken, maddened, and unhinged. His gaunt figure wasted until he became the picture of skeletonized emaciation, jealousy and fear ate like a vulture at his entrails, all of the vital energy, the power and intensity of his life, was fed into this poisonous and consuming fire and then, when it had almost wrecked his health, ruined his career, and destroyed his reason, it left him as suddenly as it came: his life reverted to its ancient and imbedded core of egotism, he grew weary of his wife, he thought of her indifferently, he forgot her.

And she, poor soul, was like a rabbit trapped before the fierce yellow eye, the hypnotic stare of a crouching tiger. She did not know whether he would spring, strike forth his paw to maul her, or walk off indifferently. She was dazed and stricken before the violence of his first passion, the unreasoning madness of his jealousy, and in the years that followed she was bewildered, resentful, and finally embittered by the abrupt indifference which succeeded it—an indifference so great that often he seemed to forget her very existence for days at a time, to live with her in a little house as if he were scarcely conscious of her presence, stumping about the place in an intensity of self-absorption while he cursed and muttered to himself, banged open furnace doors, chopped up whatever combinations of raw foods his fantastic imagination might contrive, and answering her impatiently and contemptuously when she spoke to him: "What did you *say-y?* Oh, what are you talk-ing about?"—and he would stump away again, absorbed mysteriously with his own affairs. And sometimes, if he was the victim of conspiracy in the universe—if God had forsaken him and man had tricked and cheated him, he would roll upon the floor, hammer his heels against the wall, and howl his curses at oblivious heaven.

Louise, meanwhile, her children having left her, played Wagner on the gramophone, kept her small house tidy, and learned to carry on involved and animated conversations with herself, or even with her pots and pans, for when she scrubbed and cleaned them, she would talk to them: if she dropped one, she would scold it, pick it from the floor, spank it across the bottom, saying: "No, you don't! Naughty, you bad thing, you!" And often, while he stumped through the house, these solitary conversations were interspersed by fits of laughter: she would bend double over her pots snuffling with soft laughter which was faintly broken at its climax, a long high "Who-o-op." Then she would shake her head pityingly, and be off again, but at what she was laughing she could not have said.

One night, however, she interrupted one of Bascom's stamping and howling tirades by putting on her tiny gramophone *The Ride of the Valkyries,* as recorded by the Philadelphia Symphony Orchestra. Bascom, after the first paralysis of his surprise had passed, rushed furiously toward the offending instrument that was providing such melodious but mighty competition. Then Bascom halted; for suddenly he noticed that Louise was standing beside the instrument, that she was snuffling through her nose with laughter, and that from time to time she looked craftily toward him, and broke into a high piercing cackle.

Bascom also noticed that she held a large carving knife in her hand. With a loud yell he turned and fled toward his room, where he locked the door, crying out strongly in an agony of terror: "O Momma! Momma! Save me!"

All this had amused Louise enormously. She played the record over time after time, forever snuffling with laughter and the high cackle: "Who-oo-oo!" She bent double with it.

And now, as the boy looked at the old man, he had a sense of union with the past. It seemed to him if he would only speak, the living past, the voices of lost men, the pain, the pride, the madness and despair, the million scenes and faces of the buried life—all that an old man ever knew—would be revealed to him, would be delivered to him like a priceless treasure, as an inheritance which old men owed to young, and which should be the end and effort of all living. His savage hunger was a kind of memory: he thought if he could speak, it would be fed.

And for a moment, it seemed, he saw the visages of time, dark time, the million lock-bolts shot back in man's memory, the faces of the lost Americans, and all the million casual moments of their lives, with Bascom blazing at them from a dozen pulpits, Bascom, tortured by love and madness, walking the streets of the nation, stumping the rutted roads, muttering through darkness with clasped bony hands, a gaunt and twisted figure reeling across the continent below immense and cruel skies. Light fell upon his face and darkness crossed it:—he came up from the wilderness, from derbied men and bustled women, from all of the memories of lavish brown, and from time, dark time—from a time that was further off than Saxon thanes, all of the knights, the spear-heads, and the horses.

Was all this lost?

"It was so long ago," the old man said.

Bitterly, bitterly Boston one time more: the flying leaf, the broken cloud. Was no love crying in the wilderness?

"—So long ago. I have lived so long. I have seen so much. I could tell you so many things," his uncle said huskily, with weariness and indifference. His eye was lustreless and dead, he looked for a moment tired and old.

All at once, a strange and perplexing vision, which was to return many times in the years that followed, came to the boy. It was this: there was a company of old men and women at dinner, seated together around a table. All of them were very old, older than his uncle; the faces of the old men and women were fragile and delicate like old yellowed china, their faces were frail and sexless, they had begun to look alike. In their youth all these people had known one another. The men had drunk, fought, whored, hated one another, and loved the women. Some had been devoured by the sterile and corrupt fear and envy that young men know. In secret their lips were twisted, their faces livid, and their hearts bitter; their eyes glittered with a reptilian hatred of another man—they dreaded his success, and they exulted in his failure, laughing with a delirious joy when they heard or read of his hurt, defeat, or humiliation. They had been afraid to speak or confess what was in their hearts, they feared the mockery of their fellows; with one another their words were careful, picked, and disparaging. They gave the lie to passion and belief and they said what they knew was false. And yet along dark roads at night they had shouted out into the howling winds their great goat cries of joy, exultancy and power; they had smelled snow in thick brooding air at night, and they had watched it come, softly spitting at the window glass, numbing the footfalls of the earth with its soft silent fall, filling their hearts with a dark proud ecstasy, touching their entrails with impending prophecy. Each had a thousand dark desires and fantasies; each wanted wealth, power, fame and love; each saw himself as great, good and talented; each feared and hated rivals in business or in love—and in crowds they glared at one another with hard hostile eyes, they bristled up like crested cocks, they watched their women jealously, felt looks and glances through their shoulder-blades, and hated men with white spermatic necks, amorous hair, and faces proud and insolent with female conquest.

They had been young and full of pain and combat, and now all this was dead in them: they smiled mildly, feebly, gently, they spoke in thin voices, and they looked at one another with eyes dead to desire, hostility, and passion.

As for the old women, they sat there on their yellowed and bony haunches. They were all beyond the bitter pain and ecstasy of youth—its frenzy, its hope, its sinew of bright blood and agony: they were beyond the pain and fear of anything save age and death. Here was a faithful wife, a fruitful mother; here was an adulterous and voluptuous woman, the potent mistress of a dozen men, here was her cuckold husband, who had screamed like a tortured animal when he had first found her in bed with another man, and here was the man he found her with; here was another man in whom the knowledge of his wife's infidelity had aroused only a corrupt inverted joy, he exulted in it, he urged her on into new love affairs, he besought her greedily to taunt him with it, he fed upon his pain—and now they were all old and meagre and had the look of yellowed china. They turned their mild sunken faces toward one another with looks in which there was neither hate nor love nor desire nor passion, they laughed thinly, and their memory was all of little things.

They no longer wanted to excel or to be first; they were no longer mad and jealous; they no longer hated rivals; they no longer wanted fame; they no longer cared for work or grew drunk on hope; they no longer turned into the dark and struck their bloody knuckles at the wall; they no longer writhed with shame upon their beds, cursed at the memory of defeat and desolation, or ripped the sheets between convulsive fingers. Could they not speak? Had they forgotten?

Why could not the old men speak? They had known pain, death and madness, yet all their words were stale and rusty. They had known the wilderness, the savage land, the blood of the murdered men ran down into the earth that gave no answer; and they had seen it, they had shed it. Where were the passion, pain and pride, the million living moments of their lives? Was all this lost? Were they all tongueless? It seemed to the boy that there was something sly and evil in their glances as they sat together, as if they hoarded some cunning and malevolent wisdom in their brains, as if the medicine to all our grief and error was in them, but as if through the evil and conspirate communication of their glance, they had resolved to keep it from us. Or were they simply devoured with satiety, with weariness and indifference? Did they refuse to speak because they could not speak, because even memory had gone lifeless in them?

Yes. Words echoed in their throat but they were tongueless. For them the past was dead: they poured into our hands a handful of dry dust and ashes.

The dry bones, the bitter dust? The living wilderness, the silent waste? The barren land?

Have no lips trembled in the wilderness? No eyes sought seaward from the rock's sharp edge for men returning home? Has no pulse beat more hot with love or hate upon the river's edge? Or where the old wheel and the rusted stock lie stogged in desert sand: by the horsehead a woman's skull. No love?

No lonely footfalls in a million streets, no heart that beat its best and bloodiest cry out against the steel and stone, no aching brain, caught in its iron ring, groping among the labyrinthine canyons? Naught in that immense and lonely land but incessant growth and ripeness and pollution, the emptiness of forests and deserts, the uhearted, harsh and metal jangle of a million tongues, crying the belly-cry for bread, or the great cat's snarl for meat and honey? All, then, all? Birth and the twenty thousand days of snarl and jangle—and no love, no love? Was no love crying in the wilderness?

It was not true. The lovers lay below the lilac bush; the laurel leaves were trembling in the wood.

Suddenly it seemed to the boy, that if he could put his hand upon his uncle, if he could grip his fingers in his stringy arm, his own strength and youth would go into him, and he could rekindle memory like a living flame in him, he could animate for an hour that ancient heart with the exultancy, the power, the joy that pulsed in himself, he could make the old man speak.

He wanted to speak to him as people never speak to one another, he wanted to say and hear the things one never says and hears. He wanted to know what the old man's youth beyond its grim weather of poverty, loneliness, and desperation had been like. His uncle had been over ten years old when the war had ended, and he had seen the men plod home in wreaths of dust and heard their casual voices in a room, he had breathed the air of vanished summers, he had seen cloud shadows floating on the massed green, of the wilderness, the twisting of a last lone leaf upon a bough; and he had heard the desolate and stricken voices in the South long, long ago, the quiet and casual voices of lost men, a million vanished footsteps in the streets of life. And he had known the years of brown, dark lavish brown, the lost and hypocritic years, the thunder of the wheels and hooves upon the cobbles, the color of bright blood—the savagery, the hunger and the fear.

Was the memory of all this lost?

The boy touched him—he put his hand upon his uncle's shoulder; the old man did not move. Sunken in what lost world, buried in what incommunicable and tongueless past, he said—"So long ago."

Then the boy got up and left him and went out into the streets where the singing and lyrical air, the man-swarm passing in its million-footed weft, the glorious women and the girls compacted in a single music of belly and breasts and thighs, the sea, the earth, the proud, potent, clamorous city, all of the voices of time, fused to a unity that was like a song, a token and a cry. Victoriously, he trod the neck of doubt as if it were a serpent: he was joined to the earth, a part of it, and he possessed it; he would be wasted and consumed, filled and renewed eternally; he would feel unceasingly alternate tides of life and dark oblivion; he would be emptied without weariness, replenished forever with strong joy. He had a tongue for agony, a food for hunger, a door for exile and a surfeit for insatiate desire: exultant certainty welled up in him, he thought he could possess it all, and he cried: "Yes! It will be mine!"

XIV

He had spells and rhymes of magic numbers which would enable him, he thought, to read all of the million books in the great library. This was a furious obsession with him all the time. And there were other spells and rhymes which would enable him to know the lives of 50,000,000 people, to visit every country in the world, to know a hundred languages, possess 10,000 lovely women, and yet have one he loved and honored above all, who would be true and beautiful and faithful to him.

And by the all-resuming magic of these spells he would go everywhere on earth, while keeping one place to return to; and while driven mad with thirst and hunger to have everything, he would be peacefully content with almost nothing; and while wanting to be a famous, honored, celebrated man, he would live obscurely, decently, and well, with one true love forever. In short, he would have the whole cake of the world, and eat it, too—have adventures, labors, joys, and triumphs that would exhaust the energies of ten thousand men, and yet have spells and charms for all of it, and was sure that with these charms and spells and sorceries, all of it was his.

He would rush out of the great library into the street, and take the subway into Boston. And as the train smashed and rocked along, he would sit there solemnly with his lungs expanded to the bursting point and his chest swollen and stuck out like the breast of a pouter pigeon, while his eyes bulged, the veins on his forehead stuck out, and his face slowly turned an apoplectic purple as he sat there rocking with the agony of his effort.

Then the train would roar into the Central Station, and the breath would come sobbing and soughing out of his tortured lungs like wind out of an organ bellows. And for several seconds, while the train was stopped there at the station (for in these magic formulas these stops at stations "did not count") he would pant and gasp for breath like a fish out of water, gulping a new supply ravenously down into his lungs again, as if he thought he was being shot in a projectile through the terrific vacuum of unmeasured space.

Then, as the train roared out into the tunnel's dark again, he would repeat the effort, sitting as solemn as an owl with his bulging eyes, stuck-out chest, the stolid apoplectic purple of his swollen face, while little children looked at him with frightened eyes, their mothers with a glance of nervous apprehension, and the men in all the various attitudes of gape-jawed astonishment and stupefaction. Yet, at that time, he saw nothing strange or curious in this mad behavior. Rather, to hold his breath there in the tunnel's dark, to make that mystery of rite and number, and to follow it with a maniacal devotion seemed as inevitable and natural to him as the very act of life, of breath itself, and he was sometimes bitterly incensed when people stared at him because of it.

Those faces—the secret dark, unknown, nameless faces, the faces of the million instant casual meetings of these years, in the cars of subway trains or on the swarming streets—returned in later years to haunt him with a blazing, unforgettable intensity of vision, with an overwhelming sense of strangeness, loss and sorrow, a poignancy of familiarity, affection and regret, which was somehow, unbelievably, as wordless, grievous, full of an instant rending and unfathomable pity, as those things a man has known best and loved with all the life and passion in him, and has lost forever—a child's quick laugh of innocence and exultant mirth, a woman's smile, an intonation in her voice, the naked, child-like look remembered in the eyes of simple, faithful people who have gone, or the snatches of the song one's brother sang when he lay drowned in darkness and delirium, as he died.

Why did the unknown faces of these years come back to him? For he could not forget the million obscure faces of those first years of his wandering when for the first time he walked alone the streets of a great city, a madman, a beggar, and a king, feeling the huge joy of the secret world impending over him with all the glory of its magic imminence, and when each furious prowl and quest into the swarming streets of life, each furious journey through the tunnel's depth was living with the intolerable prescience of triumph and discovery—a life more happy, fortunate, golden, and complete than any life before had ever been.

He did not know. He never knew why all those obscure, nameless and unknown faces of a million strangers who passed and vanished in an instant from his sight, or whom he passed a hundred times upon the streets without a word or sign of recognition, should return to haunt him later with a sense of loss, affection, and the familiarity of utter knowledge. But he knew that they came back to him in images of unfading brightness, and that the light of time, dark time, was on them all, and that there was revealed to him, in later years, something strange and mad and lonely in the lives of all of them, which he had accepted instantly, and felt no wonder or surprise at, when he had seen them.

But these images of the past would come back in later years, and with a feeling of bitter loss and longing he would want to find, to see, to know them all again, to ask them what their lives had been, and what had happened to them. It was a weird, strange, assorted crew—that company of memory—on whom the light of time would fall with such a lonely hue, and how they were all got together in that magic consonance, he could never tell, but he could not forget them.

One was an old man, an old man with fierce restless eyes, and bedraggled mustaches of a stained tobacco yellow who kept a lodging house where a student that he knew had rooms, and whose house, from the basement to the attic, was a museum to the old man's single mania. For that house was crowded with old tottering stacks of books, a mountain of junk, uncounted and uncountable, a weariness and desolation of old print, dusty, yellowed, and unreadable—and all were memoirs of a single man, Napoleon.

Another was a woman with a mass of henna hair, piled up in a great crown upon her head, who sat smugly, day after day, like something ageless and embalmed, a presence deathless and hermetic to all the things that change and pass, in a glass cage before a moving-picture house on Washington Street, where people thronged in the dense and narrow line before her all the time, and glass steps and a rotating stairway went steeply up beside her cage, and flashing cascades of bright water foamed and tumbled underneath the glassy stairs, as the woman with piled henna hair sat always in her cage, deathless, smug, hermetic, and embalmed.

Another was an old man with a mad, fierce, handsome face and wild strewn hair of silvery white, who never wore a hat or overcoat, and who muttered through the streets of Cambridge, over the board walks of the Harvard Yard, in every kind of weather: winter was around him always, the rugged skies of wintry sunsets, red and harsh, the frozen desolation of old snow in street and Yard and gutter, the harsh, interminable, weary savagery of gray winter.

One was a waitress in a restaurant on Tremont Street, a woman quiet, decent, and demure in manner, who wore faintly on her lips continually the most sensual, tender, and seductive mystery of a smile that he had ever seen on any woman's face, who drew him back into that place to eat a thousand times, who made him think of her at night, and prowl the streets and think of her, and go back to that restaurant night after night, with a feeling of wild joy and imminent possession when he thought of her, and yet who said, did, promised nothing that was not sedate, decent, and correct, or that could give him comfort, hope, or knowledge of her life.

He never got to know her, he never even knew her name, some secrecy and pride in him prevented him from speaking to her with familiar warmth or curiosity, but he spent thousands of good hours in thinking of her—hours filled with all the passion, dreams, and longing youth can know. The woman was no longer young; the other waitresses were younger, fresher, better-looking, had better legs and finer figures; he had no way at all of knowing the quality of her life, mind, spirit, speech —save that when he heard her speak her voice was a little husky and coarse-fibred—but that woman became the central figure of one of those glittering and impossible fantasies young men have.

It was a great legend of wealth and fame and love and glory in which this woman lived as a creature of queenly beauty, delicacy, intelligence, and grandeur of the soul—and every obstacle of cold and acid fact that interposed itself between him and his vision he would instantly destroy by the wild fantastic logic of desire.

And because of her he prowled a hundred streets, and walked three thousand miles, and ate one thousand sirloin steaks in that one restaurant. He would wait for night to come with furious impatience, and would feel his hands grow weak, his entrails numb, his heart begin to pound, and his throat to swell with this intolerable exultancy of joy as he approached the restaurant. Then when he got inside, and had gone upstairs to where the restaurant was, his whole body would be stirred with such a shifting iridescence of passion, happiness, hunger, triumph, music, and wild exuberant humor that he felt he could no longer hold the swelling power of ecstasy that he felt in him.

Everything in the restaurant would become impossibly good, wonderful, and happy. The beautifully clean, crisply waisted, and voluptuous-looking waitresses would be passing all around him bearing trays of food, the empress of his desire would pass by clean and neat and dainty, sedate and decent and demure, smiling that proud, smoke-like, faint, ghost-phantom smile of maddening tenderness and seduction, the three-piece orchestra would be playing briskly, softly, languorously, strains of popular music, filling his heart with the swelling pæans of another, prouder, grander, more triumphant music; while he listened, some robust, handsome, clear-eyed and lusty-figured New England girls would be sitting at a table, smartly, roughly dressed, their fine legs clothed with woollen stockings, their feet shod with wide-open galoshes, looking almost ripe for love and tenderness if something could be done to them—and all of this spurred his hunger with a kind of maddening relish, and made the food taste better than any he had ever had before.

Everything he saw would fill him with haunting sorrow, hunger, joy, the sense of triumph, glory, and delight, or with a limitless exuberance of wild humor. The motto of the restaurant, fixed on the wall in shields embossed with a flamboyant coat of arms, was written in a scroll beneath the coat of arms, as follows: "Luxuria Cum Economia." The effect these words wrought on his spirit was unbelievable: he could never say what he wished to say, or what he felt about them, and to say that they were "the funniest words he ever saw," would not begin to convey their real effect on him.

For what they did to him was so far beyond mere funniness that he had no name to give to the emotion they evoked. But instantly, when he saw them, the wild wordless surge of a powerful and idiot exuberance of humor would swell up in him and split his features with an exultant grin.

He would want to roar with laughter, to shout out and pound upon the table in his joy, but instead the wild voices of a goat-like exuberance would swell up in his throat until the people at the other tables would begin to stare at him as if he had gone mad. And later, on the streets, or in his room at night, he would suddenly remember them again, and then that idiot, wordless, and exultant glee would burst out of him in one roar of joy.

Yet, the words gave him a strange happiness and content, as well. He felt a feeling of tenderness for the people who had written them, for the owners of the restaurant who had solemnly and triumphantly thought them out, for all the doctrines of "taste," "class," and "refinement" they evoked, for something mistaken and most pitiful that had got into our lives, and that was everywhere, something grotesquely wrong, ridiculous and confused that made one somehow feel a warm, a wordless affection for its victims.

But this was the reason why these things could never be forgotten—because we are so lost, so naked and so lonely in America. Immense and cruel skies bend over us, and all of us are driven on forever and we have no home. Therefore, it is not the slow, the punctual sanded drip of the unnumbered days that we remember best, the ash of time; nor is it the huge monotone of the lost years, the unswerving schedules of the lost life and the well-known faces, that we remember best. It is a face seen once and lost forever in a crowd, an eye that looked, a face that smiled and vanished on a passing train, it is a prescience of snow upon a certain night, the laughter of a woman in a summer street long years ago, it is the memory of a single moon seen at the pine's dark edge in old October—and all of our lives is written in the twisting of a leaf upon a bough, a door that opened, and a stone.

For America has a thousand lights and weathers and we walk the streets, we walk the streets forever, we walk the streets of life alone.

It is the place of the howling winds, the hurrying of the leaves in old October, the hard clean falling to the earth of acorns. The place of the storm-tossed moaning of the wintry mountainside, where the young men cry out in their throats and feel the savage vigor, the rude strong energies; the place also where the trains cross rivers.

It is a fabulous country, the only fabulous country; it is the one place where miracles not only happen, but where they happen all the time.

It is the place of exultancy and strong joy, the place of the darkened brooding air, the smell of snow; it is the place of all the fierce, the bitten colors in October, when all of the wild, sweet woods flame up; it is also the place of the cider press and the last brown oozings of the York Imperials. It is the place of the lovely girls with good jobs and the husky voices, who will buy a round of drinks; it is the place where the women with fine legs and silken underwear lie in the pullman berth below you, it is the place of the dark-green snore of the pullman cars, and the voices in the night-time in Virginia.

It is the place where great boats are baying at the harbor's mouth, where great ships are putting out to sea; it is the place where great boats are blowing in the gulf of night, and where the river, the dark and secret river, full of strange time, is forever flowing by us to the sea.

The tugs keep baying in the river; at twelve o'clock the Berengaria *moans, her lights slide gently past the piers beyond Eleventh Street; and in the night a tall tree falls in Old Catawba, there in the hills of home.*

It is the place of autumnal moons hung low and orange at the frosty edges of the pines; it is the place of frost and silence; of the clean dry shocks and the opulence of enormous pumpkins that yellow on hard clotted earth; it is the place of the stir and feathery stumble of the hens upon their roost, the frosty, broken barking of the dogs, the great barn-shapes and solid shadows in the running sweep of the moon-whited countryside, the wailing whistle of the fast express. It is the place of flares and steamings on the tracks, and the swing and bob and tottering dance of lanterns in the yards; it is the place of dings and knellings and the sudden glare of mighty engines over sleeping faces in the night; it is the place of the terrific web and spread and smouldering, the distant glare of Philadelphia and the solid rumble of the sleepers; it is also the place where the Transcontinental Limited is stroking eighty miles an hour across the continent and the small dark towns whip by like bullets, and there is only the fanlike stroke of the secret, immense and lonely earth again.

I have foreseen this picture many times: I will buy passage on the Fast Express.

It is the place of the wild and exultant winter's morning and the wind, with the powdery snow, that has been howling all night long; it is the place of solitude and the branches of the spruce and hemlock piled with snow; it is the place where the Fall River boats are tethered to the wharf, and the wild gray snow of furious, secret, and storm-whited morning whips across them. It is the place of the lodge by the frozen lake and the sweet breath and amorous flesh of sinful woman; it is the place of the tragic and lonely beauty of New England; it is the place of the red barn and the sound of the stabled hooves and of bright tatters of old circus posters; it is the place of the immense and pungent smell of breakfast, the country sausages and the ham and eggs, the smoking wheat cakes and the fragrant coffee, and of lone hunters in the frosty thickets who whistle to their lop-eared hounds.

Where is old Doctor Ballard now with all his dogs? He held that they were sacred, that the souls of all the dear lost dead went into them. His youngest sister's soul sat on the seat beside him; she had long ears and her eyes were sad. Two dozen of his other cherished dead trotted around the buggy as he went up the hill past home. And that was eleven years ago, and I was nine years old; and I stared gravely out the window of my father's house at old Doctor Ballard.

It is the place of the straight stare, the cold white bellies and the buried lust of the lovely Boston girls; it is the place of ripe brainless blondes with tender lips and a flowery smell, and of the girls with shapely arms who stand on ladders picking oranges; it is also the place where large slow-bodied girls from Kansas City, with big legs and milky flesh, are sent East to school by their rich fathers, and there are also immense and lovely girls, with the grip of a passionate bear, who have such names as Neilson, Lundquist, Jorgenson, and Brandt.

I will go up and down the country, and back and forth across the country on the great trains that thunder over America. I will go out West where States are square; Oh, I will go to Boise, and Helena and Albuquerque. I will go to Montana and the two Dakotas and the unknown places.

It is the place of violence and sudden death; of the fast shots in the night, the club of the Irish cop, and the smell of brains and blood upon the pavement; it is the place of the small-town killings, and the men who shoot the lovers of their wives; it is the place where the negroes slash with razors and the hillmen kill in the mountain meadows; it is the place of the ugly drunks and the snarling voices and of foul-mouthed men who want to fight; it is the place of the loud word and the foolish boast and the violent threat; it is also the place of the deadly little men with white faces and the eyes of reptiles, who kill quickly and casually in the dark; it is the lawless land that feeds on murder.

"Did you know the two Lipe girls?" he asked. "Yes," I said. "They lived in Biltburn by the river, and one of them was drowned in the flood. She was a cripple, and she wheeled herself along in a chair. She was strong as a bull." "That's the girl," he said.

It is the place of the crack athletes and of the runners who limber up in March; it is the place of the ten-second men and the great jumpers and vaulters; it is the place where Spring comes, and the young birch trees have white and tender barks, of the thaw of the earth, and the feathery smoke of the trees; it is the place of the burst of grass and bud, the wild and sudden tenderness of the wilderness, and of the crews out on the river and the coaches coming down behind them in the motor-boats, the surges rolling out behind when they are gone with heavy sudden wash. It is the place of the baseball players, and the easy lob, the soft spring smackings of the glove and mit, the crack of the bat; it is the place of the great batters, fielders, and pitchers, of the nigger boys and the white, drawling, shirt-sleeved men, the bleachers and the resinous smell of old worn wood; it is the place of Rube Waddell, the mighty untamed and ill-fated pitcher when his left arm is swinging like a lash. It is the place of the fighters, the crafty Jewish lightweights and the mauling Italians, Leonard, Tendler, Rocky Kansas, and Dun-dee; it is the place where the champion looks over his rival's shoulder with a bored expression.

I shall wake at morning in a foreign land thinking I heard a horse in one of the streets of home.

It is the place where they like to win always, and boast about their vic-tories; it is the place of quick money and sudden loss; it is the place of the mile-long freights with their strong, solid, clanking, heavy loneliness at night, and of the silent freight of cars that curve away among raw piney desolations with their promise of new lands and unknown distances —the huge attentive gape of emptiness. It is the place where the bums come singly from the woods at sunset, the huge stillness of the water-tower, the fading light, the rails, secret and alive, and trembling with the oncoming train; it is the place of the great tramps, Oklahoma Red, Fargo Pete, and the Jersey Dutchman, who grab fast rattlers for the Western shore; it is the place of old blown bums who come up in Octo-ber skirls of dust and wind and crumpled newspapers and beg, with canned heat on their breaths: "Help Old McGuire: McGuire's a good guy, kid. You're not so tough, kid: McGuire's your pal, kid: How about McGuire, McGuire——?"

It is the place of the poolroom players and the drug-store boys; of the town whore and her paramour, the tough town driver; it is the place where they go to the woods on Sunday and get up among the laurel and dogwood bushes and the rhododendron blossoms; it is the place of the cheap hotels and the kids who wait with chattering lips while the nigger goes to get them their first woman; it is the place of the

drunken college boys who spend the old man's money and wear fur
coats to the football games; it is the place of the lovely girls up North
who have rich fathers, of the beautiful wives of business men.

*The train broke down somewhere beyond Manassas, and I went for-
ward along the tracks with all the other passengers. "What's the matter?" I said to the engineer. "The eccentric strap is broken, son," he said.
It was a very cold day, windy and full of sparkling sun. This was the
farthest north I'd ever been, and I was twelve years old and on my way
to Washington to see Woodrow Wilson inaugurated. Later I could not
forget the face of the engineer and the words "eccentric strap."*

It is the place of the immense and lonely earth, the place of fat ears
and abundance where they grow cotton, corn, and wheat, the wine-red
apples of October, and the good tobacco.

It is the place that is savage and cruel, but it is also the innocent place;
it is the wild lawless place, the vital earth that is soaked with the blood
of the murdered men, with the blood of the countless murdered men,
with the blood of the unavenged and unremembered murdered men;
but it is also the place of the child and laughter, where the young men
are torn apart with ecstasy, and cry out in their throats with joy, where
they hear the howl of the wind and the rain and smell the thunder and
the soft numb spitting of the snow, where they are drunk with the bite
and sparkle of the air and mad with the solar energy, where they
believe in love and victory and think that they can never die.

It is the place where you come up through Virginia on the great trains
in the night-time, and rumble slowly across the wide Potomac and see
the morning sunlight on the nation's dome at Washington, and where
the fat man shaving in the pullman washroom grunts, "What's this?
What's this we're coming to—Washington?"—And the thin man glanc-
ing out the window says, "Yep, this is Washington. That's what it is,
all right. You gettin' off here?"— And where the fat man grunts, "Who
—me? Naw—I'm goin' on to Baltimore." It is the place where you get
off at Baltimore and find your brother waiting.

*Where is my father sleeping on the land? Buried? Dead these seven
years? Forgotten, rotten in the ground? Held by his own great stone?
No, no! Will I say, "Father" when I come to him? And will he call me,
"Son"? Oh, no, he'll never see my face: we'll never speak except to
say——*

It is the place of the fast approach, the hot blind smoky passage, the
tragic lonely beauty of New England, and the web of Boston; the place

of the mighty station there, and engines passive as great cats, the straight dense plumes of engine smoke, the acrid and exciting smell of trains and stations, and of the man-swarm passing ever in its million-footed weft, the smell of the sea in harbors and the thought of voyages—and the place of the goat cry, the strong joy of our youth, the magic city, when we knew the most fortunate life on earth would certainly be ours, that we were twenty and could never die.

And always America is the place of the deathless and enraptured moments, the eye that looked, the mouth that smiled and vanished, and the word; the stone, the leaf, the door we never found and never have forgotten. And these are the things that we remember of America, for we have known all her thousand lights and weathers, and we walk the streets, we walk the streets forever, we walk the streets of life alone.

XV

Now at Cambridge, in the house of the Murphys on Trowbridge Street, he found himself living with the Irish for the first time, and he discovered that the Murphys were utterly different from all the Irish he had known before, and all that he had felt and believed about them. He soon discovered that the Murphys were a typical family of the Boston Irish. It was a family of five: there were Mr. and Mrs. Murphy, two sons and a daughter. Mrs. Murphy ran the house on Trowbridge Street, which they owned, and rented the rooms to lodgers, Mr. Murphy was night watchman in a warehouse on the Boston waterfront, the girl was a typist in an Irish business house in Boston, the older boy, Jimmy, had a clerical position in the Boston City Hall, and the youngest boy, Eddy, whom the youth knew best, was a student at Boston College. In addition there were two Irish lodgers who had lived with them for years: Mr. Feeney, a young man who worked at Raymond's, a department store in Washington Street, Boston, and Mr. O'Doul, a middle-aged man, unmarried, who occupied the front room upstairs just over the boy's own room. Mr. O'Doul was a civil engineer, he drank very heavily, and he would sometimes be confined to his bed for days at a time with terrible attacks of rheumatism which would bend, gnarl, and twist him, and render him incapable of movement.

But in the Murphys the boy discovered none of the richness, wildness, extravagance, and humor of such people as Mike Fogarty, Tim Donovan, or the MacReadys—the Irish he had known at home. The Murphys were hard, sterile, arid, meagre, and cruel: they were dis-

figured by a warped and infuriated puritanism, and yet they were terribly corrupt. There was nothing warm, rich, or generous about them
or their lives: it seemed as if the living roots of nature had grown
gnarled and barren among the walls and pavements of the city, it seemed
that everything that is wild, sudden, capricious, whimsical, passionate,
and mysterious in the spirit of the race had been dried and hardened
out of them by their divorce from the magical earth their fathers came
from, as if the snarl and jangle of the city streets, the barren and earthless angularity of steel and stone and brick, had entered their souls.
Even their speech had become hard, gray, and sterile: the people were
almost inarticulate, it is doubtful if one of them had three hundred words
in his vocabulary: the boy noticed that the men especially—Murphy, his
two sons, Feeney, and O'Doul—made constant use of a few arid words
and phrases, which, with the intonation of the voice, and a slight con
vulsive movement of the arms and hands, filled in enormous vacancies
in thought and feeling, and said all that they could say, or wished to
say. Chief among these words or phrases was *"You* know? . . . or *"You*
know what I mean?"—words which were uttered with a slight protesting emphasis on "You," a slight and painful movement of the hands or
shoulders, and an air that the listener must fill in for himself all that
they wanted to imply. For epithets of rich resounding rage, for curses
thick and opulent with fury, in which he had believed their tongues were
apt and their spirits prodigal, he discovered that they had no more to
offer than "Chee!" or "Jeez!" or "Ho-ly Jeez!" or "Christ!" or *"Ho*-ly
Christ!" or occasionally *"Ho*-ly Mary!" Finally, they made a constant
and stupefying use of that terrible gray abortion of a word "guy": it
studded their speech with the numberless monotony of paving brick,
without it they would have been completely speechless and would have
had to communicate by convulsions of their arms and hands and painful croakings from their tongueless throats—the word fell upon the
spirit of the listener with the gray weariness of a cold incessant drizzle,
it flowed across the spirit like a river of concrete; hope, joy, the power to
feel and think were drowned out under the relentless and pitiless aridity
of its flood.

At first, he thought these words and phrases were part of a meagre
but sufficient pattern which they had learned in order to meet the con-
tingencies of life and business with alien and Protestant spirits, as waiters
in European cafés, restaurants, and dining-cars will learn a few words
of English in order to serve the needs of British and American tourists—

he thought this because he saw something sly, closed, conspiratorial, mocking and full of hatred and mistrust, in their relations with people who were not members of their race and their religion; he thought they had a warm, secret and passionate life of their own which never could be known by a stranger. But he soon found that this belief was untrue: even in their conversations with one another, they were almost inarticulate—a race which thought, felt, and spoke with the wooden insensitivity of automatons or dummies on whose waxen souls a few banal formulas for speech and feeling had been recorded. He heard some amazing performances: every evening toward six o'clock the family would gather in their dingy living-room at the end of the hall, Mr. Feeney and Mr. O'Doul would join them, and then he could hear the voices of the men raised in argument, protest, agreement, denial, affirmation and belief, or skepticism, evoking a ghastly travesty of all of man's living moments of faith, doubt, and passion, and yet speaking for hours at a time, with the idiot repetitions of a gramophone held by its needle to a single groove, a blunted jargon of fifty meaningless words:

"What guy?"

"*Dat* guy!"

"Nah, nah, nah, not him—duh otheh guy!"

"Wich guy do yuh mean—duh big guy?"

"Nah, nah, nah—yuh got it all wrong!— Not *him*—duh little guy!"

"Guh-*wan!*"—a derisive laugh— "Guh-wan!"

"Watcha tryin' t' do—*kid* me? Dat guy neveh saw de day he could take Grogan. Grogan 'ud bat his brains out."

"Guh-*wan!* Yer full of prunes! . . . Watcha tryin' t' give me? Dat guy 'ud neveh take Tommy Grogan in a million yeahs! He couldn't take Tommy duh best day he eveh saw! Grogan 'ud have him on de floeh in thirty-seconds!"

"*Ho*-ly Chee!"

"Sure he would!"

"Guh-*wan,* Guh-*wan!* Yer *crazy! Grogan! Ho*-ly Chee!"

And this, with laughter, denial, agreement—all the appurtenances of conversation among living men—could go on unweariedly for hours at a time.

Sometimes he would interrupt these conversations for a moment: he would go back to leave a message, to pay the rent, to ask if any one had called.

As soon as he knocked, the voices would stop abruptly, the room would grow suddenly hushed, there would be whispers and a dry snickering laughter: in a moment some one would say "Come in," and he would enter a room full of hushed and suddenly straightened faces. The men would sit quietly or say a word or two of greeting, friendly enough in appearance, but swift sly looks would pass between them, and around the corners of their thin, hard mouths there would be something loose, corrupt and mocking. Mrs. Murphy would arise and come to greet him, her voice filled with a false heartiness, an unclean courtesy, a horrible and insolent travesty of friendliness, and her face would also have the look of having been suddenly straightened out and solemnly compressed, she would listen with a kind of evil attention, but she would have the same loose, mocking look, and the quiet sly look would pass between her and the others. Then, when he had left them, and the door had closed behind him, there would be the same sly silence for a moment, then a low muttering of words, a sudden violence of hard derisive laughter, and some one saying, "*Ho*-ly Jeez!*"

He despised them: he loathed them because they were dull, dirty, and dishonest, because their lives were stupid, barren, and ugly, for their deliberate and insolent unfriendliness and for the conspiratorial secrecy and closure of their petty and vicious lives, entrenched solidly behind a wall of violent and corrupt politics and religious fanaticism, and regarding the alien, the stranger, with the hostile and ignorant eyes of the peasant.

All of the men had a dry, meagre, and brutal quality: Mr. Murphy was a little man with a dry, corky figure, he had a gray face, a thin sunken mouth, around which the line of loose mockery was always playing, and a closely cropped gray moustache. The boy always found him in his shirt-sleeves, with his shoes off, and his stockinged feet thrust out upon a chair. Feeney, O'Doul, Jimmy and Eddy Murphy, although of various sizes, shapes, and ages, all had thick tallowy-looking skins, hard dull eyes and a way of speaking meagrely out of the corners of their loose thin mouths. Mrs. Murphy was physically the biggest of the lot, with a certain quality of ripeness and fertility, however blighted, that none of the others had: she was a large slatternly woman, with silvery white hair which gave her somehow a look of sly and sinister haggishness; she had a high, flaming color marked with patches of eczemic red, her voice was hearty and she had a big laugh, but her face also had the false, hostile and conspiratorial secrecy of the others.

Eddy Murphy, the youngest boy, was also the best of the crowd. All decent and generous impulse had not yet been killed or deadened in him, he still possessed a warped and blunted friendliness, the rudiments of some youthful feeling for a better, warmer, bolder, and more liberal kind of life. As time went on, he made a few awkward, shamed, and inarticulate advances toward friendship, he began to come into the young man's room from time to time, and presently to tell him a little of his life at college and his hopes for the future. He was a little fellow, with the same dry, febrile, alert, and corky figure that his father had: he was one of the dark Irish, he had black hair, and black eyes, and one of his legs was badly bowed and bent outward, the result, he said, of having broken it, in a high-school football game. The first time he came into the room, he stood around shyly, awkwardly, and mistrustfully for a spell, blurting out a few words from time to time, and looking at the books and papers with a kind of dazed and stricken stupefaction.

"Watcha do wit all dese books? Huh?"

"I read them."

"Guh-*wan!* Watcha tryin' t' hand me? Y' ain't read all dem books! Dey ain't no guy dat's read dat much."

As a matter of fact, there were only two or three hundred books in the place, but he could not have been more impressed if the entire contents of the Widener Library had been stored there.

"Well, I have read them all," the other said. "Most of them, anyway, and a lot more besides."

"Guh-*wan!* No kiddin!" he said, in a dazed tone and with an air of astounded disbelief. "Watcha want to read so much for?"

"I like to read. Don't you?"

"Oh, I don't know. *You* know," he said painfully, with the slightest convulsive movement of his hands and shoulders. ". . . 'S'all right."

"You have to read for your classes at Boston College, don't you?"

"*DO* I?" he cried, with a sudden waking to life. "I'll say I do! . . . *Ho*-ly Chee! Duh way dose guys pile it on to you is a *crime!*"

There was another awkward silence, he continued to stare at the books, and to fumble about in an embarrassed and tongue-tied manner, and suddenly he burst out explosively and triumphantly: "Shakespeare was de greatest poet dat evah lived. He wrote plays an' sonnets. A sonnet is a pome of foihteen lines: it is composed of two pahts, de sextet an' de octrave."

"That's pretty good. They must make you work out there?"

"*DO* they?" he cried. "I'll tell duh cock-eyed world dey do! . . . Do you know who de greatest prose-writeh was?" he burst out with the same convulsive suddenness.

"No . . . who was it? Jonathan Swift?"

"Guh-*wan!*"

"Addison? . . . Dryden? . . . Matthew Arnold?" the youth asked hopefully.

"Guh-*wan,* Guh-*wan!*" he shouted derisively. "Yuh're way off!"

"Am I? . . . Who was it then?"

"James Henry Cardinal Nooman," he crowed triumphantly. "Dat's who it was! . . . Father Dolan said so. . . . Chee! . . . Dey ain't nuttin' dat guy don't know! He's duh greatest English scholeh livin'! . . . Nooman wrote de *Apologia pro Vita Suo,*" he said triumphantly. "Dat's Latin."

"Well, yes, he *is* a good writer," said the other boy. "But Thomas Carlyle is a good writer, too?" he proposed argumentatively.

"Guh-*wan!*" shouted Eddy derisively. "Watcha givin' me?" He was silent a moment; then he added with a grin, "Yuh know de reason why you say dat?"

"No, why?"

"It's because yuh're a Sout'paw," and suddenly he laughed, naturally and good-naturedly.

"A Southpaw? How do you mean?"

"Oh, dat's duh name de fellows call 'em out at school," he said.

"Call who?"

"Why, guys like you," he said. "Dat's de name we call duh Protestants," he said, laughing. "We call 'em Sout'paws."

The word in its connotation of a life that was hostile, hard, fanatic, and suspicious of everything alien to itself was disgraceful and shameful but there was something irresistibly funny about it too, and suddenly they both laughed loudly.

After that, they got along together much better: Eddy came in to see the other youth quite often, he talked more freely and naturally, and sometimes he would bring his English themes and ask for help with them.

Such were the Boston Irish as he first saw them; and often as he

thought of the wild, extravagant and liberal creatures of his childhood
—of Mr. Fogarty, Tim Donovan, and the MacReadys—it seemed to
him that they belonged to a grander and completely different race; or
perhaps, he thought, the glory of earth and air and sky there had kept
them ripe and sweet as they always were, while their brothers here had
withered upon the rootless pavements, soured and sickened in the savage tumult of the streets, grown hard and dead and ugly in the barren
land.

The only person near him in the house, and the only person there the
boy saw with any regularity was a Chinese student named Wang: he
had the room next to him—in fact he had the two next rooms, for he
was immensely rich, the son of a man in the mandarin class who governed one of the Chinese provinces.

But his habits and conduct were in marked contrast to those of the
average Oriental who attends an American university. These others,
studious seekers after knowledge, had come to work. Mr. Wang, a lazy
and good-humored wastrel with more money than he could spend, had
come to play. And play he did, with a whole-hearted devotion to pleasure that was worthy of a better purpose. His pleasures were for the most
part simple, but they were also costly, running to flowered silk dressing
gowns, expensively tailored clothes cut in a rakish Broadway style, silk
shirts, five-pound boxes of chocolate creams, of which he was inordi-
nately fond, week-end trips to New York, stupendous banquets at an
expensive Chinese restaurant in Boston, phonograph records, of which
he had a great many, and the companionship of "nice flat girls"—by this
he meant to say his women should be "fat," which apparently was the
primary requisite for voluptuous pulchritude.

Mr. Wang himself was just a fat, stupid, indolent, and good-hearted
child: his two big rooms in the rear of the Murphy establishment were
lavishly furnished with carved teak-wood, magnificent screens, fat
divans, couches, and chests. The rooms were always lighted with the
glow of dim and sensual lamps, there was always an odor of sandalwood and incense, and from time to time one heard Mr. Wang's shrill
sudden scream of childish laughter. He had two cronies, young Chinese
who seemed as idle, wealthy, and pleasure-loving as himself; they came
to his rooms every night, and then one could hear them jabbering and
chattering away in their strange speech, and sometimes silence, low
eager whisperings, and then screams of laughter.

The boy had grown to know the Chinese very well; Mr. Wang had come to him to seek help on his English composition themes—he was not only stupid but thoroughly idle, and would not work at anything—and the boy had written several for him. And Mr. Wang, in grateful recompense, had taken him several times to magnificent dinners of strange delicious foods in the Chinese restaurant, and was forever urging on him chocolates and expensive cigarettes. And no matter where the Chinaman saw him now, whether in his room, or on the street, or in the Harvard Yard, he would always greet him with one joke—a joke he repeated over and over with the unwearied delight of a child or an idiot. And the joke was this: Mr. Wang would come up slyly, his fat yellow face already beginning to work, his fat throat beginning to tremble with hysterical laughter. Then, wagging his finger at the young American, the Chinaman would say:

"Lest night I see you with big flat girl. . . . Yis, yis, yis," he would scream with laughter as the young man started to protest, shaping voluptuous curves meanwhile with his fat yellow hands—"Big flat girl—like this—yis, yis, yis!" he would scream again, and bend double, choking, stamping at the ground, "nice flat girl—like this—yis, yis, yis, yis, yis."

He had perpetrated this "joke" so often, and at such unseasonable places, that it had now become embarrassing. He seemed, in fact, to delight in coming upon his victim while he was in serious conversation with some dignified-looking person, and he had already caught the boy three times in this way while he was talking to Dodd, to Professor Hatcher, and finally to a professor with a starched prim face, who had taught American Literature for thirty years, and whose name was Fust. Nothing could be done to stop him; protests at the impropriety of the proceeding only served to set him off again, he was delighted at the embarrassment he caused and he would shout down every protest rapturously, screaming, "Yis, yis, yis—nice flat girl—like this, eh," and would shape fat suggestion with his fat hands.

XVI

The purposes of Professor Hatcher's celebrated school for dramatists seemed, as stated, to be plain and reasonable enough. Professor Hatcher himself prudently forebore from making extravagant claims concerning the benefits to be derived from his course. He did not say that he could make a dramatist out of any man who came to take his

course. He did not predict a successful career in the professional theatre for every student who had been a member of his class. He did not
even say he could teach a student how to write plays. No. He made, in
fact, no claims at all. Whatever he said about his course was very reasonably, prudently, and temperately put: it was impossible to quarrel
with it.

All Professor Hatcher said about his course was that, if a man had a
genuine dramatic and theatric talent to begin with, he might be able to
derive from the course a technical and critical guidance which it would
be hard for him to get elsewhere, and which he might find for himself
only after years of painful and even wasteful experiment.

Certainly this seemed reasonable enough. Moreover, Professor
Hatcher felt that the artist would benefit by what was known as the
"round table discussion"—that is by the comment and criticism of the
various members of the class, after Professor Hatcher had read them a
play written by one of their group. He felt that the spirit of working
together, of seeing one's play produced and assisting in the production,
of being familiar with all the various "arts" of the theatre—lighting, de-
signing, directing, acting, and so on—was an experience which should
be of immense value to the young dramatist of promise and of talent.
In short, although he made no assertion that he could create a talent
where none was, or give life by technical expertness to the substance of
a work that had no real life of its own, Professor Hatcher did feel that
by the beneficent influence of this tutelage he might trim the true lamp
to make it burn more brightly.

And though it was possible to take issue with him on some of his
beliefs—that, for example, the comment and criticism of "the group,"
and a community of creative spirits was good for the artist—it was impossible to deny that his argument was reasonable, temperate, and conservative in the statement of his purposes.

And he made this plain to every member of his class. Each one was
made to understand that the course made no claims of magic alchemy—
that he could not be turned into an interesting dramatist if the talent
was not there.

But although each member of the class affirmed his understanding
of this fundamental truth, and readily said that he accepted it, most of
these people, at the bottom of their hearts, believed—pitiably and past
belief—that a miracle would be wrought upon their sterile, unproduc-
tive spirits, that for them, for *them,* at least, a magic transformation

would be brought about in their miserable small lives and feeble purposes—and all because they now were members of Professor Hatcher's celebrated class.

The members of Professor Hatcher's class belonged to the whole lost family of the earth, whose number is uncountable, and for this reason, they could never be forgotten.

And, first and foremost, they belonged to that great lost tribe of people who are more numerous in America than in any other country in the world. They belonged to that unnumbered horde who think that somehow, by some magic and miraculous scheme or rule or formula, "something can be done for them." They belonged to that huge colony of the damned who buy thousands of books that are printed for their kind, telling them how to run a tea shop, how to develop a pleasing personality, how to acquire "a liberal education," swiftly and easily and with no anguish of the soul, by fifteen minutes' reading every day, how to perform the act of sexual intercourse in such a way that your wife will love you for it, how to have children, or to keep from having children, how to write short-stories, novels, plays, and verses which are profitably salable, how to keep from having body odor, constipation, bad breath, or tartar on the teeth, how to have good manners, know the proper fork to use for every course, and always do the proper thing—how, in short, to be beautiful, "distinguished," "smart," "chic," "forceful," and "sophisticated"—finally, how to have "a brilliant personality" and "achieve success."

Yes, for the most part, the members of Professor Hatcher's class belonged to this great colony of the lost Americans. They belonged to that huge tribe of all the damned and lost who feel that everything is going to be all right with them if they can only take a trip, or learn a rule, or meet a person. They belonged to that futile, desolate, and forsaken horde who felt that all will be well with their lives, that all the power they lack themselves will be supplied, and all the anguish, fury, and unrest, the confusion and the dark damnation of man's soul can magically be healed if only they eat bran for breakfast, secure an introduction to a celebrated actress, get a reading for their manuscript by a friend of Sinclair Lewis, or win admission to Professor Hatcher's celebrated class of dramatists.

And, in a curious way, the plays written by the people in Professor Hatcher's class, illustrated, in one form or another, this desire. Few of the plays had any intrinsic reality, for most of these people were lacking in the first, the last, the foremost quality of the artist, without which he is lost: the ability to get out of his own life the power to live and work by, to derive from his own experience—as a fruit of all his seeing, feeling, living, joy and bitter anguish—the palpable and living substance of his art.

Few of the people in Professor Hatcher's class possessed this power. Few of them had anything of their own to say. Their lives seemed to have grown from a stony and a fruitless soil and, as a consequence, the plays they wrote did not reflect that life, save by a curious and yet illuminating indirection.

Thus, in an extraordinary way, their plays—unreal, sterile, imitative, and derivative as most of them indubitably were—often revealed more about the lives of the people who wrote them than better and more living work could do. For, although few of the plays showed any contact with reality—with that passionate integument of blood and sweat and pain and fear and grief and joy and laughter of which this world is made—most of them did show, in one way or another, what was perhaps the basic impulse in the lives of most of these people—the impulse which had brought them here to Professor Hatcher's class.

The impulse of the people in the class was not to embrace life and devour it, but rather to escape from it. And in one way or another most of the plays these people wrote were illustrative of this desire. For in these plays—unnatural, false, and imitative, as they were—one could discern, in however pale and feeble a design, a picture of the world not as its author had seen and lived and known it, but rather as he wished to find it, or believe in it. And, in all their several forms—whether sad, gay, comic, tragic, or fantastical—these plays gave evidence of the denial and the fear of life.

The wealthy young dawdler from Philadelphia, for example, wrote plays which had their setting in a charming little French Café. Here one was introduced to all the gay, quaint, charming Frenchmen—to Papa Duval, the jolly proprietor, and Mama Duval, his rotund and no less jolly spouse, as well as to all the quaint and curious habitués that are so prolific in theatrical establishments of this order. One met, as well, that fixture of these places: old Monsieur Vernet, the crusty, crotchety, but kindly old gentleman who is the café's oldest customer and has had the same table in the corner by the window for more than thirty years. One saw again the familiar development of the comic situation—the day when Monsieur Vernet enters at his appointed time and finds at his table a total stranger, sacrilege! Imprecations! Tears, prayers, and entreaties on the part of Papa Duval and his wife, together with the stubborn refusal of the imperious stranger to move! Climax: old Monsieur Vernet storming out of the café, swearing that he will never return. Resolution of conflict: the efforts of Papa and Mamma Duval to bring their most prized customer back into the fold again, and their final success, the pacification and return of Monsieur Vernet amid great rejoicing, thanks to a cunning stratagem on the part of Henri, the young waiter, who wins a reward for all these efforts, the hand of Mimi, Papa Duval's charming daughter, from whom he has been separated by Papa Duval's stern decree.

Thus, custom is restored, and true love re-united by one brilliant comic stroke!

And all this pretty little world, the contribution of a rich young man who came from Philadelphia! How perfectly God-damn delightful it all was, to be sure!

The plays of old Seth Flint, the sour and withered ex-reporter, were, if of a different coloring, cut from the same gaudy cloth of theatric unreality. For forty years old Seth had pounded precincts as a newsman, and had known city-rooms across the nation. He had seen every crime, ruin, and incongruity of which man's life is capable. He was familiar with every trait of graft, with every accursed smell and smear of the old red murder which ineradicably fouled the ancient soul of man, and the stench of man's falseness, treachery, cruelty, hypocrisy, cowardice, and injustice, together with the look of brains and blood upon the pavements of the nation, was no new thing to old Seth Flint.

His skin had been withered, his eyes deadened, his heart and spirit burdened wearily, his faith made cynical, and his temper soured by the black picture of mankind which he had seen as a reporter—and because of this, in spite of this, he had remained or become—how, why, in what miraculous fashion no one knew—a curiously honest, sweet, and generous person, whose life had been the record of a self-less loyalty. He had known poverty, hardship, and self-sacrifice, and endured all willingly without complaint: he had taken the savings of a lifetime to send the two sons of his widowed sister to college, he had supported this woman and her family for years, and now, when his own life was coming to its close, he was yielding to the only self-indulgence he had ever known—a year away from the city-room of a Denver newspaper, a

year away in the rare ether, among the precious and æsthetic intellects of
Professor Hatcher's celebrated course, a year in which to realize the
dream of a life-time, the vision of his youth—a year in which to write
the plays he had always dreamed of writing. And what kind of plays
did he write?

Alas! Old Seth did exactly what he set out to do, he succeeded perfectly in fulfilling his desire—and, by a tragic irony, his failure lay in
just this fact. The plays which he produced with an astounding and
prolific ease—("Three days is enough to write a play," the old man said
in his sour voice. "You guys who take a year to write a play give me
a pain. If you can't write a play a week, you can't write anything; the
play's no good")—these plays were just the plays which he had dreamed
of writing as a young man, and therein was evident their irremediable
fault.

For Seth's plays—so neat, brisk, glib, and smartly done—would have
been good plays in a commercial way, as well, if he had only done
them twenty years before. He wrote, without effort and with unerring
accuracy, a kind of play which had been immensely popular at the beginning of the twentieth century, but which people had grown tired of
twenty years before. He wrote plays in which the babies got mixed up
in the maternity ward of a great hospital, in which the rich man's child
goes to the family of the little grocer, and the grocer's child grows up
as the heir to an enormous fortune, with all the luxuries and securities
of wealth around him. And he brought about the final resolution of this
tangled scheme, the meeting of these scrambled children and their bewildered parents, with a skill of complication, a design of plot, a dex-
terity that was astonishing. His characters—all well-known types of the
theatre, as of nurse tough-spoken, shop-girl slangy, reporter cynical, and
so on—were well conceived to fret their purpose, their lives well-timed
and apt and deftly made. He had mastered the formula of an older type
of "well-made play" with astonishing success. Only, the type was dead,
the interest of the public in such plays had vanished twenty years before.

So here he was, a live man, writing, with amazing skill, dead plays
for a theatre that was dead, and for a public that did not exist.

"Chekhov! Ibsen!" old Seth would whine sourly with a dismissing
gesture of his parched old hand, and a scornful contortion of his bitter
mouth in his old mummy of a face. "You guys all make me tired the
way you worship them!" he would whine out at some of the exquisite young temperaments in Professor Hatcher's class. "Those guys

can't write a play! Take Chekhov, now!" whined Seth. "That guy
never wrote a real play in his life! He never knew how to write a play!
He couldn't have written a play if he tried! He never learned the rules
for writing a play!—That *Cherry Orchard* now," whined old Seth
with a sour sneering laugh, "—that *Cherry Orchard* that you guys
are always raving about! That's not a play!" he cried indignantly.
"What ever made you think it was a play? I was trying to read it just
the other day," he rasped, "and there's nothing there to hold your interest! It's got no *plot*! There's no story in it! There's no suspense!
Nothing happens in it. All you got is a lot of people who do nothing
but talk all the time. You never get anywhere," said Seth scornfully.
"And yet to hear you guys rave about it, you'd think it was a great
play."

"Well, what do you call a great play, then, if *The Cherry Orchard*
isn't one?" one of the young men said acidly. "Who wrote the great
plays that you talk about?"

"Why George M. Cohan wrote some," whined Seth instantly. "That's
who. Avery Hopwood wrote some great plays. We've had plenty of
guys in this country who wrote great plays. If they'd come from Russia
you'd get down and worship 'em," he said bitterly. "But just because
they came out of this country they're no good!"

In the relation of the class towards old Seth Flint, it was possible to
see the basic falseness of their relation towards life everywhere around
them. For here was a man—whatever his defects as a playwright might
have been—who had lived incomparably the richest, most varied and
dangerous, and eventful life among them; as he was himself far more
interesting than any of the plays they wrote, and as dramatists they
should have recognized and understood his quality. But they saw none
of this. For their relation towards life and people such as old Seth
Flint was not one of understanding. It was not even one of burning
indignation—of that indignation which is one of the dynamic forces
in the artist's life. It was rather one of supercilious scorn and ridicule.

They felt that they were "above" old Seth, and most of the other
people in the world, and for this reason they were in Professor Hatcher's
class. Of Seth they said:

"He's really a misfit, terribly out of place here. I wonder why he
came."

And they would listen to an account of one of Seth's latest errors in
good taste with the expression of astounded disbelief, the tones of

stunned incredulity which were coming into fashion about that time among elegant young men.

"Not really! . . . But he never really said *that*. . . . You *can't* mean it."

"Oh, but I assure you, he did!"

". . . It's simply past belief! . . . I can't believe he's as bad as *that*."

"Oh, but he *is*! It's incredible, I know, but you've no idea what he's capable of." And so on.

And yet old Seth Flint was badly needed in that class: his bitter and unvarnished tongue caused Professor Hatcher many painful moments, but it had its use—oh, it had its use, particularly when the play was of this nature:

Irene (slowly with scorn and contempt in her voice). So—it has come to this! This is all your love amounts to—a little petty selfish thing! I had thought you were bigger than that, John.

John (desperately). But—but, my God, Irene—what am I to think? I found you in bed with him—my best friend! *(with difficulty)*. You know—that looks suspicious, to say the least!

Irene (softly—with amused contempt in her voice). You poor little man! And to think I thought your love was *so big*.

John (wildly). But I do love you, Irene. That's just the point.

Irene (with passionate scorn). Love! You don't know what love means! Love is bigger than that! Love is big enough for all things, all people. *(She extends her arms in an all-embracing gesture.)* My love takes in the world—it embraces all mankind! It is glamorous, wild, free as the wind, John.

John (slowly). Then you have had other lovers?

Irene: Lovers come, lovers go. *(She makes an impatient gesture.)* What is that? Nothing! Only love endures—my love which is greater than all.

Eugene would writhe in his seat, and clench his hands convulsively. Then he would turn almost prayerfully to the bitter, mummied face of old Seth Flint for that barbed but cleansing vulgarity that always followed such a scene:

"Well?" Professor Hatcher would say, putting down the manuscript he had been reading, taking off his eye-glasses (which were attached to a ribbon of black silk) and looking around with a quizzical smile, an impassive expression on his fine, distinguished face. "Well?" he would say again urbanely, as no one answered. "Is there any comment?"

"What is she?" Seth would break the nervous silence with his rasping snarl. "Another of these society whores? You know," he continued, "you can find plenty of her kind for three dollars a throw without any of that fancy palaver."

Some of the class smiled faintly, painfully, and glanced at each other with slight shrugs of horror; others were grateful, felt pleasure well in them and said underneath their breath exultantly:

"Good old Seth! Good old Seth!"

"Her love is big enough for all things, is it?" said Seth. "I know a truck driver out in Denver I'll match against her any day."

Eugene and Ed Horton, a large and robust aspirant from the Iowa cornlands, roared with happy laughter, poking each other sharply in the ribs.

"Do you think the play will act?" some one said. "It seems to me that it comes pretty close to closet drama."

"If you ask me," said Seth, "it comes pretty close to water-closet drama. . . . No," he said sourly. "What that boy needs is a little experience. He ought to go out and get him a woman and get all this stuff off his mind. After that, he might sit down and write a play."

For a moment there was a very awkward silence, and Professor Hatcher smiled a trifle palely. Then, taking his eyeglasses with a distinguished movement, he looked around and said:

"Is there any other comment?"

XVII

OFTEN during these years of fury, hunger, and unrest, when he was trying to read all the books and know all the people, he would live for days, and even for weeks, in a world of such mad and savage concentration, such terrific energy, that time would pass by him incredibly, while he tried to eat and drink the earth, stare his way through walls of solid masonry into the secret lives of men, until he had made the substance of all life his own.

And during all this time, although he was living a life of the most savage conflict, the most blazing energy, wrestling day by day with the herculean forces of the million-footed city, listening to a million words and peering into a hundred thousand faces, he would nevertheless spend a life of such utter loneliness that he would go for days at a time without seeing a face or hearing a voice that he knew, and until the sound of his own voice seemed strange and phantasmal to him.

Then suddenly he would seem to awake out of this terrific vision, which had been so savage, mad, and literal that its very reality had a fabulous and dreamlike quality, and time, strange million-visaged time, had been telescoped incredibly, so that weeks had passed by like a single day. He would awake out of this living dream and see the minutes, hours, and days, and all the acts and faces of the earth pass by him in their usual way. And instantly, when this happened, he would feel a bitter and intolerable loneliness—a loneliness so acrid, gray, and bitter that he could taste its sharp thin crust around the edges of his mouth like the taste and odor of weary burnt-out steel, like a depleted storage battery or a light that had gone dim, and he could feel it grayly and intolerably in his entrails, the conduits of his blood, and in all the substance of his body.

When this happened, he would feel an almost unbearable need to hear the voice and see the face again of some one he had known and at such a time as this he would go to see his Uncle Bascom, that strange and extraordinary man who, born like the others in the wilderness, the hills of home, had left these hills forever.

Bascom now lived alone with his wife (for his four children were grown and would have none of him) in a dingy section of one of the innumerable suburbs that form part of the terrific ganglia of Boston, and it was here that the boy would often go on Sundays.

After a long confusing journey that was made by subway, elevated, and street car, he would leave the chill and dismal street car at the foot of a hill on a long, wide, and frozen street lined with tall rows of wintry elms, with smoky wintry houses that had a look of solid, closed and mellow warmth, and with a savage frozen waste of tidal waters on the right—those New England waters that are so sparkling, fresh and glorious, like a tide of sapphires, in the springtime, and so grim and savage in their frozen desolation in the winter.

Then the street car would bang its draughty sliding doors together, grind harshly off with its cargo of people with pinched lips, thin red pointed noses, and cod-fish faces, and vanish, leaving him with the kind of loneliness and absence which a street car always leaves when it has gone, and he would turn away from the tracks along a dismal road or street that led into the district where his uncle had his house. And stolidly he would plunge forward against the gray and frozen desolation of that place, to meet him.

And at length he would pause before his uncle's little house, and as he struck the knocker, he was always glad to hear the approaching patter of his Aunt Louise's feet, and cheered by the brightening glance of her small birdy features, as she opened the door for him, inwardly exultant to hear her confirm in her bright lady-like tones his own prediction of what she would say: "Oh, *theah* you ah! I was wondering what was keeping you."

A moment later he would be greeted from the cellar or the kitchen by his uncle Bascom's high, husky and yet strangely remote yell, the voice of a prophet calling from a mountain:

"Hello, Eugene, my boy. Is that *you?*" And a moment later the old man would appear, coming up to meet him from some lower cellar-depth, swearing, muttering, and banging doors; and he would come toward him howling greetings, buttoned to his chin in the frayed and faded sweater, gnarled, stooped and frosty-looking, clutching his great hands together at his waist; then hold one gaunt hand out to him and howl:

"Hello, hello, hello, sit down, sit down, sit down," after which, for no apparent reason, he would contort his gaunt face in a horrible grimace, convolve his amazing rubbery lips, and close his eyes and his mouth tightly and laugh through his nose in forced snarls: "Phuh! Phuh! Phuh! Phuh! Phuh!"

Bascom Pentland had been the scholar of his amazing family: he was a man of powerful intelligence and disordered emotions. Even in his youth, his eccentricities of dress, speech, walk, manner had made him an object of ridicule to his Southern kinsmen, but their ridicule was streaked with pride, since they accepted the impact of his personality as another proof that theirs was an extraordinary family. "He's one of 'em, all right," they said exultantly, "queerer than any of us!"

Bascom's youth, following the war between the States, had been seared by a bitter poverty, at once enriched and warped by a life that clung to the earth with a root-like tenacity, that was manual, painful, spare and stricken, and that rebuilt itself—fiercely, cruelly, and richly—from the earth. And, because there burned and blazed in him from the first a hatred of human indignity, a passionate avowal of man's highness and repose, he felt more bitterly than the others the delinquencies of his father, and the multiplication of his father's offspring, who came regularly into a world of empty cupboards.

"As each of them made its unhappy entrance into the world," he would say later, his voice tremulous with passion, "I went out into the woods striking my head against the trees, and blaspheming God in my anger. Yes, sir," he continued, pursing his long lip rapidly against his few loose upper teeth, and speaking with an exaggerated pedantry of enunciation, "I am not ashamed to confess that I did. For we were living in conditions un-*worthy*—*unworthy*"—his voice rising to an evangelical yell, "I had almost said—of the condition of animals. And—*say*—what do you think?"—he said, with a sudden shift in manner and tone, becoming, after his episcopal declaration, matter of fact and whisperingly confidential. "Why, do you know, my boy, at one time I had to take my *own* father aside, and point out to him we were living in no way becoming decent people."—Here his voice sank to a whisper, and he tapped Eugene on the knee with his big, stiff finger, grimacing horribly and pursing his lip against his dry upper teeth.

Poverty had been the mistress of his youth and Bascom Pentland had not forgotten: poverty had burned its way into his heart. He took what education he could find in a backwoods school, read everything he could, taught, for two or three years, in a country school and, at the age of twenty-one, borrowing enough money for railway fare, went to Boston to enroll himself at Harvard. And, somehow, because of the fire that burned in him, the fierce determination of his soul, he had been admitted, secured employment waiting on tables, tutoring, and pressing every one's trousers but his own, and lived in a room with two other starved wretches on $3.50 a week, cooking, eating, sleeping, washing, and studying in the one place.

At the end of seven years he had gone through the college and the school of theology, performing brilliantly in Greek, Hebrew, and metaphysics.

Poverty, fanatical study, the sexual meagreness of his surroundings, had made of him a gaunt zealot: at thirty he was a lean fanatic, a true Yankee madman, high-boned, with gray thirsty eyes and a thick flaring sheaf of oaken hair—six feet three inches of gangling and ludicrous height, gesticulating madly and obliviously before a grinning world. But he had a grand lean head: he looked somewhat like the great Ralph Waldo Emerson—with the brakes off.

About this time, he married a young Southern woman of a good family: she was from Tennessee, her parents were both dead, and in the 'seventies she had come North and had lived for several years with an uncle in Providence, who had been constituted guardian of her estate, amounting probably to about $75,000, although her romantic memory later multiplied the sum to $200,000. The man squandered part of her money and stole the rest: she came, therefore, to Bascom without much dowry, but she was pretty, bright, intelligent, and had a good figure. Bascom smote the walls of his room with bloody knuckles, and fell down before God.

When Bascom met her she was a music student in Boston: she had a deep full-toned contralto voice which was wrung from her somewhat tremulously when she sang. She was a small woman, birdlike and earnest, delicately fleshed and boned, quick and active in her movements and with a crisp tart speech which still bore, curiously, traces of a Southern accent. She was a brisk, serious, lady-like little person, without much humor, and she was very much in love with her gaunt suitor. They saw each other for two years: they went to concerts, lectures, sermons; they talked of music, poetry, philosophy and of God, but they never spoke of love. But one night Bascom met her in the parlor of her boarding house on Huntington Avenue, and with a voice vibrant and portentous with the importance of the words he had to utter, began as follows: "Miss Louise!" he said carefully, gazing thoughtfully over the apex of his hands, "there comes a time when a man, having reached an age of discretion and mature judgment, must begin to consider one of the *gravest*—yes! by all means one of the most important events in human life. The event I refer to is—matrimony." He paused, a clock was beating out its punctual measured tock upon the mantel, and a horse went by with ringing hoofs upon the street. As for Louise, she sat quietly erect, with dignified and lady-like composure , but it seemed to her that the clock was beating in her own breast, and that it might cease to beat at any moment.

"For a minister of the gospel," Bascom continued, "the decision is particularly grave because, for him—once made, it is *irrevocable,* once determined upon, it must be followed *inexorably, relentlessly*—aye! to the edge of the grave, to the *uttermost* gates of death, so that the possibility of an error in judgment is *fraught,*" his voice sinking to a boding whisper—"is *fraught* with the most terrible consequences. Accordingly," Uncle Bascom said in a deliberate tone, "having decided to take this step, realizing to the *full*—to the *full,* mind you—its gravity, I have searched my soul, I have questioned my heart. I have gone up into the mount-ings and out into the desert and communed with my *Maker* until," his voice rose like a demon's howl, "there no longer remains an *atom* of doubt, a *particle* of uncertainty, a *vestige* of *disbelief!* Miss Louise, I have decided that the young lady best fitted in every way to be my helpmate, the partner of my joys and griefs, the confidante of my dearest hopes, the in-*spir*-a-tion of my noblest endeavors, the companion of my declining years, and the *spirit* that shall accompany me along each step of life's vexed and troubled way, sharing with me whatever God in his *inscrutable* Providence shall will, whether of wealth or poverty, grief or happiness—I have decided, Miss Louise, that that lady must be—yourself!—and, therefore, I request," he said slowly and impressively, "the honor of your hand in mar-ri-age."

She loved him, she had hoped, prayed, and agonized for just such a moment, but now that it had come she rose immediately with lady-like dignity, and said: "Mistah Pentland: I am honuhed by this mahk of yoah esteem and affection, and I pwomise to give it my most *un*nest con-sidahwation without delay. I wealize fully, Mistah Pentland, the gwavity of the wuhds you have just uttuhed. Foh my paht, I must tell you, Mistah Pentland, that if I accept yoah pwoposal, I shall come to you without the fawchun which was *wight*fully mine, but of which I have been depwived and defwauded by the *wascality*—yes! the *wascality* of my gahdian. I shall come to you, theahfoh, without the dow'y I had hoped to be able to contwibute to my husband's fawchuns."

"Oh, my *dear* Miss Louise! My *dear* young lady!" Uncle Bascom cried, waving his great hand through the air with a dismissing gesture. "Do not suppose—do not for one instant suppose, I beg of you!—that consideration of a monetary nature could influence my decision. Oh, not in the slightest!" he cried. "Not at all, not at all!"

"Fawchnatly," Louise continued, "my inhewitance was not *wholly* dissipated by this scoundwel. A pohtion, a vewy small pohtion, re-mains."

"My dear girl! My dear young lady!" Uncle Bascom cried. "It is not of the *slightest* consequence. . . . How much did he leave?" he added.

Thus they were married.

Bascom immediately got a church in the Middle West: good pay and a house. But during the course of the next twenty years he was shifted from church to church, from sect to sect—to Brooklyn, then back to the Middle West, to the Dakotas, to Jersey City, to Western Massachusetts, and finally back to the small towns surrounding Boston.

When Bascom talked, you may be sure God listened: he preached magnificently, his gaunt face glowing from the pulpit, his rather high, enormously vibrant voice husky with emotion. His prayers were fierce solicitations of God, so mad with fervor that his audiences uncomfortably felt they came close to blasphemy. But, unhappily, on occasions his own mad eloquence grew too much for him: his voice, always too near the heart of passion, would burst in splinters, and he would fall violently forward across his lectern, his face covered by his great gaunt fingers, sobbing horribly.

This, in the Middle West, where his first church had been, does not go down so well—yet it may be successful if one weeps mellowly, joyfully—smiling bravely through the tears—at a lovely aisle processional of repentant sinners; but Bascom, who chose uncomfortable titles for his sermons, would be overcome by his powerful feelings on those occasions when his topic was "Potiphar's Wife," "Ruth, the Girl in the Corn," "The Whore of Babylon," "The Woman on the Roof," and so on.

His head was too deeply engaged with his conscience—he was in turn Episcopal, Presbyterian, Unitarian, searching through the whole roaring confusion of Protestantism for a body of doctrine with which he could agree. And he was forever finding it, and later forever renouncing what he had found. At forty, the most liberal of Unitarians, the strains of agnosticism were piping madly through his sermons: he began to hint at his new faith in prose which he modelled on the mighty utterance of Carlyle, and in poetry, in what he deemed the manner of Matthew Arnold. His professional connection with the Unitarians, and indeed with the Baptists, Methodists, Holy Rollers, and Seventh Day Adventists, came to an abrupt ending after he read from his pulpit one morning a composition in verse entitled "The Agnostic," which made up in concision what it lacked in melody, and which ended each stanza sadly, but very plainly, on this recurrence:

> "I do not know:
> It may be so."

Thus, when he was almost fifty, Bascom Pentland stopped preaching in public. There was no question where he was going. He had his family's raging lust for property. He became a "conveyancer"; he acquired enough of the law of property to convey titles; but he began to buy pieces of land in the suburbs of Boston, and to build small cheap houses, using his own somewhat extraordinary designs to save the architect's fees and, wherever possible, doing such odd jobs as laying the foundations, installing the plumbing, and painting the structure.

The small houses that he—no, he did not build them!—he went through the agonies of monstrous childbirth to produce them, he licked, nursed, and fondled them into stunted growth, and he sold them on long, but profitable terms to small Irish, Jewish, Negro, Belgian, Italian and Greek laborers and tradesmen. And at the conclusion of a sale, or after receiving from one of these men the current payment, Uncle Bascom went homeward in a delirium of joy, shouting in a loud voice, to all who might be compelled to listen, the merits of the Jews, Belgians, Irish, Swiss or Greeks.

"Finest people in the world! No question about it!"—this last being his favorite exclamation in all moments of payment or conviction.

For when they paid, he loved them. Often on Sundays they would come to pay him tramping over the frozen ground or the packed snow through street after street of smutty gray-looking houses in the flat weary-looking suburb where he lived. To this dismal heath, therefore, they came, the swarthy children of a dozen races, clad in the hard and decent blacks in which the poor pay debts and go to funerals. They would advance across the barren lands, the harsh sere earth scarred with its wastes of rust and rubbish, going stolidly by below the blank board fences of a brick yard, crunching doggedly through the lanes of dirty rutted ice, passing before the gray besmutted fronts of wooden houses which in their stark, desolate, and unspeakable ugliness seemed to give a complete and final utterance to an architecture of weariness, sterility and horror, so overwhelming in its absolute desolation that it seemed as if the painful and indignant soul of man must sicken and die at length before it, stricken, stupefied, and strangled without a tongue to articulate the curse that once had blazed in him.

And at length they would pause before the old man's little house—one of a street of little houses which he had built there on the barren flatlands of the suburb, and to which he had given magnificently his own name— Pentland Heights—although the only eminence in all that flat and weary waste was an almost imperceptible rise a half mile off. And here along this street which he had built, these little houses, warped, yet strong and hardy, seemed to burrow down solidly like moles for warmth into the ugly stony earth on which they were built and to cower and huddle doggedly below the immense and terrible desolation of the northern sky, with its rimy sun-hazed lights, its fierce and cruel rags and stripes of wintry red, its raw and savage harshness. And then, gripping their greasy little wads of money, as if in the knowledge that all reward below these fierce and cruel skies must be wrenched painfully and minutely from a stony earth, they went in to pay him. He would come up to meet them from some lower cellar-depth, swearing, muttering, and banging doors; and he would come toward them howling greetings, buttoned to his chin in the frayed and faded sweater, gnarled, stooped and frosty-looking, clutching his great hands together at his waist. Then they would wait, stiffly, clumsily, fingering their hats, while with countless squints and grimaces and pursings of the lip, he scrawled out painfully their receipts—their fractional release from debt and labor, one more hard-won step toward the freedom of possession.

At length, having pocketed their money and finished the transaction, he would not permit them to depart at once, he would howl urgently at them an invitation to stay, he would offer long weedy-looking cigars to them, and they would sit uncomfortably, crouching on their buttock bones like stalled oxen, at the edges of chairs, shyly and dumbly staring at him, while he howled question, comment, and enthusiastic tribute at them.

"Why, my dear sir!" he would yell at Makropolos, the Greek. "You have a glorious past, a history of which any nation might well be proud!"

"Sure, sure!" said Makropolos, nodding vigorously. "Beeg Heestory!"

"The isles of Greece, the isles of Greece!" the old man howled, "where burning Sappho loved and sung—" (Phuh! phuh! phuh! phuh! phuh!)

"Sure, sure!" said Makropolos again, nodding good-naturedly but wrinkling his lowering finger's-breadth of brow in a somewhat puzzled fashion. "Tha's right! You got it!"

"Why, my dear sir!" Uncle Bascom cried. "It has been the ambition of my lifetime to visit those hallowed scenes, to stand at sunrise on the Acropolis, to explore the glory that was Greece, to see the magnificent ruins of the noblest of ancient civ-i-*liz*-a-tions!"

For the first time a dark flush, a flush of outraged patriotism, began to burn upon the swarthy yellow of Mr. Makropolos's cheek: his manner became heavy and animated, and in a moment he said with passionate conviction:

"No, no, no! No ruin! Wat you t'ink, eh! Athens fine town! We got a million pipples dere!" He struggled for a word, then cupped his hairy paws indefinitely: "*You* know? *Beeg!* O, ni-ez!" he added greasily, with a smile. "Everyt'ing good! We got everyt'ing good dere as you got here! *You* know?" he said with a confiding and painful effort. "Everyt'ing ni-ez! Not old! No, no, no!" he cried with a rising and indignant vigor. "New! de same as here. Ni-ez! You get good and cheap—everyt'ing! Beeg place, new house, dumbwaiter, elevator—wat chew like!—oh, ni-ez!" he said earnestly. "Wat chew t'ink it cost, eh? Feefateen dollar a month! Sure, sure!" he nodded with a swarthy earnestness. "I wouldn't keed you!"

"Finest people on earth!" Uncle Bascom cried with an air of great conviction and satisfaction. "No question about it!"—and he would usher his visitor to the door howling farewells into the terrible desolation of those savage skies.

Meanwhile, Aunt Louise, although she had not heard a word of what was said, although she had listened to nothing except the periods of Uncle Bascom's heavily accented and particular speech, kept up a constant snuffling laughter punctuated momently by faint whoops as she bent over her pots and pans in the kitchen, pausing from time to time as if to listen, and then snuffling to herself as she shook her head in pitying mirth which rose again up to the crisis of a faint crazy cackle as she scoured the pan; because, of course, during the forty-five years of her life with him she had gone thoroughly, imperceptibly, and completely mad, and no longer knew or cared to know whether these words had just been spoken or were the echoes of lost voices long ago.

And again, she would pause to listen, with her small birdlike features uplifted gleefully in a kind of mad attentiveness as the door slammed and he stumped muttering back into the house, intent upon the secret designs of his own life, as remote and isolate from her as if they had each dwelt on separate planets, although the house they lived in was a small one.

Such had been the history of the old man. His life had come up from the wilderness, the buried past, the lost America. The potent mystery of old events and moments had passed around him, and the magic light of dark time fell across him.

Like all men in this land, he had been a wanderer, an exile on the immortal earth. Like all of us he had no home. Wherever great wheels carried him was home.

As the old man and his nephew talked together, Louse would prepare the meal in the kitchen, which gave on the living-room where they ate, by a swing door that she kept open, in order that she might hear what went on. And, while they waited, Uncle Bascom would talk to the boy on a vast range of subjects, dealing with that literature in which he had once been deep—the poetry of the Old Testament, the philosophy of Hegel, Carlyle, and Matthew Arnold, whom he worshipped, or some question in the daily papers.

Uncle Bascom, seated, his fine gaunt face grave, magnificently composed now above his arched gnarled hands, spoke with eloquent deliberation. He became triumphant reasoning mind: he talked with superb balanced judgment. All the tumult and insanity of his life had been forgotten: no question of money or of self was involved. Meanwhile, from the kitchen Aunt Louise kept up a constant snuffling laughter, punctuated momently by faint whoops. She was convinced, of course, that her husband was mad and all his opinions nonsensical. Yet she had not listened to a word of what he was saying, but only to the sound of his heavily accented, precise, and particular speech. From time to time, snuffling to herself she would look in on Eugene, trembling with laughter, and shake her head at him in pitying mirth.

"Beyond a doubt! Beyond a *doubt!"* Uncle Bascom would say. "The quality of the best writing in the books of the Old Testament may take rank with the best writing that has ever been done, but you are right in believing, too, the amount of great writing is less than it is commonly supposed to be. There are passages, nay! *books"*—his voice rising strangely to a husky howl—"of the vilest rubbish—Noah, Shem, Ham and Japheth— O vile! vile!" he cried. . . . "And Azariah begat Amariah and Amariah begat Ahitub (Phuh! Phuh! Phuh!). *Ahitub,"* he sneered. "And Azariah begat Seraiah, and Seraiah begat Jehozadak (Phuh! Phuh! Phuh!) *Jehozadak"*—he sneered with his precise articulation, finally letting out the last syllable with a kind of snarling contempt. "Can you *imagine,* can you even *dream,"* he howled, "of calling any one a name like that! 'And Jehozadak went into captivity'—as, indeed, he ought! (phuh! phuh! phuh!)—his *very* name would constitute a *penal* offense! (Phuh! Phuh! Phuh!) Jehozadak!" Uncle Bascom sneered. "But," he proceeded deliberately in a moment, as he stared calmly over his great arched hands, "—but—the quality of some of the language is God-intoxicated: the noblest poetry ever chanted in the service of eternity."

"The Book of Wevelations," cried Aunt Louise, suddenly rushing out of the kitchen with a carving knife in her hand, having returned to earth for a moment to hear him. "The Book of Wevelations!" she said in a hoarse whisper, her mouth puckered with disgust. *"Eugene!* A *wicked,* bloo-o-edy, kwu-u-el monument to supahstition. Twibute to an avenging and *muh-duh-wous Gawd!"* The last word uttered in a hoarse almost inaudible whisper would find my aunt bent double, clutching a knife in one hand, with her small bright eyes glaring madly at us.

"Oh no, my dear, oh no," said Uncle Bascom, with astonishing, unaccustomed sadness, with almost exquisite gentleness. And, his vibrant passionate voice thrilling suddenly with emotion, he added:

"The triumphant music of one of the mightiest of earth's poets: the sublime utterance of a man for whom God had opened the mysteries of heaven and hell."

He paused a moment, then quietly in a remote voice—in that remote and magnificent voice which could thrill men so deeply when it uttered poetry, he continued: " 'I am Alpha and Omega, the first and the last, the beginning and the end'—the mightiest line, my dear boy, the most magnificent poetry, that was ever written." And suddenly Uncle Bascom threw his gaunt hands before his face, and wept in strong hoarse sobs: "Oh, my God, my God!—the beauty, the pity of it all! . . . You must pardon me," he whispered after a moment, drawing his faded sweater sleeve across his eyes. "You must pardon me. It brought back —memories."

Aunt Louise, who had been stricken with a kind of fear and horror when he began to weep, now looked at Eugene with an expression of strong physical disgust, almost of nausea, shaking her head slightly in an affronted and lady-like manner as might one who, having achieved healthy and courageous discipline over all the excesses of emotion, feels only contempt for him who gives way to them.

She retired now with exaggerated dignity to the kitchen, served the meal, and addressed Eugene for some time thereafter with absurd quietness and restraint of manner, and a kind of stiff primness about her backbone. She was an excellent cook; there was magic in her treatment of food, and on the occasions when Eugene was coming out, she insisted that Bascom get her a decent piece of meat to work with.

There would be a juicy fragrant piece of lamb, or a boiled leg of mutton with currant jelly, or perhaps a small crisply browned roast of beef, with small flaky biscuits, smoking hot, two or three vegetables, and rich coffee. Uncle Bascom, quite unperturbed by his outbreak, would stamp into the kitchen, where he could be heard swearing and muttering to himself, as he searched for various things. Later he would appear at the table bearing a platter filled with some revolting mess of his own concoction,—a mixture of raw vegetables, chopped up—onions, carrots, beans, and raw potatoes—for he had the full strength of his family's mania concerning food, violent prejudices about its preparation, and deep-seated distrust of everybody's cleanliness but his own.

"Have some, my boy. Have some!" he would yell huskily, seating himself, and lunging toward Eugene with the awful mess, in a gesture of violent invitation.

"Thank you, no." Eugene would try to keep his eyes averted from the mess, and focus on the good food heaping his plate.

"You may eat that slop if you want to," Uncle Bascom would exclaim with a scornful and sneering laugh. "It would give *me* my death of dyspepsia." And the silence of their eating would be broken by the recurrent snuffling whoops of Aunt Louise, accompanied by many pitying looks and head-shakes as she trembled with laughter and hid her mouth.

Or, suddenly, in the full rich progress of the meal, Eugene would be shocked out of his pleasure in the food by the mad bright eyes of Aunt Louise bearing fiercely down upon him:

"Eugene!—don't bwood, boy! Don't bwood! You've got it in you— it's in the blood! You're one of them. You're one of *them!*—a *Pentland*," she croaked fatally.

"Ah-h—you *don't* know what you're talking about"—thus suddenly in fierce distemper Uncle Bascom. "*Scotch! Scotch*-Irish! Finest people on earth! No question about it whatever."

"Fugitive ideation! Fugitive ideation," she chattered like a monkey over a nut. "Mind goes off in all diwections. Can't stick to anything five minutes at a time. The same thing that's wong with the moduhn decadents. Wead Nordau's book, Eugene. It will open yoah eyes," and she whispered hoarsely again: "You're *oevah-sexed—all* of you!"

"Bosh! Bosh!" growled Uncle Bascom. "Some more of your psychology—the *bastard* of superstition and quackery: the black magic of little minds—the effort of a blind man (phuh! phuh! phuh!) crawling about in a dark room (phuh! phuh!) looking for a *black cat* (phuh! phuh!) that *isn't there*," he yelled triumphantly, and closed his eyes and snarled and snuffled down his nose with laughter.

He knew nothing about it: occasionally he still read Kant, and he could be as deep in absolute categories, moments of negation, and definitions of a concept, as she with all of her complicated and extensive paraphernalia of phobias, complexes, fixations, and repressions.

"Well, Eugene," thus Aunt Louise with light raillery and yet with eager curiosity, "have you found you a nice wosy-cheeked New England gul yet? You had bettah watch *out,* boy! I tell you, you had bettah watch *out!* she declared, kittenishly, wagging her finger at him, before he had time to answer.

"If he has," said Uncle Bascom grimly, "he will find her sadly lacking in the qualities of delicacy, breeding, and womanly decorum that the Southern girl has. Oh, yes! No question about that whatever!" for Uncle Bascom still had the passionate loyalty and sentimental affection for the South that many Southerners have who could not be induced, under any circumstances, to return.

"Take a Nawthun gul, Eugene." Aunt Louise became at once combative. "They're bettah for you! They are *bettah.* They are *bettah!*" she declared, shaking her head in an obdurate manner, as if further argument was useless. "Moah independence! Bettah minds! They won't choke yoah life out by hanging awound yoah neck," she concluded crisply.

"I will tell you a story," Uncle Bascom continued deliberately as if she had not spoken, "that will illustrate admirably what I mean." Here he cleared his throat, as if he were preparing to deliver a set speech, and began in a deliberate and formal tone, "Some years ago I had occasion to go to Portland, Maine, on business. When I arrived at the North Station I found a crowd waiting before the window: it was necessary for me to wait in line. I was carrying a small valise which I placed on the floor between my legs in order to get out the money for my ticket. At this moment, the woman who stood behind me, apparently not given to noticing very well where she was going," he snarled bitterly, "started to move forward and stubbed her toe against the valise. Before I had time to turn around and apologize"—he stopped abruptly, then, leaning forward with a horrible grimace, he tapped Eugene stiffly with his great bony fingers and continued in a lowered voice: "Say! Have you any idea what she did, my boy?"

"No," Eugene said.

"Why I give you my word, my boy," he whispered solemnly, "without so much as 'By your leave,' she lifted her leg and *kicked* me, *kicked* me"—he howled, "in the *stern!* And *she,* my boy, was a New England woman."

"Whoo-o-op!" Aunt Louise was off again, rocking back and forth, holding her napkin over her mouth.

"Can you *imagine,* can you *dream,*" said Bascom, his voice an intense whisper of disgust, "of a Southern lady, the flower of modesty and the old aristocracy, doing such a thing as that?"

"Yes-s," hissed Aunt Louise, her cackle subsiding, leaning intensely across the table and glaring at him, "and it *suhved* you wight! It *suhved* you wight! It *suhved* you wight! These things would nevah happen if you thought of any one's convenience but yoah own. What *wight* did you have to put youh baggage there? What *wight?*"

"Ah," he replied, with a kind of precise snarl, profoundly contemptuous of her opinion, "you-don't-know-what-you're-talk-ing-about! What *right?* she says—Why all the right in the world," he yelled. "Have you ever read the conditions enumerated upon the back of railway tickets concerning the transportation of baggage?"

"Suttinly not!" she retorted crisply. "One does not need to wead the backs of wailway tickets to learn how to behave like a civilized pusson!"

"Well, I will tell them to you," said Uncle Bascom, licking his lips, and with a look of joy upon his face. And, at great length, with infinite gusto, lip-pursing, and legal pedantry of elocution, he would enumerate them all.

"And say, by the way, Eugene," he would continue without a halt, "there is a very charming young lady who occasionally comes to my office (with her mother, of course) who is very anxious to meet you. She is a musician: she appears quite often in public. They live in Melrose, but they came, originally, I believe, from New Hampshire. Finest people in the world: no question about it," my uncle said.

And suddenly alert, scenting adventure and seduction, the young man got the address from him immediately.

"Yes, my boy," here Uncle Bascom fumbled through a mass of envelopes, "you may call her, without indiscretion, over the telephone at any time. I have spoken to her frequently about you: no doubt you'll find much in common. Or, *say!*" here a flash of inspiration aroused him to volcanic action, "I could call her now and let you talk to her." And he plunged violently toward the telephone.

"No, no, no, no, no!" Eugene sprang after him and checked him. For he wanted to make his own appointment luxuriously in private, sealed darkly in a telephone booth, craftily to feel his way, speculating on the curve of the unseen hip by the sound of the voice; probing, with the most delicate innuendo, the depth and richness of the promise. He loathed all family intercession and interference: they placed, he felt, at the outset, a crushing restraint upon the adventure from which it could never recover.

"I had rather call her myself," he added, "when I have more time. I don't know when I could see her now: it might be awkward calling at just this time."

Later, while Uncle Bascom was poking furiously at the meagre coals of the tiny furnace in the cellar, setting up a clangorous and smoky din all through the house, Aunt Louise would bear down madly upon the boy, whispering:

"Did you hear him! Did you hear him! Still mad about the women at his age! Can't keep his hands off them! The lechewous old fool!" and she cackled bitterly. Then, with a fierce change: "He's *mad* about them, Eugene. He's had one after anothah for the last twenty yeahs! He has spent *faw-chuns* on them! Have you seen that gul in his office yet? The stenographer?"

He had, and believed he had rarely seen a more solidly dull unattractive female than this pallid coarse-featured girl. But he only said: "Yes."

"He has spent thousands on her, Gene! *Thousands!* The old fool! And all they do is laugh at him behind his back. Why even at home heah," her eyes darting madly about the place, "he can hardly keep his hands off me at times! I have to lock myself in my woom to secure pwotection" and her bright old eyes muttered crazily about in her head.

He thought these outbursts the result of frantic and extravagant jealousy: fruit of some passionate and submerged affection that his aunt still bore for her husband. This, perhaps, was true, but later he was to find there was a surprising modicum of fact in what she had said.

During the wintry afternoon, he would sit and smoke one of his uncle's corn-cob pipes, filling it with the coarse cheap powerful tobacco that lay, loosely spread, upon a bread-board in the kitchen.

Meanwhile, his aunt, on these usual Sundays when she must remain at home, played entire operas from Wagner on her small victrola.

Most of the records had been given her by her two daughters, and during the week the voices of the music afforded her the only companionship she had. The boy listened attentively to all she said about music, because he knew little about it, and had got from poetry the kind of joy that music seemed to give to others. Shifting the records quickly, his aunt would point out the melodramatic effervescence of the Italians, the metallic precision, the orderly profusion, the thrill, the vibration, the emptiness of French composition. She liked the Germans and the Russians. She liked what she called the "barbaric splendor" of Rimsky, but was too late, of course, either to have heard or to care much for the modern composers.

She would play Wagner over and over again, lost in the enchanted forests of the music, her spirit wandering drunkenly down vast murky aisles of sound, through which the great hoarse throats of horns were baying faintly. And occasionally, on Sundays, on one of her infrequent excursions into the world, when her daughters bought her tickets for concerts at Symphony Hall—that great gray room lined on its sides with pallid plaster shells of Greece—she would sit perched high, a sparrow held by the hypnotic serpent's eye of music—following each motif, hearing minutely each subtle entry of the mellow flutes, the horns, the spinal ecstasy of violins—until her lonely and desolate life was spun out of her into aerial fabrics of bright sound.

During this time, Uncle Bascom, who also knew nothing about music, and cared so little for it that he treated his wife's passion for it with contempt, would bury himself in the Sunday papers, or thumb deliberately through the pages of an ancient edition of the *Encyclopædia Britannica* in search of arbitrament for some contested point.

"Ah! Here we are, just as I thought," he would declare suddenly, with triumphant satisfaction. " 'Upon the fifth, however, in spite of the heavy rains which had made of the roads quaking bogs, Jackson appeared suddenly from the South, at the head of an army of 33,000 men.' "

Then they would wrangle furiously over the hour, the moment, the place of dead event: each rushing from the room fiercely to produce the document which would support his own contention.

"Your aunt, my boy, is not the woman she once was," Bascom would say regretfully during her absence. "No question about that! At one time she was a very remarkable woman! Yes, sir, a woman of very considerable intelligence—considerable, that is, for a woman," he said, with a slight sneer.

And she, whispering, when he had gone: "You have noticed, of course, Gene?"

"What?"

"His mind's going," she muttered. "What a head he had fifteen years ago! But *now!*—Senile decay—G. Stanley Hall—forgets everything—" she whispered hoarsely, as she heard his returning footsteps.

Or, as the winter light darkened grayly, slashed on the western sky by fierce cold red, his uncle passed sheaf after sheaf of his verse to him, sniggering nosily, and prodding the boy with his great fingers, while his aunt cleared the table, or listened to the music. The great majority of these verses, labored and pedantic as they were, were variations of the motif of agnosticism, the horn on which his ministry in the Church had fatally gored itself—and still a brand that smouldered in his brain— not now so much from an all-mastering conviction, as from some desire to justify himself. These verses, which he asserted were modelled on those of his great hero, Matthew Arnold, were all remarkably like this one:

MY CREED

"Is there a land beyond the stars
Where we may find eternal day,
Life after death, peace after wars?
Is there? I cannot say.
Shall we find there a happier life,
All joy that here we never know,
Love in all things, an end of strife?
Perhaps: it may be so."

And so on.

And sniggering down his nose, Bascom would prod the young man stiffly with his great fingers, saying, as he slyly thrust another verse into his hand:

"Something in a lighter vein, my boy. Just a little foolishness, you know. (Phuh! Phuh! Phuh! Phuh! Phuh!)" Which was:

"Mary had a little calf,
It followed up her leg,
And everywhere that Mary went,
The boys were sure to beg."

And so on.

Uncle Bascom had hundreds of them: *Poems—Chiefly Religious,* he sent occasionally to the morning papers. They were sometimes printed in the Editor's Correspondence or The Open Forum. But *Poems— Chiefly Profane* he kept apparently for his own regalement.

Then, as it darkened, toward five o'clock, the boy would depart leaving them at times bitterly involved in a political wrangle, with the strewn Sunday members of *The Boston Herald* and *The Boston Post* around them, she parroting intensely the newspaper jargon, assaulting Borah and "the Senate iwwcconcilables," he angrily defending Senator Lodge as a scholar and a gentleman, with whom he had not always been in agreement, but from whom he had once received a most courteous letter—a fact which seemed to distinguish him in Bascom's mind as the paragon of statesmanship.

And as Eugene left, he would note, with a swift inchoate pang, the sudden mad loneliness in Aunt Louise's eyes, doomed for another week to her grim imprisonment. But he did not know that her distended and exhausted heart hissed audibly each time she ascended from futile labor on the cold furnace, stoked with cheap slag and coke, and that her thin blood was fed by gristly butcher's leavings, in answer to the doctor's call for meat.

And his aunt would go with Eugene to the frost-glazed door, open it, and stand huddled meagrely and hugging herself together beneath the savage desolation of the Northern cold; talking to him for a moment and calling brightly after him as he went down the icy path:

"Come again, boy! Always glad to see you!"

And in the dull cold Sunday light he strode away, his spirit braced by the biting air, the Northern cold, the ragged bloody sky, which was somehow prophetic to him of glorious fulfilment, and at the same time depressed by the gray enormous weight of Sunday tedium and dreariness all around him.

And yet, he never lost heart that out of this dulness he would draw some rich adventure. He strode away with quickening pulse, hoping to see it issue from every warmly lighted house, to find it in the street cars, the subway or at a restaurant. Then he would go back into the city and dine at one of the restaurants where the pretty waitresses served him. Later he would go out on the sparsely peopled Sunday streets, turning finally, as a last resort, into Washington Street, where the moving-picture places and cheap vaudeville houses were filled with their Sunday Irish custom.

Sometimes he went in, but as one weary act succeeded the other, and the empty brutal laughter of the people echoed in his ears, seeming to him forced and dishonest, as if people laughed at the ghosts of mirth, the rotten husks of stale wit, the sordidness, hopelessness, and sterility of their lives oppressed him hideously. On the stage he would see the comedian again display his red necktie with a leer, and hear the people laugh about it; he would hear again that some one was a big piece of cheese, and listen to them roar; he would observe again the pert and cheap young comedian with nothing to offer waste time portentously, talk in a low voice with the orchestra leader; and the only thing he liked would be the strength and balance of the acrobats.

Finally, drowned in a sea-depth of gray horror, and with the weary brutal laughter of the audience ringing in his ears, he would rush out on the street again, filled with its hideous Sunday dullness and the sterile wink of the chop-suey signs, and take the train to Cambridge.

And there, as the night grew late, his spirit would surge up in him: sunken in books at midnight, with the soft numb prescience of brooding snow upon the air, the feeling of exultancy, joy, and invincible strength would come back; and he was sure that the door would open for him, the magic word be spoken, and that he would make all of the glory, power, and beauty of the earth his own.

XVIII

ONE day the boy telephoned the girl of whom his Uncle Bascom had spoken. She was coy and cautious, but sounded hopeful: he liked her voice. When, after some subtle circumlocutions, he asked her for an early meeting, she countered swiftly by asking him to meet her the following evening at the North Station: she was coming in to town to perform at a dinner. She played the violin. He understood very well that she was really anxious to see him before admitting him to the secure license of a suburban parlor; so, he bathed himself, threw powder under his arm-pits, and put on a new shirt, which he bought for the occasion.

It was November: rain fell coldly and drearily. He buttoned himself in his long raincoat and went to meet her. She had promised to wear a red carnation; the suggestion was her own, and tickled him hugely. As the pink-faced suburbanites poured, in an icy stream, into the hot waiting-room, he looked for her. Presently he saw her: she came toward him immediately, since his height was unmistakable. They talked excitedly flustered, but gradually getting some preliminary sense of each other.

She was a rather tall, slender girl, dressed in garments that seemed to have been left over, in good condition, from the early part of the century. She wore a flat but somehow towering hat: it seemed to perch upon her head, as do those worn by the Queen of England. She was covered with a long blue coat, which flared and bustled at the hips, and had screws and curls of black corded ornament; she looked respectable and antiquated, but her costume, and a naive stupidity in her manner, gave her a quaintness that he liked. He took her to the subway, having arranged a meeting at her home for the following night.

The girl, whose name was Genevieve Simpson, lived with her mother and her brother, a heavy young lout of nineteen years, in a two-family house at Melrose. The mother, a small, full, dumpling-faced woman, whose ordinary expression in repose, in common with that of so many women of the middle class in America who have desired one life and followed another and found perhaps that its few indispensable benefits, as security, gregariousness, decorum, have not been as all-sufficient as they had hoped, was one of sullen, white, paunch-eyed discontent.

It was this inner petulance, the small carping disparagement of every one and everything that entered the mean light of her world, that made absurdly palpable the burlesque mechanism of social heartiness. Looking at her while she laughed with shrill falsity at all the wrong places, he would rock with huge guffaws, to which she would answer with eager renewal, believing that both were united in their laughter over something of which she was, it is true, a little vague.

It was, she felt, her business to make commercially attractive to every young man the beauty and comfort of the life she had made for her family, and although the secret niggling discontent of their lives was plainly described on both her own and her daughter's face, steeped behind their transparent masks in all the small poisons of irritability and bitterness, they united in their pretty tableau before the world—a tableau, he felt, something like those final exhibitions of grace and strength with which acrobats finish the act, the strained smile of ease and comfort, as if one could go on hanging by his toes forever, the grieving limbs, the whole wrought torture which will collapse in exhausted relief the second the curtain hides it.

"We want you to feel absolutely at home here," she said brightly. "Make this your headquarters. You will find us simple folk here, without any frills," she continued, with a glance around the living-room, letting her eye rest with brief satisfaction upon the striped tiles of the hearth, the flowered vases of the mantel, the naked doll, tied with a pink sash, on the piano, and the pictures of "The Horse Fair," the lovers flying before the storm, Maxfield Parrish's "Dawn," and Leonardo da Vinci's "Last Supper," which broke the spaces of the wall, "but if you like a quiet family life, a welcome is always waiting for you here. Oh, yes—every one is for each other here: we keep no secrets from each other in our little family."

Eugene thought that this was monstrous if it was true; a swift look at Genevieve and Mama convinced him, however, that not everything was being told. A mad exultancy arose in him: the old desire returned again to throw a bomb into the camp, in order to watch its effect; to express murderous opinions in a gentle Christian voice, further entrenched by an engaging matter-of-factness, as if he were but expressing the commonplace thought of all sensible people; bawdily, lewdly, shockingly with a fine assumption of boyish earnestness, sincerity, and naïveté. So, in a voice heavily coated with burlesque feeling, he said: "Thank you, thank you, Mrs. Simpson. You have no idea what it means to me to be able to come to a place like this."

"I know," said Genevieve with fine sympathy, "when you're a thousand miles from home——"

"A thousand!" he cried, with a bitter laugh, "a thousand! Say rather a million." And he waited, almost squealing in his throat, until they should bite.

"But—but your home is in the South, isn't it?" Mrs. Simpson inquired doubtfully.

"Home! Home!" cried he, with raucous laugh. "I have no home!"

"Oh, you poor boy!" said Genevieve.

"But your parents—are they *both* dead?"

"No!" he answered, with a sad smile. "They are both living."

There was a pregnant silence.

"They do not live together," he added after a moment, feeling he could not rely on their deductive powers.

"O-o-oh," said Mrs. Simpson significantly, running the vowel up and down the vocal scale. "O-o-oh!"

"Nasty weather, isn't it?" he remarked, deliberately drawing a loose cigarette from his pocket. "I wish it would snow: I like your cold Northern winters as only a Southerner can like them; I like the world at night when it is muffled, enclosed with snow; I like a warm secluded house, sheltered under heavy fir trees, with the curtains drawn across a mellow light, and books, and a beautiful woman within. These are some of the things I like."

"Gee!" said the boy, his heavy blond head leaned forward intently. "What was the trouble?"

"Jimmy! Hush!" cried Genevieve, and yet they all looked toward Eugene with eager intensity.

"The trouble?" said he, vacantly. "What trouble?"

"Between your father and mother?"

"Oh," he said carelessly, "he beat her."

"Aw-w! He hit her with his fist?"

"Oh, no. He generally used a walnut walking stick. It got too much for her finally. My mother, even then, was not a young woman—she was almost fifty, and she could not stand the gaff so well as she could in her young days. I'll never forget that last night," he said, gazing thoughtfully into the coals with a smile. "I was only seven, but I remember it all very well. Papa had been brought home drunk by the mayor."

"The *mayor?*"

"Oh, yes," said Eugene casually. "They were great friends. The mayor often brought him home when he was drunk. But he was very violent that time. After the mayor had gone, he stamped around the house smashing everything he could get his hands on, cursing and blaspheming at the top of his voice. My mother stayed in the kitchen and paid no attention to him when he entered. This, of course, infuriated him. He made for her with the poker. She saw that at last she was up against it; but she had realized that such a moment was inevitable. She was not unprepared. So she reached in the flour bin and got her revolver——"

"Did she have a revolver!"

"Oh, yes," he said nonchalantly, "my Uncle Will had given it to her as a Christmas present. Knowing my father as he did, he told her it might come in handy sometime. Mama was forced to shoot at him three times before he came to his senses."

There was a silence.

"Gee!" said the boy, finally. "Did she hit him?"

"Only once," Eugene replied, tossing his cigarette into the fire. "A flesh wound in the leg. A trifle. He was up and about in less than a week. But, of course, Mama had left him by that time."

"Well!" said Mrs. Simpson, after a yet longer silence, "I've never had to put up with anything like *that.*"

"No, thank heaven!" said Genevieve fervently. Then, curiously: "Is —is your mother Mr. Pentland's sister?"

"Yes."

"And the uncle who gave her the revolver—Mr. Pentland's brother?"

"Oh, yes," Eugene answered readily. "It's all the same family." He grinned in his entrails, thinking of Uncle Bascom.

"Mr. Pentland seems a very educated sort of man," said Mrs. Simpson, having nothing else to say.

"Yes. We went to see him when we were hunting for a house," Genevieve added. "He was very nice to us. He told us he had once been in the ministry."

"Yes," said Eugene. "He was a Man of God for more than twenty years—one of the most eloquent, passionate, and gifted soul-savers that ever struck fear into the hearts of the innumerable sinners of the American Nation. In fact, I know of no one with whom to compare him, unless I turn back three centuries to Jonathan Edwards, the Puritan divine, who evoked, in a quiet voice like the monotonous dripping of water, a picture of hell-fire so near that the skins of the more imaginative fanatics on the front rows visibly blistered. However, Edwards spoke for two and a half hours: Uncle Bascom, with his mad and beautiful tongue, has been known to drive people insane with terror in twenty-seven minutes by the clock. There are still people in the asylums that he put there," he said piously. "I hope," he added quickly, "you didn't ask him why he had left the church."

"Oh, no!" said Genevieve. "We never did that."

"Why did he?" asked Mrs. Simpson bluntly, who felt that now she had only to ask and it would be given. She was not disappointed.

"It was the centuries-old conflict between organized authority and the individual," said Eugene. "No doubt you have felt it in your own lives. Uncle Bascom was a poet, a philosopher, a mystic—he had the soul of an artist which must express divine love and ideal beauty in corporeal form. Such a man as this is not going to be shackled by the petty tyrannies of ecclesiastical convention. An artist must love, and be loved. He must be swept by the Flow of Things, he must be a constantly expanding atom in the rhythmic surges of the Life Force. Who knew this better than Uncle Bascom when he first met the choir contralto?"

"Contralto!" gasped Genevieve.

"Perhaps she was a soprano," said Eugene. "It skills not. Suffice it to say they lived, they loved, they had their little hour of happiness. Of course, when the child came——"

"The child!" screamed Mrs. Simpson.

"A bouncing boy. He weighed thirteen pounds at birth and is at the present a Lieutenant Commander in the United States Navy."

"What became of—her?" said Genevieve.

"Of whom?"

"The—the contralto."

"She died—she died in childbirth."

But—but Mr. Pentland?" inquired Mrs. Simpson in an uncertain voice. "Didn't he—marry her?"

"How could he?" Eugene answered with calm logic. "He was married to some one else."

And casting his head back suddenly he sang: "You know I'm in love with some-boddy else, so why can't you leave me alone?"

"Well, I *never!*" Mrs. Simpson stared dumbly into the fire.

"Well, *hardly* ever," Eugene became allusively Gilbertian. "She hardly ever has a Big, Big B." And he sang throatily: "Oh, yes! Oh, yes, in-deed!" relapsing immediately into a profound and moody abstraction, but noting with delight that Genevieve and her mother were looking at him furtively, with frightened and bewildered glances.

"Say!" The boy, whose ponderous jowl had been sunken on his fist for ten minutes, now at length distilled a question. "What ever became of your father? Is he still living?"

"No!" said Eugene, after a brief pause, returning suddenly to fact. "No! He's still dying."

And he fixed upon them suddenly the battery of his fierce eyes, lit with horror:

"He has a cancer." After a moment, he concluded: "My father is a very great man."

They looked at him in stricken bewilderment.

"Gee!" said the boy, after another silence. "That guy's worse than our old man!"

"Jimmy! Jimmy!" whispered Genevieve scathingly.

There was a very long, for the Simpson family, a very painful, silence.

"Aha! Aha!" Eugene's head was full of *ahas*.

"I suppose you have thought it strange," Mrs. Simpson began with a cracked laugh, which she strove to make careless, "that you have never seen Mr. Simpson about when you called?"

"Yes," he answered with a ready dishonesty, for he had never thought of it at all. But he reflected at the same moment that this was precisely the sort of thing people were always thinking of: suddenly before the embattled front of that little family, its powers aligned for the defense of reputation, he felt lonely, shut out. He saw himself looking in at them through a window: all communication with life grouped and protected seemed forever shut off.

"Mother decided some months ago that she could no longer live with Father," said Genevieve, with sad dignity.

"Sure," volunteered Jimmy, "he's livin' with another woman!"

"Jimmy!" said Genevieve hoarsely.

Eugene had a momentary flash of humorous sympathy with the departed Simpson; then he looked at her white bickering face and felt sorry for her. She carried her own punishment with her.

XIX

SHALL a man be dead within your heart before his rotten flesh be wholly dead within the ground, and before the producing fats and syrup cease to give life to his growing hair? Shall a man so soon be done with that which still provides a nest for working maggotry or shall a brother leave a brother's memory before the worms have left his tissue? This is a pregnant subject: there should be laws passed, and a discipline, which train a man to greater constancy. And suddenly, out of this dream of time in which he lived, he would awaken, and instantly, like a man freed from the spell of an enchantment which has held him captive for many years in some strange land, he would remember home with an intolerable sense of pain and loss, the lost world of his childhood, and feel the strange and bitter miracle of life and have no words for what he wished to say.

That lost world would come back to him at many times, and often for no cause that he could trace or fathom—a voice half-heard, a word far-spoken, a leaf, a light that came and passed and came again. But always when that lost world would come back, it came at once, like a sword thrust through the entrails, in all its panoply of past time, living, whole, and magic as it had always been.

And always when it came to him, and at whatever time, and for whatever reason, he could hear his father's great voice sounding in the house again and see his gaunt devouring stride as he had come muttering round the corner at the hour of noon long years before.

And then he would hear again the voice of his dead brother, and remember with a sense of black horror, dream-like disbelief, that Ben was dead, and yet could not believe that Ben had ever died, or that he had had a brother, lost a friend. Ben would come back to him in these moments with a blazing and intolerable reality, until he heard his quiet living voice again, saw his fierce scowly eyes of bitter gray, his scornful, proud and lively face, and always when Ben came back to him it was like this: he saw his brother in a single image, in some brief forgotten moment of the past, remembered him by a word, a gesture, a forgotten act; and certainly all that could ever be known of Ben's life was collected in that blazing image of lost time and the forgotten moment. And suddenly he would be there in a strange land, staring upward from his bed in darkness, hearing his brother's voice again, and living in the far and bitter miracle of time.

And always now, when Ben came back to him, he came within the frame and limits of a single image, one of those instant blazing images which from this time would haunt his memory and which more and more, as a kind of distillation—a reward for all the savage struggles of his Faustian soul with the protean and brain-maddening forms of life— were to collect and concentrate the whole material of experience and memory, in which the process of ten thousand days and nights could in an instant be resumed. And the image in which Ben now always came to him was this: he saw his brother standing in a window, and an old red light of fading day, and all the strange and tragic legend of his destiny was on his brow, and all that any man could ever see or know or under- stand of his dead brother's life was there:

Bitter and beautiful, scorn no more. Ben stands there in the window, for a moment idle, his strong, lean fingers resting lightly on his bony hips, his gray eyes scowling fiercely, bitterly and contemptuously over the laughing and exuberant faces of the crowd. For a moment more he scowls fixedly at them with an expression of almost savage contempt. Then scornfully he turns away from them. The bitter, lean and pointed face, the shapely, flashing, close-cropped head jerks upward, backward, he laughs briefly and with pitying contempt as he speaks to that un- known and invisible auditor who all his life has been the eternal con- fidant and witness of his scorn:

"Oh my God!" he says, jerking his scornful head out towards the crowd again. "Listen to this, will you?"

They look at him with laughing and exuberant faces, unwounded by his scorn. They look at him with a kind of secret and unspoken ten- derness which the strange and bitter savor of his life awakes in people always. They look at him with faith, with pride, with the joy and confidence and affection which his presence stirs in every one. And as if he were the very author of their fondest hopes, as if he were the fiat, not the helpless agent, of the thing they long to see accomplished, they yell to him in their unreasoning exuberance: "All right, Ben! Give us a hit now! A single's all we need, boy! Bring him in!" Or others, crying with the same exuberance of faith: "Strike him out, Ben! Make him fan!"

But now the crowd, sensing the electric thrill and menace of a decisive conflict, has grown still, is waiting with caught breath and pounding hearts, their eyes fixed eagerly on Ben. Somewhere, a thousand miles to the North, somewhere through the reddened, slanting and fast-fading light of that October day, somewhere across the illimitable fields and folds and woods and hills and hollows of America, across the huge brown earth, the mown fields, the vast wild space, the lavish, rude and unfenced distances, the familiar, homely, barren, harsh, strangely haunting scenery of the nation; somewhere through the crisp, ripe air, the misty, golden pollenated light of all her prodigal and careless harvest; somewhere far away at the heart of the great sky-soaring, smoke-gold, and enchanted city of the North, and of their vision—the lean right arm of the great pitcher Mathewson is flashing like a whip. A greyhound of a man named Speaker, quick as a deer to run, sharp as a hawk to see, swift as a cat to strike, stands facing him. And the huge terrific stands, packed to the eaves incredibly with mounting tiers of small white faces, now all breathless, silent, and intent, all focused on two men as are the thoughts, the hearts, the visions of these people everywhere in little towns, soar back, are flung to the farthest edges of the field in a vision of power, of distance, space and lives unnumbered, fused into a single unity that is so terrific that it bursts the measures of our comprehension and has a dream-like strangeness of reality even when we see it.

The scene is instant, whole and wonderful. In its beauty and design that vision of the soaring stands, the pattern of forty thousand em-petalled faces, the velvet and unalterable geometry of the playing field, and the small lean figures of the players, set there, lonely, tense and waiting in their places, bright, desperate solitary atoms encircled by that huge wall of nameless faces, is incredible. And more than anything, it is the light, the miracle of light and shade and color—the crisp, blue light that swiftly slants out from the soaring stands and, deepening to violet, begins to march across the velvet field and towards the pitcher's box, that gives the thing its single and incomparable beauty.

The batter stands swinging his bat and grimly waiting at the plate, crouched, tense, the catcher, crouched, the umpire, bent, hands clasped behind his back, and peering forward. All of them are set now in the cold blue of that slanting shadow, except the pitcher who stands out there all alone, calm, desperate, and forsaken in his isolation, with the gold red swiftly fading light upon him, his figure legible with all the resolution, despair and lonely dignity which that slanting, somehow fatal light can give him. Deep lilac light is eating swiftly in from every corner of the field now, and far off there is a vision of the misty, golden and October towers of the terrific city. The scene is unforgettable in the beauty, intoxication and heroic feeling of its incredible design, and yet, as overwhelming as the spectacle may be for him who sees it, it is doubt-ful if the eye-witness has ever felt its mystery, beauty, and strange love-liness as did that unseen and unseeing audience in a little town.

But now the crowd, sensing the menaceful approach of a decisive moment, has grown quiet and tense and breathless, as it stands there in the street. In the window, Ben sets the earphones firmly with his hands, his head goes down, the scowl between his gray eyes deepens to a look of listening intensity. He begins to speak sharply to a young man stand-ing at a table on the floor behind him. He snaps his fingers nervously, a card-board placard is handed to him, he looks quickly at it, and then thrusts it back, crying irritably:

"No, no, no! Strike one, I said! Damn it, Mac, you're about as much help to me as a wooden Indian!"

The young man on the floor thrusts another placard in his hand. Ben takes it quickly, swiftly takes out a placard from the complicated frame of wires and rows and columns in the window (for it is before the day of the electric scoreboard, and this clumsy and complicated system where-by every strike, ball, substitution, or base hit—every possible movement and event that can occur upon the field—must be indicated in this way by placards printed with the exact information, is the only one they know) and thrusts a new placard on the line in place of the one that he has just removed. A cheer, sharp, lusty, and immediate, goes up from the crowd. Ben speaks sharply and irritably to the dark and sullen-featured youth whose name is Foxey and Foxey runs outside quickly with another placard inscribed with the name of a new player who is coming in. Swiftly, Foxey takes out of its groove the name of the de-parting player, shoves the new one into place, and this time the rival partisans in the crowd cheer for the pinch hitter.

In the street now there is the excited buzz and hum of controversy. The people, who, with a strange and somehow moving loyalty, are divided into two groups supporting the merits of two teams which they have never seen, are eagerly debating, denying, making positive assertions of what is likely to happen, which are obviously extravagant and absurd in a contest where nothing can be predicted, and so much depends on fortune, chance, and the opportunity of the moment.

In the very forefront of the crowd, a little to the right as Ben stands facing them, a well-dressed man in the late fifties can be seen excitedly discussing the prospect of the game with several of his companions. His name is Fagg Sluder, a citizen well known to every one in town. He is a man who made a fortune as a contractor and retired from active business several years ago, investing part of his wealth in two or three large office buildings, and who now lives on the income he derives from them.

He is a nervous energetic figure of a man, of middle height, with graying hair, a short, cropped mustache, and the dry, spotted, slightly concave features which characterize many Americans of his age. A man who, until recent years, has known nothing but hard work since his childhood, he has now developed, in his years of leisure, an enthusiastic devotion to the game, that amounts to an obsession.

He has not only given to the town the baseball park which bears his name, he is also president of the local Club, and uncomplainingly makes good its annual deficit. During the playing season his whole time is spent in breathing, thinking, talking baseball all day long: if he is not at the game, bent forward in his seat behind the home plate in an attitude of ravenous absorption, occasionally shouting advice and encouragement to the players in his rapid, stammering, rather high-pitched voice that has a curiously incisive penetration and carrying power, then he is up on the Square before the fire department going over every detail of the game with his cronies and asking eager, rapid-fire questions of the young red-necked players he employs, and towards whom he displays the worshipful admiration of a school-boy.

Now this man who, despite his doctor's orders, smokes twenty or thirty strong black cigars a day, and in fact is never to be seen without a cigar in his fingers or in his mouth—may be heard all over the crowd speaking eagerly in his rapid, stammering voice to a man with a quiet and pleasant manner who stands behind him. This is the assistant chief of the fire department and his name is Bickett:

"Jim," Mr. Jordan is saying in his eager and excited way, "I—I—I—I tell you what I think! If—if—if Speaker comes up there again with men on bases—I—I—I just believe Matty will strike him out—I swear I do. What do you think?" he demands eagerly and abruptly.

Mr. Bickett, first pausing to draw slowly and languorously on a cigarette before casting it into the gutter, makes some easy, quiet and non-committal answer which satisfies Mr. Jordan completely, since he is paying no attention to him anyway. Immediately, he claps the chewed cigar which he is holding in his stubby fingers into his mouth, and nodding his head briskly and vigorously, with an air of great decision, he stammers out again:

"Well—I—I—I just believe that's what he's going to do: I—I—I don't think he's afraid of that fellow at all! I—I—I think he knows he can strike him out any time he feels like it."

The boy knows every one in the crowd as he looks around him. Here are the other boys of his own age, and older—his fellow route-boys in the morning's work, his school companions, delivery boys employed by druggists, merchants, clothiers, the sons of the more wealthy and prominent people of the town. Here are the boys from the eastern part of town from which he comes and in which his father's house is built—the older, homelier, and for some reason more joyful and confident part of town to him—though why he does not know, he cannot say. Perhaps it is because the hills along the eastern borders of the town are near and close and warm, and almost to be touched. But in the western part of town, the great vistas of the soaring ranges, the distant summits of the Smokies fade far away into the west, into the huge loneliness, the haunting desolation of the unknown distance, the red, lonely light of the powerful retreating sun.

But now the old red light is slanting swiftly, the crowd is waiting tense and silent, already with a touch of sorrow, resignation, and the winter in their hearts, for summer's over, the game is ending, and October has come again, has come again. In the window, where the red slant of the sun already falls, Ben is moving quickly, slipping new placards into place, taking old ones out, scowling, snapping his hard, white fingers in command, speaking curtly, sharply, irritably to the busy figures, moving at his bidding on the floor. The game—the last game of the series—is sharp, close, bitterly contested. No one can say as yet which way the issue goes, which side will win, when it will end—but that fatality of red slanting light, the premonitory menace of the frost, the fatal certitude of victory and defeat, with all the sorrow and regret that both can bring to men, are in their hearts.

From time to time, a wild and sudden cheer breaks sharply from the waiting crowd, as something happens to increase their hope of victory, but for the most part they are tense and silent now, all waiting for the instant crisis, the quick end.

Behind Ben, seated in a swivel chair, but turned out facing toward the crowd, the boy can see the gouty bulk of Mr. Flood, the owner of the paper. He is bent forward heavily in his seat, his thick apoplectic fingers braced upon his knees, his mouth ajar, his coarse, jowled, venously empurpled face and bulging yellow eyes turned out upon the crowd, in their constant expression of slow stupefaction. From time to time, when the crowd cheers loudly, the expression of brutal surprise upon Mr. Flood's coarse face will deepen perceptibly and comically, and in a moment he will say stupidly, in his hoarse and phlegmy tones:

"Who done that? . . . What are they yelling for? . . . Which side's ahead now? . . . What happened that time, Ben?"

To which Ben usually makes no reply whatever, but the savage scowl between his gray eyes deepens with exasperation, and finally, cursing bitterly, he says:

"Damn it, Flood! What do you think I am—the whole damned newspaper? For heaven's sake, man, do you think all I've got to do is answer damn-fool questions! If you want to know what's happening, go outside where the rest of them are!"

"Well, Ben, I just wanted to know how—" Mr. Flood begins hoarsely, heavily, and stupidly.

"Oh, for God's sake! Listen to this, won't you?" says Ben, laughing scornfully and contemptuously as he addresses the invisible auditor of his scorn, and jerking his head sideways toward the bloated figure of his employer as he does so, "Here!" he says, in a disgusted manner. "For God's sake, some one go and tell him what the score is, and put him out of his misery!" And scowling savagely, he speaks sharply into the mouthpiece of the phone and puts another placard on the line.

And suddenly, even as the busy figures swarm and move there in the window before the waiting crowd, the bitter thrilling game is over! In waning light, in faint shadows, far, far away in a great city of the North, the 40,000 small empetalled faces bend forward, breathless, waiting— single and strange and beautiful as all life, all living, and man's destiny. There's a man on base, the last flash of the great right arm, the crack of the bat, the streaking white of a clean-hit ball, the wild, sudden, solid roar, a pair of flashing legs have crossed the rubber, and the game is over!

And instantly, there at the city's heart, in the great stadium, and all across America, in ten thousand streets, ten thousand little towns, the crowd is breaking, flowing, lost forever! That single, silent, most intolerable loveliness is gone forever. With all its tragic, proud and waiting unity, it belongs now to the huge, the done, the indestructible fabric of the past, has moved at last out of that inscrutable maw of chance we call the future into the strange finality of dark time.

Now it is done, the crowd is broken, lost, exploded, and 10,000,000 men are moving singly down 10,000 streets—toward what? Some by the light of Hesperus which, men say, can bring all things that live on earth to their own home again—flock to the fold, the father to his child, the lover to the love he has forsaken—and the proud of heart, the lost, the lonely of the earth, the exile and the wanderer—to what? To pace again the barren avenues of night, to pass before the bulbous light of lifeless streets with half averted faces, to pass the thousand doors, to feel again the ancient hopelessness of hope, the knowledge of despair, the faith of desolation.

And for a moment, when the crowd has gone, Ben stands there silent, lost, a look of bitter weariness, disgust, and agony upon his gray gaunt face, his lonely brow, his fierce and scornful eyes. And as he stands there that red light of waning day has touched the flashing head, the gaunt, starved face, has touched the whole image of his fiercely wounded, lost and scornful spirit with the prophecy of its strange fatality. And in that instant as the boy looks at his brother, a knife is driven through his entrails suddenly, for with an instant final certitude, past reason, proof, or any visual evidence, he sees the end and answer of his brother's life. Already death rests there on his proud head like a coronal. The boy knows in that one instant Ben will die.

XX

He visited Genevieve frequently over a period of several months. As his acquaintance with the family deepened, the sharpness of his appetite for seduction dwindled, and was supplanted by an ecstatic and insatiable glee. He felt that he had never in his life been so enormously and constantly amused: he would think exultantly for days of an approaching visit, weaving new and more preposterous fables for their consumption, bursting into violent laughter on the streets as he thought of past scenes, the implication of a tone, a gesture, the transparent artifice of mother and daughter, the incredible exaggeration of everything.

He was charmed, enchanted: his mind swarmed daily with monstrous projects—his heart quivered in a tight cage of nervous exultancy
as he thought of the infinite richness of absurdity that lay stored for
him. His ethical conscience was awakened hardly at all—he thought of
these three people as monsters posturing for his delight. His hatred of
cruelty, the nauseating horror at the idiot brutality of youth, had not
yet sufficiently defined itself to check his plunge. He was swept along
in the full tide of his adventure: he thought of nothing else.

Through an entire winter, and into the spring, he went to see this
little family in a Boston suburb. Then, he got tired of the game and the
people as suddenly as he had begun, with the passionate boredom, weariness, and intolerance of which youth is capable. And now that the affair
was ending, he was at last ashamed of the part he had played in it, and of
the arrogant contempt with which he had regaled himself at the expense of other people. And he knew that the Simpsons had themselves
at length become conscious of the meaning of his conduct, and saw that,
in some way, he had made them the butt of a joke. And when they saw
this, the family suddenly attained a curious quiet dignity, of which he
had not believed them capable and which later he could not forget.

One night, as he was waiting in the parlor for the girl to come down,
her mother entered the room, and stood looking at him quietly for a
moment. Presently she spoke:

"You have been coming here for some time, now," she said, "and we
were always glad to see you. My daughter liked you when she met you
—she likes you yet—" the woman said slowly, and went on with obvious difficulty and embarrassment. "Her welfare means more to me
than anything in the world—I would do anything to save her from un-
happiness or misfortune." She was silent a moment, then said bluntly,
"I think I have a right to ask you a question:—what are your intentions
concerning her?"

He told himself that these words were ridiculous and part of the
whole comic and burlesque quality of the family, and yet he found now
that he could not laugh at them. He sat looking at the fire, uncertain of
his answer, and presently he muttered:

"I have no intentions concerning her."

"All right," the woman said quietly. "That is all I wanted to know.
. . . You are a young man," she went on slowly after a pause, "and very
clever and intelligent—but there are still a great many things you do

not understand. I know now that we looked funny to you and you have amused yourself at our expense. . . . I don't know why you thought it was such a joke, but I think you will live to see the day when you are sorry for it. It's not good to make a joke of people who have liked you and tried to be your friends."

"I know it's not," he said, and muttered: "I'm sorry for it now."

"Still, I can't believe," the woman said, "that you are a boy who would wilfully bring sorrow and ruin to any one who had never done you any harm. . . . The only reason I am saying this is for my daughter's sake."

"You don't need to worry about that," he said. "I'm sorry now for acting as I have—but you know everything I've done. And I'll not come back again. But I'd like to see her, and tell her that I'm sorry before I go."

"Yes," the woman said, "I think you ought."

She went out and a few minutes later the girl came down, entered the room, and he said good-bye to her. He tried to make amends to her with fumbling words, but she said nothing. She stood very still as he talked, almost rigid, her lips pressed tightly together, her hands clenched, winking back the tears.

"All right," she said finally, giving him her hand. "I'll say good-bye to you without hard feelings. . . . Some day . . . some day," her voice choked and she winked furiously— "I hope you'll understand—oh, good-bye!" she cried, and turned away abruptly. "I'm not mad at you any longer—and I wish you luck. . . . You know so many things, don't you? —You're so much smarter than we are, aren't you? . . . And I'm sorry for you when I think of all you've got to learn . . . of what you're going through before you do."

"Good-bye," he said.

He never saw any of them again, but he could not forget them. And as the years went on, the memory of all their folly, falseness, and hypocrisy was curiously altered and subdued and the memory that grew more vivid and dominant was of a little family, one of millions huddled below the immense and timeless skies that bend above us, lost in the darkness of nameless and unnumbered lives upon the lonely wilderness of life that is America, and banked together against these giant antagonists, for comfort, warmth, and love, with a courage and integrity that would not die, and could not be forgotten.

XXI

ONE afternoon early in May, Helen met McGuire upon the street. He had just driven in behind Wood's Pharmacy on Academy Street, and was preparing to go in to the prescription counter when she approached him. He got out of his big dusty-looking roadster with a painful grunt, slammed the door, and began to fumble slowly in the pockets of his baggy coat for a cigarette. He turned slowly as she spoke, grunted, "Hello, Helen," stuck the cigarette on his fat under-lip and lighted it, and then looking at her with his brutal, almost stupid, but somehow kindly glance, he barked coarsely:

"What's on your mind?"

"It's about Papa," she began in a low, hoarse and almost morbid tone— "Now I want to know if this last attack means that the end has come. You've got to tell me—we've got the right to know about it——"

The look of strain and hysteria on her big-boned face, her dull eyes fixed on him in a morbid stare, the sore on her large cleft chin, above all, the brooding insistence of her tone as she repeated phrases he had heard ten thousand times before suddenly rasped upon his frayed nerves, stretched them to the breaking point; he lost his air of hard professionalism and exploded in a flare of brutal anger:

"You want to know what? You've got a right to be told what? For God's sake,"—his tone was brutal, rasping, jeering—"pull yourself together and stop acting like a child." And then, a little more quietly, but brusquely, he demanded:

"All right. What do you want to know?"

"I want to know how long he's going to last," she said with morbid insistence. "Now, you're a doctor," she wagged her large face at him with an air of challenge that infuriated him, "and you ought to tell us. We've got to know!"

"Tell you! Got to know!" he shouted. "What the hell are you talking about? What do you expect to be told?"

"How long Papa has to live," she said with the same morbid insistence as before.

"You've asked me that a thousand times," he said harshly. "I've told you that I didn't know. He may live another month, he may be here a year from now—how can we tell about these things," he said in an exasperated tone, "particularly where your father is concerned. Helen, three or four years ago I might have made a prediction. I did make them—I didn't see how W. O. could go on six months longer. But he's fooled us all—you, me, the doctors at Johns Hopkins, every one who's had anything to do with the case. The man is dying from malignant carcinoma—he has been dying for years—his life is hanging by a thread, and the thread may break at any time—but when it is going to break I have no way of telling you."

"Ah-hah," she said reflectively. Her eyes had taken on a dull appeased look as he talked to her, and now she had begun to pluck at her large cleft chin. "Then you think—" she began.

"I think nothing," he shouted. "And for God's sake stop picking at your chin!"

For a moment he felt the sudden brutal anger that one sometimes feels toward a contrary child. He felt like taking her by the shoulders and shaking her. Instead, he took it out in words and scowling at her, said with brutal directness:

"Look here! . . . You've got to pull yourself together. You're becoming a mental case—do you hear me? You wander around like a person in a dream, you ask questions no one can answer, you demand answers no one can give—you work yourself up into hysterical frenzies and then you collapse and soak yourself with drugs, patent medicines, corn licker—anything that has alcohol in it—for days at a time. When you go to bed at night you think you hear voices talking to you, some one coming up the steps, the telephone. And really you hear nothing: there is nothing there. Do you know what that is?" he demanded brutally. "Those are symptoms of insanity—you're becoming unbalanced, if it keeps on they may have to send you to the crazy-house to take the cure."

"Ah-hah! Uh-huh!" she kept plucking at her big chin with an air of abstracted reflection, and with a curious look of dull appeasement in her eyes as if his brutal words had really given her some comfort. Then she suddenly came to herself, looked at him with clear eyes, and, her generous mouth touched at the corners with the big lewd tracery of her earthy humor, she sniggered hoarsely, and prodding him in his fat ribs with a big bony finger, she said:

"You think I've got 'em, do you? Well—" she nodded seriously in agreement, frowning a little as she spoke, but with the faint grin still legible around the corners of her mouth,—"I've often thought the same thing. You may be right," she nodded seriously again. "There are times when I do feel off—you know?—*queer*—looney—crazy—like there was a screw loose somewhere— Brrr!" and with the strange lewd mixture of frown and grin, she made a whirling movement with her finger towards her head. "What do you think it is?" she went on with an air of seriousness. "Now, I'd just like to know. What is it that makes me act like that? . . . Is it woman-business?" she said with a lewd and comic look upon her face. "Am I getting funny like the rest of them— now I've often thought the same—that maybe I'm going through a change of life—is that it? Maybe——"

"Oh, change of life be damned!" he said in a disgusted tone. "Here you are a young woman thirty-two years old and you talk to me about a change of life! That has about as much sense to it as a lot of other things you say! The only thing you change is your mind—and you do that every five minutes!" He was silent for a moment, breathing heavily and staring at her coarsely with his bloated and unshaven face, his veined and weary-looking eyes. When he spoke again his voice was gruff and quiet, touched with a burly, almost paternal tenderness:

"Helen," he said, "I'm worried about you—and not about your father. Your father is an old man now with a malignant cancer and with no hope of ever getting well again. He is tired of life, he wants to die— for God's sake why do you want to prolong his suffering, to try to keep him here in a state of agony, when death would be a merciful release for him? . . . I know there is no hope left for your father: he has been doomed for years, the sooner the end comes the better——"

She tried to speak but he interrupted her brusquely, saying:

"Just a minute. There's something that I want to say to you—for God's sake try to use it, if you can. The death of this old man seems strange and horrible to you because he is your father. It is as hard for you to think about his death as it is to think about the death of God Almighty; you think that if your father dies there will be floods and earthquakes and convulsions throughout nature. I assure you that this is not true. Old men are dying every second of the day, and nothing happens except they die——"

"Oh, but Papa was a wonderful man," she said. "I *know!* I *know!* Everybody who ever knew him said the same."

"Yes," McGuire agreed, "he was—he was one of the most remarkable men I ever knew. And that is what makes it all the harder now."

She looked at him eagerly, and said:

"You mean—his dying?"

"No, Helen," McGuire spoke quietly and with a weary patience.

"There's nothing very bad about his dying. Death seems so terrible to you because you know so little about it. But I have seen so much of death, I have seen so many people die—and I know there is really nothing very terrible about it, and about the death of an old man ravaged by disease there is nothing terrible at all. It seems terrible to those looking on—there are," he shrugged his fat shoulders, "there are sometimes—physical details that are unpleasant. But the old man knows little of all that: an old man dies as a clock runs down—he is worn out, has lost the will to live, he wants to die, and he just stops. That is all. And that will happen to your father."

"Oh, but it will be so strange now—so hard to understand!" she muttered with a bewildered look in her eyes. "We have expected him to die so many times—we have been fooled so often—and now I can't believe that it will ever happen. I thought that he would die in 1916, I never expected him to live another year; in 1918, the year that Ben died, none of us could see how he'd get through the winter—and then Ben died! No one had even thought of Ben—" her voice grew cracked and hoarse and her eyes glistened with tears. "We had forgotten Ben—every one was thinking about Papa—and then when Ben died, I turned against Papa for a time. For a while I was bitter against him—it seemed that I had done everything for this old man, that I had given him everything I had—my life, my strength, my energy—all because I thought that he was going to die—and then Ben, who had never been given anything—who had had nothing out of life—who had been neglected and forgotten by us all and who was the best one—the most decent one of the whole crowd—Ben was the one who had to go. For a time after his death I didn't care what happened—to Papa or to any one else. I was so bitter about Ben's death—it seemed so cruel, so rotten and unjust—that it had to be Ben of all the people in the world—only twenty-six years old and without a thing to show for his life—no love, no children, no happiness, cheated out of everything, when Papa had had so much—I couldn't stand the thought of it, even now I hate to go to Mama's house, it almost kills me to go near Ben's room, I've never been in it since the night he died—and somehow I was bitter against Papa! It seemed to me that he had cheated me, tricked me—at times I got so bitter that I thought that he was responsible in some way for Ben's death. I said I was through with him, that I would do nothing else for him, that I had done all that I intended to do, and that somebody else would have to take care of him. . . . But it all came back; he had another bad spell and I was afraid that he was going to die, and I couldn't stand the thought of it. . . . And it has gone on now so long, *year* after year, and *year* after year," she said in a frenzied tone, "always thinking that he couldn't last and seeing him come back again, that I couldn't believe that it would ever happen. I can't believe it now. . . . And what am I going to do?" she said hoarsely and desperately, clutching McGuire by the sleeve, "what am I going to do now if he really dies? What is there left for me in life with Papa gone?" Her voice was almost sobbing now with grief and desperation— "He's all I've got to live for, Doctor McGuire. I've got nothing out of life that I wanted or expected—it's all been so different from the way I thought it was—I've had nothing—no fame, no glory, no success, no children—everything has gone—Papa is all that I have left! If he dies what shall I do?" she cried frantically, shaking him by the sleeve. "That old man is all I've got—the only thing I've got left to live for; to keep him alive, to make him comfortable, to ease his pain, to see he gets good food and attention—somehow, somehow," she panted desperately, clasping her big bony hands in a gesture of unconscious but pitiable entreaty, and beginning to rock unsteadily on her feet as she spoke—"somehow, somehow, to keep life in him, to keep him here, not to let him go—that's all I've got to live for—what in the name of God am I going to do when that is taken from me?"

And she paused, panting and exhausted by her tirade, her big face strained and quivering, glaring at him with an air of frantic entreaty as if it was in his power to give the answers to these frenzied questions. And for a moment he said nothing; he just stood there looking at her with the coarse and brutal stare of his blotched face, his venous yellowed eyes, the wet cigarette stuck comically at the corner of one fat lip.

"What are you going to do?" he barked, presently. "You're going to get hold of yourself—pull yourself together—amount to something, be somebody!" He coughed chokingly to one side, for a moment there was just the sound of his thick short breathing, then he flung the cigarette away, and said quietly:

"Helen, for God's sake, don't throw your life away! Don't destroy the great creature that lies buried in you somewhere—wake it up, make it come to life. Don't talk to me of this old man's life as if it were your own——"

"It is, it is!" she said in a brooding tone of morbid fatality.

"It is not!" he said curtly, "unless you make it so—unless you play the weakling and the fool and throw yourself away. For God's sake, don't let that happen to you. I have seen it happen to so many people—some of them fine people like yourself, full of energy, imagination, intelligence, ability—all thrown away, frittered away like that," he flung fat fingers in the air—"because they did not have the guts to use what God had given them—to make a new life for themselves—to stand on their own feet and not to lean upon another's shoulder! . . . Don't die the death!" he rasped coarsely, staring at her with his brutal face. "Don't die the rotten, lousy, dirty death-in-life—the only death that's really horrible! For God's sake, don't betray life and yourself and the people who love you by dying that kind of death! I've seen it happen to so many people—and it was always so damned useless, such a rotten waste! That's what I was trying to say to you a few minutes ago—it's not the death of the dying that is terrible, it is the death of the living. And we always die that death for the same reason:—because our father dies, and takes from us his own life, his world, his time—and we haven't courage enough to make a new life, a new world for ourselves. I wonder if you know how often that thing happens—how often I have seen it happen—the wreck, the ruin, and the tragedy it has caused in life! When the father goes, the whole structure of the family life goes with him—and unless his children have the will, the stuff, the courage to make something of their own, they die, too. . . . With you, it's going to be very hard when your father dies; he was a man of great vitality and a strong personality who has left a deep impression on every one who knew him. And for seven years now, your father's death has been your life. . . . It has become a part of you, you have brooded over it, lived with it, soaked in it, been tainted by it—and now it is going to be hard for you to escape. But escape you must, and stand on your own feet—or you are lost. . . . Helen!" he barked sharply, and fixed her with his coarse and brutal stare—"listen to me:—your childhood, Woodson Street, getting your father over drunks, cooking for him, nursing him, feeding him, dressing and undressing him—I know about it all, I saw it all—and now!"—he paused, staring at her, then made a sudden gesture outward, palms downward, of his two thick hands—"over, done for, gone forever! It's no good any more, it won't work any more, it can't be brought back any more—forget about it!"

"Oh, I can't! I can't!" she said desperately. "I can't give him up—I can't let him go—he's all I've got. Doctor McGuire," she said earnestly, "ever since I was a kid of ten and you first came to get Papa over one of his sprees, I've fairly worshipped you! I've always felt down in my

heart that you were one of the most wonderful people—the most wonderful doctor—in the world! I've always felt that at the end you could
do anything—perform a miracle—bring him back. For God's sake, don't
go back on me now! Do something—anything you can—but save him,
save him."

He was silent for a moment, and just stared at her with his yellow,
venous eyes. And when he spoke his voice was filled with the most
quiet and utter weariness of despair that she had ever heard:

"Save him?" he said. "My poor child, I can save no one—nothing—
least of all myself."

And suddenly she saw that it was true; she saw that he was lost, that
he was done for, gone, and that he knew it. His coarse and bloated face
was mottled by great black purplish patches, his yellow weary eyes already had the look of death in them; the knowledge of death rested
with an unutterable weariness in his burly form, was audible in the
short thick labor of his breath. She saw instantly that he was going to
die, and with that knowledge her heart was torn with a rending pity as
if a knife had been driven through it and twisted there; all of the brightness dropped out of the day, and in that moment it seemed that the
whole substance and structure of her life was gone.

The day was a shining one, full of gold and sapphire and sparkle, and
in the distance, toward the east, she could see the sweet familiar green
of hills. She knew that nothing had been changed at all, and yet even
the brightness of the day seemed dull and common to her. It served
only to make more mean and shabby the rusty buildings and the street
before her. And the bright light filled her with a nameless uneasiness
and sense of shame: it seemed to expose her, to show her imperfections
nakedly, and instinctively she turned away from it into the drugstore,
where there were coolness, artificial lights and gaiety, the clamor of
voices and people that she knew. And she knew that most of them had
come here for the same reason—because the place gave them a sort of
haven, however brief and shabby, from the naked brightness of the day
and their sense of indefinable uncertitude and shame—because "it was
the only place there was to go."

Several young people, two girls and a boy were coming down among
the crowded tables towards one of the mirrored booths against the
wall, where another boy and girl were waiting for them. As they approached, she heard their drawling voices, talking "cute nigger-talk"
as her mind contemptuously phrased it, the vapid patter phrased to a

monotonous formula of "charm," inane, cheap, completely vulgar, and as if they had been ugly little monsters of some world of dwarfs she listened to them with a detached perspective of dislike and scorn.

One of the girls—the one already in the booth—was calling to the others in tones of playful protest, in her "cute," mannered, empty little voice:

"*Hey,* theah, you all! *Wheah* you been! Come *on,* heah, man!" she cried urgently and reproachfully toward the approaching youth— "We been lookin' up an' down faw you! What you been doin', anyhow?" she cried with reproachful curiosity. "We been *waitin'* heah an' waitin' heah until it seemed lak you nevah *would* come! We wuh about to give you up!"

"Child!" another of the girls drawled back, and made a languid movement of the hand—a move indicative of resignation and defeat. "Don't tawk! I thought we nevah would get away. . . . That Jawdan woman came in to see Mothah just as me an' Jim was fixin' to go out, an' child!"—again the languid movement of exhaustion and defeat— "when that woman gits stahted tawkin' you might as well give up! No one else can git a wuhd in edgeways. I'll declayah!" the voice went up, and the hand again made its languid movement of surrender— "I nevah huhd the lak of it in all mah days! That's the tawkinest woman that evah lived. You'd a-died if you could a-seen the way Jim looked. I thought he was goin' to pass right out befoah we got away from theah!"

"Lady," said Jim, who had as yet taken no part in the conversation, "you *said* it! It sho'ly is the truth! That sho is *one* tawkin' woman— an' I don't mean *maybe,* eithah!" He drawled these words out with an air of pert facetiousness, and then looked round him with a complacent smirk on his young, smooth, empty face to see if his display of wit had been noticed and properly appreciated.

And Helen, passing by, kept smiling, plucking at her chin abstractedly, feeling toward these young people a weary disgust that was tinged with a bitter and almost personal animosity.

"Awful little made up girls . . . funny-looking little boys . . . nothing to do but hang out here and loaf . . . walk up and down the street . . . and drink coca-cola all day long . . . and to think it seemed so wonderful to me when I was a kid, to dress up and go up town and come in here where Papa was. . . . How dull and cheap and dreary it all is!"

XXII

A LITTLE after three o'clock one morning in June, Hugh McGuire was seated at his desk in the little office which stood just to the left of the entrance hall at the Altamont Hospital, of which institution he was chief of staff and principal owner. McGuire's burly bloated form was seated in a swivel chair and sprawled forward, his fat arms resting on the desk which was an old-fashioned roll-top affair with a number of small cubby-holes above and with two parallel rows of drawers below. In the space below the desk and between the surgeon's fat legs there was a gallon jug of corn whiskey.

And on the desk there was a stack of letters which had also been delivered to him the day before. The letters had been written to one of McGuire's own colleagues by a certain very beautiful lady of the town, of whom it is only necessary to say that she was not McGuire's wife and that he had known her for a long time. The huge man—curiously enough, not only a devoted father and a loyal husband, but a creature whose devotion to his family had been desperately intensified by the bitter sense of his one unfaith—had been for many years obsessed by one of those single, fatal and irremediable passions which great creatures of this sort feel only once in life, and for just one woman. Now the obsession of that mad fidelity was gone—exploded in an instant by a spidery scheme of words upon a page, a packet of torn letters in a woman's hand. Hence, this sense now of a stolid, slow, and cureless anguish in the man, the brutal deliberation of his drunkenness. Since finding these letters upon his desk when he had returned at seven o'clock the night before from his visit to Gant, McGuire had not left his office or moved in his chair, except to bend with a painful grunt from time to time, feel between his legs with a fat hand until he found the jug, and then, holding it with a bear-like solemnity between his paws, drink long and deep of the raw, fiery, and colorless liquid in the jug. He had done this very often, and now the jug was two-thirds empty. As he read, his mouth was half open and a cigarette was stuck on the corner of one fat lip, a look that suggested a comical drunken stupefaction. The hospital had long since gone to sleep, and in the little office there was no sound save the ticking of a clock and McGuire's short, thick, and stertorous breathing. Then when he had finished a letter, he would fold it carefully, put it back in its envelope, rub his thick fingers across the stubble of brown-reddish beard that covered his bloated and discolored face, reach with a painful grunt for the glass jug, drink, and open up another letter.

And from time to time he would put a letter down before he had finished reading it, take up a pen, and begin to write upon a sheet of broad hospital stationery, of which there was a pad upon the desk. And McGuire wrote as he read, slowly, painfully, carefully, with a fixed and drunken attentiveness, no sound except the minute and careful scratching of the pen in his fat hands, and the short, thick stertorous breathing as he bent over the tablet, his cigarette plastered comically at the edge of one fat lip.

McGuire would read the letters over and over, slowly, carefully, and solemnly. Burly, motionless and with no sound save for the short and stertorous labor of his breath he stared with drunken fixity at the pages which he held close before his yellowed eyes, his bloated face. He had read each letter at least a dozen times during the course of the long evening. And each time that he finished reading it, he would fold it carefully with his thick fingers, put it back into its envelope, bend and reach down between his fat legs with a painful grunt, fumble for the liquor jug, and then drink long and deep.

It seemed that a red-hot iron had been driven through his heart and twisted there; the liquor burned in his blood and guts like fire; and each time that he had finished reading that long letter, he would grunt, reach for the jug again, and then slowly and painfully begin to scrawl some words down on the pad before him.

He had done this at least a dozen times that night, and each time after a few scrawled lines, he would grunt impatiently, wad the paper up into a crumpled ball and throw it into the waste-paper basket at his side. Now, a little after three o'clock in the morning, he was writing steadily; there was no sound now in the room save for the man's thick short breathing, and the minute scratching of his pen across the paper. An examination of these wadded balls of paper, however, in the order in which they had been written, would have revealed perfectly the successive states of feeling in the man's spirit.

The first, which was written after his discovery of the letters, was just a few scrawled words without punctuation or grammatical coherence, ending abruptly in an explosive splintered movement of the pen, and read simply and expressively as follows:

"You bitch you damned dirty trollop of a lying whore you——"

And this ended here in an explosive scrawl of splintered ink, and had been wadded up and thrown away into the basket.

XXIII

HELEN had lain awake for hours in darkness, in a strange comatose state of terror and hallucination. There was no sound save the sound of Barton's breathing beside her, but in her strange drugged state she would imagine she heard all kinds of sounds. And she lay there in the dark, her eyes wide open, wide awake, plucking at her large cleft chin abstractedly, in a kind of drugged hypnosis, thinking like a child:

"What is that? ... Some one is coming! ... That was a car that stopped outside. ... Now they're coming up the steps. ... There's some one knocking at the door. ... Oh, my God! ... It's about Papa! ... He's had another attack, they've come to get me ... he's dead! ... Hugh! Hugh! Wake up!" she said hoarsely, and seized him by the arm. And he woke, his sparse hair touselled, grumbling sleepily.

"Hugh! Hugh!" she whispered. "It's Papa—he's dying ... they're at the door now! ... oh, for heaven's sake, get up!" she almost screamed, in a state of frenzied despair and exasperation. "Aren't you good for anything! ... Don't lie there like a dummy—Papa may be dying! Get up! Get up! There's some one at the door! My God, you can at least go and find out what it is! Oh, get up, get up, I tell you! ... Don't leave everything to me! You're a man—you can at least do that much!" —and by now her voice was almost sobbing with exasperation.

"Well, *all* right, *all* right!" he grumbled in a tone of protest, "I'm going! Only give me a moment to find my slippers and my bath-robe, won't you?"

And, hair still twisted, tall, bony, thin to emaciation, he felt around with his bare feet until he found his slippers, stepped gingerly into them, and put on his bath-robe, tying the cord around his waist, and looking himself over in the mirror carefully, smoothing down his rumpled hair and making a shrugging motion of the shoulders. And she looked at him with a tortured and exasperated glare, saying:

"Oh, slow, slow, slow! ... My God, you're the slowest thing that ever lived! ... I could walk from here to California in the time it takes you to get out of bed."

"Well, *I'm* going, *I'm* going," he said again with surly protest. "I don't want to go to the front door naked—only give me a minute to get ready, won't you?"

"Then, go, go, go!" she almost screamed at him. "They've been there for fifteen minutes. . . . They're almost hammering the door down—for God's sake go and find out if they've come because of Papa, I beg of you."

And he went hastily, still preserving a kind of dignity as he stepped along gingerly in his bath-robe and thin pyjamaed legs. And when he got to the door, there was no one, nothing there. The street outside was bare and empty, the houses along the street dark and hushed with their immense and still attentiveness of night and silence and the sleepers, the trees were standing straight and lean with their still young leafage—and he came back again growling surlily.

"Ah-h, there's no one there! You didn't hear anything! . . . You imagined the whole thing!"

And for a moment her eyes had a dull appeased look, she plucked at her large cleft chin and said in an abstracted tone: "Ah-hah! . . . Well, come on back to bed, honey, and get some sleep."

"Ah, get some sleep!" he growled, scowling angrily as he took off his robe—and scuffed the slippers from his feet. "What chance do I have to get any sleep any more with you acting like a crazy woman half the time?"

She snickered hoarsely and absently, still plucking at her chin, as he lay down beside her; she kissed him, and put her arms around him with a mothering gesture:

"Well, I know, Hugh," she said quietly, "you've had a hard time of it, but someday we will get away from it and live our own life. I know you didn't marry the whole damn family—but just try to put up with it a little longer: Papa has not got long to live, he's all alone over there in that old house—and she can't realize—she doesn't understand that he is dying—she'll never wake up to the fact until he's gone! I lie here at night thinking about it—and I can't go to sleep . . . I get funny notions in my head." As she spoke these words the dull strained look came into her eyes again, and her big-boned generous face took on the warped outline of hysteria— "You know, I get queer." She spoke the word in a puzzled and baffled way, the dull strained look becoming more pronounced— "I think of him over there all alone in that old house, and then I think they're coming for me—" she spoke the word "they" in this same baffled and puzzled tone, as if she did not clearly understand who "they" were— "I think the telephone is ringing, or that some one is coming up the steps and then I hear them knocking at the door, and then I hear them talking to me, telling me to come quick, he needs me—

and then I hear him calling to me 'Baby! Oh, baby—come quick, baby, for Jesus' sake!' "

"You've been made the goat," he muttered, "you've got to bear the whole burden on your shoulders. You're cracking up under the strain. If they don't leave you alone I'm going to take you away from here."

"Do you think it's right?" she demanded in a frenzied tone again, responding thirstily to his argument. "Why, good heavens, Hugh! I've got a right to my own life the same as anybody else. Don't you think I have? I married *you!*" she cried, as if there were some doubt of the fact. "I wanted a home of my own, children, my own life—good heavens, we have a right to that just the same as any one else! Don't you think we have?"

"Yes," he said grimly, "and I'm going to see we get it. I'm tired of seeing you made the victim! If they don't give you some peace or quiet we'll move away from this town."

"Oh, it's not that I mind doing it for Papa," she said more quietly. "Good heavens, I'll do anything to make that poor old man happier. If only the rest of them—well, honey," she said, breaking off abruptly, "let's forget about it! It's too bad you've got to go through all this now, but it won't last forever. After Papa is gone, we'll get away from it. Some day we'll have a chance to lead our own lives together."

"Oh, it's all right about me, dear," the man said quietly, speaking the word "dear" in the precise and nasal way Ohio people have. He was silent for a moment, and when he spoke again, his lean seamed face and care-worn eyes were quietly eloquent with the integrity of devotion and loyalty that was of the essence of his life. "I don't mind it for myself—only I hate to see you get yourself worked up to this condition. I'm afraid you'll crack under the strain: that's all I care about."

"Well, forget about it. It can't be helped. Just try to make the best of it. Now go on back to sleep, honey, and try to get some rest before you have to get up."

And returning her kiss, with an obedient and submissive look on his lean face, he said quietly, "Good night, dear," turned over on his side and closed his eyes.

She turned the light out, and now again there was nothing but darkness, silence, the huge still hush and secrecy of night, her husband's quiet breath of sleep as he lay beside her. And again she could not sleep, but lay there plucking absently at her large cleft chin, her eyes open, turned upward into darkness in a stare of patient, puzzled, and abstracted thought.

XXIV

For a long time now, McGuire had sat there without moving, sprawled out upon the desk in a kind of drunken stupor. About half-past three the telephone upon the desk began to ring, jangling the hospital silence with its ominous and insistent clangor, but the big burly figure of the man did not stir, he made no move to answer. Presently he heard the brisk heel-taps of Creasman, the night superintendent, coming along the heavy oiled linoleum of the corridor. She entered, glanced quickly at him, and saying, "Shall I take it?" picked up the phone, took the receiver from its hook, said "hello" and listened for a moment. He did not move.

In a moment, the night superintendent said quietly:

"Yes, I'll ask him."

When she spoke to him, however, her tone had changed completely from the cool professional courtesy of her speech into the telephone: putting the instrument down upon the top of the desk, and covering the mouth-piece with her hand, she spoke quietly to him, but with a note of cynical humor in her voice, bold, coarse, a trifle mocking.

"It's your wife," she said. "What shall I tell her?"

He regarded her stupidly for a moment before he answered.

"What does she want?" he grunted.

She looked at him with hard eyes touched with pity and regret.

"What do you think a woman wants?" she said. "She wants to know if you are coming home tonight."

He stared at her, and then grunted:

"Won't go home."

She took her hand away from the mouth-piece instantly, and taking up the phone again, spoke smoothly, quietly, with cool crisp courtesy:

"The doctor will not be able to go home tonight, Mrs. McGuire. He has to operate at seven-thirty. . . . Yes. . . . Yes. . . . At seven-thirty. . . . He has decided it is best to stay here until the operation is over. . . . Yes. . . . I'll tell him. . . . Thank *you*. . . . Good-bye."

She hung up quietly and then turning to him, her hands arched cleanly on starched hips, she looked at him for a moment with a bold sardonic humor.

"What did she say?" he mumbled thickly.

"Nothing," she said quietly. "Nothing at all. What else is there to say?"

He made no answer but just kept staring at her in his bloated drunken way with nothing but the numb swelter of that irremediable anguish in his heart. In a moment, her voice hardening imperceptibly, the nurse spoke quietly again:

"Oh, yes—and I forgot to tell you—you had another call tonight."

He moistened his thick lips, and mumbled:

"Who was it?"

"It was that woman of yours."

There was no sound save the stertorous labor of his breath; he stared at her with his veined and yellowed eyes, and grunted stolidly:

"What did she want?"

"She wanted to know if the doc-taw was theah," Creasman said in a coarse and throaty parody of refinement. "And is he coming in tonight? Really, I should like to know. . . . Ooh, yaas," Creasman went on throatily, adding a broad stroke or two on her own account. "I simply must find out! I cawn't get my sleep in until I do. . . . Well," she demanded harshly, "what am I going to tell her if she calls again?"

"What did she say to tell me?"

"She said"—the nurse's tone again was lewdly tinged with parody—"to tell you that she is having guests for dinner tomorrow night—this evening—and that you simply *got* to be thöh, you, and your wife, too—ooh, Gawd, yes!—the Reids are comin', don't-cherknow—and if you are not thöh Gawd only knows what will happen!"

He glowered at her drunkenly for a moment, and then, waving thick fingers at her in disgust, he mumbled:

"You got a dirty mouth . . . don't become you. . . . Unlady-like. . . . Don't like a dirty-talkin' woman. . . . Never did. . . . Unbecomin'. . . . Unlady-like. . . . Nurses all alike . . . all dirty talkers . . . don't like 'em."

"Oh, dirty talkers, your granny!" she said coarsely. "Now you leave the nurses alone. . . . They're decent enough girls, most of 'em, until they come here and listen to you for a month or two. . . . You listen to me, Hugh McGuire; don't blame the nurses. When it comes to dirty talking, you can walk off with the medals any day in the week. . . . Even if I am your cousin, I had a good Christian raising out in the country before I came here. So don't talk to me about nurses' dirty talk: after a few sessions with you in the operating room even the Virgin Mary could use language fit to make a monkey blush. So don't blame it on the nurses. Most of them are white as snow compared to you."

"You're dirty talkers—all of you," he muttered, waving his thick fingers in her direction. "Don't like it. . . . Unbecomin' in a lady."

For a moment she did not answer, but stood looking at him, arms akimbo on her starched white hips, a glance that was bold, hard, sardonic, but somehow tinged with a deep and broad affection.

Then, taking her hands off her hips, she bent swiftly over him, reached down between his legs, and got the jug and lifting it up to the light in order to make her cynical inspection of its depleted contents more accurate, she remarked with ironic approbation:

"My, my! You're doing pretty well, aren't you? . . . Well, it won't be long *now*, will it?" she said cheerfully, and then turning to him abruptly and accusingly, demanded:

"Do you realize that you were supposed to call Helen Gant at twelve o'clock?" She glanced swiftly at the clock. "Just three and a half hours ago. Or did you forget it?"

He passed his thick hand across the reddish unshaved stubble of his beard.

"Who?" he said stupidly. "Where? What is it?"

"Oh, nothing to worry about," she said with a light hard humor. "Just a little case of carcinoma of the prostate. He's going to die anyway, so you've got nothing to worry about at all."

"Who?" he said stupidly again. "Who is it?"

"Oh, just a man," she said gaily. "An old, old man named Mr. Gant.— You've been his physician for twenty years, but maybe you've forgotten him. You know—they come and go; some live and others die—it's all right,—this one's going to die. They'll bury him—it'll all come out right one way or the other—so you've nothing to worry about at all. . . . Even if you kill him," she said cheerfully. "He's just an old, old man with cancer, and bound to die anyway, so promise me you won't worry about it too much, will you?"

She looked at him a moment longer; then, putting her hand under his fat chin, she jerked his head up sharply. He stared at her stupidly with his yellowed drunken eyes, and in them she saw the mute anguish of a tortured animal, and suddenly her heart was twisted with pity for him.

"Look here," she said, in a hard and quiet voice, "what's wrong with you?"

In a moment he mumbled thickly:

"Nothing's wrong with me."

"Is it the woman business again? For God's sake, are you never going to grow up, McGuire? Are you going to remain an overgrown school-boy all your life? Are you going to keep on eating your heart out over a bitch who thinks that spring is here every time her hind end itches? Are you going to throw your life away, and let your work go to smash because some damned woman in the change of life has done you dirt! What kind of man are you, anyway?" she jeered. "Jesus God! If it's a woman that you want the woods are full of 'em. Besides," she added, "what's wrong with your own wife! She's worth a million of those flossy sluts."

He made no answer and in a moment she went on in a harsh and jeering tone that was almost deliberately coarse:

"Haven't you learned yet, with all you've seen of it, that a piece of tail is just a piece of tail, and that in the dark it doesn't matter one good God-damn whether it's brown, black, white, or yellow?"

Even as she spoke, something cold and surgical in his mind, which no amount of alcohol seemed to dull or blur, was saying accurately: "Why do they all feel such contempt for one another? What is it in them that makes them despise themselves?"

Aloud, however, waving his thick fingers at her in a gesture of fat disgust, he said:

"Creasman, you got a dirty tongue. . . . Don't like to hear a woman talk like that. . . . Never liked to hear a dirty-talkin' woman. . . . You're no lady!"

"Ah-h! No lady!" she said bitterly, and let her hands fall in a ges-ture of defeat. "All right, you poor fool, if that's the way you feel about it, go ahead and drink yourself to death over your 'lady.' That's what's wrong with you."

And, muttering angrily, she left him. He sat there stupidly, without moving, until her firm heel-taps had receded down the silent hall, and he heard a door close. Then he reached down between his knees, and got the jug, and drank again. And again there was nothing in the place ex-cept the sound of silence, the rapid ticking of a little clock, the thick short breathing of the man.

XXV

SOMEWHERE, far away, across the cool sweet silence of the night, Helen heard the sound of a train. For a moment she could hear the faint and ghostly tolling of its bell, the short explosive blasts of its hard labor, now muted almost into silence, now growing near, immediate as it labored out across the night from the enclosure of a railway cut down by the river's edge; and for an instant she heard the lonely wailing and receding cry of the train's whistle, and then the long heavy rumble of its wheels; and then nothing but silence, darkness, the huge hush and secrecy of night again.

And still plucking at her chin, thinking absently, but scarcely conscious of her thinking, like a child in revery, she thought:

"There is a freight-train going west along the river. Now, by the sound, it should be passing below Patton Hill, just across from where Riverside Park used to be before the flood came and washed it all away. . . . Now it is getting farther off, across the river from the casket factory. . . . Now it is almost gone, I can hear nothing but the sound of wheels . . . it is going west toward Boiling Springs . . . and after that it will come to Wilson City, Tennessee . . . and then to Dover. . . . Knoxville . . . Memphis—after that? I wonder where the train is going . . . where it will be tomorrow night? . . . Perhaps across the Mississippi River, and then on through Arkansas . . . perhaps to St. Louis . . . and then on to—what comes next?" she thought absently, plucking at her chin—"to Kansas City, I suppose . . . and then to Denver . . . and across the Rocky Mountains . . . and across the desert . . . and then across more mountains and then at last to California."

And still plucking at her chin, and scarcely conscious of her thought —not *thinking* indeed so much as reflecting by a series of broken but powerful images all cogent to a central intuition about life—her mind resumed again its sleepless patient speculation:

"How strange and full of mystery life is. . . . Tomorrow we shall all get up, dress, go out on the streets, see and speak to one another—and yet we shall know absolutely nothing about any one else. . . . I know almost every one in town—the bankers, the lawyers, the butchers, the bakers, the grocers, the clerks in the stores, the Greek restaurant man, Tony Scarsati the fruit dealer, even the niggers down in Niggertown— I know them all, as well as their wives and children—where they came from, what they are doing, all the lies and scandals and jokes and mean stories, whether true or false, that are told about them—and yet I really know nothing about any of them. I know nothing about any one, not even about myself—" and suddenly, this fact seemed terrible and grotesque to her, and she thought desperately:

"What is wrong with people? . . . Why do we never get to know one another? . . . Why is it that we get born and live and die here in this world without ever finding out what any one else is like? . . . No, what is the strangest thing of all—why is it that all our efforts to know people in this world lead only to greater ignorance and confusion than before? We get together and talk, and say we think and feel and believe in such a way, and yet what we really think and feel and believe we never say at all. Why is this? We talk and talk in an effort to understand another person, and yet almost all we say is false: we hardly ever say what we mean or tell the truth—it all leads to greater misunderstanding and fear than before—it would be better if we said nothing. Tomorrow I shall dress and go out on the street and bow and smile and flatter people, laying it on with a trowel, because I want them to like me, I want to make 'a good impression,' to be a 'success'—and yet I have no notion what it is all about. When I pass Judge Junius Pearson on the street, I will smile and bow, and try to make a good impression on him, and if he speaks to me I shall almost fawn upon him in order to flatter my way into his good graces. Why? I do not like him, I hate his long pointed nose, and the sneering and disdainful look upon his face: I think he is 'looking down' on me—but I know that he goes with the 'swell' social set and is invited out to all the parties at Catawba House by Mrs. Goulderbilt and is received by them as a social equal. And I feel that if Junius Pearson should accept me as *his* social equal it would help me— get me forward somehow—make me a success—get *me* an invitation to Catawba House. And yet it would get me nothing; even if I were Mrs. Goulderbilt's closest friend, what good would it do me? But the people I really like and feel at home with are working people of Papa's kind. The people I really like are Ollie Gant, and old man Alec Ramsay, and big Mike Fogarty, and Mr. Jannadeau, and Myrtis, my little nigger servant girl, and Mr. Luther, the fish man down in the market, and the nigger Jacken, the fruit and vegetable man, and Ernest Pegram, and Mr. Duncan and the Tarkintons—all the old neighbors down on Woodson Street—and Tony Scarsati and Mr. Pappas. Mr. Pappas is just a Greek lunchroom proprietor, but he seems to me to be one of the finest people I have ever known, and yet if Junius Pearson saw me talking to him I should try to make a joke out of it—to make a joke out of talking to a Greek who runs a restaurant. In the same way, when some of my new friends see me talking to people like Mr. Jannadeau or Mike Fogarty or Ollie or Ernest Pegram or the Tarkintons or the old Woodson Street crowd, I feel ashamed or embarrassed, and turn it off as a big joke. I laugh about Mr. Jannadeau and his dirty fingers and the way he picks his nose, and old Alec Ramsay and Ernest Pegram spitting tobacco while they talk, and then I wind up by appearing to be democratic and saying in a frank and open manner— 'Well, I like them ... I don't care what any one says' (when no one has said anything!), 'I like them, and always have. If the truth is told, they're just as good as any one else!'—as if there is any doubt about it, and as if I should have to justify myself for being 'democratic.' Why 'democratic'? Why should I apologize or defend myself for liking people when no one has accused me?

"I'm pushing Hugh ahead now all the time; he's tired and sick and worn-out and exhausted—but I keep 'pushing him ahead' without knowing what it is we're pushing ahead toward, where it will all wind up. What is it all about? I've pushed him ahead from Woodson Street up here to Weaver Street: and now this neighborhood has become old-fashioned—the swell society crowd is all moving out to Grovemont— opposite the golf-course; and now I'm pushing him to move out there, build upon the lot we own, or buy a house. I've 'pushed' him and myself until now he belongs to the Rotary Club, and I belong to the Thursday Literary Club, the Orpheus Society, the Saturday Musical Guild, the Woman's Club, the Discussion Group, and God knows what else—all these silly and foolish little clubs in which we have no interest—and yet it would kill us if we did not belong to them, we feel that they are a sign that we are 'getting ahead.' Getting ahead to what?

"And it is the same with all of us: pretend, pretend, pretend—show-off, show-off, show-off—try to keep up with the neighbors and to go ahead of them—and never a word of truth; never a word of what we really feel, and understand and know. The one who shouts the loudest goes the farthest:—Mrs. Richard Jeter Ebbs sits up on top of the whole heap, she goes everywhere and makes speeches; people say 'Mrs. Richard Jeter Ebbs said so-and-so'—and all because she shouts out everywhere that she is a lady and a member of an old family and the widow of Richard Jeter Ebbs. And no one in town ever met Richard Jeter Ebbs, they don't know who he was, what he did, where he came from; neither do they know who Mrs. Richard Jeter Ebbs was, or where she came from, or who or what her family was.

"Why are we all so false, cowardly, cruel, and disloyal toward one an-other and toward ourselves? Why do we spend our days in doing useless things, in false-pretense and triviality? Why do we waste our lives—exhaust our energy—throw everything good away on falseness and lies and emptiness? Why do we deliberately destroy ourselves this way, when we want joy and love and beauty and it is all around us in the world if we would only take it? Why are we so afraid and ashamed when there is really nothing to be afraid and ashamed of? Why have we wasted everything, thrown our lives away, what is this horrible thing in life that makes us throw ourselves away—to hunt out death when what we want is life? Why is it that we are always strangers in this world, and never come to know one another, and are full of fear and shame and hate and falseness, when what we want is love? Why is it? Why? Why? Why?"

And with that numb horror of disbelief and silence and the dark about her, in her, filling her, it seemed to her suddenly that there was some monstrous and malevolent force in life that held all mankind in its spell and that compelled men to destroy themselves against their will. It seemed to her that everything in life—the things men did and said, the way they acted—was grotesque, perverse, and accidental, that there was no reason for anything.

A thousand scenes from her whole life, seen now with the terrible detachment of a spectator, and dark and sombre with the light of time, swarmed through her mind: she saw herself as a child of ten, hanging on grimly to her father, a thin fury of a little girl, during his sprees of howling drunkenness—slapping him in the face to make him obey her, feeding him hot soup, undressing him, sending for McGuire, "sobering him up" and forcing him to obey her when no one else could come near him. And she saw herself later, a kind of slavey at her mother's boarding house in St. Louis during the World's Fair, drudging from morn to night, a grain of human dust, an atom thrust by chance into the great roar of a distant city, or on an expedition as blind, capricious, and fatally mistaken as all life. Later, she saw herself as a girl in high school, she remembered her dreams and hopes, the pitiably mistaken innocence of her vision of the world; her grand ambitions to "study music," to follow a "career in grand opera"; later still, a girl of eighteen or twenty, amorous of life, thirsting for the great cities and voyages of the world, playing popular songs of the period— "Love Me and the World Is Mine," "I Wonder Who's Kissing Her Now," "Till the Sands of the Desert Grow Cold," and so on—for her father, as he sat, on summer evenings, on his porch; a little later, "touring" the little cities of the

South, singing and playing the popular "rhythm" and sentimental ballads of the period in vaudeville and moving-picture houses. She remembered how she had once been invited to a week-end house party with a dozen other young men and women of her acquaintance, and of how she had been afraid to go, and how desperately ashamed she was when she had "to go in swimming" with the others, and to "show her figure," her long skinny legs, even when they were concealed by the clumsy bathing dress and the black stockings of the period. She remembered her marriage then, the first years of her life with Barton, her tragic failure to have children, and the long horror of Gant's last years of sickness—the years of sombre waiting, the ever-impending terror of his death.

A thousand scenes from this past life flashed through her mind now, as she lay there in the darkness, and all of them seemed grotesque, accidental and mistaken, as reasonless as everything in life.

And filled with a numb, speechless feeling of despair and nameless terror, she heard, somewhere across the night, the sound of a train again, and thought:

"My God! My God! What is life about? We are all lying here in darkness in ten thousand little towns—waiting, listening, hoping—for what?"

And suddenly, with a feeling of terrible revelation, she saw the strangeness and mystery of man's life; she felt about her in the darkness the presence of ten thousand people, each lying in his bed, naked and alone, united at the heart of night and darkness, and listening, as she, to the sounds of silence and of sleep. And suddenly it seemed to her that she knew all these lonely, strange, and unknown watchers of the night, that she was speaking to them, and they to her, across the fields of sleep, as they had never spoken before, that she knew men now in all their dark and naked loneliness, without falseness and pretense as she had never known them. And it seemed to her that if men would only listen in the darkness, and send the language of their naked lonely spirits across the silence of the night, all of the error, falseness and confusion of their lives would vanish, they would no longer be strangers, and each would find the life he sought and never yet had found.

"If we only could!" she thought. "If we only could!"

Then, as she listened, there was nothing but the huge hush of night and silence, and far away the whistle of a train. Suddenly the phone rang.

XXVI

A few minutes after four o'clock that morning as McGuire lay there sprawled upon his desk, the phone rang again. And again he made no move to answer it: he just sat there, sprawled out on his fat elbows, staring stupidly ahead. Creasman came in presently, as the telephone continued to disturb the silence of the hospital with its electric menace and this time, without a glance at him, answered.

It was Luke Gant. At four o'clock his father had had another hemorrhage, he had lost consciousness, all efforts to awaken him had failed, they thought he was dying.

The nurse listened carefully for a moment to Luke's stammering and excited voice, which was audible across the wire even to McGuire. Then, with a troubled and uncertain glance toward the doctor's sprawled and drunken figure, she said quietly:

"Just a minute. I don't know if the doctor is in the hospital. I'll see if I can find him."

Putting her hand over the mouthpiece, keeping her voice low, she spoke urgently to McGuire:

"It's Luke Gant. He says his father has had another hemorrhage and that they can't rouse him. He wants you to come at once. What shall I tell him?"

He stared drunkenly at her for a moment, and then waving his finger at her in a movement of fat impatience, he mumbled thickly:

"Nothing to do.... No use.... Can't be stopped.... People expect miracles.... Over.... Done for.... Tell him I'm not here ... gone home," he muttered, and sprawled forward on the desk again.

Quietly, coolly, the nurse spoke into the phone again:

"The doctor doesn't seem to be here at the hospital, Mr. Gant. Have you tried his house? I think you may find him at home."

"No, G-g-g-god-damn it!" Luke fairly screamed across the wire. "He's not at home. I've already t-t-tried to get him there.... N-n-n-now you look here, Miss Creasman!" Luke shouted angrily. "You c-c-can't kid me: I know where he is— He's d-d-down there at the hospital right now—wy-wy-wy—stinkin' drunk! You t-t-tell him, G-g-g-god-damn his soul, that if he d-d-doesn't come, wy-wy-wy—P-p-p-papa's in a bad way and and and f-f-frankly, I f'ink it's a rotten shame for McGuire to act this way, wy-wy-wy after he's b-b-been Papa's doctor all these years. F-f-frankly, I do!"

"Nothing to be done," mumbled McGuire. "No use.... All over."

"I'll see what I can do, Mr. Gant," said Creasman quietly. "I'll let the doctor know as soon as he comes in!"

"C-c-c-comes in, hell!" Luke stammered bitterly. "I'm c-c-comin' down there myself and g-g-get him if I have to wy wy wy d-d-drag him here by the s-s-scruff of his neck!" And he hung up the receiver with a bang.

The nurse put the phone down on the desk, and turning to McGuire, said:

"He's raving. He says if you don't go, he'll come for you and get you himself. Can't you pull yourself together enough to go? If you can't drive the car, I'll send Joe along to drive it for you—" Joe was a negro orderly in the hospital.

"What's the use?" McGuire mumbled thickly, a little angrily. "What the hell do these people expect anyway? .. I'm a doctor, not a miracle man.... The man's gone, I tell you ... the whole gut and rectum is eaten away ... he can't live over a day or two longer at the most.... It's cruelty to prolong it: why the hell should I try to?"

"All right," she said resignedly. "Do as you please. Only, he'll probably be here for you himself in a few minutes. And since they do feel that way about it, I think you might make the effort just to please them."

"Ah-h," he muttered wearily. "People are all alike. . . . They all want miracles."

"Are you just going to sit here all night?" she said with a rough kindliness. "Aren't you going to try to get a little sleep before you operate?"

He waved fat fingers at her, and did not look at her.

"Leave me alone," he mumbled; and she left him.

When she had gone, he fumbled for the jug and drank again. And then, while time resumed its sanded drip, and he sat there in the silence, he thought again of the old dying man whom he had known first when he was a young doctor just beginning and with whom his own life had been united by so many strange and poignant memories. And thinking of Gant, the strangeness of the human destiny returned to haunt his mind; there was something that he could not speak, a wonder and a mystery he could not express.

He fumbled for the jug again, and holding it solemnly in his bearish paws, drained it. Then he sat for several minutes without moving. Finally, he got up out of his chair, grunting painfully, and fumbling for the walls, lurched out into the hall, and began to grope his way across the corridor toward the stairs. And the first step fooled him as it had done so many time before; he missed his step, even as a man stepping out in emptiness might miss, and came down heavily upon his knees. Then, pushing with his hands, he slid out peacefully on the oiled green linoleum, pillowed his big head on his arms with a comfortable grunt, and sprawled out flat, already half dead to the world. It was in this position—also a familiar one—that Creasman, who had heard his thump when falling, found him. And she spoke sharply and commandingly as one might speak to a little child:

"You get right up off that floor and march upstairs," she said. "If you want to sleep you're going to your room; you'll not disgrace us sleeping on that floor."

And like a child, as he had done so many times before, he obeyed her. In a moment, as her sharp command reached his drugged consciousness, he grunted, stirred, climbed painfully to his knees, and then, pawing carefully before him like a bear, unable or unwilling to stand up, he began to crawl slowly up the stairs.

And it was in this position, half-way up, pawing his burly and cumbersome way on hands and knees, that Luke Gant found him. Cursing bitterly, and stammering with wild excitement, the young man pulled him to his feet, Creasman sponged off the great bloated face with a cold towel and assisted by Joe Corpering, the negro man, they got him down the stairs and out of the hospital into Luke's car.

Dawn was just breaking, a faint glimmer of blue-silver light, with the still purity of the earth, the sweet fresh stillness of the trees, the bird-song waking. The fresh sweet air, Luke's breakneck driving through the silent streets, the roaring motor—finally, the familiar and powerfully subdued emotion of a death chamber, the repressed hysteria, the pain and tension and the terror of shocked flesh, the aura of focal excitement around the dying man revived McGuire.

Gant lay still and almost lifeless on the bed, his face already tinged with the ghostly shade of death, his breath low, hoarse, faintly rattling, his eyes half-closed, comatose, already glazed with death.

McGuire sighted at his shining needle, and thrust a powerful injection of caffeine, sodium, and benzoate into the arm of the dying man. This served partially to revive him, got him through the low ebb of the dark, his eyes opened, cleared, he spoke again. Bright day and morning came, and Gant still lived. And with the light, their impossible and frenzied hopes came back again, as they have always been revived in desperate men. And Gant did not die that day. He lived on.

XXVII

By the middle of the month Gant had a desperate attack; for four days now he was confined to bed, he began to bleed out of the bowels, he spent four sleepless days and nights of agony, and with the old terror of death awake again and urgent, Helen telegraphed to Luke, who was in Atlanta, frantically imploring him to come home at once.

With the arrival of his son and under the stimulation of Luke's vital and hopeful nature, the old man revived somewhat: they got him out of bed, and into a new wheel-chair which they had bought for the purpose, and the day of his arrival Luke wheeled his father out into the bright June sunshine, and through the streets of the town, where he again saw friends, and renewed acquaintances he had not known in years.

The next day Gant seemed better. He ate a good breakfast, by ten o'clock he was up and Luke had dressed him, got him into the new wheel-chair and was wheeling him out on the streets again in the bright sunshine. All along the streets of the town people stopped and greeted the old man and his son, and in Gant's weary old brain there may perhaps have been a flicker of an old hope, a feeling that he had come to life again.

"Wy-wy-wy-wy, he's f-f-f-fine as silk!" Luke would sing out in answer to the question of some old friend or acquaintance, before his father had a chance to answer. "Aren't you, C-C-C-Colonel? Wy-wy-wy-wy Lord God! Mr. P-p-p-p-parker, you couldn't k-k-k-kill him with a wy wy wy wy wy with a b-b-butcher's cleaver. He'll be here when you and I bofe are p-p-p-pushing daisies." And Gant, pleased, would smile feebly, puffing from time to time at a cigar in the unaccustomed, clumsy, and pitifully hopeful way sick men have.

Towards one o'clock Gant began to moan with pain again, and to entreat his son to make haste and take him home. When they got back before the house, Luke brought the wheel chair to a stop, and helped his father to get up. His stammering solicitude and over-extravagant offers of help served only to exasperate and annoy the old man who, still moaning feebly, and sniffling with trembling lip, said petulantly:

"No, no, no. Just leave me alone to try to get a moment's peace, I beg of you, I ask you, for Jesus' sake."

"Wy-wy-wy-wy, all right, P-p-p-papa," Luke stammered with earnest cheerfulness. "Wy-wy-wy, you're the d-d-d-doctor. Wy-wy, I'll just wheel the chair up on the porch and then I'll c-c-come back to your room and f-f-f-fix you up in a j-j-j-j-jiffy."

"Oh, Jesus, I don't care what you do. . . . Do what you like," Gant moaned. "I'm in agony. . . . O Jesus!" he wept. "It's fearful, it's awful, it's cruel—just leave me alone, I beg of you," he sniffled.

"Wy-wy-wy, yes, sir, P-p-p-papa—wy, you're the doctor," Luke said. "Can you make it by yourself all right?" he said anxiously, as his father, leaning heavily upon his cane, started up the stone steps toward the walk that led up to the house.

"Why, yes, now, son," Eliza, who had heard their voices and come out on the porch, now said diplomatically, seeing that Luke's well-meant but stammering solicitude had begun to irritate his father. "Mr. Gant doesn't want any help—you put the car up, son, and leave him alone, he's able to manage all right by himself."

And Luke, muttering respectfully, "Wy-wy-wy, yes, sir, P-p-p-papa, you're the d-d-doctor," stopped then, lifted the chair up to the walk, and begun to push it toward the house, not however without a troubled glance at the old man who was walking slowly and feebly toward the porch steps. And for a moment, Eliza stood surveying them and then turned, to stand looking at her house reflectively before she entered it again, her hands clasped loosely at her waist, her lips pursed in a strong reflective expression in which the whole pride of possession, her living and inseparable unity with this gaunt old house, was powerfully evident.

It was at this moment while she stood planted there upon the sidewalk looking at the house, that the thing happened. Gant, still moaning feebly to himself, had almost reached the bottom of the steps when suddenly he staggered, a scream of pain and horror was torn from him; in that instant, the walking cane fell with a clatter to the concrete walk, his two great hands went down to his groin in a pitiable clutching gesture and crying out loudly: "O Jesus! Save me! Save me!" he fell to his knees, still clutching at his entrails with his mighty hands.

Even before Eliza got to him, her flesh turned rotten at the sight. Blood was pouring from him; the bright arterial blood was already running out upon the concrete walk, the heavy black cloth of Gant's trousers was already sodden, turning purplish with the blood; the blood streamed through his fingers, covering his great hands. He was bleeding to death through the genital organs.

Eliza rushed toward him at a strong clumsy gait; she tried to lift him, he was too big for her to handle, and she screamed to Luke for help. He came at once, running at top speed across the yard and, scarcely pausing in his stride, he picked up Gant's great figure in his arms—it felt as light and fleshless as a bundle of dry sticks—and turning to his mother, said curtly:

"Call Helen! Quick! I'll take him to his room and get his clothes off."

And holding the old man as if he were a child, he fairly raced up the steps and down the hall, leaving a trail of blood behind him as he went.

Eliza, scarcely conscious of what she did, paused just long enough to pick up Gant's black felt hat and walking stick which had fallen to the walk. Then, her face white and set as a block of marble, she rushed up the steps and down the hall toward the telephone. Now that the end had come, after all the years of agony and waiting, the knowledge filled her with an unbelievable, an incredulous horror. In another moment she was talking to her daughter:

"Oh, child, child," she said in a low tone of utter terror, "come quick! . . . Your father's bleeding to death!"

There was a gasp, a sob of anguish and surprise, half broken in the throat, the receiver was banged on the hook without an answer: within four minutes Helen had arrived, Barton, usually a deliberate and cautious driver, having taken the dangerous hills and curves between at murderous speed.

As she entered the hall, her mother had just finished phoning to McGuire. Without a word of greeting the two women rushed back through the rear hall towards Gant's room; when they got there Luke had already finished undressing him. Gant lay half propped on pillows still holding his great hands clutched around his genitals, the sheet beneath him was already soaked with blood, a red wet blot that spread horribly, sickeningly even as they looked. Gant's cold-gray eyes were bright with terror. As his daughter entered the room, he looked at her with the pitiable entreaty of a child, a look that tore at her heart, that begged her —the only one on earth who could, the only one who through black years of horror actually had—by some miracle of strength and grace to save him. And even as he looked at her with pitiable entreaty, she saw that he was gone, that he was dying, and that he knew it. Cold terror drank her heart; without a word she seized a towel, pulled his great hands away from that fount of jetting blood and covered him. By the time McGuire arrived, they had got a fresh sheet under him: but the spreading horror of the great red blot could not be checked, the sheet was soaking in bright blood the moment that they got it down.

McGuire came in and took one look, then turned toward the window, fumbling in his pocket for a cigarette. Helen came to him and seized him by his burly arms, unconsciously shaking him in the desperation of her entreaty.

"You've got to make it stop," she said hoarsely, "you've got to! You've got to!"

He stared at her for a moment, then stuck the cigarette in the corner of his thick lip, and barked coarsely:

"Stop what? What the hell do you think I am—Jehovah?"

"You've got to! You've got to!" she muttered again, her large gaunt face strained with hysteria—and then, suddenly, abruptly, quietly:

"What's to be done?"

He did not answer for a moment; he stared out the window, his coarse, bloated and brutally good face patched and mottled in late western light.

"You'd better wire the others," he grunted. "That is, if you want them here. Tell Steve and Daisy to come on. They may make it. Where's Eugene?"

"Boston."

He shrugged his burly shoulders and said nothing for a moment.

"All right. Tell him to come on."

"How long?" she whispered.

Again he shrugged his burly shoulders, but made no answer. He lit his cigarette, and turned toward the bed: nothing could be heard except Luke's heavy and excited breathing. Both towel and sheet were red and wet again. Gant remained motionless, his great hands clasped upon the towel, his eyes bright with terror and pitiable entreaty. McGuire opened his old leather case, squinted at the needle, and loaded it. Then, the cigarette still plastered on his fat lip, coiling smoke, he walked over to the bed and even as Gant raised his fear-bright eyes to him, he took him by his stringy arm, and grunting "All right, W. O.," he plunged the needle in above the elbow. Gant moaned a little, and relaxed insensibly after the needle had gone in: in a few minutes his eyes grew dull, and his great hands loosened in their clutch.

XXVIII

He bled incredibly. It was unbelievable that an old cancer-riddled spectre of a man should have so much blood in him. One has often heard the phrase "bled white," and that is literally what happened to him. Some liquid still came from him, but it was almost colorless, like water. There was no more blood left in him. And even then he did not die. Instead, as if to compensate him for all these years of agony and mortal terror, this bitter clutch on life so desperately relinquished, there came now a period of almost total peace and clarity. And Helen, grasping hope fiercely from that unaccustomed tranquillity, tried to hearten him and herself with futile words; she even seized him by his shoulders and shook him a little, saying:

"Why, you're all right! You're going to be all right now! The worst is over—you'll get well now! Don't you know it?"

And Gant covered her fingers with his own great hand and, smiling a little and shaking his head, looked at her, saying in a low and gentle voice:

"Oh, no, baby. I'm dying. It's all right now."

And in her heart, she knew at last that she was beaten; yet she would not give up. The final stop of that horrible flow of blood which had continued unabated for a day, the unaccustomed tranquil clarity of Gant's voice and mind, awakened in her again all the old unreasoning hopefulness of her nature, its desperate refusal to accept the ultimate.

"Oh," she said that night to Eliza, shaking her head with a strong movement of negation—"you can't tell me! Papa's not going to die yet! He'll pull through this just like he's pulled through all those other spells. Why, his mind is as clear and sound as a bell! He knows everything that's going on around him! He hasn't talked in years as he talked to me tonight—he was more like his old self than he's been since he took sick."

"Why, yes," Eliza answered instantly, eagerly catching up the drift of her daughter's talk, and pursuing it with the web-like, invincibly optimistic hopefulness of her own nature.

"Why, yes," she went on, pursing her lips reflectively and speaking in a persuasive manner. "And, see here, now!—Say!—Why, you know, I got to studyin' it over tonight and it's just occurred to me—now I'll tell you what *my* theory is! I believe that that old growth—that awful old thing—that—well, I suppose, now, you might say—that *cancer*," she said, making a gesture of explanation with her broad hand—"whatever it is, that awful old thing that has been eating away inside him there for years—" here she pursed her lips powerfully and shook her head in a short convulsive tremor of disgust—"well, now, I give it as my theory that the whole thing tore loose in him yesterday—when he had that attack—and," she paused deliberately, looked her daughter straight in the eyes, and went on with a slow and telling force—"and that he has simply gone and got that rotten old thing out of his system."

"Then, you mean—" Helen began eagerly, seizing at this fantastic straw as if it were the rock by which her drowning hope might be saved—"you mean, Mama——"

"Yes, sir!" said Eliza, shaking her head slowly and positively. "That's exactly what I mean! I think nature has taken its own course—I think nature has succeeded in doing what all the doctors and hospitals in the world were not able to do—for you can rest assured," and here she paused, looking her daughter gravely in the eyes—"you can rest assured that nature is the best physician in the end! Now, I've always said as much, and all the best authorities agree with me. Why, yes, now!—here! —say!—wasn't I readin' in the paper—oh! here along, you know a week or so ago—Doctor Royal S. Copeland!—yes, sir!—that was the very feller—why, he said, you know—" she went on in explanatory fashion.

"Oh, but, Mama!" Helen said, desperately, unable to make her mind believe this grotesque reasoning, and yet clutching at every word with a pleading entreaty that begged to be convinced.

"Oh, but, Mama, surely Wade Eliot and all those other men at Hopkins couldn't have been wrong! Why, Mama," she cried furiously, yet pleadingly—"you know they couldn't—after all these years—after taking him there for treatment a dozen times or more! Why, Mama, those men are *famous*—the greatest doctors in the world! Oh, surely not! Surely not!" she said desperately, and then gazed at Eliza pleadingly again.

"H'm!" said Eliza, pursing her lips with a little scornful smile. "It won't be the first time that a doctor has been wrong—I don't care how famous they may be! You can rest assured of that! It's always been my opinion that they're wrong about as often as they're right—only you can't prove it on 'em. They *bury* their mistakes." She was silent a moment, looking at her daughter in a sudden, straight and deadly fashion, with a little smile at the corners of her mouth. "Now, child, I want to tell you something. . . . I want to tell you what I saw today." Again she was silent, looking straight in her daughter's eyes, smiling her quiet little smile.

"What? What was it, Mama?" Helen demanded eagerly.

"Did you ever take a good look at that maple tree out front that stands on your right as you come in the house?"

"Why, no," Helen said in a bewildered tone. "How do you mean?"

"Well," said Eliza calmly, yet with a certain triumph in her voice, "you just take a good look at it tomorrow. That's all."

"But why—I can't see—how do you mean, Mama?"

"Now, child—" Eliza pursued her subject deliberately, with a ruminant relish of her strong pursed lips—"I was born and brought up in the country—close to the lap of Mother Earth, as the sayin' goes—and when it comes to *trees*—why, I reckon there's mighty little about 'em that I don't know. . . . Now here," she said abruptly, coming to the centre of her argument—"did you ever see a tree that had a big hollow gash down one side—that looked like it had all been eaten an' rotted out by some disease that had been destroyin' it?"

"Why, yes," Helen said, in a puzzled voice. "But I don't see yet——"

"Well, child, I'll tell you, then," said Eliza, both voice and worn brown eyes united in their portents of a grave and quiet earnestness—"that tree doesn't *always* die! You'll see trees that have had that happen to them—and they *cure* themselves! You can see where some old rotten growth has eaten into them—and then you can see where the tree has got the best of it—and grown up again—as sound and healthy as it *ever* was—around that old rotten growth. And that," she said triumphantly, "that is just exactly what has happened to that maple in the yard. Oh, you can *see* it!" she cried positively, at the same time making an easy descriptive gesture with her wide hand—"you can see where it has lapped right around that old growth—made a sort of fold, you know—and here it is just as sound and healthy as it ever was!"

"Then you mean?——"

"I mean," said Eliza in her straight and deadly fashion—"I mean that if a tree can do it, a *man* can do it—and I mean that if any man alive could do it your daddy is that man—for he's had as much strength and vitality as any man I ever saw—and *more* than a tree!" she cried. "Lord! I've seen him do enough to kill a *hundred* trees—the things *he's* done and managed to get over would kill the strongest tree that ever lived!"

"Oh, but Mama, surely not!" said Helen, laughing, and beginning to pluck at her chin in an abstracted manner, amused and tickled in spite of herself by her mother's extraordinary reasoning. "You know that a man is not built the same way as a tree!"

"Why," Eliza cried impatiently, "why not! They're both Nature's products, aren't they? Now, here," she said persuasively, "just stop and consider the thing for a moment. Just imagine for a moment that *you're* the tree." Here she took her strong worn fingers and traced a line down Helen's stomach. "Now," she went on persuasively, "you've got some kind of growth inside you—call it what you like—a tumor, a growth, a cancer—anything you will—and your *healthy* tissues get to work to get the *best* of that growth—to build up a wall around it—to destroy it—to replace it with sound tissues, weed it out! Now," she said, clenching her fingers in a loose but powerful clasp—"if a *tree* can do that, doesn't it stand to reason that a *man* can do the same! Why, I wouldn't doubt it for a moment!" she cried powerfully. "Not a bit of it."

Thus the two women talked together according to the laws of their nature—the one with an invincible and undaunted optimism that persuaded itself in the octopal pursuit of its own reasonings, the other clutching like a drowning person at a straw.

XXIX

HE had not heard from any of his family in some weeks but late that night, while he was reading in his room on Trowbridge Street, he received the following telegram from home: "Father very ill doctor says cannot live come at once." The telegram was signed by his mother.

He telephoned the railway information offices and was informed that there was a train for New York and the South in about an hour. If he hurried, he could make it. He did not have enough money for the fare, he knew that he might hunt up Starwick, Dodd, Professor Hatcher, or other people that he knew, and get the money, but the delay would make him miss the train. Accordingly, he appealed to the person he knew best in the house, and who would be, he thought, most likely to help him. This was Mr. Wang, the Chinese student.

Mr. Wang was as good-hearted as he was stupid and childlike and now, faced with the need of getting money at once, the boy appealed to him. Mr. Wang came to his door and blinked owlishly; behind him the room was a blur of smoke and incense, and the big cabinet victrola was giving forth for the dozenth time that evening the hearty strains of "Yes, We Have No Bananas."

When Mr. Wang saw him, his round yellow face broke into a foolish crease of merriment, he began to shake his finger at the young man waggishly, and his throat already beginning to choke and squeak a little with his jest, he said:

"I s'ink lest night I see you with nice—" Something in the other's manner cut him short; he stopped, his round foolish face grew wondering and solemn, and in a doubtful and inquiring tone, he said:

"You say——?"

"Listen, Wang: I've just got this telegram from home. My father is very sick—they think that he is dying. I've got to get money to go home at once. I need fifty dollars: can you let me have it?"

As Mr. Wang listened, his sparkling eyes grew dull as balls of tar, his round yellow moon of face grew curiously impassive. When the boy had finished, the Chinese thrust his hands into the wide flowered sleeves of his dressing gown, and then with a curious formal stiffness said:

"Will you come in? Please."

The boy entered, and Mr. Wang, closing the door, turned, thrust his hand in his sleeves again, marched across the room to a magnificent teak-wood desk and opening a small drawer, took out a roll of bills, peeled off two twenties and a ten, and coming back to where his visitor was standing, presented the money to him with a stiff bow, and his round face still woodenly impassive, said again:

"Please."

The young man seized the money and saying, "Thank you, Wang, I'll send it to you as soon as I get home," ran back to his room and began to hurl clothing, shirts, socks, toilet articles, into his valise as hard as he could. He had just finished when there was a tapping on the door and the Chinese appeared again. He marched into the room with the same ceremonious formality that had characterized his former conduct and bowing stiffly again, presented the boy with two magnificent fans of peacock feathers of which the lacquered blades were delicately and beautifully engraved.

And bowing stiffly again, and saying, "Please!" he turned and marched out of the room, his fat hands thrust into the wide sleeves of the flowered dressing gown. The boy never saw him again.

Thirty minutes later he was on his way, leaving behind him, in the care of Mrs. Murphy, most of his belongings—the notebooks, letters, books, old shoes, worn-out clothes and battered hats, the thousands of pages of manuscript that represented the accretions of three years— that immense and nondescript collection of past events, foredone accomplishment, and spent purposes, the very sight of which filled him with weariness and horror but which, with the huge acquisitive mania of his mother's blood, he had never been able to destroy.

In this way he left Cambridge and a life he had known for two years; instantly re-called, drawn back by the hand of death into the immediacy of a former life that had grown strange as dreams. It was toward the end of June, just a day or two before the commencement exercises at the university. That year he had been informed of his eligibility for the Master's degree—a degree he had neither sought nor known he had earned and, at the time he had received the telegram, he had been waiting for the formal exercises at which he would receive the degree—a wait prompted more by his total indecision as to his future purpose than by any other cause. Now, with explosive sudden- ness, his purpose had been shaped, decided for him, and with the old feeling of groping bewilderment, he surveyed the history of the last two years and wondered why he had come, why he was here, toward what blind goal he had been tending: all that he had to "show" for these years of fury, struggle, homelessness and hunger was an academic distinction which he had not aimed at, and on which he placed small value.

And it was in this spirit that he left the place. Rain had begun to fall that night, it fell now in torrential floods. The gay buntings and Japanese lanterns with which the Harvard Yard were already decked were reduced to sodden ruin, and as he raced towards the station in a taxi, the streets of Cambridge, and the old, narrow, twisted and familiar lanes of Boston were deserted—pools of wet light and glittering ribbons swept with storm.

When he got to the South station he had five minutes left to buy his ticket and get on his train. In spite of the lashing storm and the lateness of the hour, that magnificent station, which at that time—before the later "improvements" had reduced it to a glittering sterility of tile and marble—was one of the most thrilling and beautiful places in the world, was still busy with the tides of people that hurry forever through the great stations of America, and that no violence of storm can check.

The vast dingy sweep of the cement concourse outside the train-gates was pungent, as it had always been, with the acrid and powerfully ex- citing smell of engine smoke, and beyond the gates, upon a dozen tracks, great engines, passive and alert as cats, purred and panted softly, with the couched menace of their tremendous stroke. The engine smoke rose up straight in billowing plumes to widen under vaulting arches, to spread foggily throughout the enormous spaces of the grimy sheds. And beside the locomotives, he could see the burly denimed figures of the engineers, holding flaming torches and an oil-can in their hands as they peered and probed through the shining flanges of terrific pistoned wheels much taller than their heads. And forever, over the enormous cement concourse and down the quays beneath the powerful groomed attentiveness of waiting trains the tides of travellers kept passing, passing, in their everlasting change and weft, of voyage and return—of speed and space and movement, morning, cities, and new lands.

And caught up in the vaulting arches of those immense and grimy sheds he heard again the murmurous sound of time—that sound remote and everlasting, distilled out of all the movement, frenzy, and unceasing fury of our unresting lives, and yet itself detached, as calm and imperturbable as the still sad music of humanity, and which, made up out of our million passing lives, is in itself as fixed and everlasting as eternity.

They came, they paused and wove and passed and thrust and vanished in their everlasting tides, they streamed in and out of the portals of that enormous station in unceasing swarm; great trains steamed in to empty them, and others steamed out loaded with their nameless motes of lives, and all was as it had always been, moving, changing, swarming on forever like a river, and as fixed, unutterable in unceasing movement and in changeless change as the great river is, and time itself.

And within ten minutes he himself, another grain of dust borne onward on this ceaseless tide, another nameless atom in this everlasting throng, another wanderer in America, as all his fathers were before him, was being hurled into the South again in the huge projectile of a train. The train swept swiftly down the gleaming rails, paused briefly at the Back-Bay station, then was on its way again, moving smoothly, powerfully, almost noiselessly now, through the outer stretches of the small dense web of Boston. The town swept smoothly past: old blanks of wall, and old worn brick, and sudden spokes of streets, deserted, lashed with rain, set at the curbs with glittering beetles of its wet machinery and empetalled with its wet and sudden blooms of life. The flushed spoke-wires crossed his vision, lost the moment that he saw them, his forever, gone, like all things else, and never to be captured, seen a million times, yet never known before—as haunting, fading, deathless as a dream, as brief as is the bitter briefness of man's days, as lost and lonely as his life upon the mighty breast of earth, and of America.

Then the great train, gathering now in speed, and mounting smooth-ly to the summit of its tremendous stroke, was running swiftly through the outskirts of the city, through suburbs and brief blurs of light and then through little towns and on into the darkness, the wild and secret loneliness of earth. And he was going home again into the South and to a life that had grown strange as dreams, and to his father who was dying and who had become a ghost and shadow of his father to him, and to the bitter reality of grief and death. And—how, why, for what reason he could not say—all he felt was the tongueless swelling of wild joy. It was the wild and secret joy that has no tongue, the impossible hope that has no explanation, the savage, silent, and sweet exultancy of night, the wild and lonely visage of the earth, the imperturbable stroke and calmness of the everlasting earth, from which we have been de-rived, wherein again we shall be compacted, on which all of us have lived alone as strangers, and across which, in the loneliness of night, we have been hurled onward in the projectile flight of mighty trains —America.

Then the great train was given to the night and darkness, the great train hurtled through the night across the lonely, wild, and secret earth, bearing on to all their thousand destinations its freight of unknown lives—some to morning, cities, new lands, and the joy of voyages, and some to known faces, voices, and the hills of home—but which to cer-tain fortune, peace, security, and love, no man could say.

The news that Gant was dying had spread rapidly through the town and, as often happens, that news had brought him back to life again in the heart and living memory of men who had known him, and who had scarcely thought of him for years. That night—the night of his death— the house was filled with some of the men who had known him best since he came to the town forty years before.

Among these people were several of the prominent and wealthy busi-ness men of the community: these included, naturally, Eliza's brothers, William and James Pentland, both wealthy lumber dealers, as well as one of her younger brothers, Crockett, who was Will Pentland's book-keeper, a pleasant, ruddy, bucolic man of fifty years. Among the other men of wealth and influence who had been Gant's friends there was Fagg Sluder, who had made a fortune as a contractor and retired to in-

vest his money in business property, and to spend his time seated in an
easy creaking chair before the fire department, in incessant gossip about
baseball with the firemen and the young professional baseball players
whose chief support he was, whose annual deficit he cheerfully supplied,
and to whom he had given the local baseball park, which bore his name.
He had been one of Gant's best friends for twenty years, he was immensely fond of him, and now, assembled in the broad front hall in
earnest discussion with the Pentlands and Mike Fogarty, another of
Gant's friends, and armed with the invariable cigar (despite his doctor's
orders he smoked thirty or forty strong black cigars every day), which he
chewed on, took out of his mouth, and put back again, with quick,
short, unconscious movements, he could be heard saying in the rapid,
earnest, stammering tone that was one of the most attractive qualities of
his buoyant and constantly hopeful nature:

"I-I-I-I just believe he's going to pull right out of this and-and-and-
get well! Why-why-why-why-when I went in there tonight he spoke
right up and-and-and knew me right away!" he blurted out, sticking
the cigar in his mouth and chewing on it vigorously a moment—"why-
why-why his mind is-is-is-is just as clear—as it always was—spoke
right up, you know, says 'Sit down, Fagg'—shook hands with me—
knew me right away—talked to me just the same way he always talked—
says 'Sit down, Fagg. I'm glad to see you. How have you been?' he
says—and-and-and—I just believe he's going to pull right out of this,"
Mr. Sluder blurted out,—"be damned if I don't—what do *you* say,
Will?" and snatching his chewed cigar butt from his mouth he turned
eagerly to Will Pentland for confirmation. And Will, who, as usual,
had been paring his stubby nails during the whole course of the conversation, his lips pursed in their characteristic family grimace, now
studied his clenched fingers for a moment, pocketed his knife and turning to Fagg Sluder, with a little bird-like nod and wink, and with the
incomparable Pentland drawl, at once precise, and full of the relish of
self-satisfaction, said:

"Well, if any man alive can do it, W. O. is that man. I've seen him
time and again when I thought every breath would be his last—and he's
got over it every time. I've always said," he went on precisely, and with
a kind of deadly directness in his small compact and almost wizened
face, "that he has more real vitality than any two men that I ever knew
—he's got out of worse holes than this before—and he may do it again."

He was silent a moment, his small packed face pursed suddenly in its animal-like grimace that had an almost savage ferocity and a sense of deadly and indomitable power.

Even more astonishing and troubling was the presence of these four older members of the Pentland family gathered together in his mother's hall. As they stood there talking—Eliza with her hands held in their loose and powerful clasp across her waist, Will intently busy with his finger-nails, Jim listening attentively to all that was said, his solid porcine face and small eyes wincing from time to time in a powerful but unconscious grimace, and Crockett, gentlest, ruddiest, most easy-going and dreamy of them all, speaking in his quiet drawling tone and stroking his soft brown mustaches in a gesture of quiet and bucolic meditation, Luke could not recall having seen so many of them together at one time and the astonishing enigma of their one-ness and variety was strikingly apparent.

What was it?—this indefinable tribal similarity that united these people so unmistakably. No one could say: it would have been difficult to find four people more unlike in physical appearance, more strongly marked by individual qualities. Whatever it was—whether some chemistry of blood and character, or perhaps some physical identity of broad and fleshy nose, pursed reflective lips and flat wide cheeks, or the engines of powerfully concentrated egotisms—their kinship with one another was astonishing and instantly apparent.

XXX

In a curious and indefinable way the two groups of men in the hallway had become divided: the wealthier group of prominent citizens, which was composed of the brothers William, James, and Crockett Pentland, Mr. Sluder and Eliza, stood in a group near the front hall door, engaged in earnest conversation. The second group, which was composed of working men, who had known Gant well, and worked for or with him —a group composed of Jannadeau the jeweller, old Alec Ramsay and Saul Gudger, who were stonecutters, Gant's nephew, Ollie Gant, who was a plasterer, Ernest Pegram, the city plumber, and Mike Fogarty, who was perhaps Gant's closest friend, a building contractor—this group, composed of men who had all their lives done stern labor with their hands, and who were really the men who had known the stone-cutter best, stood apart from the group of prominent and wealthy men who were talking so earnestly to Eliza.

And in this circumstance, in this unconscious division, in the air of constraint, vague uneasiness and awkward silence that was evident among these working men, as they stood there in the hallway dressed in their "good clothes," nervously fingering their hats in their big hands, there was something immensely moving. The men had the look that working people the world over have always had when they found themselves suddenly gathered together on terms of social intimacy with their employers or with members of the governing class.

And Helen, coming out at this instant from her father's room into the hall, suddenly saw and felt the awkward division between these two groups of men, as she had never before felt or noticed it, as sharply as if they had been divided with a knife.

And, it must be admitted, her first feeling was an unworthy one—an instinctive wish to approach the more "important" group, to join her life to the lives of these "influential" people who represented to her a "higher" social level. She found herself walking towards the group of wealthy and prominent men at the front of the hall, and away from the group of working men who had really been Gant's best friends.

But seeing the brick-red face of Alec Ramsay, the mountainous figure of Mike Fogarty, suddenly with a sense of disbelief, and almost terrified revelation of the truth, she thought: "Why-why-why—these men are really the closest friends he's got—not rich men like Uncle Will or Uncle Jim or even Mr. Sluder—but men like Mike Fogarty—and Jannadeau—and Mr. Duncan—and Alec Ramsay—and Ernest Pegram—and Ollie Gant—but—but—good heavens, no!" she thought, almost desperately—"surely these are not his closest friends—why-why—of course, they're decent people—they're honest men—but they're only common people—I've always considered them as just *working* men—and-and-and—my God!" she thought, with that terrible feeling of discovery we have when we suddenly see ourselves as others see us—"do you suppose that's the way people in this town think of Papa? Do you suppose they have always thought of him as just a common working man—oh, no! but of course not!" she went on impatiently, trying to put the troubling thought out of her mind. "Papa's not a working man—Papa is a *business* man—a well thought of business man in this community. Papa has always owned property since he came here—he has always had his own shop"—she did not like the sound of the word shop, and in her mind she hastily amended it to "place"—"he's always had his own place, up on the public

square—he's—he's rented places to other people—he's—he's—oh, of
course not!—Papa is different from men like Ernest Pegram, and Ollie,
and Jannadeau and Alec Ramsay—why, they're just working men—they
work with their hands—Ollie's just an ordinary plasterer—and-and—
Mr. Ramsay is nothing but a stone-cutter.'

And a small insistent voice inside her said most quietly: "And your
father?"

And suddenly Helen remembered Gant's great hands of power and
strength, and how they now lay quietly beside him on the bed, and
lived and would not die, even when the rest of him had died, and she
remembered the thousands of times she had gone to his shop in the afternoon and found the stonecutter in his long striped apron bending with
delicate concentration over a stone inscription on a trestle, holding in his
great hands the chisel and the heavy wooden mallet the stonecutters use,
and remembering, the whole rich and living compact of the past came
back to her, in a rush of tenderness and joy and terror, and on that
flood a proud and bitter honesty returned. She thought: "Yes, he was a
stonecutter, no different from these other men, and these men were his
real friends."

And going directly to old Alec Ramsay she grasped his blunt thick
fingers, the nails of which were always whitened a little with stone
dust, and greeted him in her large and spacious way:

"Mr. Ramsay," she said, "I want you to know how glad we are that
you could come. And that goes for all of you—Mr. Jannadeau, and Mr.
Duncan, and Mr. Fogarty, and you, Ernest, and you, too, Ollie—you are
the best friends Papa has, there's no one he thinks more of, and no one
he would rather see."

Mr. Ramsay's brick-red face and brick-red neck became even red-
der before he spoke, and beneath his grizzled brows his blue eyes suddenly were smoke blue. He put his blunt hand to his mustache for a
moment, and tugged at it, then he said in his gruff, quiet, and matter-
of-fact voice:

"I guess we know Will about as well as any one, Miss Helen. I've
worked for him off and on for thirty years."

At the same moment, she heard Ollie Gant's easy, deep, and powerful
laugh, and saw him slowly lift his cigarette in his coarse paw; she saw
Jannadeau's great yellow face and massive domy brow, and heard him
laugh with guttural pleasure, saying, "Ah-h! I tell you vat! Dat girl
has alvays looket out for her datty—she's de only vun dat coult hantle

him; efer since she vas ten years olt it has been de same." And she was overwhelmingly conscious of that immeasurable mountain of a man, Mike Fogarty, beside her, the sweet clarity of his blue eyes, and the almost purring music of his voice as he gently laid his mutton of a hand upon her shoulder for a moment, saying,

"Ah, Miss Helen, I don't know how Will could have got along all these years without ye—for he has said the same himself a thousand times—aye! that he has!"

And instantly, having heard these words, and feeling the strong calm presences of these powerful men around her, it seemed to Helen she had somehow re-entered a magic world that she thought was gone forever. And she was immensely content.

At the same moment, with a sense of wonder, she discovered an astonishing thing, that she had never noticed before, but that she must have heard a thousand times;—this was that of all these people, who knew Gant best, and had a deep and true affection for him, there were only two—Mr. Fogarty and Mr. Ramsay—who had ever addressed him by his first name. And so far as she could now remember, these two men, together with Gant's mother, his brothers, his sister Augusta, and a few of the others who had known him in his boyhood in Pennsylvania, were the only people who ever had. And this revelation cast a strange, a lonely and a troubling light upon the great gaunt figure of the stonecutter, which moved her powerfully and which she had never felt before. And most strange of all was the variety of names by which these various people called her father.

As for Eliza, had any of her children ever heard her address her husband as anything but "Mr. Gant"—had she ever called him by one of his first names—their anguish of shame and impropriety would have been so great that they could hardly have endured it. But such a lapse would have been incredible: Eliza could no more have addressed Gant by his first name, than she could have quoted Homer's Greek; had she tried to address him so, the muscles of her tongue would have found it physically impossible to pronounce the word. And in this fact there was somehow, now that Gant was dying, an enormous pathos. It gave to Eliza's life with him a pitiable and moving dignity, the compensation of a proud and wounded spirit for all the insults and injuries that had been heaped upon it. She had been a young country woman of twenty-four when she had met him, she had been ignorant of life, and innocent of the cruelty, the violence, the drunkenness and abuse of which men

are capable, she had borne this man fifteen children, of whom eight had
come to life, and had for forty years eaten the bread of blood and tears
and joy and grief and terror, she had wanted affection and had been
given taunts, abuse, and curses, and somehow her proud and wounded
spirit had endured with an anguished but unshaken fortitude all the
wrongs and cruelties and injustices of which he had been guilty toward
her. And now at the very end her pride still had this pitiable distinction,
her spirit still preserved this last integrity: she had not betrayed her
wounded soul to a shameful familiarity, he had remained to her—in
mind and heart and living word—what he had been from the first day
that she met him; the author of her grief and misery, the agent of her
suffering, the gaunt and lonely stranger who had come into her hills
from a strange land and a distant people—that furious, gaunt, and
lonely stranger with whom by fatal accident her destiny—past hate or
love or birth or death or human error and confusion—had been in-
solubly enmeshed, with whom for forty years she had lived, a wife, a
mother, and a stranger—and who would to the end remain to her a
stranger—"Mr. Gant."

What was it? What was the secret of this strange and bitter mystery
of life that had made of Gant a stranger to all men, and most of all a
stranger to his wife? Perhaps some of the answer might have been
found in Eliza's own unconscious words when she described her meeting with him forty years before:

"It was not that he was old," she said,—"he was only thirty-three—but
he *looked* old—his *ways* were old—he had lived so much among old people.—Pshaw!" she continued, with a little puckered smile, "if any one
had told me that night I saw him sitting there with Lydia and old Mrs.
Mason—that was the very day they moved into the house, the night he
gave the big dinner—and Lydia was still alive and, of course, she was
ten years older than he was, and that may have had something to do with
it—but I got to studying him as he sat there, of course, he was tired and
run down and depressed and worried over all that trouble that he'd had
in Sidney before he came up here, when he lost everything, and he
knew that Lydia was dying, and that was preyin' on his mind—but he
looked old, thin as a rake you know, and sallow and run down, and
with those *old* ways he had acquired, I reckon, from associatin' with
Lydia and old Mrs. Mason and people like that—but I just sat there
studying him as he sat there with them and I said— 'Well, you're an old
man, aren't you, sure enough?'—pshaw! if any one had told me that

night that some day I'd be married to him I'd have laughed at them—
I'd have considered that I was marrying an old man—and that's just
exactly what a lot of people thought, sir, when the news got out that I
was goin' to marry him—I know Martha Patton came running to me,
all excited and out of breath—said, 'Eliza! You're not going to marry
that old man—you know you're not!'—you see, his *ways* were old, he
looked old, *dressed* old, *acted* old—everything he did was old; there was
always, it seemed, something strange and old-like about him, almost
like he had been born that way."

And it was at this time that Eliza met him, saw him first—"Mr. Gant"
—an immensely tall, gaunt, cadaverous-looking man, with a face stern
and sad with care, lank, drooping mustaches, sandy hair, and cold-gray
staring eyes—"not so old, you know—he was only thirty-three—but he
looked old, he *acted* old, his *ways* were old—he had lived so much
among older people he seemed older than he was—I thought of him as
an old man."

This, then, was "Mr. Gant" at thirty-three, and since then, although
his fortunes and position had improved, his character had changed little. And now Helen, faced by all these working men, who had known,
liked, and respected him, and had now come to see him again before he
died—suddenly knew the reason for his loneliness, the reason so few
people—least of all, his wife—had ever dared address him by his first
name. And with a swift and piercing revelation, his muttered words,
which she had heard him use a thousand times when speaking of his
childhood— "We had a tough time of it—I tell you what, we did!"—
now came back to her with the unutterable poignancy of discovery. For
the first time she understood what they meant. And suddenly, with the
same swift and nameless pity, she remembered all the pictures which
she had seen of her father as a boy and a young man. There were a half
dozen of them in the big family album, together with pictures of his
own and Eliza's family: they were the small daguerreotypes of fifty years
before, in small frames of faded plush, with glass covers, touched with
the faint pale pinks with which the photographers of an earlier time
tried to paint with life the sallow hues of their photography. The first
of these pictures showed Gant as a little boy; later, a boy of twelve, he
was standing in a chair beside his brother Wesley, who was seated, with
a wooden smile upon his face. Later, a picture of Gant in the years in
Baltimore, standing, his feet crossed, leaning elegantly upon a marble
slab beside a vase; later still, the young stonecutter before his little shop

in the years at Sidney; finally, Gant, after his marriage with Eliza, standing with gaunt face and lank drooping mustaches before his shop upon the square, in the company of Will Pentland, who was at the time his business partner.

And all these pictures, from first to last, from the little boy to the man with the lank drooping mustaches, had been marked by the same expression: the sharp thin face was always stern and sad with care, the shallow cold-gray eyes always stared out of the bony cage-formation of the skull with a cold mournfulness—the whole impression was always one of gaunt sad loneliness. And it was not the loneliness of the dreamer, the poet, or the misjudged prophet, it was just the cold and terrible loneliness of man, of every man, and of the lost American who has been brought forth naked under immense and lonely skies, to "shift for himself," to grope his way blindly through the confusion and brutal chaos of a life as naked and unsure as he, to wander blindly down across the continent, to hunt forever for a goal, a wall, a dwelling place of warmth and certitude, a light, a door.

And for this reason, she now understood something about her father, this great gaunt figure of a stonecutter that she had never understood or thought about before: she suddenly understood his order, sense of decency and dispatch; his love of cleanness, roaring fires, and rich abundance, his foul drunkenness, violence, and howling fury, his naked shame and trembling penitence, his good clothes of heavy monumental black that he always kept well pressed, his clean boiled shirts, wing collars, and his love of hotels, ships, and trains, his love of gardens, new lands, cities, voyages. She knew suddenly that he was unlike any other man that ever lived, and that every man that ever lived was like her father. And remembering the cold and mournful look in his shallow staring eyes of cold hard gray, she suddenly knew the reason for that look, as she had never known it before, and understood now why so few men had ever called him by his first name—why he was known to all the world as "Mr. Gant."

Having joined this group of working men, Helen immediately felt an indefinable but powerful sense of comfort and physical well-being which the presence of such men as these always gave to her. And she did not know why; but immediately, once she had grasped Mr. Ramsay by the hand, and was aware of Mike Fogarty's mountainous form and clear-blue eye above her, and Ollie Gant's deep and lazy laugh, and the deliberate and sensual languor with which he raised his cigarette to his lips with his powerful plasterer's hand, drawing the smoke deep into his strong lungs and letting it trickle slowly from his nostrils as he talked —she was conscious of a feeling of enormous security and relief which she had not known in years.

And this feeling, as with every person of strong sensuous perceptions, was literal, physical, chemical, astoundingly acute. She not only felt an enormous relief and joy to get back to these working people, it even seemed to her that everything they did—the way Mr. Duncan held his strong cheap cigar in his thick dry fingers, the immense satisfaction with which he drew on it, the languid and sensual trickling of cigarette smoke from Ollie Gant's nostrils, his deep, good-natured, indolently lazy laugh, even the perceptible bulge of tobacco-quid in Alec Ramsay's brick-red face, his barely perceptible rumination of it—all these things, though manlike in their nature, seemed wonderfully good and fresh and living to her—the whole plain priceless glory of the earth restored to her—and gave her a feeling of wonderful happiness and joy.

And later that night when all these men, her father's friends, had gone into his room, filling it with their enormous and full-blooded vitality, as she saw him lying there, wax-pale, bloodless, motionless, yet with a faint grin at the edge of his thin mouth as he received them, as she heard their deep full-fibred voices, Mike Fogarty's lilting Irish, Mr. Duncan's thick Scotch burr, Ollie Gant's deep and lazy laugh, and the humor of Alec Ramsay's deep, gruff and matter-of-fact tone, relating old times—"God, Will!" he said, "at your worst, you weren't in it compared to Wes! He was a holy terror when he drank! Do you remember the day he drove his fist through your plate-glass window right in the face of Jannadeau—and went home then and tore all the plumbing out of the house and pitched the bathtub out of the second-storey window into Orchard Street—God! Will!—you weren't in it compared to Wes"—as she heard all this, and saw Gant's thin grin and heard his faint and rusty cackle, his almost inaudible "E'God! Poor Wes!"—she could not believe that he was going to die, the great full-blooded working men filled the room with the vitality of a life which had returned in all its rich and living flood, and seemed intolerably near and familiar—and she kept thinking with a feeling of wonderful happiness and disbelief: "Oh, but Papa's not going to die! It's not possible! He can't! He can't!"

XXXI

THE dying man himself was no longer to be fooled and duped by hope; he knew that he was done for, and he no longer cared. Rather, as if that knowledge had brought him a new strength—the immense and measureless strength that comes from resignation, and that has vanquished terror and despair—Gant had already consigned himself to death, and now was waiting for it, without weariness or anxiety, and with a perfect and peaceful acquiescence.

This complete resignation and tranquillity of a man whose life had been so full of violence, protest, and howling fury stunned and silenced them, and left them helpless. It seemed that Gant, knowing that often he had lived badly, was now determined to die well. And in this he succeeded. He accepted every ministration, every visit, every stammering reassurance, or frenzied activity, with a passive gratefulness which he seemed to want every one to know. On the evening of the day after his first hemorrhage, he asked for food and Eliza, bustling out, pathetically eager to do something, killed a chicken and cooked it for him.

And as if, from that infinite depth of death and silence from which he looked at her, he had seen, behind the bridling brisk activity of her figure, forever bustling back and forth, saying confusedly— "Why, yes! The very thing! This very minute, sir!"—had seen the white strained face, the stricken eyes of a proud and sensitive woman who had wanted affection all her life, had received for the most part injury and abuse, and who was ready to clutch at any crust of comfort that might console or justify her before he died—he ate part of the chicken with relish, and then looking up at her, said quietly:

"I tell you what—that was a good chicken."

And Helen, who had been sitting beside him on the bed, and feeding him, now cried out in a tone of bantering and good-humored challenge:

"What! Is it better than the ones *I* cook for you! You'd better not say it is—I'll beat you if you do."

And Gant, grinning feebly, shook his head, and answered:

"Ah-h! Your mother is a good cook, Helen. You're a good cook, too—but there's no one else can cook a chicken like your mother!"

And stretching out his great right hand, he patted Eliza's worn fingers with his own.

And Eliza, suddenly touched by that word of unaccustomed praise

and tenderness, turned and rushed blindly from the room at a clumsy
bridling gait, clasping her hands together at the wrist, her weak eyes
blind with tears—shaking her head in a strong convulsive movement,
her mouth smiling a pale tremulous smile, ludicrous, touching, made unnatural by her false teeth, whispering over and over to herself, "Poor
fellow! Says, 'There's no one else can cook a chicken like your mother.'
Reached out and patted me on the hand, you know. Says 'I tell you what,
there's no one who can cook a chicken like your mother.' I reckon he
wanted to let me know, to tell me, but says, 'The rest of you have all
been good to me, Helen's a good cook, but there's no one else can cook
like your mother.' "

"Oh, here, here, here," said Helen, who, laughing uncertainly had
followed her mother from the room when Eliza had rushed out, and
had seized her by the arms, and shook her gently, "good heavens! *Here!*
You mustn't carry on like this! You mustn't take it this way! Why,
he's all right!" she cried out heartily and shook Eliza again. "Papa's
going to be all right! Why, what are you crying for?" she laughed.
"He's going to get well now—don't you know that?"

And Eliza could say nothing for a moment but kept smiling that
false trembling and unnatural smile, shaking her head in a slight convulsive movement, her eyes blind with tears.

"I tell you what," she whispered, smiling tremulously again and
shaking her head, "there was something about it—you know, the way he
said it—says, 'There's no one who can come up to your mother'—there
was something in the way he said it! Poor fellow, says, 'None of the rest
of you can cook like her'—says, 'I tell you what, that was certainly a
good chicken'— Poor fellow! It wasn't so much what he said as the
way he said it—there was something about it that went through me
like a knife—I tell you what it did!"

"Oh, here, here, here!" Helen cried again, laughing. But her own
eyes were also wet, the bitter possessiveness that had dominated all her
relations with her father, and that had thrust Eliza away from him, was
suddenly vanquished. At that moment she began to feel an affection for
her mother that she had never felt before, a deep and nameless pity
and regret, and a sense of sombre satisfaction.

"Well," she thought, "I guess it's all she's had, but I'm glad she's got
that much to remember. I'm glad he said it: she'll always have that now
to hang on to."

And Gant lay looking up from that sunken depth of death and silence, his great hands of living power quiet with their immense and passive strength beside him on the bed.

XXXII

Towards one o'clock that night Gant fell asleep and dreamed that he was walking down the road that led to Spangler's Run. And although he had not been along that road for fifty years everything was as fresh, as green, as living and familiar as it had ever been to him. He came out on the road from Schaefer's farm, and on his left he passed by the little white frame church of the United Brethren, and the graveyard about the church where his friends and family had been buried. From the road he could see the line of family gravestones which he himself had carved and set up after he had returned from serving his apprenticeship in Baltimore. The stones were all alike: tall flat slabs of marble with plain rounded tops, and there was one for his sister Susan, who had died in infancy, and one for his sister Huldah, who had died in childbirth while the war was on, and one for Huldah's husband, a young farmer named Jake Lentz who had been killed at Chancellorsville, and one for the husband of his oldest sister, Augusta, a man named Martin, who had been an itinerant photographer and had died soon after the war, and finally one for Gant's own father. And since there were no stones for his brother George or for Elmer or for John, and none for his mother or Augusta, Gant knew that he was still a young man, and had just recently come home. The stones which he had put up were still white and new, and in the lower right hand corner of each stone, he had carved his own name: W. O. Gant.

It was a fine morning in early May and everything was sweet and green and as familiar as it had always been. The graveyard was carpeted with thick green grass, and all around the graveyard and the church there was the incomparable green velvet of young wheat. And the thought came back to Gant, as it had come to him a thousand times, that the wheat around the graveyard looked greener and richer than any other wheat that he had ever seen. And beside him on his right were the great fields of the Schaefer farm, some richly carpeted with young green wheat, and some ploughed, showing great bronze-red strips of fertile nobly swelling earth. And behind him on the great swell of the land, and commanding that sweet and casual scene with the majesty of its incomparable lay was Jacob Schaefer's great red barn and to the right the neat brick house with the white trimming of its windows, the white picket fence, the green yard with its rich tapestry of flowers and lilac bushes and the massed leafy spread of its big maple trees. And behind the house the hill rose, and all its woods were just greening into May, still smoky, tender and unfledged, gold-yellow with the magic of young green. And before the woods began there was the apple orchard halfway up the hill; the trees were heavy with the blossoms and stood there in all their dense still bloom incredible.

And from the greening trees the bird-song rose, the grass was thick with the dense gold glory of the dandelions, and all about him were a thousand magic things that came and went and never could be captured. Below the church, he passed the old frame house where Elly Spangler, who kept the church keys, lived, and there were apple trees behind the house, all dense with bloom, but the house was rickety, unpainted and dilapidated as it had always been, and he wondered if the kitchen was still buzzing with a million flies, and if Elly's half-wit brothers, Jim and Willy, were inside. And even as he shook his head and thought, as he had thought so many times "Poor Elly," the back door opened and Willy Spangler, a man past thirty wearing overalls, and with a fond, foolish witless face, came galloping down across the yard toward him, flinging his arms out in exuberant greeting, and shouting to him the same welcome that he shouted out to every one who passed, friends and strangers all alike— "I've been lookin' fer ye! I've been lookin' fer ye, Oll," using, as was the custom of the friends and kinsmen of his Pennsylvania boyhood, his second name—and then, anxiously, pleadingly, again the same words that he spoke to every one: "Ain't ye goin' to stay?"

And Gant, grinning, but touched by the indefinable sadness and pity which that kind and witless greeting had always stirred in him since his own childhood, shook his head, and said quietly:

"No, Willy. Not to-day. I'm meeting some one down the road"—and straightway felt, with thudding heart, a powerful and nameless excitement, the urgency of that impending meeting—why, where, with whom, he did not know—but all-compelling now, inevitable.

And Willy, still with wondering, foolish, kindly face followed along beside him now, saying eagerly, as he said to every one:

"Did ye bring anythin' fer me? Have ye got a chew?"

And Gant, starting to shake his head in refusal, stopped suddenly, seeing the look of disappointment on the idiot's face, and putting his hand in the pocket of his coat, took out a plug of apple-tobacco, saying:

"Yes. Here you are, Willy. You can have this."

And Willy, grinning with foolish joy, had clutched the plug of to-bacco and, still kind and foolish, had followed on a few steps more, saying anxiously:

"Are ye comin' back, Oll? Will ye be comin' back real soon?"

And Gant, feeling a strange and nameless sorrow, answered:

"I don't know, Willy"—for suddenly he saw that he might never come this way again.

But Willy, still happy, foolish, and contented, had turned and gal-loped away toward the house, flinging his arms out and shouting as he went:

"I'll be waitin' fer ye. I'll be waitin' fer ye, Oll."

And Gant went on then, down the road, and there was a nameless sorrow in him that he could not understand, and some of the brightness had gone out of the day.

When he got to the mill, he turned left along the road that went down by Spangler's run, crossed by the bridge below, and turned from the road into the wood-path on the other side. A child was standing in the path, and turned and went on ahead of him. In the wood the sunlight made swarming moths of light across the path, and through the leafy tangle of the trees: the sunlight kept shifting and swarming on the child's gold hair, and all around him were the sudden noises of the wood, the stir, the rustle, and the bullet thrum of wings, the cool broken sound of hidden water.

The wood got denser, darker as he went on and coming to a place where the path split away into two forks, Gant stopped, and turning to the child said, "Which one shall I take?" And the child did not answer him.

But some one was there in the wood before him. He heard footsteps on the path, and saw a footprint in the earth, and turning took the path where the footprint was, and where it seemed he could hear some one walking.

And then, with the bridgeless instancy of dreams, it seemed to him that all of the bright green-gold around him in the wood grew dark and sombre, the path grew darker, and suddenly he was walking in a strange and gloomy forest, haunted by the brown and tragic light of dreams. The forest shapes of great trees rose around him, he could hear no bird-song now, even his own feet on the path were soundless, but he always thought he heard the sound of some one walking in the wood before him. He stopped and listened: the steps were muffled, softly thunderous, they seemed so near that he thought that he must catch up with the one he followed in another second, and then they seemed immensely far away, receding in the dark mystery of that gloomy wood. And again he stopped and listened, the footsteps faded, vanished, he shouted, no one answered. And suddenly he knew that he had taken the wrong path, that he was lost. And in his heart there was an immense and quiet sadness, and the dark light of the enormous wood was all around him; no birds sang.

XXXIII

GANT awoke suddenly and found himself looking straight up at Eliza who was seated in a chair beside the bed.

"You were asleep," she said quietly with a grave smile, looking at him in her direct and almost accusing fashion.

"Yes," he said, breathing a little hoarsely, "what time is it?"

It was a few minutes before three o'clock in the morning. She looked at the clock and told him the time: he asked where Helen was.

"Why," said Eliza quickly, "she's right here in this hall room: I reckon she's asleep, too. Said she was tired, you know, but that if you woke up and needed her to call her. Do you want me to get her?"

"No," said Gant. "Don't bother her. I guess she needs the rest, poor child. Let her sleep."

"Yes," said Eliza, nodding, "and that's exactly what you must do, too, Mr. Gant. You try to go on back to sleep now," she said coaxingly, "for that's what we all need. There's no medicine like sleep—as the fellow says, it's Nature's sovereign remedy," said Eliza, with that form of sententiousness that she was very fond of—"so you go on, now, Mr. Gant, and get a good night's sleep, and when you wake up in the morning, you'll feel like a new man. That's half the battle—if you can get your sleep, you're already on the road to recovery."

"No," said Gant, "I've slept enough."

He was breathing rather hoarsely and heavily and she asked him if he was comfortable and needed anything. He made no answer for a moment, and then muttered something under his breath that she could not hear plainly, but that sounded like "little boy."

"Hah? What say? What is it, Mr. Gant?" Eliza said. "Little boy?" she said sharply, as he did not answer.

"Did you see him?" he said.

She looked at him for a moment with troubled eyes, then said:

"Pshaw, Mr. Gant, I guess you must have been dreaming."

He did not answer, and for a moment there was no sound in the room but his breathing, hoarse, a little heavy. Then he muttered:

"Did some one come into the house?"

She looked at him sharply, inquiringly again, with troubled eyes:

"Hah? What say? Why, no, I think not," she said doubtfully, "unless you may have heard Gilmer come in an' go up to his room."

And Gant was again silent for several moments, breathing a little heavily and hoarsely, his hands resting with an enormous passive strength, upon the bed. Presently he said quietly:

"Where's Bacchus?"

"Hah? Who's that?" Eliza said sharply, in a startled kind of tone. "Bacchus? You mean Uncle Bacchus?"

"Yes," said Gant.

"Why, pshaw, Mr. Gant!" cried Eliza laughing—for a startled moment she had wondered if "his mind was wanderin'," but one glance at his quiet eyes, the tranquil sanity of his quiet tone, reassured her——

"Pshaw!" she said, putting one finger up to her broad nose-wing and laughing slyly. "You must have been havin' queer dreams, for a fact!"

"Is he here?"

"Why, I'll vow, Mr. Gant!" she cried again. "What on earth is in your mind? You know that Uncle Bacchus is way out West in Oregon—it's been ten years since he came back home last—that summer of the reunion at Gettysburg."

"Yes," said Gant. "I remember now."

And again he fell silent, staring upward in the semi-darkness, his hands quietly at rest beside him, breathing a little hoarsely, but without pain. Eliza sat in the chair watching him, her hands clasped loosely at her waist, her lips pursed reflectively, and a puzzled look in her eyes: "Now I wonder what ever put that in his mind?" she thought. "I wonder what made him think of Bacchus. Now his mind's not wanderin'—that's one thing sure. He knows what he's doing just as well as I do—I reckon he must have dreamed it—that Bacchus was here—but that's certainly a strange thing, that he should bring it up like this."

He was so silent that she thought he might have gone to sleep again, he lay motionless with his eyes turned upward in the semi-darkness of the room, his hands immense and passive at his side. But suddenly he startled her again by speaking, a voice so quiet and low that he might have been talking to himself.

"Father died the year before the war," he said, "when I was nine years old. I never got to know him very well. I guess Mother had a hard time of it. There were seven of us—and nothing but that little place to live on—and some of us too young to help her much—and George away at war. She spoke pretty hard to us sometimes—but I guess she had a hard time of it. It was a tough time for all of us," he muttered, "I tell you what, it was."

"Yes," Eliza said, "I guess it was. I know she told me—I talked to her, you know, the time we went there on our honeymoon—whew! what about it?" she shrieked faintly, and put her finger up to her broad nose-wing with the same sly gesture—"it was all I could do to keep a straight face sometimes—why, you know, the way she had of talkin'— the expressions she used—oh! came right out with it, you know—sometimes I'd have to turn my head away so she wouldn't see me laughin'— says, you know, 'I was left a widow with seven children to bring up, but I never took charity from no one; as I told 'em all, I've crawled under the dog's belly all my life; now I guess I can get over its back.'"

"Yes," said Gant with a faint grin. "Many's the time I've heard her say that."

"But she told it then, you know," Eliza went on in explanatory fashion, "about your father and how he'd done hard labor on a farm all his life and died—well, I reckon you'd call it consumption."

"Yes," said Gant. "That was it."

"And," Eliza said reflectively, "I never asked—of course, I didn't want to embarrass her—but I reckon from what she said, he may have been— well, I suppose you might say he was a drinkin' man."

"Yes," said Gant, "I guess he was."

"And I know she told it on him," said Eliza, laughing again, and passing one finger slyly at the corner of her broad nose-wing, "how he went to town that time—to Brant's Mill, I guess it was—and how she was afraid he'd get to drinkin', and she sent you and Wes along to watch him and to see he got home again—and how he met up with some fellers there and, sure enough, I guess he started drinkin' and stayed away too long—and then, I reckon he was afraid of what she'd say to him when he got back—and that was when he bought the clock—it's that very clock upon the mantel, Mr. Gant—but that was when he got the clock, all right—I guess he thought it would pacify her when she started out to scold him for gettin' drunk and bein' late."

"Yes," said Gant, who had listened without moving, staring at the ceiling, and with a faint grin printed at the corners of his mouth, "well do I remember: that was it, all right."

"And then," Eliza went on, "he lost the way comin' home—it had been snowin', and I reckon it was getting dark, and he had been drinkin' —and instead of turnin' in on the road that went down by your place he kept goin' on until he passed Jake Schaefer's farm—an' I guess Wes and you, poor child, kept follerin' where he led, thinkin' it was all right—and when he realized his mistake he said he was tired an' had to rest a while and—I'll vow! to think he'd go and do a thing like that," said Eliza, laughing again—"he lay right down in the snow, sir, with the clock beside him—and went sound to sleep."

"Yes," said Gant, "and the clock was broken."

"Yes," Eliza said, "she told me about that too—and how she heard you all come creepin' in real quiet an' easy-like about nine o'clock that night, when she and all the children were in bed—an' how she could hear him whisperin' to you and Wes to be quiet—an' how she heard you all come creepin' up the steps—and how he came tip-toein' in real easy-like an' laid the clock down on the bed—I reckon the glass had been broken out of it—hopin' she'd see it when she woke up in the morning an' wouldn't scold him then for stayin' out——"

"Yes," said Gant, still with the faint attentive grin, "and then the clock began to strike."

"Whew-w!" cried Eliza, putting her finger underneath her broad nose-wing—"I know she had to laugh about it when she told it to me— she said that all of you looked so sheepish when the clock began to strike that she didn't have the heart to scold him."

And Gant, grinning faintly again, emitted a faint rusty cackle that sounded like "E'God!" and said: "Yes, that was it. Poor fellow."

"But to think," Eliza went on, "that he would have no more sense than to do a thing like that—to lay right down there in the snow an' go to sleep with you two children watchin' him. And I know how she told it, how she questioned you and Wes next day, and I reckon started in to scold you for not takin' better care of him, and how you told her, 'Well, Mother, I thought that it would be all right. I kept steppin' where he stepped, I thought he knew the way.' And said she didn't have the heart to scold you after that—poor child, I reckon you were only eight or nine years old, and boy-like thought you'd follow in your father's footsteps and that everything would be all right."

"Yes," said Gant, with the faint grin again, "I kept stretchin' my legs to put my feet down in his tracks— it was all I could do to keep up with him. . . . Ah, Lord," he said, and in a moment said in a faint low voice, "how well I can remember it. That was just the winter before he died."

"And you've had that old clock ever since," Eliza said. "That very clock upon the mantel, sir—at least, you've had it ever since I've known you, and I reckon you had it long before that—for I know you told me how you brought it South with you. And that clock must be all of sixty or seventy years old—if it's a day."

"Yes," said Gant, "it's all of that."

And again he was silent, and lay so still and motionless that there was no sound in the room except his faint and labored breathing, the languid stir of the curtains in the cool night breeze, and the punctual tocking of the old wooden clock. And presently, when she thought that he might have gone off to sleep again, he spoke, in the same remote and detached voice as before:

"Eliza,"—he said—and at the sound of that unaccustomed word, a name he had spoken only twice in forty years—her white face and her worn brown eyes turned toward him with the quick and startled look of an animal—"Eliza," he said quietly, "you have had a hard life with me, a hard time. I want to tell you that I'm sorry."

And before she could move from her white stillness of shocked surprise, he lifted his great right hand and put it gently down across her own. And for a moment she sat there bolt upright, shaken, frozen, with a look of terror in her eyes, her heart drained of blood, a pale smile trembling uncertainly and foolishly on her lips. Then she tried to withdraw her hand with a clumsy movement, she began to stammer with an air of ludicrous embarrassment, she bridled, saying—"Aw-w, now, Mr. Gant. Well, now, I reckon,"—and suddenly these few simple words of regret and affection did what all the violence, abuse, drunkenness and injury of forty years had failed to do. She wrenched her hand free like a wounded creature, her face was suddenly contorted by that grotesque and pitiable grimace of sorrow that women have had in moments of grief since the beginning of time, and digging her fist into her closed eye quickly with the pathetic gesture of a child, she lowered her head and wept bitterly:

"It was a hard time, Mr. Gant," she whispered, "a hard time, sure enough. . . . It wasn't all the cursin' and the drinkin'—I got used to that. . . . I reckon I was only an ignorant sort of girl when I met you and I guess," she went on with a pathetic and unconscious humor, "I didn't know what married life was like . . . but I could have stood the rest of it . . . the bad names an' all the things you called me when I was goin' to have another child . . . but it was what you said when Grover died . . . accusin' me of bein' responsible for his death because I took the children to St. Louis to the Fair—" and at the words as if an old and lacerated wound had been re-opened raw and bleeding, she wept hoarsely, harshly, bitterly—"that was the worst time that I had—sometimes I prayed to God that I would not wake up—he was a fine boy, Mr. Gant, the best I had—like the write-up in the paper said he had the sense an' judgment of one twice his age . . . an' somehow it had grown a part of me, I expected him to lead the others—when he died it seemed like everything was gone . . . an' then to have you say that I had—" her voice faltered to a whisper, stopped: with a pathetic gesture she wiped the sleeve of her old frayed sweater across her eyes and already ashamed of her tears, said hastily:

"Not that I'm blamin' you, Mr. Gant. . . . I reckon we were both at fault . . . we were both to blame . . . if I had it to do all over I know I could do better . . . but I was so young and ignorant when I met you, Mr. Gant . . . knew nothing of the world . . . there was always something strange-like about you that I didn't understand."

Then, as he said nothing, but lay still and passive, looking at the ceiling, she said quickly, drying her eyes and speaking with a brisk and instant cheerfulness, the undaunted optimism of her ever-hopeful nature:

"Well, now, Mr. Gant, that's all over, and the best thing we can do is to forget about it. . . . We've both made our mistakes—we wouldn't be human if we didn't—but now we've got to profit by experience—the worst of all this trouble is all over—you've got to think of getting well now, that's the only thing you've got to do, sir," she said pursing her lips and winking briskly at him—"just set your mind on getting well— that's all you've got to do now, Mr. Gant—and the battle is half won. For half our ills and troubles are all imagination," she said sententiously, "and if you'll just make up your mind now that you're going to get well—why, sir, you'll do it," and she looked at him with a brisk nod. "And we've both got years before us, Mr. Gant—for all we know, the best years of our life are still ahead of us—so we'll both go on and profit by the mistakes of the past and make the most of what time's left," she said. "That's just exactly what we'll do!"

And quietly, kindly, without moving, and with the impassive and limitless regret of a man who knows that there is no return, he answered: "Yes, Eliza. That is what we'll do."

"And now," she went on coaxingly, "why don't you go on back to sleep now, Mr. Gant? There's nothin' like sleep to restore a man to health—as the feller says, it's Nature's sovereign remedy, worth all the doctors and all the medicine on earth," she winked at him, and then concluded on a note of cheerful finality, "so you go on and get some sleep now, and tomorrow you will feel like a new man."

And again he shook his head in an almost imperceptible gesture of negation:

"No," he said, "not now. Can't sleep."

He was silent again, and presently, his breath coming somewhat hoarse and labored, he cleared his throat, and put one hand up to his throat, as if to relieve himself of some impediment.

Eliza looked at him with troubled eyes and said:

"What's the matter, Mr. Gant? There's nothing hurtin' you?"

"No," he said. "Just something in my throat. Could I have some water?"

"Why, yes, sir! That's the very thing!" She got up hastily, and looking about in a somewhat confused manner, saw behind her a pitcher of water and a glass upon his old walnut bureau, and saying "This very minute, sir!" started across the room.

And at the same moment, Gant was aware that some one had entered the house, was coming towards him through the hall, would soon be with him. Turning his head towards the door he was conscious of something approaching with the speed of light, the instancy of thought, and at that moment he was filled with a sense of inexpressible joy, a feeling of triumph and security he had never known. Something immensely bright and beautiful was converging in a flare of light, and at that instant, the whole room blurred around him, his sight was fixed upon that focal image in the door, and suddenly the child was standing there and looking towards him.

And even as he started from his pillows, and tried to call his wife he felt something thick and heavy in his throat that would not let him speak. He tried to call to her again but no sound came, then something wet and warm began to flow out of his mouth and nostrils, he lifted his hands up to his throat, the warm wet blood came pouring out across his fingers; he saw it and felt joy.

For now the child—or some one in the house was speaking, calling to him; he heard great footsteps, soft but thunderous, imminent, yet immensely far, a voice well-known, never heard before. He called to it, and then it seemed to answer him; he called to it with faith and joy to give him rescue, strength, and life, and it answered him and told him that all the error, old age, pain and grief of life was nothing but an evil dream; that he who had been lost was found again, that his youth would be restored to him and that he would never die, and that he would find again the path he had not taken long ago in a dark wood.

And the child still smiled at him from the dark door; the great steps, soft and powerful, came ever closer, and as the instant imminent approach of that last meeting came intolerably near, he cried out through the lake of jetting blood, "Here, Father, here!" and heard a strong voice answer him, "My son!"

At that instant he was torn by a rending cough, something was wrenched loose in him, the death gasp rattled through his blood, and a mass of greenish matter foamed out through his lips. Then the world was blotted out, a blind black fog swam up and closed above his head, some one seized him, he was held, supported in two arms, he heard some one's voice saying in a low tone of terror and of pity, "Mr. Gant! Mr. Gant! Oh, poor man, poor man! He's gone!" And his brain faded into night. Even before she lowered him back upon the pillows, she knew that he was dead.

Eliza's sharp scream brought three of her children—Daisy, Steve, and Luke, and the nurse, Bessie Gant, who was the wife of Gant's nephew Ollie—running from the kitchen. At the same moment Helen, who had taken an hour's sleep—her first in two days—in the little hall-bedroom off the porch, was wakened by her mother's cry, the sound of a screen-door slammed, and the sound of footsteps running past her window on the porch. Then, for several minutes she had no consciousness of what she did, and later she could not remember it. Her actions were those of a person driven by a desperate force, who acts from blind intuition, not from reason. Instantly, the moment that she heard her mother scream, the slam of the screen-door, and the running feet, she knew what had happened, and from that moment she knew only one frenzied desire; somehow to get to her father before he died.

The breath caught hoarse and sharp in her throat in a kind of nervous sob, it seemed that her heart had stopped beating and that her whole life-force was paralyzed; but she was out of her bed with a movement that left the old springs rattling, and she came across the back-porch with a kind of tornado-like speed that just came instantly from nowhere: in a moment she was standing in the open door with the sudden bolted look of a person who has been shot through the heart, staring at the silent group of people, and at the figure on the bed, with a dull strained stare of disbelief and horror.

All the time, although she was not conscious of it, her breath kept coming in a kind of hoarse short sob, her large big-boned face had an almost animal look of anguish and surprise, her mouth was partly open, her large chin hung down, and at this moment, as they turned towards her she began to moan, "Oh-h, oh-h, oh-h, oh-h!" in the same unconscious way, like a person who has received a heavy blow in the pit of the stomach. Then her mouth gaped open, a hoarse and ugly cry was torn from her throat—a cry not of grief but loss—and she rushed forward like a mad woman. They tried to stop her, to restrain her, she flung them away as if they had been rag dolls and hurled herself down across the body on the bed, raving like a maniac.

"Oh, Papa, Papa. . . . Why didn't they tell me? . . . Why didn't they let me know? . . . Why didn't they call me? . . . Oh, Papa, Papa, Papa! . . . dead, dead, dead . . . and they didn't tell me . . . they didn't let me know . . . they let you die . . . and I wasn't here! . . . I wasn't here!"—and she wept harshly, horribly, bitterly, rocking back and forth like a mad woman, with a dead man in her arms. She kept moaning, ". . . They didn't tell me . . . they let you die without me . . . I wasn't here . . . I wasn't here . . ."

And even when they lifted her up from the bed, detached her arms from the body they had held in such a desperate hug, she still kept moaning in a demented manner, as if talking to the corpse, and oblivious of the presence of these living people:

"They never told me . . . they never told me. . . . They let you die here all by yourself . . . and I wasn't here . . . I wasn't here."

All of the women, except Bessie Gant, had now begun to weep hysterically, more from shock, exhaustion, and the nervous strain than from grief, and now Bessie Gant's voice could be heard speaking to them sharply, coldly, peremptorily, as she tried to bring back order and calmness to the distracted scene:

"Now, you get out of here—all of you! . . . There's nothing more any of you can do—I'll take care of all the rest of it! . . . Get out, now . . . I can't have you in the room while there's work to do. . . . Helen, go on back to bed and get some sleep. . . . You'll feel better in the morning."

"They never told me! . . . They never told me," she turned and stared stupidly at Bessie Gant with dull glazed eyes. "Can't you do something? . . . Where's McGuire? Has any one called him yet?"

"No," said the nurse sharply and angrily, "and no one's going to. You're not going to get that man out of bed at this hour of the night when there's nothing to be done. . . . Get out of here, now, all of you," she began to push and herd them towards the door. "I can't be bothered with you. . . . Go somewhere—anywhere—get drunk—only don't come back in here."

The whole house had come to life; in the excitement, shock, and exhaustion of their nerves the dead man still lying there in such a grotesque and twisted position, was forgotten. One of Eliza's lodgers, a man named Gilmer, who had been in the house for years, was wakened, went out, and got a gallon of corn whiskey; every one drank a great deal, became, in fact, somewhat intoxicated; when the undertakers came to take Gant away, none of the family was present. No one saw it. They were all in the kitchen seated around Eliza's battered old kitchen table, with the jug of whiskey on the table before them. They drank and talked together all night long until dawn came.

XXXIV

THE morning of Gant's funeral the house was filled with people who had known him and the air was heavy with the sweet, cloying fragrance of the funeral flowers: the odors of lilies, roses, and carnations. His coffin was banked with flowers, but in the centre there was a curious and arresting plainness, a simple wreath of laurel leaves. Attached to the wreath was a small card on which these words were written: "Hugh McGuire."

And people passing by the coffin paused for a moment and stared at the name with a feeling of unspoken wonder in their hearts. Eliza stood looking at the wreath a moment with hands clasped across her waist, and then turned away, shaking her head rapidly, with a short convulsive pucker of her lips, as she spoke to Helen in a low voice:

"I tell you what—it's pretty strange when you come to think of it—it gives you a queer feeling—I tell you what, it does."

And this expressed the emotion that every one felt when they saw the wreath. For Hugh McGuire had been found dead at his desk at six o'clock that morning, the news had just spread through the town, and now, when people saw the wreath upon Gant's coffin, there was something in their hearts they could not utter.

Gant lay in the splendid coffin, with his great hands folded quietly on his breast. Later, the boy could not forget his father's hands. They were the largest, most powerful, and somehow the most shapely hands he had ever seen. And even though his great right hand had been so crippled and stiffened by an attack of inflammatory rheumatism ten years before that he had never regained the full use of it, and since that time could only hold the great wooden mallet that the stone-cutters use in a painful and clumsy half-clasp between the thumb and the big stiffened fingers, his hands had never lost their character of life, strength, and powerful shapeliness.

The hands had given to the interminable protraction of his living death a kind of concrete horror that it otherwise would not have had. For as his powerful gaunt figure waned and wasted under the ravages of the cancer that was consuming him until he had become only the enfeebled shadow of his former self, his gaunt hands, on which there was so little which death could consume, lost none of their former rock-like heaviness, strength and shapely power. Thus, even when the giant figure of the man had become nothing but a spectral remnant of itself, sunk in a sorrow of time, awaiting death, those great, still-living hands of power and strength hung incredibly, horribly, from that spectral form of death to which they were attached.

And for this reason those powerful hands of life evoked, as nothing else could have done, in an instant searing flash of memory and recognition the lost world of his father's life of manual power, hunger, fury, savage abundance and wild joy, the whole enchanted structure of that lost life of magic he had made for them. Constantly, those great hands of life joined, with an almost grotesque incongruity, to that scarecrow form of wasting death would awake for them, as nothing else on earth could do, all of the sorrowful ghosts of time, the dream-like spell and terror of the years between, the years of phantom death, the horror of unreality, strangeness, disbelief, and memory, that haunted them.

So was it now, even in death, with his father's hands. In their powerful, gaunt and shapely clasp, as he lay dead in his coffin, there seemed to be held and gathered, somehow, all of his life that could never die—a living image of the essential quality of his whole life with its fury and unrest, desire and hunger, the tremendous sweep and relish of its enormous appetites and the huge endowment of its physical and sensual powers.

Thus, one could suppose that on the face of a dead poet there might remain—how, where or in what way we could not tell, a kind of flame, a light, a glory,—the magic and still living chrysm of his genius. And on the face of the dead conqueror we might still see living, arrogant, and proud with all its dark authorities the frown of power, the inflexible tyranny of stern command, the special infinitude of the invincible will that would not die with life, and that incredibly remains, still dark and living in its scorn and mockery of time.

Then, on the face of an old dead prophet or philosopher there would live and would not die the immortality of proud, lonely thought. We could not say just where that spirit rested. Sometimes it would seem to rest upon the temples of the grand and lonely head. Sometimes we would think it was a kind of darkness in the shadows of the closed and sunken eyes, sometimes the marsh fire of a dark and lambent flame that hovered round the face, that could never be fixed, but that we always knew was there.

And just as poet, prophet, priest and conqueror might each retain in death some living and fitting image of his whole life's truth, so would the strength, the skill, all of the hope, hunger, fury, and unrest that had lashed and driven on through life the gaunt figure of a stonecutter be marvellously preserved in the granite power and symmetry of those undying hands.

Now the corpse was stretched out on the splendid satin cushions of the expensive coffin. It had been barbered, powdered, disembowelled, and pumped full of embalming fluid. And as it lay there with its waxen head set forward in its curious gaunt projectiveness, the pale lips firmly closed and with a little line of waxen mucous in the lips, the women came forward with their oily swollen faces, and a look of ravenous eagerness in their eyes, stared at it hard and long, lifted their sodden handkerchiefs slowly to their oily mouths, and were borne away, sobbing hysterically, by their equally oily, ravenous, sister orgiasts in sorrow.

Meanwhile his father's friends, the stonecutters, masons, building contractors, butchers, business men and male relatives were standing awkwardly about, dressed in their good, black clothes which they seemed not to wear so much as to inhabit with a kind of unrestful itchiness, lowering their eyes gravely and regretfully as the women put on their revolting show, talking together in low voices, and wondering when it would all be over.

These circumstances, together with the heavy unnatural languor of the funeral smells, the sweet-sick heaviness of the carnations, the funereal weepy blacks in which the women had arrayed themselves, the satiny sandalwood scent that came from the splendid coffin, and the fragrant faintly acrid odor of embalmed flesh, particularly when blended with the smell of cooking turnip greens, roast pork and apple sauce out in the kitchen, combined to create an atmosphere somewhat like a dinner party in a comfortably furnished morgue.

In all this obscene pomp of burial there was something so grotesque, unnatural, disgusting, and remote from all he could remember of the dead man's life and personality that everything about him—even the physical horror of his bloody death—now seemed so far away he could hardly believe it ever happened. Therefore, he stared at this waxen and eviscerated relic in the coffin with a sense of weird disbelief, unable to relate it to the living man who had bled great lakes of blood the night before.

Yet, even in his death, his father's hands still seemed to live, and would not die. And this was the reason why the memory of those hands haunted him then and would haunt him forever after. This was the reason why, when he would try to remember how he looked when dead, he could remember nothing clearly except the powerful sculptured weight and symmetry of his tremendous hands as they lay folded on his body in the coffin. The great hands had a stony, sculptured and yet living strength and vitality, as if Michelangelo had carved them. They seemed to rest there upon the groomed, bereft and vacant horror of the corpse with a kind of terrible reality as if there really is, in death, some energy of life that will not die, some element of man's life that must persist and that resumes into a single feature of his life the core and essence of his character.

XXXV

STARWICK had now become his best and closest friend. Suddenly, it occurred to him with a strange and bitter sense of loss and lack that. Starwick was the only friend of his own age that he had ever known to whom he had fully and passionately revealed his own life, of whose fellowship and comradeship he had never grown weary. Friends he had had—friends in the casual and indifferent sense in which most friendship is understood—but until now he had never held a friend like Starwick in his heart's core.

Why was it? What was this grievous lack or loss—if lack or loss it was—in his own life? Why was it that, with his fierce, bitter, and insatiate hunger for life, his quenchless thirst for warmth, joy, love, and fellowship, his constant image, which had blazed in his heart since childhood, of the enchanted city of the great comrades and the glorious women, that he grew weary of people almost as soon as he met them? Why was it that he seemed to squeeze their lives dry of any warmth and interest they might have for him as one might squeeze an orange, and then was immediately filled with boredom, disgust, dreary tedium, and an impatient weariness and desire to escape so agonizing that it turned his feeling almost into hatred?

Why was it that his spirit was now filled with this furious unrest and exasperation against people because none of them seemed as good as they should be? Where did it come from—this improvable and yet unshakable conviction that grew stronger with every rebuff and disappointment— that the enchanted world was here around us ready to our hand the moment that we chose to take it for our own, and that the impossible magic in life of which he dreamed, for which he thirsted, had been denied us not because it was a phantom of desire, but because men had been too base and weak to take what was their own?

Now, with Starwick, and for the first time, he felt this magic constantly—this realization of a life forever good, forever warm and beautiful, forever flashing with the fires of passion, poetry and joy, forever filled with the swelling and triumphant confidence of youth, its belief in new lands, morning, and a strange city, its hope of voyages, its conviction of a fortunate, good and happy life—an imperishable happiness and joy—that was impending, that would be here at any moment.

For a moment he looked at the strange and delicate face of the young man beside him, reflecting, with a sense of wonder, at his communion with this other life, so different from his own in kind and temper. What was it? Was it the sharp mind, that original and penetrating instrument which picked up the old and weary problems of the spirit by new handles, displaying without labor planes and facets rarely seen? With what fierce joy he welcomed those long walks together in the night, along the quiet streets of Cambridge, or by the marvellous river that wound away small and magical in the blazing moonlight into the sweet, dark countryside! What other pleasure, what other appeasement of his mind and sense had been so complete and wonderful as that which came from this association as, oblivious of the world, they carried on their fierce debate about all things under heaven; his own voice, passionate, torrential, and wild, crying out against the earth, the moon, invoking all the gods of verse and magic while his mind played rivers of lightning across the vast fields of reading and experience!

And how eagerly he waited for the answers of that other voice, quiet, weary, drawling—how angrily he stormed against its objections, how hungrily and gratefully he fed upon its agreement! What other tongue had had the power to touch his pride and his senses as this one had— how cruelly had its disdain wounded him, how magnificently had its praise filled his heart with glory! On these nights when he and Starwick had walked along the river in these vehement, passionate, and yet affectionate debates, he would relive the scene for hours after it had ended, going over their discussion again and again, remembering every gesture, every intonation of the voice, every flash of life and passion in the face. Late in the night he would pace up and down his room, or pause dreaming by his window, still carrying on in his mind the debate with his friend, inventing and regretting splendid things he might have said, exulting in those he had said and in every word of approval or burst of laughter he had provoked. And he would think: Ah, but I was *good* there! I could see how he admired me, how high a place I have in his affection. For when he says a thing he *means* it: he called me a poet, his voice was quiet and full of passion, he said my like had never been, that my destiny was great and sure.

Was this, then, the answer?

Until this period of his life he had drunk very little: in spite of the desperate fear his mother had that each of her children inherited the whiskey disease—"the curse of licker," as she called it—from their father, he felt no burning appetite for stimulant. Alone, he never sought it out, he never bought a bottle for himself: solitary as his life had become, the idea of solitary drinking, of stealthy alley potations from a flask, filled him with sodden horror.

Now, in the company of Starwick, he was drinking more frequently than he had ever done before. Alcohol, indeed, until his twentieth year had been only a casual and infrequent spirit—once, in his seventeenth year, when he had come home from college at the Christmas vacation, he had got very drunk on various liquors which his brother Luke had brought home to his father, and which he had mixed together in a tumbler, and drunk without discretion. And there had been two or three casual sprees during his years at college, but until this time he had never known the experience of frequent intoxication.

But now, in the company of Frank Starwick, he went every week or so to a little restaurant which was situated in the Italian district of the eastern quarter of town, beyond Scollay Square and across Washington Street. The place was Starwick's own discovery, he hoarded his knowledge of it with stern secrecy, yielding it up only to a few friends—a few rare and understanding spirits who would not coarsely abuse the old-world spirit of this priceless place because, he said:

"It would be a pity if it ever got known about. It really would, you know. . . . I mean, the kind of people who would begin to go there would ruin it. . . . They really would. . . . I mean, it's *quite* astonishing to find a place of that sort here in Boston."

It was the beginning of that dark time of blood, and crime, and terror which the years of prohibition brought and which was to leave its hideous mutilation not only upon the soul and conscience of the nation, but upon the lives of millions of people—particularly the young everywhere. At this time, however, the ugly, jeering, open arrogance of the later period—the foul smell of privilege and corruption, the smirk of protection, and the gangster's sneer, were not so evident as they became in the years that followed. At this time, it was by no means easy "to get a drink": the speakeasy had already started on its historic career, but was still more or less what its name suggested—a place to be got at quietly and by stealth, a place of low voices, furtive and suspicious eyes, and elaborate precautions.

The place which Starwick had "discovered," and which he hoarded with such precious secrecy, was a small Italian restaurant known as Posillipo's, which occupied the second floor of an old brick building in an obscure street of the Italian quarter. Frank pronounced the name strongly and lovingly—"Pothillippo's"—in the mannered voice, and with the affected accent which all foreign and exotic names—particularly those that had a Latin flavoring—inspired in him.

Arrived at "Pothillippo's," Frank, who even at this time did all things with the most lavish and lordly extravagance, and who tipped generously at every opportunity, would be welcomed obsequiously by the proprietor and the waiters, and then would order with an air of the most refined and sensual discrimination from his favorite waiter, a suave and fawning servitor named Nino. There were other waiters just as good as Nino, but Frank expressed an overwhelming preference for him above all others because, he said, Nino had the same face as one of the saints in a painting by Giotto, and because he professed to find all of the ancient, grave and exquisite rhythm of the ancient Tuscan nobility composed in the one figure of this waiter.

"But have you noticed the way he uses his hands while talking?" Frank would say in a tone of high impassioned earnestness,—"Did you notice that last gesture? It is the same gesture that you find in the figure of the disciple Thomas in Leonardo's painting of 'The Last Supper.' It really is, you know. . . . Christ!" he would cry, in his high, strange, and rather womanish tone. "The centuries of art, of living, of culture—the terrific knowledge *all* these people have—the kind of thing you'll never find in people in this country, the kind of thing that no amount of college education or books can give you—all expressed in a single gesture of the hands of this Italian waiter. . . . The whole thing's *quite* astonishing, it really is, you know."

The real reason, however, that Frank preferred Nino to all the other waiters in "Pothillippo's" establishment was that he liked the sound of the word "Nino," and pronounced it beautifully.

"Nino!" Frank would cry, in a high, strange, and rather womanish voice—"Nino!"

"Si, signor," Nino would breathe unctuously, and would then stand in an attitude of heavy and prayerful adoration, awaiting the young lord's next commands.

"Nino," Frank would then go on in the tone and manner of a sensuous and weary old-world sophisticate. "Quel vin avez-vous? . . . Quel vin—rouge—du—très—bon. Vous—comprenez? said Frank, using up in one speech most of his French words, but giving a wonderful sense of linguistic mastery and complete eloquence in two languages.

"Mais si, signor!" Nino would answer immediately, skilfully buttering

Frank on both sides—the French and the Italian—with three masterly words.

"Le Chianti est *très, très* bon! . . . C'est parfait, monsieur," he whispered, with a little ecstatic movement of his fingers. "Admirable!"

"Bon," said Frank with an air of quiet decision. "Alors, Nino," he continued, raising his voice as he pronounced these two words, which were among his favorites. "Alors, une bouteille du Chianti—n'est-ce pas——"

"Mais si, signor!" said Nino, nodding enthusiastically. "Si—et pour manger?" he went on coaxingly.

"Pour manger?" Frank began—"Ecoute, Nino—vous pouvez recommander quelque-chose—quelque-chose *d'extraordinaire!*" Frank cried in a high impassioned tone. "Quelque-chose de la *maison!*" he concluded triumphantly.

"Mais, si!" Nino cried enthusiastically. "Si, signor. . . . Permettez-moi! . . . Le spaghetti," he whispered seductively, rolling his dark eyes rapturously aloft, and making a little mincing movement, indicative of speechless ecstasy, of his thumb and forefinger. "Le spaghetti . . . de la . . . maison . . . ah, signor," Nino breathed—"le spaghetti avec la sauce de la maison est merveilleuse . . . merveilleuse!" he whispered.

"Bon," said Starwick nodding. "Alors, Nino—le spaghetti pour deux —vous comprenez?"

"Mais si, signor! Si," Nino breathed. "Parfaitement"—and wrote the miraculous order on his order pad. "Et puis, monsieur," said Nino coaxingly, and with complete humility. "Permettez moi de recommander—le poulet," he whispered rapturously—"le poulet roti," he breathed, as if unveiling the rarest secrets of cookery that had been revealed since the days of Epicurus—"le poulet roti . . . de la maison," again he made the little speechless movement of the finger and the thumb, and rolled his rapturous eyes around—"ah, signor," said Nino, "Vous n'aurez pas de regrets si vous commandez le poulet."

"Bon. . . . Bon," said Starwick quietly and profoundly. "Alors, Nino —deux poulets rotis, pour moi et pour monsieur," he commanded.

"Bon, bon," said Nino, nodding vigorously and writing with enthusiasm—"et pour la salade, messieurs," he paused—looking inquiringly and yet hopefully at both his lordly young patrons.

And so it went, until the menu had all been gone through in mangled French and monosyllabic Italian. When this great ceremony was over, Frank Starwick had done nothing more nor less than order the one-dollar table d'hôte dinner which Signor "Pothillippo" provided for all the patrons of his establishment and whose order—soup, fish, spaghetti, roasted chicken, salad, ice-cream, cheese, nuts and bitter coffee—was unchangeable as destiny, and not to be altered by the whims of common men, whether they would or no.

And yet Frank's manner of ordering his commonplace rather dreary meal was so touched by mystery, strangeness, an air of priceless rarity and sensual refinement, that one would smack his lips over the various dishes with a gourmandizing gusto, as if the art of some famous chêf had really been exhausted in their preparation.

And this element of Frank Starwick's character was one of the finest and most attractive things about him. It was, perhaps as much as anything else, the reason why people of all kinds were drawn to him, delighted to be with him, and why Frank could command the boundless affection, devotion, and support of people more than any one the other boy had ever known.

For, in spite of all Frank's affectations of tone, manner, gesture, and accent, in spite of the elaborately mannered style of his whole life—no! really *because* of them (for what were all these manners and affectations except the evidence of Frank's constant effort to give qualities of strangeness, mystery, rareness, joy and pleasure to common things that had none of these qualities in themselves)—the deep and passionate desire in Frank's spirit to find a life that would always be good, beautiful, and exciting was apparent.

And to an amazing degree, Frank Starwick succeeded in investing all the common and familiar acts and experiences of this world with this strange and romantic color of his own personality.

When one was with him, everything—"le Chianti de la maison," a cigarette, the performance of a play, a poem or a book, a walk across the Harvard Yard, or along the banks of the Charles River—became strange and rare and memorable, and for this reason Frank, in spite of the corrupt and rotten spot which would develop in his character and eventually destroy him, was one of the rarest and highest people that ever lived, and could never be forgotten by any one who had ever known him, and been his friend.

For, by a baffling paradox, these very affectations of Frank's speech and dress and carriage, the whole wrought manner of his life, which caused many people who disbelieved him to dismiss him bitterly as an affected and artificial poseur, really came from something innocent and naive and good in Frank's character—something as innocent and familiar as the affectations of Tom Sawyer when he told tall stories, invented wild, complicated, and romantic schemes, when none was necessary, or used big words to impress his friends, the nigger Jim, or Huckleberry Finn.

Thus, the two young men would stay in "Pothillippo's" until late at night when the place closed, drinking that wonderful "Chianti de la maison," so preciously and lovingly described, which was really nothing but "dago red," raw, new, and instantaneous in its intoxication, filled with headaches and depression for tomorrow morning, but filled now with the mild, soaring, jubilant and triumphant drunkenness that only youth can know.

And they would leave this place of Latin mystery and languor at one o'clock in the morning, Frank shouting in a high drunken voice before he left, 'Nino! Nino!—Il faut quelque chose à boire avant de partir—Nino!—Nino!—Encora! Encora!"—pronouncing his last Italian word victoriously.

"Mais si, signor," Nino would answer, smiling somewhat anxiously. "Du vin?"

"Mais non, mais non, Nino" Frank would cry violently. "Pas de vin —du wis-kee, Nino! Du wis-kee!"

Then they would gulp down drinks of the raw and powerful beverage to which the name of whiskey had been given in that era, and leaving a dim blur of lights, a few dim blots of swarthy, anxiously smiling faces behind them, they would reel dangerously down the rickety stairs and out into the narrow, twisted streets, the old grimed web of sleeping quietness, the bewildering, ancient, and whited streets of Boston.

Above them, in the cool sweet skies of night, the great moons of the springtime, and New England, blazed with a bare, a lovely and enchanted radiance. And around them the great city, and its thousand narrow twisted streets lay anciently asleep beneath that blazing moon, and from the harbor came the sound of ships, the wasting, fresh, half-rotten harbor-smells, filled with the thought of ships, the sea, the proud exultancy of voyages. And out of the cobbled streets and from the old grimed buildings—yes! from the very breast and bareness of that springtime moon and those lovely lilac skies, there came somehow—God knows how—all of the sweet wildness of New England in the month of May, the smell of the earth, the sudden green, the glorious blossoms

—all that was wild, sweet, strange, simple, instantly familiar—that impossible loveliness, that irresistible magic, that unutterable hope for the magic that could not be spoken, but that seemed almost in the instant to be seized, grasped, and made one's own forever—for the hunger, possession and fulfilment—and for God knows what—for that magic land of green, its white and lovely houses, and the white flesh, the moon-dark hair, the depthless eyes and everlasting silence of its secret, dark, and lavish women.

Dark Helen in our hearts forever burning—oh, no more!

Then the two young men would thread that maze of drunken moonlit streets, and feel the animate and living silence of the great city all around them, and look then at the moon with drunken eyes, and see the moon, all bare and drunken in the skies, the whole earth and the ancient city drunk with joy and sleep and springtime and the enchanted silences of the moon-drunk squares. And they would come at length to Cambridge, to find the moonlight dark upon the sleeping silence of the university and Harvard Square, and exultancy and joy welled up in them forever, wild shouts and songs and laughter were torn from their throats and rang out through the sleeping streets of Cambridge, filling the moon-sweet air with jubilation, for they were drunken, young, and twenty—immortal confidence and victorious strength possessed them—and they knew that they could never die.

Immortal drunkenness! What tribute can we ever pay, what song can we ever sing, what swelling praise can ever be sufficient to express the joy, the gratefulness, and the love which we, who have known youth and hunger in America, have owed to alcohol?

We are so lost, so lonely, so forsaken in America: immense and savage skies bend over us, and we have no door.

But you, immortal drunkenness, came to us in our youth when all our hearts were sick with hopelessness, our spirits maddened with unknown terrors, and our heads bowed down with nameless shame. You came to us victoriously, to possess us, and to fill our lives with your wild music, to make the goat-cry burst from our exultant throats, to make us know that here upon the wilderness, the savage land, that here beneath immense, inhuman skies of time, in all the desolation of the cities, the gray unceasing flood-tides of the manswarm, our youth would soar to fortune, fame, and love, our spirits quicken with the power of mighty poetry, our work go on triumphantly to fulfilment until our lives prevailed.

What does it matter then if since that time of your first coming, magic drunkenness, our head has grown bald, our young limbs heavy, and if our flesh has lain battered, bleeding in the stews?

You came to us with music, poetry, and wild joy when we were twenty, when we reeled home at night through the old moon-whitened streets of Boston and heard our friend, our comrade, and our dead companion, shout through the silence of the moonwhite square: "You are a poet and the world is yours."

And victory, joy, wild hope, and swelling certitude and tenderness surged through the conduits of our blood as we heard that drunken cry, and triumph, glory, proud belief was resting like a chrysm around us as we heard that cry, and turned our eyes then to the moon-drunk skies of Boston, knowing only that we were young, and drunk, and twenty, and that the power of mighty poetry was within us, and the glory of the great earth lay before us—because we were young and drunk and twenty, and could never die!

XXXVI

WHEN Oswald Ten Eyck left his $8000 job on the Hearst Syndicate and came to Cambridge to enroll in Professor Hatcher's celebrated course for dramatists, he had saved a sum rare in the annals of journalism—$700. When he got through paying the tuition, admission, and other accessory fees that would entitle him to a membership in good standing in the graduate school of the university, something less than $500 remained. Oswald got an attic room in Cambridge, in a square, smut-gray frame house which was the home of an Irish family named Grogan. To reach his room, he had to mount a rickety flight of stairs that was almost as steep as a ladder, and when he got there, he had to manage his five feet five of fragile stature carefully in order to keep from cracking his head upon the sloping white-washed walls that followed the steep pitch of the roof with painful fidelity. The central part of Oswald's room, which was the only place in which the little man could stand erect, was not over four feet wide: there was a single window at the front where stood his writing table. He had a couple of straight chairs, a white iron cot pushed in under the eave of the left side, a few bookshelves pushed in under the eave of the right. It could literally be said that the playwright crawled to bed, and when he read he had to approach the poets as a poet should—upon his knees.

For this austere cell, Professor Hatcher's dramatist paid Mrs. Mary Grogan fifteen dollars every month. Therefore, when the primary fees of tuition and matriculation and the cell in Mrs. Grogan's house had been accounted for, Oswald Ten Eyck had all of $300 left to take care of clothing, food, tobacco, books, and plays during the ensuing period of nine months. This sum perhaps was adequate, but it was not grand, and Ten Eyck, poet though he was, was subject to all those base cravings of sensual desire that 100 pounds of five feet five is heir to.

This weakness of the flesh was unhappily reflected in the artist's work. During the brief period of his sojourn in Professor Hatcher's class, his plays were numerous but for the most part low. Ten Eyck turned them out with the feverish haste which only a trained newspaper man can achieve when driven on by the cherished ambition of a lifetime and the knowledge that art is long and $300 very fleeting. He had started out most promisingly in the fleshless ethers of mystic fantasy, but he became progressively more sensual until at the end he was practically wallowing in a trough of gluttony.

The man, in fact, became all belly when he wrote—and this was strange in a frail creature with the large burning eyes of a religious zealot, hands small-boned, fleshless as a claw, and a waist a rubber band would have snapped round comfortably. He seemed compact of flame and air and passion and an agonizing shyness. Professor Hatcher had great hopes for him—the whole atom was framed, Professor Hatcher thought, for what the true Hatcherian called "the drama of revolt," but the flaming atom fooled him, fooled him cruelly. For after the brilliant promise of that first beginning—a delicate, over-the-hills-and-far-away fantasy reminiscent of Synge, Yeats, and the Celtic Dawn—brain bowed to belly, Ten Eyck wrote of food.

His second effort was a one-act play whose action took place on the sidewalk in front of a Childs restaurant, while a white-jacketed attendant deftly flipped brown wheat-cakes on a plate. The principal character, and in fact the only speaker in this play, was a starving poet who stood before the window and delivered himself of a twenty-minute monologue on a poet's life and the decay of modern society, in the course of which most of the staple victuals on the Childs menu were mentioned frequently and with bitter relish.

Professor Hatcher felt his interest waning: he had hoped for finer things. Yet a wise caution learned from errors in the past had taught him to forbear. He knew that out of man's coarse earth the finer flow-

OF TIME AND THE RIVER

ers of his spirit sometimes grew. Some earlier members of his class had taught him this, some who had written coarsely of coarse things. They wrote of sailors, niggers, thugs, and prostitutes, of sunless lives and evil strivings, of murder, hunger, rape, and incest, a black picture of man's life unlighted by a spark of grace, a ray of hope, a flicker of the higher vision. Professor Hatcher had not always asked them to return—to "come back for a second year," which was the real test of success and future promise in the Hatcherian world. And yet, unknighted by this accolade, some had gone forth and won renown: their grim plays had been put on everywhere and in all languages. And the only claim the true Hatcherian could make of them was: "Yes, they were with us but not of us: they were not asked to come back for a second year."

There were some painful memories, but Professor Hatcher had derived from them a wise forbearance. His hopes for Oswald Ten Eyck were fading fast, but he had determined to hold his judgment in abeyance until Oswald's final play. But, as if to relieve his distinguished tutor from a painful choice, Ten Eyck himself decided it. After his third play there was no longer any doubt of the decision. For that play, which Oswald called "Dutch Fugue," would more aptly have been titled "No Return."

It was a piece in four acts dealing with the quaintly flavored life and customs of his own people, the Hudson River Dutch. The little man was hotly proud of his ancestry, and always insisted with a slight sneer of aristocratic contempt: "Not the Pennsylvania Dutch—Good God, no! *They're* not Dutch but German: the *real* Dutch, the *old* Dutch, *Catskill* Dutch!" And if Ten Eyck's interest in food had been uncomfortably pronounced in his earlier work, in this final product of his curious genius, his sensual appetites became indecent in their unrestraint. It is doubtful if the long and varied annals of the stage have ever offered such a spectacle: the play became a sort of dramatic incarnation of the belly, acted by a cast of fourteen adults, male and female, all of whom were hearty eaters.

The central events of that extraordinary play, which were a birth, a death, a wedding, were all attended by eating, drinking, and the noises of the feast. Scene followed scene with kaleidoscopic swiftness: the jubilant merry-making of the christening had hardly died away before the stage was set, the trestles groaning, with the more sombre, sober and substantial victuals of the funeral; and the wheels of the hearse had hardly echoed away into the distance before the scene burst out in all the boisterous reel and rout and feasting of the wedding banquet. Of no play that was ever written could it be more aptly said that the funeral baked meats did coldly furnish forth the marriage tables, and what is more, they almost furnished forth the casket and the corpse as well. Finally, the curtain fell as it had risen, upon a groaning table surrounded by the assembled cast of fourteen famished gluttons—a scene in which apparently the only sound and action were provided by the thrust of jowl and smack of lip, a kind of symphonic gluttony of reach and grab, cadenced by the stertorous breathing of the eaters, the clash of crockery, and the sanguinary drip of rare roast beef—the whole a prophetic augury that flesh was grass and man's days fleeting, that life would change and reappear in an infinite succession of births and deaths and marriages, but that the holy rites of eating and the divine permanence of good dinners and roast beef were indestructible and would endure forever.

Ten Eyck read the play himself one Friday afternoon to Professor Hatcher and his assembled following. He read in a rapid high-pitched voice, turning the pages with a trembling claw, and thrusting his long fingers nervously through his disordered mop of jet-black hair. As he went on, the polite attention of the class was changed insensibly to a paralysis of stupefaction. Professor Hatcher's firm thin lips became much firmer, thinner, tighter. A faint but bitter smile was printed at the edges of his mouth. Then, for a moment, when the playwright finished, there was silence: Professor Hatcher slowly raised his hand, detached his gold-rimmed glasses from his distinguished nose, and let them fall and dangle on their black silk cord. He looked around the class; his cultivated voice was low, controlled, and very quiet.

"Is there any comment?" Professor Hatcher said.

No one answered for a moment. Then Mr. Grey, a young patrician from Philadelphia, spoke:

"I think," he said with a quiet emphasis of scorn, "I think he might very well get it produced in the Chicago Stock Yards."

Mr. Grey's remark was ill-timed. For the Stock Yards brought to Ten Eyck's mind a thought of beef, and beef brought back a memory of his palmy days with Mr. Hearst when beef was plenty and the pay-checks fat, and all these thoughts brought back the bitter memory of the day before which was the day when he had eaten last: a single meal, a chaste and wholesome dinner of spaghetti, spinach, coffee, and a roll. And thinking, Ten Eyck craned his scrawny neck convulsively along the edges of his fraying collar, looked desperately at Professor Hatcher, who returned his gaze inquiringly; ducked his head quickly, bit his nails and craned again. Then, suddenly, seeing the cold patrician features of young Mr. Grey, his blue shirt of costly madras, his limp crossed elegance of legs and pleated trousers, the little man half rose, scraping his chair back from the table round which the class was sitting, and with an inclusive gesture of his claw-like hand, screamed incoherently:

"These! These! . . . We have the English. . . . As for the Russians. . . . Take the Germans—Toller—Kaiser—the Expressionists. . . . But the Dutch, the Dutch, the *Catskill* Dutch. . . ." Pointing a trembling finger towards Mr. Grey, he shrieked: "The Philadelphia Cricket Club. . . . God! God!" he bent, racked with soundless laughter, his thin hands pressed against his sunken stomach. "That it should come to this!" he said, and suddenly, catching Professor Hatcher's cold impassive eye upon him, he slumped down abruptly in his seat, and fell to biting his nails: "Well, I don't know," he said with a foolish little laugh. "Maybe—I guess . . . " his voice trailed off, he did not finish.

"Is there any other comment?" said Professor Hatcher.

There was none.

"Then," said Professor Hatcher, "the class is dismissed until next Monday."

Professor Hatcher did not look up as Ten Eyck went out.

When Oswald got out into the corridor, he could hear the last footfalls of the departing class echoing away around the corner. For a moment, he leaned against the wall: he felt hollow, weak, and dizzy: his knees bent under him like rubber, and his head, after its recent flood of blood and passion, felt swollen, light, and floating as a toy balloon. Suddenly he remembered that it was Friday. Saturday, the day on which he could next allow himself to take a little from his dwindling hoard—for such was the desperate resolution made at the beginning and adhered to ever since—Saturday shone desperately far away, a small and shining disc of light at the black mouth of an interminable tunnel, and all giddy, weak, and hollow as he was, he did not see how he could wait! So he surrendered. He knew that if he hurried now he would be just in time for old Miss Potter's Friday afternoon. And torn between hunger and disgust, Ten Eyck gave in again to hunger as he had done a score of times before, even when he knew that he must face again that crowning horror of modern life, the art party.

Miss Potter was a curious old spinster of some property, and she lived, with a companion, in a pleasant house on Garden Street, not far from the University. Miss Potter's companion was also an aged spinster: her name was Miss Flitcroft; the two women were inseparable. Miss Potter was massively constructed: a ponderous woman who moved heavily and with wheezing difficulty, and whose large eyes bulged comically out of a face on which a strange fixed grin was always legible.

Miss Flitcroft was a wren of a woman, with bony little hands, and an old withered, rather distinguished-looking face: she wore a band of velvet around her stringy neck. She was not only a companion, she was also a kind of nurse to Miss Potter, and she could give relief and comfort to the other woman as no one else could.

For Miss Potter was really very ill: she had a savage love of life, a desperate fear of death, and she knew that she was dying. But even the woman's sufferings, which were obviously intense, were touched by that grotesque and ridiculous quality that made Ten Eyck want to howl with explosive laughter, even when he felt a rending pity for her. Thus, at table sometimes, with all her tribe of would-be poets, playwrights, composers, novelists, painters, critics, and enfeebled litterateurs gathered around her, putting away the delicious food she had so abundantly provided, Miss Potter would suddenly begin to choke, gasp, and cough horribly; her eyes would bulge out of her head in a fish-like stare, and looking desperately at Miss Flitcroft with an expression of unutterable terror, she would croak: . . . "Dying! Dying! I tell you I'm dying!"

"Nonsense!" Miss Flitcroft would answer tartly, jumping up and running around behind Miss Potter's chair. "You're no such thing! . . . You've only choked yourself on something you have eaten! There!" and she would deliver herself straightway of a resounding whack upon Miss Potter's meaty, mottled back (for on these great Friday afternoons, Miss Potter came out sumptuously in velvet, which gave ample glimpses of her heavy arms and breasts and the broad thick surface of her shoulders).

"If you didn't eat so fast these things would never happen!" Miss Flitcroft would say acidly, as she gave Miss Potter another resounding whack on her bare shoulders. "Now you get over this nonsense!" . . .

whack! "There's nothing wrong with you—do you hear?" . . . whack!
"You're frightened half out of your wits," . . . whack! . . . "just because you've tried to stuff everything down your throat at once!" whack!
whack!

And by this time, Miss Potter would be on the road to recovery, gasping and panting more easily now, as she continued to look up with a
fixed stare of her bulging eyes at Miss Flitcroft, with an expression full
of entreaty, dawning hopefulness, apology, and pitiable gratitude.

As for Ten Eyck, his pain and embarrassment when one of these
catastrophes occurred were pitiable. He would scramble to his feet, stand
helplessly, half-crouched, casting stricken glances toward the most con-
venient exit as if contemplating the possibility of a sudden and in-
glorious flight. Then he would turn again toward the two old women,
his dark eyes fixed on them in a fascinated stare in which anguish, sympathy, helplessness and horror were all legible.

For several years, in spite of her ill health, Miss Potter had fiddled
around on the edges of Professor Hatcher's celebrated course at the
university. She had written a play or two herself, took a passionate interest in what she called "the work," was present at the performances
of all the plays, and was a charter member of Professor Hatcher's carefully selected and invited audiences. Now, whether by appointment or
self-election, she had come to regard herself as a kind of embassadress
for Professor Hatcher's work and was the chief sponsor of its social life.

The grotesque good old woman was obsessed by that delusion which
haunts so many wealthy people who have no talent and no understanding, but who are enchanted by the glamour which they think surrounds
the world of art. Miss Potter thought that through these Friday afternoons she could draw together all the talent, charm, and brilliance of the
whole community. She thought that she could gather here not only
Professor Hatcher's budding dramatists and some older representatives
of the established order, but also poets, painters, composers, philosophers,
"radical thinkers," people "who did interesting things," of whatever
kind and quality. And she was sure that from this mad mélange every
one would derive a profitable and "stimulating" intercourse.

Here, from the great "art community" of Cambridge and Boston, came
a whole tribe of the feeble, the sterile, the venomous and inept—the meagre little spirits of no talent and of great pretensions: the people who had
once got an essay printed in *The Atlantic Monthly* or published "a

slender volume" of bad verse; the composers who had had one dull academic piece performed a single time by the Boston Symphony; the novelists, playwrights, painters, who had none of the "popular success" at which they sneered and which they pretended to despise, but for which each would have sold his shabby little soul; the whole wretched poisonous and embittered crew of those who had "taken" some one's celebrated course, or had spent a summer at the MacDowell Colony—in short, the true philistines of art—the true enemies of the artist's living spirit, the true defilers and betrayers of creation—the impotent fumbling little half men of the arts whose rootless, earthless, sunless lives have grown underneath a barrel, and who bitterly nurse their fancied injuries, the swollen image of their misjudged worth, and hiss and sting in all the impotent varieties of their small envenomed hate; who deal the stealthy traitor's blow in darkness at the work and talent of far better men than they.

Usually, when Ten Eyck went to Miss Potter's house he found several members of Professor Hatcher's class who seemed to be in regular attendance on all these Friday afternoons. These others may have come for a variety of reasons: because they were bored, curious, or actually enjoyed these affairs, but the strange, horribly shy and sensitive little man who bore the name of Oswald Ten Eyck came from a kind of desperate necessity, the ravenous hunger of his meagre half-starved body, and his chance to get his one good dinner of the week.

It was evident that Ten Eyck endured agonies of shyness, boredom, confusion, and tortured self-consciousness at these gatherings but he was always there, and when they sat down at the table he ate with the voracity of a famished animal. The visitor to Miss Potter's reception room would find him, usually backed into an inconspicuous corner away from the full sound and tumult of the crowd, nervously holding a tea-cup in his hands, talking to some one in the strange blurted-out desperate fashion that was characteristic of him, or saying nothing for long periods, biting his nails, thrusting his slender hands desperately through his mop of black disordered hair, breaking from time to time into a shrill, sudden, almost hysterical laugh, blurting out a few volcanic words, and then relapsing into his desperate hair-thrusting silence.

The man's agony of shyness and tortured nerves was painful to watch: it made him say and do sudden, shocking and explosive things that could suddenly stun a gathering such as this, and plunge him back immediately into a black pit of silence, self-abasement and despair. And as great as his tortured sensitivity was, it was greater for other people than for himself. He could far better endure a personal affront, a wounding of his own quick pride, than see another person wounded. His anguish, in fact, when he saw this kind of suffering in other people would become so acute that he was no longer responsible for his acts: he was capable of anything on such an occasion.

And such occasions were not lacking at Miss Potter's Friday afternoons. For even if the entire diplomatic corps had gathered there in suavest mood, that good grotesque old woman with her unfailing talent for misrule, would have contrived to set every urbane minister of grace snarling for the other's blood before an hour had passed. And with that museum collection of freaks, embittered æsthetes and envenomed misfits of the arts, that did gather there, she never failed. Her genius for confusion and unrest was absolute.

If there were two people in the community who had been destined from birth and by every circumstance of education, religious belief, and temperament, to hate each other with a murderous hatred the moment that they met, Miss Potter would see to it instantly that the introduction was effected. If Father Davin, the passionate defender of the faith, and the foe of modernism in all its hated forms, had been invited to one of Miss Potter's Friday afternoons, he would find himself shaking hands before he knew it with Miss Shanksworth, the militant propagandist for free love, sterilization of the unfit, and the unlimited practice of birth control by every one, especially the lower classes.

If the editor of *The Atlantic Monthly* should be present, he would find himself, by that unerring drawing together of opposites which Miss Potter exercised with such accuracy, seated next to the person of one Sam Shulemovitch, who as leader and chief editorial writer of an organ known as *Red Riot* or *The Worker's Dawn*, had said frequently and with violence that the sooner *The Atlantic Monthly* was extinguished, and its writers, subscribers, and editorial staff embalmed and put on exhibition in a museum, the better it would be for every one.

If the radical leader who had just served a sentence in prison for his speeches, pamphlets, and physical aggressions against the police, or members of the capitalist class, should come to one of Miss Potter's Friday afternoons, he would find himself immediately debating the merits of the present system and the need for the swift extinction of the wealthy parasite with a maiden lady from Beacon Street who had a parrot, two Persian kittens, and a Pekinese, three maids, a cook, a butler, chauffeur and motor car, a place at Marblehead, and several thousand shares of Boston and Maine.

And so it went, all up and down the line, at one of Miss Potter's Friday afternoons. There, in her house, you could be sure that if the lion and the lamb did not lie down together their hostess would seat them in such close proximity to each other that the ensuing slaughter would be made as easy, swift, and unadorned as possible.

And as the sound of snarl and curse grew louder in the clamorous tumult of these Friday afternoons, as the face grew livid with its hate, as the eye began to glitter, and the vein to swell upon the temple, Miss Potter would look about her with triumphant satisfaction, seeing that her work was good, thinking with delight:

"How stimulating! How fine it is to see so many interesting people together—people who are really doing things! To see the flash and play of wit, to watch the clash of brilliant intellects, to think of all these fine young men and women have in common, and of the mutual benefits they will derive from contact with one another!—ah-ha! What a delightful thing to see—but who is this that just came—" she would mutter, peering toward the door, for she was very near-sighted—"who? Who?—O-oh! Professor Lawes of the Art Department—oh, Professor Lawes, I'm so glad you could come. We have the most *interesting* young man here today—Mr. Wilder, who painted that picture every one's talking about—"Portrait of a Nude Falling Upon Her Neck in a Wet Bathroom"— Mr. Wilder, this is Doctor Lawes, the author of *Sanity and Tradition in the Renaissance*—I know you're going to find *so* much in common."

And having done her duty, she would wheeze heavily away, looking around with her strange fixed grin and bulging eyes to see if she had left anything or anyone undone or whether there was still hope of some new riot, chaos, brawl, or bitter argument.

And yet there was a kind of wisdom in her too, that few who came there to her house suspected: a kind of shrewdness in the fixed bulging stare of her old eyes that sometimes saw more than the others knew. Perhaps it was only a kind of instinct of the old woman's warm humanity that made her speak to the fragile little man with burning eyes more gently than she spoke to others, to seat him on her right hand at the dinner table, and to say from time to time: "Give Mr. Ten Eyck some more of that roast beef. Oh, Mr. Ten Eyck, *do*—you've hardly eaten anything."

And he, stretched out upon the rack of pride and all the bitter long-ing of his hunger, would crane convulsively at his collar and laugh with a note of feeble protest, saying "Well—I don't know . . . I really think . . . if you want me to. . . . Oh! all right then," as a plate smoking with her lavish helping was placed before him, and would straight-way fall upon it with the voracity of a famished wolf.

When Ten Eyck reached Miss Potter's on that final fateful Friday, the other guests were already assembled. Miss Thrall, a student of the woman's section of Professor Hatcher's course, was reading her own translation of a German play which had only recently been produced. Miss Potter's reception rooms—which were two large gabled rooms on the top floor of her house, ruggedly festooned with enormous fishing nets secured from Gloucester fishermen—were crowded with her motley parliament, and the whole gathering was discreetly hushed while the woman student read her play.

It was a scene to warm the heart of any veteran of æsthetic parties. The lights were soft, shaded, quietly and warmly subdued: the higher parts of the room were pools of mysterious gloom from which the Gloucester fishing nets depended, but within the radius of the little lamps, one could see groups of people tastefully arranged in all the atti-tudes of rapt attentiveness. Some of the young women slouched dream-ily upon sofas, their faces and bodies leaning toward the reader with a yearning movement, other groups could be vaguely discerned leaning upon the grand piano, or elegantly slumped against the walls with tea-cups in their hands. Mr. Cram, the old composer, occupied a chosen seat on a fat sofa; he drew voluptuously on a moist cigarette which he held daintily between his dirty fingers, his hawk-like face turned meditatively away into the subtle mysteries of the fishing nets. From time to time he would thrust one dirty hand through the long sparse locks of his gray hair, and then draw deeply, thoughtfully on his cigarette.

Some of the young men were strewn about in pleasing postures on the floor, in attitudes of insouciant grace, gallantly near the ladies' legs. Ten Eyck entered, looked round like a frightened rabbit, ducked his head, and then sat down jack-knife fashion beside them.

Miss Thrall sat on the sofa with the old composer, facing her audi-ence. The play that she was reading was one of the new German Ex-pressionist dramas, at that time considered one of "the most vital movements in the world theatre," and the young lady's translation of the play which bore the vigorous title of *You Shall Be Free When You Have Cut Your Father's Throat,* ran somewhat in this manner:

Elektra: (advancing a step to the top of the raised dais, her face blue with a ghastly light, and her voice low and hoarse with passion as she addresses the dark mass of men below her.) Listen, man! To you it is now proper that I speak must. Do you by any manner of means know who this woman who now before you speaking stands may be? (With a sudden swift movement she, the purple-reddish silk-stuff of the tunic which she wearing is, asunder in two pieces rips, her two breasts exposing.)

(A low swiftly-growing-and-to-the-outer-edges-of-the-crowd-thunder-becoming mutter of astonishment through the great crowd surges.)

Elektra: (Thunder louder becomes, and even with every moment growing yet) Elektra! (The sound to a mighty roar arisen has, and now from every throat is in a single shout torn.) ELEKTRA!

Elektra: (quietly) Ja! Man, thou hast said it. I am Elektra!

The Crowd: (with from their throats an even-stronger roar yet) E L E K - T R A . It is E l e k t r a !

Elektra: (her voice even lower and more hoarse becoming, her eyes with the red blood-pains of all her heart-grief with still greater love-sorrow at the man-mass gleaming.) Listen, man. Slaves, workers, the of your fathers' sons not yet awakened—hear! Out of the night-dark of your not yet born souls to deliver you have I come! So, hear! (Her voice even lower with the low blood-pain heart-hate hoarse becoming.) Tonight must you your old with-crime-blackened and by-ignorance-blinded father's throat cut! I have spoken: so must it be.

A Voice, Homunculus: (from the crowd, pleadingly, with protest.) Ach! Elektra! Spare us! Please! With the blood-lust malice-blinded your old father's throat to cut not nice is.

Elektra: (raising her arm with a cold imperious gesture of command.) As I have spoken, must it be! Silence!

(Homunculus starts to interrupt: again she speaks, her voice more loud and stern becoming.) Silence! Silence!

At this moment there was a loud and sibilant hiss from the door. Miss Potter, who had been on the point of entering the room, had been halted by the sight of Miss Thrall's arm uplifted in command and by the imperious coldness of her voice as she said "Silence!" Now as Miss Thrall stopped and looked up in a startled manner, Miss Potter, still hissing loudly, tip-toed ponderously into the room. The old woman advanced with the grace of a hydroptic hippopotamus, laying her finger to her lips as she came on, looking all around her with her fixed grin and bulging eyes, and hissing loudly for the silence she had thus violently disrupted every time she laid her finger to her lips.

Every one *stared* at her in a moment of blank and horrible fascination. As for Miss Thrall, she gaped at her with an expression of stupefaction which changed suddenly to a cry of alarm as Miss Potter, tiptoeing blindly ahead, barged squarely into the small crouched figure of Oswald Ten Eyck, and went plunging over him to fall to her knees with a crash that made the fish-nets dance, the pictures swing, and even drew a sympathetic resonant vibration from the polished grand piano.

Then, for one never-to-be-forgotten moment, while every one *stared* at her in a frozen paralysis of horrified astonishment, Miss Potter stayed there on her knees, too stunned to move or breathe, her eyes bulging from her head, her face turned blindly upward in an attitude of grotesque devotion. Then as she began to gasp and cough with terror, Ten Eyck came to life. He fairly bounded off the floor, glanced round him like a startled cat, and spying a pitcher on a tray, rushed toward it wildly, seized it in his trembling hands, and attempted to pour a glass of water, most of which spilled out. He turned, still clutching the glass in his hand, and panting out "Here! Here! . . . Take this!" he rushed toward Miss Potter. Then, terrified by her apoplectic stare, he dashed the contents of the glass full in her face.

A half dozen young men sprang to her assistance and lifted her to her feet. The play was forgotten, the whole gathering broke into excited and clamorous talk, above which could be heard Miss Flitcroft's tart voice, saying sharply, as she whacked the frightened and dripping old woman on the back:

"Nonsense! You're not! You're no such thing! . . . You're just frightened out of your wits, that's all that's the matter with you— If you ever stopped to look where you were going, these things would never happen!"

Whack!

Both Oswald and Miss Potter had recovered by the time the guests were assembled round the table. As usual, Oswald found he had been seated on Miss Potter's right hand: and the feeling of security this gave him, together with the maddening fragrance of food, the sense of ravenous hunger about to be appeased, filled him with an almost delirious joy, a desire to shout out, to sing. Instead, he stood nervously beside his chair, looking about with a shy and timid smile, passing his fingers through his hair repeatedly, waiting for the other guests to seat themselves. Gallantly, he stood behind Miss Potter's chair, and pushed it under her as she sat down. Then, with a feeling of jubilant elation, he sat down beside her and drew his chair up. He wanted to talk, to prove himself a brilliant conversationalist, to surprise the whole gathering with his wit, his penetration, his distinguished ease. Above all, he wanted to eat and eat and eat! His head felt light and drunk and giddy, but gloriously so—he had never been so superbly confident in his life. And in this mood, he unfolded his napkin, and smiling brightly, turned to dazzle his neighbor on his right with the brilliant effervescence of wit that already seemed to sparkle on his lips. One look, and the bright smile faded, wit and confidence fell dead together, his heart shrank instantly and seemed to drop out of his very body like a rotten apple. Miss Potter had not failed. Her unerring genius for calamity had held out to the finish. He found himself staring into the poisonous face of the one person in Cambridge that he hated most—the repulsive visage of the old composer, Cram.

An old long face, yellowed with malevolence, a sudden fox-glint of small eyes steeped in a vitriol of ageless hate, a beak of cruel nose, and thin lips stained and hardened in a rust of venom, the whole craftily, slantingly astare between a dirty frame of sparse lank locks. Cackling with malignant glee, and cramming crusty bread into his mouth, the old composer turned and spoke:

"Heh! Heh! Heh!"—Crunch, crunch— "It's *Mister* Ten Eyck, isn't it? The man who wrote that play Professor Hatcher put on at his last performance—that mystical fantasy kind of thing. That was *your* play, wasn't it?"

The old yellow face came closer, and he snarled in a kind of gloating and vindictive whisper: "Most of the audience *hated* it! They thought it very *bad,* sir—very bad!" Crunch, crunch. "I am only telling you because I think you ought to know—that you may profit by the criticism."

And Ten Eyck, hunger gone now, shrank back as if a thin poisoned blade had been driven in his heart and twisted there. "I—I—I thought some of them rather liked it. Of course I don't know—I can't say—" he faltered hesitantly, "but I—I really thought some of the audience—liked it."

"Well, they *didn't,"* the composer snarled, still crunching on his crust of bread. "Every one that I saw thought that it was terrible. Heh! Heh! Heh! Heh! Except my wife and I—" Crunch, crunch. "We were the only ones who thought that it was any good at all, the only ones who thought there would ever be any *hope* for you. And we found parts of it—a phrase or sentence here and there—now and then a scene—that we *liked*. As for the rest of them," he suddenly made a horrible downward gesture with a clenched fist and pointing thumb, "it was *thumbs down,* my boy! Done for! No good. . . . That's what they thought of *you,* my boy. And that," he snarled suddenly, glaring round him, "*that* is what they've thought of *me* all these years—of *me,* the greatest composer that they have, the man who has done more for the cause of American music than all the rest of them combined—*me! me! me!* the prophet and the seer!" he fairly screamed, "*thumbs down!* Done for! No good any more!"

Then he grew suddenly quiet, and leaning toward Ten Eyck with a gesture of horrible clutching intimacy, he whispered: "And *that's* what they'll always think of you, my boy—of any one who has a grain of talent— Heh! Heh ! Heh! Heh!" Peering into Ten Eyck's white face, he shook him gently by the arm, and cackled softly a malevolent tenderness, as if the evidence of the anguish that his words had caused had given him a kind of paternal affection for his victim. "That's what they said about your play, all right, but don't take it too seriously. It's live and learn, my boy, isn't it—profit by criticism—a few hard knocks will do you no harm. Heh! Heh! Heh! Heh! Heh!"

And turning, satisfied with the anguish he had caused, he thrust out his yellowed face with a vulture's movement of his scrawny neck, and smacking his envenomed lips with relish, drew noisily inward with slobbering suction on a spoon of soup.

As for Ten Eyck, all hunger now destroyed by his sick shame and horror and despair, he turned, began to toy nervously with his food, and forcing his pale lips to a trembling and uncertain smile, tried desperately to compel his brain to pay attention to something that was being said by the man across the table who was the guest of honor for the day, and whose name was Hunt.

Hunt had been well-known for his belligerent pacifism during the war, had been beaten by the police and put in jail more times than he could count, and now that he was temporarily out of jail, he was carrying on his assault against organized society with more ferocity than ever. He was a man of undoubted courage and deep sincerity, but the suffering he had endured, and the brutal intolerance of which he had been the victim, had left its mutilating mark upon his life. His face was somehow like a scar, and his cut, cruel-looking mouth could twist like a snake to the corner of his face when he talked. And his voice was harsh and jeering, brutally dominant and intolerant, when he spoke to any one, particuarly if the one he spoke to didn't share his opinions.

On this occasion, Miss Potter, with her infallible talent for error, had seated next to Hunt a young Belgian student at the university, who had little English, but a profound devotion to the Roman Catholic Church. Within five minutes, the two were embroiled in a bitter argument, the Belgian courteous, but desperately resolved to defend his faith, and because of his almost incoherent English as helpless as a lamb before the attack of Hunt, who went for him with the rending and pitiless savagery of a tiger. It was a painful thing to watch: the young man, courteous and soft-spoken, his face flushed with embarrassment and pain, badly wounded by the naked brutality of the other man's assault.

As Ten Eyck listened, his spirit began to emerge from the blanket of shame and sick despair that had covered it, a spark of anger and resentment, hot and bright, began to glow, to burn, to spread. His large dark eyes were shining now with a deeper, fiercer light than they had had before, and on his pale cheeks there was a flush of angry color. And now he no longer had to force himself to listen to what Hunt was saying: anger had fanned his energy and his interest to a burning flame, he listened tensely, his ears seemed almost to prick forward on his head, from time to time he dug his fork viciously into the table cloth. Once or twice, it seemed that he would interrupt. He cleared his throat, bent forward, nervously clutching the table with his claw-like hands, but each time ended up thrusting his fingers through his mop of hair, and gulping down a glass of wine.

As Hunt talked, his voice grew so loud in its rasping arrogance that every one at the table had to stop and listen, which was what he most desired. And there was no advantage, however unjust, which the man did not take in this bitter argument with the young Belgian. He spoke jeeringly of the fat priests of the old corrupt church, fattening themselves on the blood and life of the oppressed workers; he spoke of the bigotry, oppression, and superstition of religion, and of the necessity for the workers to destroy this monster which was devouring them. And when the young Belgian, in his faltering and painful English, would try to reply to these charges, Hunt would catch him up on his use of words, pretend to be puzzled at his pronunciation, and bully him brutally in this manner:

"You think *what?* ... *What?* ... I don't understand what you're saying half the time. . . . It's very difficult to talk to a man who can't speak decent English."

"I—vas—say—ink," the young Belgian would answer slowly and painfully, his face flushed with embarrassment— "—vas—say—ink—zat—I sink—zat you—ex—ack—sher—ate——"

"That I *what?*— *What?* What is he trying to say, anyway?" demanded Hunt, brutally, looking around the table as if hoping to receive interpretation from the other guests. "Oh-h!" he cried suddenly, as if the Belgian's meaning had just dawned on him. "*Exaggerate!* That's the word you're trying to say!" and he laughed in an ugly manner.

Oswald Ten Eyck had stopped eating and turned white as a sheet. Now he sat there, looking across in an agony of tortured sympathy at the young Belgian, biting his nails nervously, and thrusting his hands through his hair in a distracted manner. The resentment and anger that he had felt at first had now burned to a white heat of choking, murderous rage. The little man was taken out of himself entirely. Suddenly his sense of personal wrong, the humiliation and pain he had himself endured, was fused with a white-hot anger of resentment for every injustice and wrong that had ever been done to the wounded soul of man. United by that agony to a kind of savage fellowship with the young Belgian, with the insulted and the injured of the earth, of whatsoever class or creed, that burning coal of five feet five flamed in one withering blaze of wrath, and hurled the challenge of its scorn at the oppressor.

The thing happened like a flash. At the close of one of Hunt's jeering tirades, Ten Eyck jumped from his chair, and leaning half across the table, cried out in a high shrill voice that cut into the silence like a knife:

"Hunt! You are a swine, and every one who ever had anything to do with you is likewise a swine!" For a moment he paused, breathing hard, clutching his napkin in a bony hand. Slowly his feverish eyes went round the table, and suddenly, seeing the malevolent stare of the old composer Cram fixed upon him, he hurled the wadded napkin down and pointing a trembling finger at that hated face, he screamed: "And that goes for you as well, you old bastard! . . . It goes for all the rest of you," he shrieked, gesturing wildly. "Hunt . . . Cram! *Cram!* . . . God!" he cried, shaking with laughter. "*There's* a name for you! . . . It's perfect. . . . Yes, you! You swine!" he yelled again, thrusting his finger at Cram's yellowed face so violently that the composer scrambled back with a startled yelp. "And all the rest of you!" he pointed towards Miss

Thrall— "You—the Expressionist!" And he paused, racked terribly again by soundless laughter— "The Greeks—the Russians— Oh, how we love in Spain!—and fantasy—why, Goddam my soul to hell, but it's delightful!" he fairly screamed, and then pointing a trembling finger at several in succession he yelled "You?—And you?—And you?—What the hell do you know about anything? . . . Ibsen—Chekov—the Celtic Dawn— *Balls!*" he snarled, "Food! Food! Food!—you Goddam fools! . . . That's all that matters." He picked up a morsel of his untouched bread and hurled it savagely upon the table— "Food! Food!—Ask Cram—he knows. . . . Now," he said, panting for breath and pointing a trembling finger at Miss Potter— "Now," he panted, "I want to tell *you* something."

"Oh . . . Mr. . . . Ten . . . Eyck," the old woman faltered in a tone of astonished reproach, "I . . . never . . . believed it possible . . . you could——"

Her voice trailed off helplessly, and she looked at him.

And Ten Eyck, suddenly brought to himself by the bulging stare of that good old creature fixed on him with wounded disbelief, suddenly laughed again, shrilly and hysterically, thrust his fingers through his hair, looked about him at the other people whose eyes were fixed on him in a stare of focal horror, and said in a confused, uncertain tone: "Well, I don't know—I'm always—I guess I said something that oh, damn it, what's the use!" and with a desperate, stricken laugh, he slumped suddenly into his chair, craned convulsively at his collar, and seizing a decanter before him poured out a glass of wine with trembling haste and gulped it down.

Meanwhile, all around the table people began to talk with that kind of feverish eagerness that follows a catastrophe of this sort, and Hunt resumed his arguments, but this time in a much quieter tone, and with a kind of jeering courtesy, accompanying his remarks from time to time with a heavy sarcasm directed toward Ten Eyck— "If I may say so— since, of course, Mr. Ten Eyck considers me a swine" *or* "if you will pardon such a remark from a swine like me"—or—"as Mr. Ten Eyck has told you I am nothing but a swine," and so on.

The upshot of it was that Ten Eyck gulped down glass after glass of the strong wine, which raced instantly through his frail starved body like a flame.

He got disgracefully drunk, sang snatches of bawdy songs, screamed with maudlin laughter, and began to pound enthusiastically on the

table, shaking his head to himself and shouting from time to time:
"You're right, Hunt! ... God-damn it, man, you're right! ... Go on!
... Go on! I agree with you! You're right! Everybody else is wrong
but Hunt and Cram! ... Words by Hunt, music by Cram ... no one's
right but Hunt and Cram!"

They tried to quiet him, but in vain. Suddenly Miss Potter began to
cough and choke and gasp, pressed both hands over her heart, and
gasped out in a terror-stricken voice:

"Oh, my God, I'm dying!"

Miss Flitcroft jumped to her feet and came running to her friend's
assistance, and then while Miss Flitcroft pounded the old woman on her
back, and the guests scrambled up in a general disruption of the party,
Oswald Ten Eyck staggered to the window, flung it open, and looking
out across one of the bleak snow-covered squares of Cambridge,
screamed at the top of his voice:

"Relentless! ... Relentless! ... Juh sweez un art-e-e-este!" Here he
beat on his little breast with a claw-like hand and yelled with drunken
laughter, "And, Goddamn it, I will always be relentless ... relentless
... relentless!"

The cool air braced him with its cleansing shock: for a moment, the
fog of shame and drunkenness shifted in his brain, he felt a vacancy of
cold horror at his back, and turning suddenly found himself confronted
by the frozen circle of their faces, fixed on him. And even in that instant glimpse of utter ruin, as the knowledge of this final castastrophe
was printed on his brain, over the rim of frozen faces he saw the dial-
hands of a clock. The time was seven-fifty-two: he knew there was a
train at midnight for New York—and work, food, freedom, and forgetfulness. He would have four hours to go home and pack: if he hurried
he could make it.

Little was heard of him thereafter. It was rumored that he had gone
back to his former lucrative employment with Mr. Hearst: and Professor
Hatcher smiled thinly when he heard the news; the young men looked
at one another with quiet smiles.

And yet he could not wholly be forgotten: occasionally some one
mentioned him.

"A strange case, wasn't it?" said Mr. Grey. "Do you remember how
he looked? Like ... like ... really, he was like some mediæval ascetic.
I thought he had something. I thought he would do something ... I

really did, you know! And then—heavens!—that last play!" He tossed his cigarette away with a movement of dismissal. "A strange case," he said with quiet finality. "A man who looked as if he had it and who turned out—all belly and no brain."

There was silence for a moment while the young men smoked.

"I wonder what it was," another said thoughtfully at length. "What happened to him? I wonder why."

There was no one there who knew the answer. The only one on earth, perhaps, who could have given it was that curious old spinster named Miss Potter. For blind to many things that all these clever young men knew, that good grotesque old empress of confusion still had a wisdom that none of them suspected. But Miss Potter was no longer there to tell them, even if she could. She had died that spring.

Later it seemed to Gene that the cold and wintry light of desolation— the red waning light of Friday in the month of March—shone forever on the lives of all the people. And forever after, when he thought of them, their lives, their faces and their words—all that he had seen and known of them—would be fused into a hopeless, joyless image which was somehow consonant to that accursed wintry light that shone upon it. And this was the image:

He was standing upon the black and grimy snow of winter before Miss Potter's house, saying good-bye to a group of her invited guests. The last red wintry light of Friday afternoon fell on their lives and faces as he talked to them, and made them hateful to him, and yet he searched those faces and talked desperately to see if he could find there any warmth or love or joy, any ring of hope for himself which would tell him that his sick heart and leaden spirit would awake to life and strength again, that he would get his hands again on life and love and labor, and that April would come back again.

But he found nothing in these cold and hateful faces but the lights of desolation, the deadly and corrupt joy that took delight in its own death, and breathed, without any of the agony and despair he felt, the poisonous ethers of its own dead world. In those cold hateful faces as that desolate and wintry light fell on them he could find no hope for his own life or the life of living men. Rather, he read in their pale faces, and in their rootless and unwholesome lives, which had come to have for him the wilted yellow pallor of nameless and unuseful plants such as flourish under barrels, a kind of cold malicious triumph, a momentary gleam in pale fox eyes, which said that they looked upon his desperate life and knew the cause of his despair, and felt a bitter triumph over it. The look on their cold faces and in their fox eyes said to him that there was no hope, no work, no joy, no triumph, and no love for such as he, that there could be nothing but defeat, despair and failure for the living of this world, that life had been devoured and killed by such as these, and had become rat's alley, death-in-life forever.

And yet he searched their hated faces desperately in that cold red light, he sought frantically in their loathed faces for a ray of hope, and in his drowning desolation shameful words were wrenched from him against his will—words of entreaty, pleading, pitiful begging for an alms of mercy, a beggarly scrap of encouragement, even a word of kindly judgment on his life, from these cold and hateful faces that he loathed.

"But my work—this last work that I did—don't you think—didn't it seem to you that there was something good in it—not much, perhaps, but just enough to give me hope? . . . Don't you think if I go on I may do something good some day—for God's sake, tell me if you do?—or must I die here in this barren and accursed light of Friday afternoon, must I drown and smother in this poisonous and lifeless air, wither in this rootless, yellow, barren earth below the barrel, die like a mad-dog howling in the wilderness, with the damned, cold, hateful sneer of your impotent lives upon me?

"Tell me, in God's name, man, is there no life on earth for such as I? Has the world been stripped for such as you? Have all joy, hope, health, sensual love, and warmth and tenderness gone out of life—are living men the false men, then, and is all truth and work and wisdom owned by rat's alley and the living dead such as yourself?—For God's sake, tell me if there is no hope for me! Let me have the worst, the worst, I beg of you. Is there nothing for me now but the gray gut, the sick heart, and the leaden spirit? Is there nothing now but Friday afternoon in March, Miss Potter's parties, and your damned poisonous, sterile, cold, life-hating faces? For God's sake tell me now if I am no good, am false while you, the living dead, are true—and had better cut my throat or blow my brains out than stay on longer in this world of truth, where joy is dead, and only the barren rootless lives of dead men live!—In God's name, tell me now, if this is true—or do you find a rag of hope for me?"

"Ah," the old composer Cram would answer, arranging the folds of his dirty scarf, and peering out malevolently underneath his sparse lank webs of dirty gray, as the red and wintry light fell hopelessly on his poisonous old face. "—Ah-h," he rasped bitterly, "—my wife and I liked some things in that play of yours that Professor Hatcher put on in his Playshop. . . . My wife and I liked one or two speeches in that play," he rasped, "but"—for a moment a fox's glittering of malevolent triumph shone in his eyes as he drove the fine blade home "—no one else did! —No one else thought it was any good at all!" he cackled malevolently. "I heard people saying all around me that they *hated* it," he gloated, "—that you had no talent, no ability to write, and had better go back where you came from—live some other kind of life—or *kill* yourself," he gloated— "That's the way it is, my boy!—Nothing but defeat and misery and despair for such as you in life! . . . That has been my lot, too," he cackled vindictively, rubbing his dry hands in glee. "They've always hated what I did—if I ever did anything good I was lucky if I found two people who liked it. The rest of them *hated* it," he whispered wildly. "There's no hope for you—so *die, die, die,*" he whispered, and cackling with malevolent triumph, he rubbed his dry hands gleefully.

"Meeker, for God's sake," the boy cried, turning to the elegant figure of the clergyman, who would be carefully arranging around his damned luxurious neck the rich folds of a silk blue scarf— "Meeker, do you feel this way about it, too? . . . Is that your opinion? . . . Do you find nothing good in what I do?"

—"You see, old chap, it's this way," Meeker answered, in his soft voice, and drew with languor on one of his expensive straw-tipped cigarettes— "You have lots of ability, I am sure"—here he paused to inhale meditatively again— "but don't you think, old boy, it's critical rather than creative?—now with Jim here it's different," he continued, placing one hand affectionately on Hogan's narrow shoulders— "Jim here's a great genius—like Shelley—with a great gift waiting for the world"— Here Hogan lowered his pale weak face with a simpering smile of modesty, but not before the boy had seen the fox's glitter of vindictive triumph in his pale dull eyes—"but you have nothing of that sort to give. Why don't you try to make the best of what you have?" he said with hateful sympathetic urbanity and put the cigarette to elegant and reflective lips again.

"Hogan," the boy cried hoarsely, turning to the poet,"—is that your answer, too? Have you no word of hope for me?—but no, you damned, snivelling, whining upstart—you are gloating at your rotten little triumph, aren't you? I'd get nothing out of you, would I?"

"Come on, Jim," said Meeker quietly. "He's becoming abusive. . . .

The kind of attack you make is simply stupid," he now said. "It will get you nowhere."

"And so raucous—so raucous," said Hogan, smirking nervously. "It means nothing."

And the three hated forms of death would go away then rapidly, snickering among themselves, and he would turn again, filled with the death of life, the end of joy, again, again, to prowl the wintry, barren, and accursed streets of Friday night.

XXXVII

It had been almost two years since Eugene had last seen Robert Weaver, but now, by one of those sudden weavings of blind chance that for a moment bring men's lives together, and in an instant show them more than years together could have done, he was to see the other youth again.

One night in his second year at Cambridge he was reading in his room at about two o'clock in the morning, at the heart and core of the brooding silence of night that had come to mean so much to him, and that had the power to stir him as no other time of day could do with a feeling of swelling and exultant joy. The house had gone to sleep long before and there was no sound anywhere: it was late in winter, along in March, and the ice and snow had been packed and frozen on the earth for months with a kind of weary permanence—with a tenacity that gave to winter a harsh and dreary reality, a protraction of gray days and grim gray light which made the memory of other seasons, and particularly the hope of spring, remote and almost unbelievable. The street outside was frozen in this living and animate silence of great cold: suddenly this still perfection of night and darkness was shattered by the engines of a powerful motor which turned into the end of the street from Massachusetts Avenue, and tore along before the house at drunken speed with a roaring explosion of sound. Then, without slacking its speed, the brakes were jammed on, the car skidded murderously to a halt on the slippery pavement, and immediately backed up at full speed until it came before the house again, skidded to a halt and was abruptly silent.

Some one got out with the same violent impatience, slammed the door, and then for a moment, he could hear him hunting along the street, swearing and muttering to himself, at length he came back to the house, started up the steps on which he slipped or stumbled and fell heavily, after which he heard Robert cursing in a tone of hoarse and feverish discontent: "The God-damnedest place I ever saw. . . . Did they never hear of a light around here? . . . Who the hell would want to live in a place like this?"

He began to hammer at the front door and to bawl out Eugene's name at the top of his voice: then he came up outside his windows and began to knock on the glass impatiently with his fist. Eugene went to the door and let him in: he entered the room without a word, and with the intent driving movement of a man who is very drunk, then he looked at him scornfully and accusingly, and barked out: "What time do you go to bed? . . . Do you stay up all night? . . . What do you do, sleep all morning?" . . . He looked around the room: the floor was strewn with books he had been reading and littered with pieces of paper on which he had been writing. Robert broke into his sudden, hoarse, falsetto laugh: "The damndest place I ever saw!" he said. "Do you sleep on that thing?" he said contemptuously, pointing to his cot bed which stood along the wall in one corner of the room.

"No, Robert," he said, "I sleep on the floor. I use that for an ice box."

"What's that in the corner?" Robert asked pointing to some dirty shirts he had thrown there. "Shirts? . . . How long has it been since you sent anything to the laundry? . . . What do you do when you want a shirt, go out and buy one? . . . Do you ever take a bath? . . . Have you had a bath since you came to Harvard?" He laughed suddenly, hoarsely and wildly again, hurled himself into a chair, sighed sharply with a weary and impatient discontent, began to pass his hand across his forehead with an abstracted and weary movement, and said, "Lord! Lord! Lord! . . . The things I've done!" he shook his head mournfully. "Why it's awful," he said, and he started to shake his head again.

"Why don't you try to talk a little louder?" Eugene suggested. "I think there are a few people over in South Boston who haven't heard you yet."

He laughed, hoarsely and abruptly, and then resumed his abstracted and repentant shaking of the head, sighing heavily from time to time and saying, "Lord!"

It was the first time Eugene had seen Robert in two years. Under the hard light that he kept burning in his room he now looked closely at him: he wore a derby hat that became his small lean head well, and he had on a magnificent fur coat, such as the rich Harvard boys wear, that came down almost to his shoe-tops. For the rest, he was quietly and elegantly tailored with the distinction he had always seemed to get into his clothes—there was always, even in his boyhood, a kind of formal dignity in his dress: he always wore a stiff, starched collar.

Robert's face had grown thinner, he looked haggard and a good deal older: the lines of his sharp, incisive features were more deeply cut and his eyes, now injected and bloodshot from heavy drinking, were more wild and feverish in their restless discontent than they had ever been—he seemed to be lashed and driven by a savage and desperate hunger which he could neither satisfy nor articulate: he was being consumed and torn to pieces by a torment of desire and longing, the cause of which he could not define, and which he had no means to assuage or quench.

He had a bottle half filled with whiskey in the pocket of his fur coat: he took it out and offered Eugene a drink and after he had drunk, he put the bottle to his lips and gulped down all that remained in a single draught. Then he flung the empty bottle away impatiently on the table: it was obvious that the liquor, instead of giving him some peace or comfort, acted as savagely and immediately as oil poured on the tumult of a raging fire—it fed and spurred the madness in him and gave him no release until he had drunk himself into a state of paralysis and stupefaction. He was one of those men for whom alcohol was a fatal and uncontrollable stimulant: having once drawn the cork from a bottle and tasted his first drink he was then powerless to resist or stop: he drank until he could drink no more, and he would beg, fight, lie, cheat, crawl or walk or incur any desperate risk or danger to get more drink. Yet, he told Eugene that until his twenty-first year he had never tasted liquor: he began to drink during his last year in college, and during the two years that followed he had gone far on the road toward alcoholism.

Eugene asked him how he had found out where he lived and, still passing his hand across his forehead, he answered in an impatient and abstracted tone: "Oh . . . I don't know. . . . Some one told me, I guess. . . . I think it was Arthur Kittrell," and then he fell to shaking his head again, and saying, "Awful! awful! awful! . . . Do you know how much money I've spent so far this year. . . . Forty-eight hundred dollars. . . . So help me God, I hope I may die if I'm not telling you the truth! Why it's awful!" he said, and burst into a laugh.

"Have you travelled around a lot?" Gene asked.

"Have I? My God, I've spent only one week-end in New Haven since the beginning of the year," he said. "Why it's terrible! . . . Do you know who I'm rooming with?" he demanded.

"No."

"Andy Westerman," he said impressively and then, as the name communicated none of its significance to Gene, he added impatiently: "Why you've heard of the Westermans, haven't you? . . . My God, what have you been doing all your life? . . . You've heard of the Westerman vacuum cleaners and electric refrigerators, haven't you? . . . Why, he's worth $20,000,000 if he's worth a cent! . . . The craziest man that ever lived!" he said, breaking suddenly into a sharp recollective laugh.

"Who? Westerman?"

"No. . . . My room-mate . . . that damned Andy Westerman. . . . Do you want to meet him?"

"Is he up here with you?"

"Why, that's what I'm telling you," he said impatiently.

"Where is he?"

"I don't know," said Robert with a laugh. "In jail by now, I reckon. . . . I left him down at the Copley Plaza an hour ago stopping every one who came in and asking him if he'd ever been to Harvard. . . . If the man said yes, Andy would haul off and hit him as hard as he could. . . . God! the craziest man!" he said. Then, in a feverish staccato monolog, he continued: "The damnedest story you ever heard. . . . You never heard anything like the way I met him in your life. . . . Passed right out in the gutter on Park Avenue one night. . . . All alone. . . . They'd given me knockout drops in some joint and robbed me. . . . Waked up in the most magnificent apartment you ever saw in your life. . . . Most beautiful woman you ever saw sitting right there on the bed holding my hand. . . . Andy Westerman's sister. . . . God! they've got stuff in that place that cost a fortune. . . . They've got one picture that the old man paid a hundred thousand dollars for. . . . Damned little thing that doesn't take up a foot of space. . . . Twenty million dollars! Yes, sir! . . . And those two get it all. . . . Why, it'll ruin me!" he burst out. "It takes every cent I can get to keep up with 'em. . . . My God! I never saw a place like this in my life! . . . These people up here think no more of spending a thousand dollars than we'd think of fifty cents down home. . . . God! I've got to do something. . . . I've got to get money somehow. . . . Yes, sir, Robert is going to be right up there among them. . . . Apartment on Park Avenue and everything. . . . God! that's the most beautiful woman in the world! All I want is to sleep with her just once. . . . Yes, sir, just once. . . .

"And to think that she'd go and throw herself away on that damned consumptive little . . .!" he fairly ground his teeth together, turned away abruptly, and did not finish.

"Throw herself away on who? Who is this, Robert?"

"Ah-h! that damned little fellow Upshaw that she's married to: been waiting—praying—hoping that he'd die for months—she'll marry me just as soon as he's out of the way—and he knows it! The damned little rat!" He gnashed his teeth savagely. "He's hanging on just as long as he can to spite us!" And he cursed bitterly, with a terrible unconscious humor, against a man who was too subborn to oblige him by an early death.

Then he jumped up and said abruptly: "Do you want to go to New York with me?"

"When?"

"Right now!" said Robert. "I'm ready to go this very minute. Come on!"—and he started impatiently toward the door.

When Eugene made no move to follow him, he turned and came back, saying in a resentful tone: "Well, are you coming, or are you just trying to bluff about it?"

For a moment, the boy was infected by the other's madness, too near akin to his own ever to be wholly strange to him. The prospect of that reckless, drunken, purposeless flight through darkness towards the magic city held him with hypnotic power. Then, rudely, painfully, he broke the spell and answered curtly:

"I wouldn't go as far as Harvard Square with you tonight, Robert. Not if you're going to drive that car. You're too drunk to know what you're doing and you'll have a smash-up as sure as you live if you try to drive."

He was, in fact, wildly and dangerously drunk by now and Eugene began to think of some way of persuading him to go to sleep and of finding some place where he could spend the night: in his own room there was only a single cot, and it was too late to rouse the Murphys—they had been in bed for hours. Then he remembered that Mr. Wang had an extra couch in one of his rooms: it was a very comfortable one and he did not think that Wang would make any objection to Robert's sleeping there if he explained the situation to him. Therefore, he cautioned Robert to keep quiet, and went to Wang's door and knocked. Presently he appeared sleepily, thrusting out his fat, drowsy, and troubled face to see what the trouble was: when Eugene told him he agreed very generously and readily to let Robert sleep upon the couch and thus the young man got him settled at length although not before the sudden apparition of a dragon with a scaly tail—one of the drawings that hung above the couch—had wrested from him a howl of terror: he had sprung out of bed and rushed out of Wang's apartment and into Eugene's, saying hoarsely, and in a tone of frightened indignation: "Do you expect me to spend the night alone in there with that damned Chinaman and his dragon? . . . How do I know what he'll do? . . . One of those people would cut your throat while you're asleep and think nothing of it. . . . I'm not going to stay in there." Gene finally persuaded him of Wang's innocence and kindness, and at length he went off to sleep after drinking the better part of a bottle of Wang's rice wine.

XXXVIII

ONE Sunday morning early in the month of May, Starwick and Eugene had crossed the bridge that led to the great stadium, and turned right along a path that followed the winding banks of the Charles River. Spring had come with the sudden, almost explosive loveliness that marks its coming in New England: along the banks of the river the birch trees leaned their slender, white and beautiful trunks, and their boughs were coming swiftly into the young and tender green of May.

That spring—which, for Eugene, would be the third and last of his years in Cambridge—Starwick had become more mannered in his dress and style than ever before. During the winter, much to Professor Hatcher's concern—a concern which constantly became more troubled and which he was no longer able to conceal—the darling protégé on whom his bounty and his favor had been lavished, and to whom, he had fondly hoped, he would one day pass on the proud authorities of his own position when he himself should become too old to carry on "the work," had begun to wear spats and carry a cane and be followed by a dog.

Now, with the coming of spring, Frank had discarded the spats, but as they walked along beside the Charles, he twirled his elegant light stick with an air of languid insouciance, interrupting his conversation with his friend now and then to speak sharply to the little dog that frisked and scampered along as if frantic with the joy of May, crying out to the little creature sharply, commandingly, and in a rather womanish tone from time to time:

"Heel, Tang! Heel, I say!"

And the dog, a shaggy little terrier—the gift of some wealthy and devoted friends of Frank's on Beacon Hill—would pause abruptly in its frisking, turn its head, and look towards its owner with the attentive, puzzled, and wistfully inquiring look that dogs and little children have, as if to say: "What is it, master? Are you pleased with me or have I done something that was wrong?"

And in a moment, in response to Frank's sharper and more peremptory command, the little dog, with a crestfallen and somewhat apologetic look, would scamper back from its wild gaieties along the green banks of the Charles, to trot meekly along the path behind the two young men, until its exuberant springtime spirits got the best of it again.

From time to time, they would pass other students, in pairs or groups, striding along the pleasant path; and when these young men saw Starwick twirling his stick and speaking to the little dog, they would grin broadly at each other, and stare curiously at Starwick as they passed.

Once Starwick paused to call "Heel!" sharply to the little dog at the very moment it had lifted its leg against a tree, and the dog, still holding its leg up, had looked inquiringly around at Starwick with such a wistful look that some students who were passing had burst out in hearty laughter. But Starwick, although the color of his ruddy face deepened a shade, had paid no more attention to these ruffians than if they had been scum in the gutter. Rather, he snapped his fingers sharply, and cried, "Heel!" again, at which the little dog left its tree and came trotting meekly back to its obedient position.

Suddenly, while one of these episodes was being enacted, Eugene heard the bright wholesome tones of a familiar voice, and turning around with a startled movement, found himself looking straight into the broad and beaming countenance of Effie Horton, and her husband Ed.

"*Well!*" Effie was saying in her rich bright voice of Iowa. "Look who's here! I *thought* those long legs looked familiar," she went on in her tone of gay and lightsome, and yet wholesome, banter, "even from a distance! I told Pooly—" this, for an unknown reason, was the affectionate nickname by which Horton was known to his wife, and all his friends from Iowa—"I told Pooly that there was only one pair of legs as long as that in Cambridge. 'It *must* be Eugene,' I said.—Yes, sir!" she went on brightly, shaking her head with a little bantering movement, her broad and wholesome face shining with good nature all the time. "It *is* Eugene —and *my! my! my!*—I just wish you'd look at him," she went on gaily, in her tones of full rich fellowship and banter in which, however, a trace of something ugly, envious, and mocking was evident—"all dressed up in his Sunday-go-to-meeting clothes out for a walk this fine morning just to give the pretty girls a treat! Yes, sir!" she cried again, shaking her head in wondering admiration, and with an air of beaming satisfaction, "I'll *bet* you that's *just* what he's going to do."

He flushed, unable to think of an apt reply to this good-natured banter, beneath whose hearty good-fellowship he felt the presence of something that was false, ugly, jeering and curiously tormented, and while he was blundering out a clumsy greeting, Horton, laughing with lazy good-nature at his confusion, slapped him on the back and said:

"How are yuh, kid? . . . Where the hell have you been keeping yourself, anyway?"

The tone was almost deliberately coarse and robust in its hearty masculinity, but beneath it one felt the same false and spurious quality that had been evident in the woman's tone.

—"And here is *Mister* Starwick!" Effie now cried brightly. "—And I *wish* you'd *look!*" she went on, as if enraptured by the spectacle—"all dressed up with a walking stick and a dog—and yes, *sir!*" she exclaimed ecstatically, after an astonished examination of Frank's sartorial splendor —"wearing a *bee-yew-teeful* brown tweed suit that looks as if it just came out of the shop of a London tailor! . . . *My! My! My!* . . . I tell *you!*" she went on admiringly—"I just wish the folks back home could see us now, Pooly——"

Horton laughed coarsely, with apparent good nature, but with an ugly jeering note in his voice.

"—I just wish they could see us now!" she said. "It's not every one can say they knew two London swells—and here they are—Mr. Starwick with his cane and his dog—and Eugene with his new suit—yes, *sir!*— and talking to us just as if we were their equals."

Eugene flushed, and then with a stiff and inept sarcasm, said:

"I'll try not to let it make any difference between us, Effie."

Horton laughed coarsely and heartily again, with false good nature, and then smote the boy amiably on the back, saying:

"Don't let her kid you, son! Tell her to go to hell if she gets fresh with you!"

"—And how is Mr. Starwick these fine days!" cried Effie gaily, now directing the artillery of her banter at his unworthy person— "Where is that great play we've all been waiting for so eagerly for lo these many years! I tell *you!*" she exclaimed with rich conviction—"I'm going to be right there on the front row the night it opens up on Broadway!—I know that a play that has taken any one so many years will be a masterpiece— every word pure gold—I don't want to miss a *word* of it."

"Quite!" said Starwick coldly, in his mannered and affected tone. His ruddy face had flushed crimson with embarrassment; turning, he called sharply and coldly to the little dog, in a high and rather womanish voice:

"Heel, Tang! Heel, I say!"

He snapped his fingers and the little dog came trotting meekly toward him. Before Starwick's cold and scornful impassivity, Effie's broad and wholesome face did not alter a jot from its expression of radiant good-will, but suddenly her eyes, which, set in her robust and friendly countenance, were the tortured mirror of her jealous, envious, possessive, and ravenously curious spirit, had grown hard and ugly, and the undernote of malice in her gay tones was more apparent than ever when she spoke again:

"Pooly," she said, laughing, taking Horton affectionately by the arm, and drawing close to him with the gesture of a bitterly jealous and possessive female, who, by the tortured necessity of her own spirit, must believe that "her man" is the paragon of the universe, and herself the envy of all other women, who lust to have him, but must gnash their teeth in vain—"Pooly," she said lightly, and drawing close to him—"maybe that's what's wrong with us! . . . Maybe that's what it takes to make you write a great play! . . . Yes, *sir!*" she said gaily, "I believe that's it! . . . I believe I'll save up all my spending money until I have enough to buy you a bee-yew-teeful tailored suit just like the one that Mr. Starwick has on. . . . Yes, *sir!*" She nodded her head emphatically in a convinced manner. "That's just *exactly* what I'm going to do! . . . I'm going to get Mr. Starwick to give me the address of his tailor—and have him make you a *bee-yew-teeful* new suit of English clothes—and then, maybe, you'll turn into a great genius like Mr. Starwick and Eugene!"

"The hell you will!" he said coarsely and heartily. "What's wrong with the one I got on? I only had it three years—why, it's as good as the day I bought it." And he laughed with hearty, robust masculinity.

"Why, Poo-o-ly!" she said reproachfully. "It's turning *green!* And I do so want you to get dressed up and be a *genius* like Mr. Starwick!"

"Nope!" he said in his tone of dominant finality. "I'll wear this pair of pants till it falls off me. Then I'll go into Filene's bargain basement and buy another pair. Nope! You can't make an æsthete out of me! I can write just as well with a hole in the seat of my britches as not." And laughing coarsely, with robust and manly good nature, he smote Eugene on the back again, and rasped out heartily:

"Ain't that right, kid?"

"Oh, *Pooly!*" cried Effie reproachfully— "And I do *so* want you to be a genius—like Mr. Starwick!"

"Now, wait a minute! Wait a minute!" he rasped, lifting a commanding hand, as he joined with her in this ugly banter. "That's different! Starwick's an artist—I'm nothing but a writer. They don't understand the way we artists work—do they, Starwick? Now an artist is sensitive to all these things," he went on in a jocose explanatory tone to his wife. "He's got to have the right *atmosphere* to work in. Everything's got to be just right for we artists—doesn't it, Starwick?"

"Quite!" said Starwick coldly.

"Now with me it's different," said Horton heavily. "I'm just one of those big crude guys who can write anywhere. I get up in the morning and write, whether I feel like it or not. But it's different with us artists, isn't it, Starwick? Why, with a real honest-to-God-dyed-in-the-wool *artist* like Starwick, his whole life would be ruined for a *month* if his pants didn't fit, or if his necktie was of the wrong shade. . . . Ain't that right, Starwick?"

And he laughed heavily, apparently with robust fellowship, hearty good nature, but his eyes were ugly, evil, jeering, as he spoke.

"Quite!" said Starwick as before; and, his face deeply flushed, he called sharply to his dog, and then, turning inquiringly to Eugene, said quietly: "Are we ready?"

Oh, I *see*, I *see!*" cried Effie, with an air of gay enlightenment. "That's what every one is all dressed up about!—You're out for a walk, aren't you—all among the little birdies, and the beeses, and the flowers! *My! My!* How I wish I could go along! Pooly!" she said coaxingly, "why don't you take *me* for a walk sometime? I'd love to hear the little birdies sing! Come on, dear. Won't you?" she said coaxingly.

"Nope!" he boomed out finally. "I walked you across the bridge and I walked to the corner this morning for a paper. That's all the walking that I'm going to do today. If you want to hear the little birdies sing, I'll buy you a canary." And turning to Eugene, he smote him on the shoulder again, and laughing with coarse laziness, said:

"You know me, kid. . . . You know how I like exercise, don't you?"

"Well, then, if we can't go along to hear the little birdies sing to Mr.

Starwick and Eugene, I suppose we'll have to say good-bye," said Effie regretfully. "We've got no right to keep them from the little birdies any longer—have we, dear? And think what a treat it will be for all the little birdies. . . . And you, Eugene!" she cried out gaily and reproachfully, but now with real warmth and friendship in her voice. "We haven't seen you at our home in a-a-ages! What's *wrong* with you? . . . You come up soon or I'll be mad at you."

"Sure," Horton came out in his broad Iowa accent, putting his hand gently on the boy's shoulder. "Come up to see us, kid. We'll cook some grub and chew the rag a while. You know, I'm not coming back next year—" for a moment Horton's eyes were clear, gray, luminous, deeply hurt, and full of pride and tenderness. "We're going to New Hampshire with Jim Madden. So come up, kid, as soon as you can: we ought to have one more session before I go."

And the boy, suddenly touched and moved, felt the genuine affection, the real friendliness—an animal-like warmth and kindliness and affection that was the truest and most attractive element in Horton's personality.

And nodding his head, suddenly feeling affection for them both again, he said:

"All right, Ed. I'll see you soon. So long, Effie. Good-bye. Good-bye, Ed."

"Good-bye, kid. So long, Starwick," Horton said in a kindly tone. "We'll be looking for you, 'Gene— So long!"

Then they parted, in this friendly manner, and Starwick and Eugene continued their walk along the river. Starwick walked quietly, saying nothing; from time to time he called sharply to the little dog, commanding him to come to "heel" again.

The two young men had not seen each other for two months, save at Professor Hatcher's class, and then their relations had been formal, cold, and strained. Now Starwick, with a quick friendly and generous spontaneity, had broken through the stubborn and resentful pride of the other youth, had made the first advance towards reconciliation, and, as he was able to do with every one when and where he pleased, had instantly conquered his friend's resentful feelings, and won him back with the infinite grace, charm, and persuasiveness of his own personality.

Yet, during the first part of their walk along the river their conversation, while friendly, had almost been studiously detached and casual, and was the conversation of people still under the constraint of embarrassment and diffidence, who are waiting for the moment to speak things in which their lives and feelings are more intimately concerned.

At length, they came to a bending in the river where there was a bank of green turf on which in the past they had often sat and smoked and talked while that small and lovely river flowed before them. Seated here again, and provided with cigarettes, a silence came between them, as if each was waiting for the other one to speak.

Presently when Eugene looked towards his companion, Starwick's pleasant face with the cleft chin was turned towards the river in a set stare, and even as the other young man looked at him, his ruddy countenance was contorted by the animal-like grimace swift and instant, which the other boy had often seen before, and which had in it, somehow, a bestial and inarticulate quality, a kind of unspeakable animal anguish that could find no release.

In a moment, lowering his head, and staring away into the grassy turf, Starwick said quietly:

"Why have you not been in to see me these last two months?"

The other young man flushed, began to speak in a blundering and embarrassed tone and then, angered by his own confusion, burst out hotly:

"Look here, Frank—why have you got to be so damned mysterious and secretive in everything you do?"

"Am I?" said Starwick quietly.

"Yes, you are! You've been that way ever since I met you."

"In what way?" Starwick asked.

"Do you remember the first time I met you?" the other one demanded.

"Perfectly," Starwick said. "It was during your first year in Cambridge, a few days after you arrived. We met for dinner at the Cock Horse Tavern."

"Yes," the other said excitedly. "Exactly. You had written me a note inviting me to dinner, and asking me to meet you there. Do you remember what was in that note?"

"No. What was it?"

"Well, you said: 'Dear Sir—I should be pleased if you will meet me for dinner at seven-thirty Wednesday evening at the Cock Horse Tavern on Brattle Street.' And the note was signed, 'Francis Starwick.'"

"Well?" Starwick demanded quietly. "And what was wrong with that?"

"Nothing!" the other young man cried, his face flushing to a darker hue, and the excitement of his manner growing. "Nothing, Frank! Only, if you were going to invite a stranger—some one you had never met before—to dinner—why the hell couldn't you have told him who you are, and the purpose of the meeting?"

"I should think the purpose of the meeting was self-evident," said Starwick calmly. "The purpose was to have dinner together. Does that demand a whole volume of explanation? No," he said coldly, "I confess I see nothing extraordinary about that at all."

"Of course there wasn't!" the other youth exclaimed with vehement excitement. "Of course there was nothing extraordinary about it! Why, then, did you attempt, Frank, to make something extraordinary out of it?"

"It seems to me that you're the one who's doing that!" Starwick answered.

"Yes, but, damn it, man," the other cried angrily "—don't you see the point? You're that way with everything you do! You try to surround the simplest act with this great air of mystery and secrecy," he said bitterly. "Inviting me to dinner was all right—it was fine!" he shouted. "I was a green kid of twenty who knew no one here, and I was scared to death. It was wonderful to get an invitation from some one asking me to dinner. But when you sent the invitation, why couldn't you have added just a word or two by way of explanation? Why couldn't you have stated one or two simple facts that would have made the reason for your invitation clear?"

"For example?" Starwick said.

"Why, Frank, simply that you were Professor Hatcher's assistant in the course, and that this thing of inviting people out to dinner was just a way you and Professor Hatcher had of getting acquainted with the new people," the other youth said angrily. "After all, you can't get an invitation to dinner from some one you don't know without wondering what it's all about."

"And yet you came," said Starwick.

"Yes, of course I came! I think I would have come if I had never heard of you before—I was so bewildered and rattled by this new life, and so overwhelmed by living in a big city for the first time in my life that I would have accepted any kind of invitation—jumped at the chance of meeting any one! However, I already knew who you were when your invitation came. I had heard that a man named Starwick was Hatcher's assistant. I figured therefore that the invitation had something

to do with your connection with Professor Hatcher and the course—
that you were inviting me to make me feel more at home up here, to
establish a friendly relation, to give me what information you could, to
help the new people out in any way you could. But when I met you,
what happened?" he went on indignantly. "Never a word about the
course, about Professor Hatcher, about your being his assistant—you
pumped me with questions as if I were a prisoner on the witness stand
and you the prosecuting lawyer. You told me nothing about yourself
and asked a thousand questions about me—and then you shook hands
coldly, and departed!—Always this air of secrecy and mystery, Frank!"
the boy went on angrily. "That's always the way it is with you—in
everything you do! And yet you wonder why people are surprised at
your behavior! For weeks at a time I see you every day. We get together in your rooms and talk and argue about everything on earth.
You come and yell for me in my place at midnight and then we walk
all over Cambridge in the dead of night. We go over to Posillippo's
place in Boston and eat and drink and get drunk together, and when
you pass out, I bring you home and carry you upstairs and put you to
bed. Then the next day, when I come around again," the boy cried bitterly, "what has happened? I ring the bell. Your voice comes through
the place as cold as hell— 'Who is it?' you say. 'Why,' I say, 'it's your
old friend and drunken companion, Eugene Gant, who brought you
home last night.'—'I'm sorry,' you say, in a tone that would freeze a polar
bear— 'I can't see you. I'm busy now'—and then you hang up in my
face. The season of the great mystery has now begun," he went on sar-
castically. "The great man is closeted in his sanctum *composing*," he
sneered. "Not *writing*, mind you, but *composing* with a gold-tipped
quill plucked from the wing of a Brazilian condor—so, out, out, damned
spot—don't bother me, Gant—begone, you low fellow—on your way,
bum!—the great master, Signor Francis Starwick, is upstairs in a purple
cloud, having a few immortal thoughts today with Amaryllis, his pet
muse——"

"Gene! Gene!" said Starwick laughing, a trace of the old mannered
accent returning to his voice again. "You are *most* unfair! You really
are, you know!"

"No—but Frank, that's just the way you act," the other said. "You
can't see enough of some one for weeks at a time and then you slam the
door in his face. You pump your friends dry and tell them nothing
about yourself. You try to surround everything you do with this grand

romantic air of mysterious secrecy—this there's-more-to-this-than-meets-the-eye manner. Frank, who the hell do you think you are, anyway, with these grand airs and mysterious manners that you have? Is it that you're not the same as other men?" he jeered. "Is it that like Cæsar you were from your mother's womb untimely ripped! Is it that you are made from different stuff than the damned base clay of blood and agony from which the rest of us have been derived?"

"What have I ever done," said Starwick flushing, "to give you the impression that I think of myself that way?"

"For one thing, Frank, you act sometimes as if the world exists solely for the purpose of being your oyster. You sometimes act as if friendship, the affection of your friends, is something that exists solely for your pleasure and convenience and may be turned on and off at will like a hot-water faucet—that you can use their time, their lives, their feelings when they amuse and interest you—and send them away like whipped dogs when you are bored, tired, indifferent, or have something else it suits you better to do."

"I am not aware that I have ever done that," said Starwick quietly. "I am sorry if you think I have."

"No, but, Frank—what can you expect your friends to think? I have told you about my life, my family, the kind of place and people I came from—but you have told me nothing. You are the best friend I have here in Cambridge—I think," the boy said slowly, flushing, and with some difficulty, "one of the best friends I have ever had. I have not had many friends—I have known no one like you—no one of my own age to whom I could talk as I have talked to you. I think I enjoy being with you and talking to you more than to any one I have ever known. This friendship that I feel for you has now become a part of my whole life and has got into everything I do. And yet, at times, I run straight into a blank wall I could no more separate my friendship for you from the other acts and meetings of my life than I could divide into two parts of my body my father's and my mother's blood. With you it's different. You seem to have all your friends partitioned off and kept separate from one another in different cells and sections of your life. I know now that you have three or four sets of friends and yet these different groups of people never meet one another. You go about your life with all these different sets of people in this same secret and mysterious manner that characterizes everything you do. You have these aunts and cousins here in Cambridge that you see every week, and who, like every one else, lay themselves out to do everything they can to make your life comfortable and pleasant. You know these swells over on Beacon Hill in Boston, and you have some grand, mysterious and wealthy kind of life with them. Then you have another group here at the university—people like Egan, and Hugh Dodd and myself. And at the end, Frank," the boy said almost bitterly—"what is the purpose of all this secrecy and separation among your friends? There's something so damned arrogant and cold and calculating about it—it's almost as if you were one of these damned, wretched, self-centred fools who have their little time and place for everything—an hour for social recreation and an hour for useful reading, another hour for healthy exercise, and then four hours for business, an hour for the concert and an hour for the play, an hour for "business contacts" and an hour for friendship— Surely to God, Frank, you of all people on earth are not one of these damned, smug, vain, self-centred egotists—who would milk this earth as if it were a great milk cow here solely for their enrichment, and who, at the end, in spite of all their damned, miserable, self-seeking profit for themselves remain nothing but the God-damned smug, sterile, misbegotten set of impotent and life-hating bastards that they are— Surely to God, you, of all people in the world are not one of these," he fairly yelled, and sat there panting, exhausted by the tirade, and glaring at the other youth with wild, resentful eyes.

"Eugene!" cried Starwick sharply, his ruddy features darkened with an angry glow. "You are being most unjust! What you are saying simply is not true." He was silent a moment, his face red and angry-looking, as he stared out across the river— "If I had known that you felt this way," he went on quietly, "I should have introduced you to my other friends—what you call these separate groups of people—long ago. You may meet them any time you wish," he concluded. "It simply never occurred to me that you would be interested in knowing them."

"Oh, Frank, I'm not!" the other boy cried impatiently, with a dismissing movement of the hand. "I don't want to meet them—I don't care who they are—or how rich and fashionable or 'artistic' they may be. The thing I was kicking about was what seemed to me to be your air of secrecy—the mysterious manner in which you go about things: it seemed to me that there was something deliberately calculating and secretive in the way you shut one part of your life off from the people who know and like you best."

Starwick made no answer for a moment, but sat looking out across the river. And for a moment, the old grimace of bestial, baffled pain passed swiftly across his ruddy features, and then he said, in a quiet and weary tone:

"Perhaps you are right. I had never thought about it in that way. Yes, I can see now that you have told me much more about yourself— your family, your life before you came here, than I have told you about mine. And yet it never occurred to me that I was being mysterious or secretive. I think it is easier for you to speak about these things than it is for me. There is a great river of energy in you and it keeps bursting over and breaking loose. You could not hold it back if you tried. With me, it's different. I have not got that great well of life and power in me, and I could not speak as you do if I tried. Yet, Gene, if there is anything you want to know about my life before I came here, or what kind of people I came from I would tell you willingly."

"I have wanted to know more about you, Frank," the other young man said. "All that I know about your life before you came here is that you come from somewhere in the Middle West, and yet are completely different from any one I ever knew who came from there."

"Yes," said Starwick quietly. "From Horton, for example?" his tone was still quiet, but there was a shade of irony in it.

"Well," the other boy said, flushing, but continuing obstinately, "— yes, from Horton. He is from Iowa, you can see, smell, read, feel Iowa all over him, in everything he says and does——"

"'It's—a—*darn—good—yarn,*'" said Starwick, beginning to burble with laughter as he imitated the heavy, hearty, sonorous robustiousness of Horton's voice when he pronounced his favorite judgment.

"Yes," said Eugene, laughing at the imitation, "that's it, all right—'it's a *darn good yarn.*' Well, Frank, you couldn't be more different from Horton if you had come from the planet Mars, and yet the place you come from out there in the Middle West, the kind of life you knew when you were growing up—could not have been so different from Ed Horton's."

"No," said Starwick quietly. "As a matter of fact, I know where he is from—it's not over fifty miles from the town I was born in, which is in Illinois, and the life in both places is much the same."

He was silent a moment longer, as he stared across the river, and then continued in a quiet voice that had a calm, weary, and almost inert detachment that characterized these conversations with his friend, and that was almost entirely free of mannered speech:

"As to the kind of people that we came from," he continued, "I can't say how different they may be, but I should think it very likely that Horton's people are much the same kind of people as my own——"

"His father is a Methodist minister," the other young man quickly interposed. "He told me that."

"Yes," said Starwick in his quiet and inert voice—"and Horton is the rebel of the family." His tone had not changed apparently in its quality by an atom, yet the quiet and bitter irony with which he spoke was evident.

"How did you know that?" the other youth said in a surprised tone. "Yes—that's true. His wife told me that Ed and his father are scarcely on speaking terms—the old man prays for the salvation of Ed's soul three times a day, because he is trying to write plays and wants to get into the theatre. Effie Horton says Ed's father still writes Ed letters begging him to repent and mend his ways before his soul is damned forever: she says the old man calls the theatre the Devil's Workshop."

"Yes," said Starwick in his quiet and almost lifeless tone that still had curiously the cutting edge of a weary and detached sarcasm—"and Horton has bearded the philistines in their den, hasn't he, and given all for art?"

"Isn't that a bit unjust? I know you don't think very highly of Ed Horton's ability, but, after all, the man must have had some genuine desire to create something—some real love for the theatre—or he would not have broken with his family, and come here."

"Yes. I suppose he has. Many people have that desire," said Starwick wearily. "Do you think it is enough?"

"No, I do not. And yet I think a man who has it is better off—will have a better life, somehow—than the man who does not have it at all."

"Do you?" Starwick answered in a dead tone. "I wish I thought so, too."

"But don't you, Frank? Surely it is better to have some kind of talent, however small, than none at all."

"Would you say, then," Starwick answered, "that it was better to have some kind of child—however puny, feeble, ugly, and diseased—as King Richard said about himself, brought into the world 'scarce half made up'—than to have no child at all?"

"I would not think so. No."

"Have you ever thought, Eugene, that the great enemy of life may not be death, but life itself?" Starwick continued. "Have you never noticed that the really evil people that one meets—the people who are filled with hatred, fear, envy, rancour against life—who wish to destroy the artist and his work—are not figures of satanic darkness, who have been born with a malignant hatred against life, but rather people who have had the seeds of life within themselves, and been destroyed by them? They are the people who have been given just enough to get a vision of the promised land—however brief and broken it may be——"

"But not enough to get there? Is that what you mean?"

"Exactly," Starwick answered. "They are left there in the desert, maddened by the sight of water they can never reach, and all the juices of their life then turn to gall and bitterness—to envy and malignant hate. They are the old women in the little towns and villages with the sour eyes and the envenomed flesh who have so poisoned the air with their envenomed taint that everything young and beautiful and full of joy that lives there will sicken and go dead and vicious and malignant as the air it breathes. They are the lecherous and impotent old men of the world, those foul, palsied creatures with small rheumy eyes who hate the lover and his mistress with the hate of hell and eunuchry—who try to destroy love with their hatred, and the slanderous rumor of their poisoned tongues. And, finally, they are the eunuchs of the arts—the men who have the lust, without the power, for creation, and whose life goes dead and rotten with its hatred of the living artist and the living man."

"And you think that Horton will be one of these?"

Again Starwick was silent for a moment, staring out across the river. When he spoke again, he did not answer his companion's question directly, but in a quiet and inert tone in which the cutting edge of irony was barely evident, he said:

"My *God,* Eugene"—his voice was so low and wearily passionate with revulsion that it was almost inaudible—"if ever you may come to know, as I have known all my life, the falseness in a hearty laugh, the envy and the malice in a jesting word, the naked hatred in a jeering eye, and all the damned, warped, poisonous constrictions of the heart—the horrible fear and cowardice and cruelty, the naked shame, the hypocrisy, and the pretense, that is masked there behind the full hearty tones, the robust manliness of the Hortons of this earth . . ." He was silent a moment longer, and then went on in a quiet, matter-of-fact tone— "I was the youngest in a family of nine children—the same kind of family that you will find everywhere. I was the only delicate flower among them," he went on with a cold impassive irony. "We were not rich people . . . a big family growing up with only a small income to support us. They were all good people," he said quietly. "My father was superintendent of a small farm-machinery plant, and before that they were farming people, but they sent me to school, and after that to college. I was the 'bright boy' of the town"—again the weary irony of his voice was evident—"the local prodigy, the teacher's pet. . . . Perhaps that is my destiny; to have something of the artist's heart, his soul, his understanding, his perceptions—never to have his power, the hand that shapes, the tongue that can express—oh, God! Eugene! is *that* to be my life—to have all that I know and feel and would create rot still-born in my spirit, to be a wave that breaks forever in mid-ocean, the shoulder of a strength without the wall—my God! My God! to come into this world scarce half made up, to have the spirit of the artist and to lack his hide, to feel the intolerable and unspeakable beauty, mystery, loveliness, and terror of this immortal land—this great America—and a skin too sensitive, a hide too delicate and rare—" his voice was high and bitter with his passion—"to declare its cruelty, its horror, falseness, hunger, the warped and twisted soul of its frustration, and lacking hide and toughness, born without a skin, to make an armor, school a manner, build a barrier of my own against its Hortons——"

"And is that why—?" the other boy began, flushed, and quickly checked himself.

"Is that why—what?" said Starwick turning, looking at him. Then as he did not answer, but still remained silent, flushed with embarrassment, Starwick laughed, and said: "Is that why I am an affected person—a poseur—what Horton calls a 'damned little æsthete'—why I speak and act and dress the way I do?"

The other flushed miserably and muttered:

"No, I didn't say that, Frank!"

Starwick laughed suddenly, his infectious and spontaneous laugh, and said:

"But why not? Why shouldn't you say it? Because it is the truth. It really is, you know," and almost mockingly at these words, his voice assumed its murmured and affected accent. Then he said quietly again:

"Each man has his manner—with each it comes for his own reason— Horton's, so that his hearty voice and robust way may hide the hatred in his eyes, the terror in his heart, the falseness and pretense in his pitiable warped small soul. He has his manner, I have mine—his for concealment, mine for armor, because my native hide was tender and my skin too sensitive to meet the Hortons of the earth—and somewhere, down below our manner, stands the naked man." Again he was silent and in a moment he continued quietly:

"My father was a fine man and we never got to know each other very well. The night before I went away to college he 'took me to one side' and talked to me—he told me how they had their hearts set on me, and he asked me to become a good and useful man—a good American."

"And what did you say, Frank?"

"Nothing. There was nothing I could say. . . . Our house stands on a little butte above the river," he went on quietly in a moment, "and when he had finished talking I went out and stood there looking at the river."

"What river, Frank?"

"There is only one," he answered. "The great slow river—the dark and secret river of the night—the everlasting flood—the unceasing Mississippi. . . . It is a river that I know so well, with all my life that I shall never tell about. Perhaps you will some day—perhaps you have the power in you— And if you do—" he paused.

"And if I do?"

"Speak one word for a boy who could not speak against the Hortons of this land, but who once stood above a river—and who knew America as every other boy has known it." He turned, smiling: "If thou did'st ever hold me in thy heart, absent thee from felicity awhile, and in this harsh world draw thy breath in pain, to tell my story."

In a moment he got up, and laughing his infectious laugh, said:

"Come on, let's go."

And together they walked away.

BOOK III
TELEMACHUS

XXXIX

OCTOBER had come again, and that year it was sharp and soon: frost was early, burning the thick green on the mountain sides to massed brilliant hues of blazing colors, painting the air with sharpness, sorrow and delight—and with October. Sometimes, and often, there was warmth by day, an ancient drowsy light, a golden warmth and pollenated haze in afternoon, but over all the earth there was the premonitory breath of frost, an exultancy for all the men who were returning, a haunting sorrow for the buried men, and for all those who were gone and would not come again.

His father was dead, and now it seemed to him that he had never found him. His father was dead, and yet he sought him everywhere, and could not believe that he was dead, and was sure that he would find him. It was October and that year, after years of absence and of wandering, he had come home again.

He could not think that his father had died, but he had come home in October, and all the life that he had known there was strange and sorrowful as dreams. And yet he saw it all in shapes of deathless brightness—the town, the streets, the magic hills, and the plain prognathous faces of the people he had known. He saw them all in shapes of deathless brightness, and everything was instantly familiar as his father's face, and stranger, more phantasmal than a dream.

Their words came to him with the accents of an utter naturalness, and yet were sorrowful and lost and strange like voices speaking in a dream, and in their eyes he read a lost and lonely light, as if they were all phantoms and all lost, or as if he had revisited the shores of this great earth again with a heart of fire, a cry of pain and ecstasy, a memory of intolerable longing and regret for all the glorious and exultant life that he had known and which he must visit now forever as a fleshless ghost, never to touch, to hold, to have its palpable warmth and substance for his own again. He had come home again, and yet he could not believe his father was dead, and he thought he heard his great voice ringing in the street again, and that he would see him striding toward him across the Square with his gaunt earth-devouring stride, or find him waiting every time he turned the corner, or lunging toward the house bearing the tremendous provender of his food and meat, bringing to them all the deathless security of his strength and power and passion, bringing to them all again the roaring message of his fires that shook the fire-full chimney throat with their terrific blast, giving to them all again the exultant knowledge that the good days, the magic days, the golden weather of their lives would come again, and that this dream-like and phantasmal world in which they found themselves would waken instantly, as it had once, to all the palpable warmth and glory of the earth, if only his father would come back to make it live, to give them life, again.

Therefore, he could not think that he was dead, and yet it was October, and that year he had come home again. And at night, in his mother's house, he would lie in his bed in the dark, hearing the wind that rattled dry leaves along the empty pavement, hearing far-off across the wind, the barking of a dog, feeling dark time, strange time, dark secret time, as it flowed on around him, remembering his life, this house, and all the million strange and secret visages of time, dark time, thinking, feeling, thinking:

"October has come again, has come again. . . . I have come home again, and found my father dead . . . and that was time . . . time . . . time. . . . Where shall I go now? What shall I do? For October has come again, but there has gone some richness from the life we knew, and we are lost."

Storm shook the house at night—the old house, his mother's house—where he had seen his brother die. The old doors swung and creaked in darkness, darkness pressed against the house, the darkness filled them, filled the house at night, it moved about them soft and secret, palpable, filled with a thousand secret presences of sorrowful time and memory, moving about him as he lay below his brother's room in darkness, while storm shook the house in late October, and something creaked and rattled in the wind's strong blast. It was October, and he had come home again: he could not believe that his father was dead.

Wind beat at them with burly shoulders in the night. The darkness moved there in the house like something silent, palpable—a spirit breathing in his mother's house, a demon and a friend—speaking to him its silent and intolerable prophecy of flight, of darkness and the storm, moving about him constantly, prowling about the edges of his life, ever beside him, with him, in him, whispering:

"Child, child—come with me—come with me to your brother's grave tonight. Come with me to the places where the young men lie whose bodies have long since been buried in the earth. Come with me where they walk and move again tonight, and you shall see your brother's face again, and hear his voice, and see again, as they march toward you from their graves the company of the young men who died, as he did, in October, speaking to you their messages of flight, of triumph, and the all-exultant darkness, telling you that all will be again as it was once."

October had come again, and he would lie there in his mother's house at night, and feel the darkness moving softly all about him, and hear the dry leaves scampering on the street outside, and the huge and burly rushes of the wind. And then the wind would rush away with huge caprice, and he could hear it far off roaring with remote demented cries in the embraces of great trees, and he would lie there thinking:

"October has come again—has come again"—feeling the dark around him, not believing that his father could be dead, thinking: "The strange and lonely years have come again. . . . I have come home again . . . come home again . . . and will it not be with us all as it has been?"—feeling the darkness as it moved about him, thinking, "Is it not the same darkness that I knew in childhood, and have I not lain here in bed before, and felt this darkness moving all about me? . . . Did we not hear dogs that barked in darkness, in October?" he then thought. "Were not their howls far broken by the wind? . . . And hear dry leaves that scampered on the streets at night . . . and the huge and burly rushes of the wind . . . and hear huge limbs that stiffly creak in the remote demented howlings of the burly wind . . . and something creaking in the wind at night . . . and think, then, as we think now, of all the men who have gone and never will come back again, and of our friends and brothers who lie buried in the earth? . . . Oh, has not October now come back again?" he cried. "As always—as it always was?"—and hearing the great darkness softly prowling in his mother's house at night, and thinking, feeling, thinking, as he lay there in the dark:

"Now October has come again which in our land is different from October in the other lands. The ripe, the golden month has come again, and in Virginia the chinkapins are falling. Frost sharps the middle music of the seasons, and all things living on the earth turn home again. The country is so big you cannot say the country has the same October. In Maine, the frost comes sharp and quick as driven nails, just for a week or so the woods, all of the bright and bitter leaves, flare up: the maples turn a blazing bitter red, and other leaves turn yellow like a living light, falling about you as you walk the woods, falling about you like small pieces of the sun so that you cannot say where sunlight shakes and flutters on the ground, and where the leaves.

"Meanwhile the Palisades are melting in massed molten colors, the season swings along the nation, and a little later in the South dense woodings on the hill begin to glow and soften, and when they smell the burning wood-smoke in Ohio children say: 'I'll bet that there's a forest fire in Michigan.' And the mountaineer goes hunting down in North Carolina, he stays out late with mournful flop-eared hounds, a rind of moon comes up across the rude lift of the hills: what do his friends say to him when he stays out late? Full of hoarse innocence and laughter, they will say: 'Mister, yore ole woman's goin' to whup ye if ye don't go home.'"

Oh, return, return!

"October is the richest of the seasons: the fields are cut, the granaries are full, the bins are loaded to the brim with fatness, and from the cider-press the rich brown oozings of the York Imperials run. The bee bores to the belly of the yellowed grape, the fly gets old and fat and blue, he buzzes loud, crawls slow, creeps heavily to death on sill and ceiling, the sun goes down in blood and pollen across the bronzed and mown fields of old October.

"The corn is shocked: it sticks out in hard yellow rows upon dried ears, fit now for great red barns in Pennsylvania, and the big stained teeth of crunching horses. The indolent hooves kick swiftly at the boards, the barn is sweet with hay and leather, wood and apples—this, and the clean dry crunching of the teeth is all: the sweat, the labor, and the plow is over. The late pears mellow on a sunny shelf; smoked hams hang to the warped barn rafters; the pantry shelves are loaded with 300 jars of fruit. Meanwhile the leaves are turning, turning, up in Maine, the chestnut burrs plop thickly to the earth in gusts of wind, and in Virginia the chinkapins are falling.

"There is a smell of burning in small towns in afternoon, and men with buckles on their arms are raking leaves in yards as boys come by with straps slung back across their shoulders. The oak leaves, big and brown, are bedded deep in yard and gutter: they make deep wadings to the knee for children in the streets. The fire will snap and crackle like a whip, sharp acrid smoke will sting the eyes, in mown fields the little vipers of the flame eat past the black coarse edges of burned stubble like a line of locusts. Fire drives a thorn of memory in the heart.

"The bladed grass, a forest of small spears of ice, is thawed by noon: summer is over but the sun is warm again, and there are days throughout the land of gold and russet. But summer is dead and gone, the earth is waiting, suspense and ecstasy are gnawing at the hearts of men, the brooding prescience of frost is there. The sun flames red and bloody as it sets, there are old red glintings on the battered pails, the great barn gets the ancient light as the boy slops homeward with warm foaming milk. Great shadows lengthen in the fields, the old red light dies swiftly, and the sunset barking of the hounds is faint and far and full of frost: there are shrewd whistles to the dogs, and frost and silence—this is all. Wind stirs and scuffs and rattles up the old brown leaves, and through the night the great oak leaves keep falling.

"Trains cross the continent in a swirl of dust and thunder, the leaves fly down the tracks behind them: the great trains cleave through gulch and gulley, they rumble with spoked thunder on the bridges over the powerful brown wash of mighty rivers, they toil through hills, they skirt the rough brown stubble of shorn fields, they whip past empty stations in the little towns and their great stride pounds its even pulse across America. Field and hill and lift and gulch and hollow, mountain and plain and river, a wilderness with fallen trees across it, a thicket of bedded brown and twisted undergrowth, a plain, a desert, and a plantation, a mighty landscape with no fenced niceness, an immensity of fold and convolution that can never be remembered, that can never be forgotten, that has never been described—weary with harvest, potent with every fruit and ore, the immeasurable richness embrowned with autumn, rank, crude, unharnessed, careless of scars or beauty, everlasting and magnificent, a cry, a space, an ecstasy!—American earth in old October.

"And the great winds howl and swoop across the land: they make a distant roaring in great trees, and boys in bed will stir in ecstasy, thinking of demons and vast swoopings through the earth. All through the night there is the clean, the bitter rain of acorns, and the chestnut burrs are plopping to the ground.

"And often in the night there is only the living silence, the distant frosty barking of a dog, the small clumsy stir and feathery stumble of the chickens on limed roosts, and the moon, the low and heavy moon of autumn, now barred behind the leafless poles of pines, now at the pine-woods' brooding edge and summit, now falling with ghost's dawn of milky light upon rimed clods of fields and on the frosty scurf on pumpkins, now whiter, smaller, brighter, hanging against the steeple's slope, hanging the same way in a million streets, steeping all the earth in frost and silence.

"Then a chime of frost-cold bells may peal out on the brooding air, and people lying in their beds will listen. They will not speak or stir, silence will gnaw the darkness like a rat, but they will whisper in their hearts:

" 'Summer has come and gone, has come and gone. And now—?' But they will say no more, they will have no more to say: they will wait listening, silent and brooding as the frost, to time, strange ticking time, dark time that haunts us with the briefness of our days. They will think of men long dead, of men now buried in the earth, of frost and silence long ago, of a forgotten face and moment of lost time, and they will think of things they have no words to utter.

"And in the night, in the dark, in the living sleeping silence of the towns, the million streets, they will hear the thunder of the fast express, the whistles of great ships upon the river.

"What will they say then? What will they say?"

Only the darkness moved about him as he lay there thinking, feeling in the darkness: a door creaked softly in the house.

"October is the season for returning: the bowels of youth are yearning with lost love. Their mouths are dry and bitter with desire: their hearts are torn with the thorns of spring. For lovely April, cruel and flowerful, will tear them with sharp joy and wordless lust. Spring has no language but a cry; but crueller than April is the asp of time.

"October is the season for returning: even the town is born anew," he thought. "The tide of life is at the full again, the rich return to business or to fashion, and the bodies of the poor are rescued out of heat and weariness. The ruin and horror of the summer is forgotten—a memory of hot cells and humid walls, a hell of ugly sweat and labor and distress and hopelessness, a limbo of pale greasy faces. Now joy and hope have revived again in the hearts of millions of people, they breathe the air again with hunger, their movements are full of life and energy. The mark of their summer's suffering is still legible upon their flesh, there is something starved and patient in their eyes, and a look that has a child's hope and expectation in it.

"All things on earth point home in old October: sailors to sea, travellers to walls and fences, hunters to field and hollow and the long voice of the hounds, the lover to the love he has forsaken—all things that live upon this earth return, return: Father, will you not, too, come back again?

"Where are you now, when all things on the earth come back again? For have not all these things been here before, have we not seen them, heard them, known them, and will they not live again for us as they did once, if only you come back again?

"Father, in the night time, in the dark, I have heard the thunder of the fast express. In the night, in the dark, I have heard the howling of the winds among great trees, and the sharp and windy raining of the acorns. In the night, in the dark, I have heard the feet of rain upon the roofs, the glut and gurgle of the gutter spouts, and the soaking gulping throat of all the mighty earth, drinking its thirst out in the month of May—and heard the sorrowful silence of the river in October. The hill-streams foam and welter in a steady plunge, the mined clay drops and melts and eddies in the night, the snake coils cool and glistening under dripping ferns, the water roars down past the mill in one sheer sheet-like plunge, making a steady noise like wind, and in the night, in the dark, the river flows by us to the sea.

"The great maw slowly drinks the land as we lie sleeping: the mined banks cave and crumble in the dark, the earth melts and drops into its tide, great horns are baying in the gulph of night, great boats are baying at the river's mouth. Thus, darkened by our dumpings, thickened by our stains, rich, rank, beautiful, and unending as all life, all living, the river, the dark immortal river, full of strange tragic time is flowing by us—by us—by us—to the sea.

"All this has been upon the earth, and will abide forever. But you are gone; our lives are ruined and broken in the night, our lives are mined below us by the river, our lives are whirled away into the sea and dark-ness, and we are lost unless you come to give us life again.

"Come to us, Father, in the watches of the night, come to us as you al-ways came, bringing to us the invincible sustenance of your strength, the limitless treasure of your bounty, the tremendous structure of your life that will shape all lost and broken things on earth again into a golden pattern of exultancy and joy. Come to us, Father, while the winds howl in the darkness, for October has come again bringing with it huge prophecies of death and life and the great cargo of the men who will re-turn. For we are ruined, lost, and broken if you do not come, and our lives, like rotten chips, are whirled about us onward in darkness to the sea."

So, thinking, feeling, speaking, he lay there in his mother's house, but there was nothing in the house but silence and the moving darkness: storm shook the house and huge winds rushed upon them, and he knew then that his father would not come again, and that all the life that he had known was now lost and broken as a dream.

XL

DURING the whole course of that last October—the last October he would spend at home—he was waiting day by day with a desperation of wild hope for a magic letter—one of those magic letters for which young men wait, which are to bring them instantly the fortune, fame, and triumph for which their souls thirst and their hearts are panting, and which never come.

Each morning he would get up with a pounding heart, trembling hands, and chattering lips, and then, like a man in prison who is waiting feverishly for some glorious message of release or pardon which he is sure will come that day, he would wait for the coming of the postman. And when he came, even before he reached the house, the moment that Eugene heard his whistle, he would rush out into the street, tear the mail out of his astounded grasp, and begin to hunt through it like a madman for the letter which would announce to him that fortune, fame, and glittering success were his. He was twenty-two years old, a madman and a fool, but every young man in the world has been the same.

Then, when the wonderful letter did not come, his heart would sink down to his bowels like lead, all of the brightness, gold, and singing would go instantly out of the day and he would stamp back into the house, muttering to himself, sick with despair and misery and thinking that now his life was done for, sure enough. He could not eat, sleep, stand still, sit down, rest, talk coherently, or compose himself for five minutes at a time. He would go prowling and muttering around the house, rush out into the streets of the town, walk up and down the main street, pausing to talk with the loafers before the principal drug store, climb the hills and mountains all around the town and look down on the town with a kind of horror and disbelief, an awful dreamlike unreality because the town, since his long absence and return to it, and all the people in it, now seemed as familiar as his mother's face and stranger than a dream, so that he could never regain his life or corporeal substance in it, any more than a man who revisits his

youth in a dream, and so that, also, the town seemed to have shrunk together, got little, fragile, toy-like in his absence, until now when he
walked in the street he thought he was going to ram his elbows through
the walls, as if the walls were paper, or tear down the buildings, as if
they had been made of straw.

Then he would come down off the hills into the town again, go home,
and prowl and mutter around the house, which now had the same real-
unreal familiar-strangeness that the town had, and his life seemed to
have been passed there like a dream. Then, with a mounting hope and
a pounding heart, he would begin to wait for the next mail again; and
when it came, but without the letter, this furious prowling and lashing
about would start all over. His family saw the light of madness in his
eyes, and in his disconnected movements, and heard it in his incoherent
speech. He could hear them whispering together, and sometimes when
he looked up he could see them looking at him with troubled and bewildered faces. And yet he did not think that he was mad, nor know
how he appeared to them.

Yet, during all this time of madness and despair his people were as
kind and tolerant as any one on earth could be.

His mother, during all this time, treated him with kindness and
tolerance, and according to the law of her powerful, hopeful, brooding,
octopal, and web-like character, with all its meditative procrastination,
never coming to a decisive point, but weaving, re-weaving, pursing her
lips, and meditating constantly and with a kind of hope, even though in
her deepest heart she really had no serious belief that he could succeed
in doing the thing he wanted to do.

Thus, as he talked to her sometimes, going on from hope to hope, his
enthusiasm mounting with the intoxication of his own vision, he would
paint a glittering picture of the fame and wealth he was sure to win in
the world, as soon as his play was produced. And his mother would
listen thoughtfully, pursing her lips from time to time, in a meditative
fashion, as she sat before the fire with her hands folded in a strong loose
clasp above her stomach. Then, finally, she would turn to him and with
a proud, tremulous, and yet bantering smile playing about her mouth,
such as she had always used when he was a child, and had perhaps
spoken of some project with an extravagant enthusiasm, she would say:

"Hm, boy! I tell you what!" his mother said, in this bantering tone,
as if he were still a child. "That's mighty big talk—as the sayin' goes,"
here she put one finger under her broad red nose-wing and laughed

shyly, but with pleasure—"as the sayin' goes, mighty big talk for poor-folks!" said his mother. "Well, now," she said in a thoughtful and hope-ful tone, after a moment's pause, "you may do it, sure enough. Stranger things than that have happened. Other people have been able to make a success of their writings—and there's one thing sure!" His mother cried out strongly with the loose, powerful and manlike gesture of her hand and index finger which was characteristic of all her family—"there's one thing sure!—what one man has done another can do if he's got grit and determination enough!" His mother said, putting the full strength of her formidable will into these words— "Why, yes, now!" she now said, with a recollective start, "Here, now! Say!" she cried—"wasn't I reading?—didn't I see? Why, pshaw!—yes! just the other day—that all these big writers—yes, sir! Irvin S. Cobb—there was the very feller!" cried his mother in a triumphant tone— "Why, you know," she continued, pursing her lips in a meditative way, "—that he had the very same trials and tribulations—as the sayin' goes—as every one else! Why, yes!—here he told it on himself—admitted it, you know—that he kept writin' these stories for years, sendin' them out, I reckon, to all the editors and magazines—and having them all sent back to him. That's the way it was," she said, "and now—look at him! Why, I reckon they'd pay him hundreds of dollars for a single piece—yes! and be glad of the chance to get it," said his mother.

Then for a space his mother sat looking at the fire, while she slowly and reflectively pursed her lips.

"Well," she said slowly at length, "you may do it. I hope you do. Stranger things than that have happened.—Now, there's one thing sure," she said strongly, "you have certainly had a good education—there's been more money spent upon your schoolin' than on all the rest of us put together—and you certainly ought to know enough to write a story or a play!—Why, yes, boy! I tell you what," his mother now cried in the old playful and bantering tone, as if she were speaking to a child, "if I had *your* education I believe I'd try to be a writer, too! Why, yes! I wouldn't mind getting out of all this drudgery and house-work for a while—and if I could earn my living doin' some light easy work like that, why, you can bet your bottom dollar, I'd do it!" cried his mother. "But, say, now! See here!" his mother cried with a kind of jocose seriousness—"maybe that'd be a good idea, after all! Suppose you write the stories," she said, winking at him,—"and I tell you what I'll do!—Why, I'll *tell* 'em to you!

Now, if I had your education, and your command of language," said his mother, whose command of language was all that any one could wish—"I believe I could tell a pretty good story—so if you'll write 'em out," she said, with another wink, "I'll tell you what to write—and I'll *bet* you—I'll *bet* you," said his mother, "that we could write a story that would beat most of these stories that I read, all to pieces! Yes, sir!" she said, pursing her lips firmly, and with an invincible conviction—"and I bet you people would buy that story and come to see that play!" she said. "Because I know what to tell 'em, and the kind of thing people are interested in hearing," she said.

Then for a moment more she was silent and stared thoughtfully into the fire.

"Well," she said slowly, "you may do it. You may do it, sure enough! Now, boy," she said, levelling that powerful index finger toward him, "I want to tell you! Your grandfather, Tom Pentland, was a remarkable man—and if he'd had your education he'd a-gone far! And every one who ever knew him said the same! . . . Oh! stories, poems, pieces in the paper—why didn't they print something of his every week or two!" she cried. "And that's exactly where you get it," said his mother. "—But, say, now," she said in a persuasive tone, after a moment's meditation, "I've been thinkin'—it just occurred to me—wouldn't it be a good idea if you could find some work to do—I mean, get you a job somewheres of some light easy work that would give you plenty of time to do your writin' as you went on! Now, Rome wasn't built in a day, you know!" his mother said in the bantering tone, "—and you might have to send that play around to several places before you found the one who could do it right for you! So while you're waitin'," said his mother persuasively, "why wouldn't it be a good idea if you got a little light newspaper work, or a job teachin' somewheres—pshaw! you could do it easy as falling off a log," his mother said contemptuously. "I taught school myself before I got married to your papa, and I didn't have a bit of trouble! And all the schoolin' that I ever had—all the schoolin' that I ever had," she cried impressively, "was six months one time in a little backwoods school! Now if I could do it, there's one thing sure, with all your education you ought to be able to do it, too! Yes, sir, that's the very thing!" she said. "I'd do it like a shot if I were you."

He said nothing, and his mother sat there for a moment looking at the fire. Suddenly she turned, and her face had grown troubled and sorrowful, and her worn and faded eyes were wet with tears. She stretched her strong rough hand out and put it over his, shaking her head a little before she spoke:

"Child, child!" she said. "It worries me to see you act like this! I hate to see you so unhappy! Why, son," his mother said, "what if they shouldn't take it now! You've got long years ahead of you, and if you can't do it now, why, maybe, some day you will! And if you don't!" his mother cried out strongly and formidably, "why, Lord, boy, what about it! You're a young man with your whole life still before you—and if you can't do this thing, why there are other things you can do! . . . Pshaw, boy, your life's not ended just because you find out that you weren't cut out to be a playwriter," said his mother. "There are a thousand things a young man of your age could do! Why, it wouldn't faze me for a moment!" cried his mother.

And he sat there in front of her invincible strength, hope, and fortitude and her will that was more strong than death, her character that was as solid as a rock; he was as hopeless and wretched as he had ever been in his life, wanting to say a thousand things to her and saying none of them, and reading in her eyes the sorrowful message that she did not believe he would ever be able to do the thing on which his heart so desperately was set.

At this moment the door opened and his brother entered the room. As they stared at him with startled faces, he stood there looking at them out of his restless, tormented gray eyes, breathing his large and unhappy breath of unrest and nervousness, a harassed look on his handsome and generous face, as with a distracted movement he thrust his strong, impatient fingers through the flashing mop of his light brown hair, that curled everywhere in incredible whorls and screws of angelic brightness.

"Hah?" his mother sharply cried, as she looked at him with her white face, the almost animal-like quickness and concentration of her startled attention. "What say?" she said in a sharp startled tone, although as yet my brother had said nothing.

"W-w-w-wy!" he began in a distracted voice, as he thrust his fingers through his incredible flashing hair, and his eyes flickered about absently and with a tormented and driven look, "I was just f-f-f-finkin'—" he went on in a dissonant and confused tone, then, suddenly catching sight of her white startled face, he smote himself suddenly and hard upon his temple with the heel of one large hand, and cried out, "Haw!" in a tone of such idiot exuberance and exultancy that it is impossible to reproduce in words the limitless and earthy vulgarity of its humor. At the same time he prodded his mother stiffly in the ribs with his clumsy fingers, an act that made her shriek out resentfully, and then say in a vexed and fretful tone:

"I'll vow, boy! You act like a regular idiot! If I didn't have any more sense than to go and play a trick like that—I'd be ash-a-a-med—ash-a-a-a-med," she whispered, with a puckered mouth, as she shook her head at him in a movement of strong deprecation, scorn, and reproof. "I'd be *ashamed* to let any one know I was such a fool," his mother said.

"Whah! *Whah!*" Luke shouted with his wild, limitlessly exuberant laugh, that was so devastating in its idiot exultancy that all words, reproaches, scorn, or attempts at reason were instantly reduced to nothing by it. "Whee!" he cried, prodding her in her resentful ribs again, his handsome face broken by his huge and exuberant smile. Then, as if cherishing something secret and uncommunicably funny in its idiot humor, he smote himself upon the forehead again, cried out, "Whah—*Whah!*" and then, shaking his grinning face to himself in this movement of secret and convulsive humor, he said: "Whee! Go-o-d-damn!" in a tone of mincing and ironic refinement.

"Why, what on earth has got into you, boy!" his mother cried out fretfully. "Why, you're actin' like a regular simpleton, I'll vow you are!"

"Whah! *Whah!*" Luke cried exultantly.

"Now, I don't know where it comes from," said his mother judicially, with a deliberate and meditative sarcasm, as if she were seriously considering the origin of his lunacy. "There's one thing sure: you never got it from me. Now, all my people had their wits about them—now, say what you please," she went on in a thoughtful tone, as she stared with puckered mouth into the fire, "I never heard of a weak-minded one in the whole crowd——"

"Whah—*whah!*" he cried.

"—So you didn't get it from any of my people," she went on with deliberate and telling force—"no, you didn't!" she said.

"*Whah-h!*" he prodded her in the ribs again, and then immediately, and in a very earnest tone, he said:

"W-w-w-wy, I was just f-f-f-finkin' it would be a good idea if we all

w-w-w-went for a little ride. F-f-f-frankly, I fink it would do us good,"
he said, looking at Eugene with a very earnest look in his restless and
tormented eyes. "I fink we need it! F-f-f-frankly, I fink we do," he
said, and then added abruptly and eagerly as he thrust his clumsy fingers
through his hair: "W-w-w-wy, what do you say?"

"Why, yes!" his mother responded with an instant alacrity as she got
up from her chair. "That's the very thing! A little breath of fresh air
is just the thing we need—as the feller says," she said, turning to Eugene
now and beginning to laugh slyly, and with pleasure, passing one
finger shyly underneath her broad red nose-wing as she spoke—, "as the
feller says, it costs nothin' and it's Nature's sovereign remedy, good for
man and good for beast!—So let's all get out into the light of open day
again," she said with rhetorical deliberation, "and breathe in God's
fresh air like He intended we should do—for there's one thing sure,"
his mother went on in tones of solemn warning, which seemed directed
to a vast unseen audience of the universe rather than to themselves,
"there's one thing sure—you can't violate the laws of God or nature," she said decisively, "or you'll pay for it—as sure as you're born.
As sure as you're born," she whispered. "Why, yes, now!"—she went on,
with a start of recollective memory— "Here now!—Say!—Didn't I see
it—wasn't I readin'— Why, here, you know, the other day," she went
on impatiently, as if the subject of these obscure broken references must
instantly be clear to every one—"why, it was in the paper, you know—
this article written by Doctor Royal S. Copeland," his mother said, nodding her head with deliberate satisfaction over his name, and pronouncing the full title sonorously with the obvious satisfaction that titles and
distinctions always gave her—"that's who it was all right, sayin' that
fresh air was the thing that every one must have, and that all of us
should take good care to——"

"Now, M-m-m-m-mama," said Luke, who had paid no attention at all
to what she had been saying, but had stood there during all the time she
was speaking, breathing his large, weary, and unhappy breath, thrusting
his clumsy fingers through his hair, as his harassed and tormented eyes
flickered restlessly about the room in a driven but unseeing stare:—
"Now, M-m-m-mama!" he said in a tone of exasperated and frenzied impatience, "if we're g-g-g-going we've g-g-g-got to get started! N-n-n-now
I d-d-don't mean next W-w-w-w-Wednesday," he snarled, with exasperated sarcasm, "I d-d-d-don't m-m-m-mean the fifteenth of next July.
But—*now—now—now,*" he muttered crazily, coming to her with his

large hands lifted like claws, the fingers working, and with a look of
fiendish madness in his eyes.

"Now!" he whispered hoarsely. "This week! Today! This afternoon! A-a-a-a-at once!" he barked suddenly, jumping at her comically,
then thrusting his hand through his hair again, he said in a weary and
exasperated voice:

"M-m-m-mama, will you please get ready! I b-b-b-beg of you. I beseech you—*please!*" he said, in tortured entreaty.

"*All* right! *All* right!" his mother replied instantly in a tone of the
heartiest and most conciliatory agreement. "I'll be ready in five minutes!
I'll just go back here and put on a coat over this old dress—so folks won't
see me," she laughed shyly, "an' I'll be ready before you know it!—
Pshaw, boy!" she now said in a rather nettled tone, as if the afterthought
of his impatience had angered her a little, "now you don't need to
worry about *my* being ready," she said, "because when the time comes
—I'll be *there!*" she said, with the loose, deliberate, man-like gesture of
her right hand and in tones of telling deliberation. "Now you worry
about yourself!" she said. "For I'll be ready before *you* are—yes, and
I'm never late for an appointment, either," she said strongly, "and that's
more than *you* can say—for I've seen you miss 'em time an' time again."

During all this time Luke had been thrusting his fingers through his
hair, breathing heavily and unhappily, and pawing and muttering
over a mass of thumbed envelopes and papers which were covered
with the undecipherable scrawls and jottings of his nervous hand:
"T-t-t-Tuesday," he muttered, "Tuesday . . . Tuesday in Blackstone—
B-b-b-b-Blackstone—Blackstone—Blackstone, South Car'lina," he muttered in a confused and distracted manner, as if these names were completely meaningless to him, and he had never heard them before. "Now
—*ah!*" he suddenly sang out in a rich tenor voice, as he lifted his hand,
thrust his fingers through his hair, and stared wildly ahead of him—
"meet Livermore in Blackstone Tuesday morning—see p-p-p-p-prospect
in G-g-g-g-Gadsby Tuesday afternoon about—about—about— Wheet!"
—here he whistled sharply, as he always did when hung upon a word—
"about a new set of batteries for his Model X—Style 37—lighting system
—which the cheap p-p-p-penny-pinching South Car'lina bastard w-w-w-
wants for nothing—Wednesday m-m-m-morning b-b-b-back to Blackstone—F'ursday . . . w-w-w-wy," he muttered pawing clumsily and confusedly at his envelopes with a demented glare— "F-f-f-f-f'ursday—you
—ah—j-j-j-jump over to C-c-c-Cavendish to t-t-t-try to persuade that

ignorant red-faced nigger-Baptist son-of-a-bitch that it's f-f-f-for his own
b-b-b-best interests to scrap the-the-w-w-w-wy the d-d-d-decrepit pile
of junk he's been using since S-s-s-Sherman marched through Georgia
and b-b-b-buy the new X50 model T Style 46 transmission——

"M-m-m-mama!" he cried suddenly, turning toward her with a movement of frenzied and exasperated entreaty. "Will you *please* kindly
have the g-g-g-goodness and the m-m-m-mercy to do me the favor to
b-b-b-begin to commence—w-w-w-w-wy—to start—to make up your
mind—to get ready," he snarled bitterly. "W-w-w-w-wy sometime before
midnight—I b-b-b-beg of you . . . I beseech you . . . I ask it of you p-p-p-
please, for *my* sake—for *all* our sakes—for *God's* sake!" he cried with
frenzied and maddened desperation.

"*All* right! *All* right!" his mother cried hastily in a placating and reassuring tone beginning to move with an awkward, distracted, bridling
movement that got her nowhere, since there were two doors to the parlor and she was trying to go out both of them at the same time. "*All*
right!" she said decisively, at length getting started toward the door
nearest her. "I'll just go back there an' slip on a coat—and *I'll be with you*
in a jiffy!" she said with comforting assurance.

"If you *please!*" Luke said with an ironic and tormented obsequiousness of entreaty, as he fumbled through his mass of envelopes. "If you
please! W-w-w-wy I'd certainly be m-m-m-m-much obliged to you if
you would!" he said.

At this moment, however, a car halted at the curb outside, some one
got out, and in a moment more they could hear Helen's voice, as she
came towards the house, calling back to her husband in tones of exasperated annoyance:

"All *right,* Hugh! All *right!* I'm coming!"—although she was really
going toward the house. "Will you *kindly* leave me alone for just a
moment! Good heavens! Will I never get a little peace? All right!
All right! I'm coming! For God's sake, leave me *alone* for just five
minutes, or you'll drive me crazy!" she stormed, and with a high-cracked
note of frenzied strain and exasperation that was almost like hysteria.

"All right, Mr. Barton," she now said to her husband in a more
good-humored tone. "Now you just hold your horses for a minute and
I'll come on out. The house is not going to burn down before we get
there."

His lean, seamed, devoted face broke into a slow, almost unwilling
grin, in which somehow all of the submission, loyalty and goodness of

his soul was legible, and Helen turned, came up on the porch, opened the hall door, and came into the parlor where they were, beginning to speak immediately in a tone of frenzied and tortured exacerbation of the nerves and with her large, gaunt, liberal features strained to the breaking point of nervous hysteria.

"My *God!*" she said in a tone of weary exasperation. "If I don't get away from them soon I'm going to lose my mind! . . . From the moment that I get up in the morning I never get a moment's peace! Some one's after me all day long from morn to night! Why, good heavens, Mama!" she cried out in a tone of desperate fury, and as if Eliza had contradicted something she had said, "I've got troubles enough of my own, without any one else putting theirs on me! Have they got no one else they can go to? Haven't they got homes of their own to look after? Do I have to bear the burden of it all for every one *all* my life?" she stormed in a voice that was so hoarse, strained and exasperated now that she was almost weeping. "Do I have to be the goat *all* my life? Oh, I want a little peace," she cried desperately. "I just want to be left alone by myself once in a while!—The rest of you don't have to worry!" she said accusingly. "You don't have to stand for it. You can get away from it!" she cried. "You don't know— you don't *know!*" she said furiously, "what I put up with—but if I don't get away from it soon, I'm going all to pieces."

During all the time that Helen had been pouring out her tirade of the wrongs and injuries that had been inflicted on her, Luke had acted as a kind of dutiful and obsequious chorus, punctuating all the places where she had to pause to pant for breath, with such remarks as——

"W-w-w-w-well, you d-d-do too much for every one and they don't appreciate it—that's the trouble," or, "I f-f-f-f-fink I'd tell them all to p-p-p-p-politely step to hell—f-f-frankly I fink you owe it to yourself to do it! W-w-w-wy you'll only w-w-w-wear yourself out doing for others and in the end you d-d-d-don't get so m-m-m-much as one good God-damn for all your t-t-t-trouble! Frankly, I mean it!" he would say with a very earnest look on his harassed and drawn face. "W-w-w-wy here-after I'd let 'em g-g-g-g-go to hell!"

—"If they'd only show a little appreciation once in a while I wouldn't mind so much," she panted. "But do you think they care? Do you think it ever occurs to them to lift a hand to help me when they see me working my fingers to the bone for them? Why," and here her big-boned generous face worked convulsively, "if I should work myself to death for them, do you think any of them would even so much as send a bunch of flowers to the funeral?"

Luke laughed with jeering scorn: "W-w-w-wy," he said, "it is to laugh! It is to laugh! They w-w-wouldn't send a G-g-g-g-God-damn thing—n-n-n-not even a ten-cent b-b-b-bunch of-of-w-w-w-w-wy—of turnip-greens!" he said.

"All *right!* All *right!*" Helen again cried furiously through the door, as Barton sounded a long imperative blast of protest and impatience on his horn. "All *right,* Hugh! I'm coming! Good heavens, can't you leave me in peace for just five minutes! . . . Hugh, *please!* Please!" she stormed in a tone of frenzied exasperation as he sourly answered her. "Give me a little time alone, I beg of you—or I'll go mad!"—And she turned to them again, panting and with the racked and strained expression of hysteria on her big-boned features. In a moment, her harassed and driven look relaxed somewhat, and the big rough bawdy smile began to shape itself again around the corners of her generous mouth.

"My God, Mama," she said in a tone of quiet and weary despair, but with this faint lewd smile about her mouth and growing deeper as she spoke, "what am I going to do about it? Will you please tell me that? Did you have to put up with that when you and Papa were together? Is that the way it is? Is there no such thing as peace and privacy in this world? Now, I'd like to know. When you marry one of them, does that mean that you'll never get a moment's peace or privacy alone as long as you live? Now, there are some things you like to do alone"—she said, and by this time the lewd smile had deepened perceptibly around her mouth. "Why, it's got so," she said, "that I'm almost afraid to go to the bath-room anymore——"

"Whew-w!" shrieked Eliza, laughing, putting one finger underneath her nose.

"Yes, sir," Helen said quietly, with the lewd smile now deep and loose around her mouth. "I've just got so I'm almost afraid to go, I don't know from one moment to the next whether one of them is going to come in and keep me company or not."

"Whew!" Eliza cried. "Why, you'll have to put up signs! 'No Visitors Allowed!'—that's exactly what you ought to say! I'd fix 'em! I'd do it like a shot," she said.

Helen sniggered hoarsely, and absently began to pluck at her chin.

"But *oh!*" she said with a sigh. "If only they'd leave me alone an hour a day! If only I could get away for just an hour——"

"W-w-w-wy!" Luke began. "Why don't you c-c-come with us! F-f-f-frankly, I fink you ought to do it! I fink the change would do you good," he said.

"Why?" she said rather dully, yet curiously. "Where are you going?"

"W-w-w-wy," he said, "we were just starting for a little ride. . . . Mama!" he burst out suddenly in a tone of exasperated entreaty— "Will you k-k-k-kindly go and get yourself ready? W-w-wy, its g-g-g-going to get d-d-d-dark before we get started," he said bitterly, as if she had kept him waiting all this time. "Now, *please*—I b-b-b-beg of you—to g-g-g-get ready—wy-wy-wy without f-f-f-further delay—now, I ask it of you, for God's sake!" he said, and then turning to Helen with a movement of utter exasperation and defeat, he shuddered convulsively, thrust his fingers through his hair, and moaned "Ah-h-h-h-h-h!" after which he began to mutter "My God! My God! My God!"

"All *right,* sir! All *right!*" Eliza said briskly, in a conciliating tone. "I'll just go right back here and put my coat and hat on and I won't keep you waitin' *five*——"

"Wy, wy, wy. If you p-p please, Mama," said Luke with a tortured and ironic bow. "If you p-p-please."

At length, they really did get out of the house and were assembled on the curb in the last throes of departure. Luke, breathing stertorously his large unhappy breath, began to walk about his battered little car, casting uneasy and worried looks at it and falling upon it violently from time to time, kicking it in the tires with his large flat feet, smiting it with a broad palm and seizing it by the sides and shaking it so savagely that its instant dissolution seemed inevitable. Meanwhile Eliza stood planted solidly, facing her house, her hands clasped loosely at the waist, and her powerful and delicate mouth pursed reflectively as she surveyed her property—a characteristic gesture that always marked every departure from the house and every return to it, in which the whole power and relish of possession was evident. As for Barton, while these inevitable ceremonies were taking place, he just sat in his car with a kind of sour resigned patience, and waited. And Helen, while this was going on, had taken Eugene by the arm and walked a few paces down the street with him, talking all the time in a broken and abstracted way, of which the reference could only be inferred:

"You see, don't you? . . . You see what I've got to put up with, don't you? . . . You only get it for a little while when you come here, but with me it's *all* the time and *all* the time"— Suddenly she turned to him, looked him directly in the eye, and speaking quietly to him, but with a curious, brooding and disturbing inflection in her voice, she said:

"Do you know what day this is?"

"No."

"Do you realize that Ben died five years ago this morning?—I was thinking of it yesterday when she was talking about getting that room ready for those people who are coming," she muttered, and with a note of weary bitterness in her voice. For a moment her big-boned face was marked with the faint tension of hysteria, and her eyes looked dark and lustreless and strained as she plucked absently at her large chin. "But do you see how she can do it?" she went on in a low tone of brooding and weary resignation. "Do you understand how she can ever bear to go back in there? Do you see how she can rent that room out to any cheap roomer who comes along? Do you realize that she's got the same bed in there he died on," she said morbidly, "the same mattress?—K-k-k-k-k-k!" she laughed softly and huskily, poking at his ribs. "She'll have you sleeping on it next"——

"I'll be damned if she does!"

"K-k-k-k-k-k-k!"

"Do you think I could be sleeping on it now!" Eugene said with a feeling of black horror and dread around his heart.

"K-k-k-k-k-k!" she snickered. "Would you like that? Would you sleep better if you knew it was? . . . No," she said quietly, shaking her head. "Uh-uh. I don't think so. It's still up there in the same room. She may have painted the bed, but otherwise I don't think she's changed a thing. Have you ever been back up there since he died?" she said curiously.

"My *God,* no! Have you?"

She shook her head: "Not I," she said with weary finality. "I've never even been up-stairs since that morning. . . . Hugh hates the place," she muttered, looking towards him. "He doesn't even like to stop and wait for me. He won't come in."

Then she was silent for a moment as they looked at the gaunt ugly bay of the room upstairs where Ben had died. In the yard the maple trees were thinning rapidly; the leaves were sere and yellow and were floating to the ground. And the old house stood there in all its ugly, harsh, and prognathous bleakness, its paint of rusty yellow scaling from it in patches, and weathered and dilapidated as Eugene had never seen it before, but incredibly near, incredibly natural and familiar, so that all its ghosts of pain and grief and bitterness, its memories of joy and magic and lost time, the thousand histories of all the vanished people it had sheltered, whom all of them had known, revived instantly with an intolerable and dream-like strangeness and familiarity.

And now, as they looked up at the bleak windows of the room in which he died, the memory of his death's black horror passed across their souls a minute, and then was gone, leaving them only with the fatality of weary resignation which they had learned from it. In a moment, with a look of ancient and indifferent weariness and grief in her eyes, Helen turned to him, and with a faint rough smile, around her mouth, said quietly:

"Does he ever bother you at night? When the wind begins to howl around the house, do you ever hear him walking up there? Has he been in to see you yet?—K-k-k-k-k!" she poked him with her big stiff finger, laughing huskily, and then in a low, sombrely brooding tone, as if the grisly suggestion were his, she shook her head, saying:

"Forget about it! They don't come back, Eugene! I used to think they did, but now I know they never do.—He won't come," she muttered, as she shook her head. "Forget about it. He won't come. Just forget about it," she continued, looking at Eliza with weary resignation. "It's not her fault. I used to think that you could change them. But you can't. Uh-uh," she muttered, plucking at her large, cleft chin. "It can't be done. They never change."

Luke stood distractedly for a moment on the curbstone, breathing his large unhappy breath and thrusting his clumsy fingers strongly through the flashing whirls and coils of his incredible hair:

"Now—ah!" he sang out richly. "Let me see! I—wy—I fink! M-m-m-mama, if you *please!*" he said. "Wy if you *please!*" with an exasperated and ironic obsequiousness.

She had been standing there, planted squarely on the sidewalk, facing her house. She stood with her hands clasped loosely across her stomach, and as she looked at the gaunt weathered shape of the old house, her mouth was puckered in an expression of powerful rumination in which the whole terrible legend of blood and hunger and desperate tenacity—the huge clutch of property and possession which, with her, was like the desperate clutch of life itself—was evident.

What was this great claw in her life—this thing that was stronger than life or death or motherhood—which made her hold on to anything which had ever come into her possession, which made her cling desperately to everything which she had ever owned—old bottles, papers, pieces of string, worn-out gloves with all the fingers missing, frayed cast-off sweaters which some departed boarder had left behind him, postcards, souvenirs, sea-shells, cocoanuts, old battered trunks, dilapidated furniture which could be no longer used, calendars for the year 1906, showing coy maidens simpering sidewise out beneath the crisply ruffled pleatings of a Japanese parasol—a mountainous accumulation of old junk for which the old dilapidated house had now become a fit museum.

Then in the wink of an eye she would pour thousands of dollars after the crazy promises of boom-town real-estate speculation that by comparison made the wildest infatuation of a drunken race-track gambler look like the austere process of a coldly reasoning mind.

Even as she stood there staring at her house with her pursed mouth of powerful and ruminant satisfaction, another evidence of this madness of possession was staring in their face. At the end of the alley slope, behind the house, there was a dilapidated old shed or house of whitewashed boards, which had been built in earlier times as a carriage house. Now through the open entrance of this shed, they could see the huge and dusty relic of Eliza's motor car. She had bought it four years before, and bought it instantly one day before they knew about it, and paid $2000 in hard cash for it—and why she bought it, what mad compulsion of her spirit made her buy it, no one knew, and least of all Eliza.

For from that day to this that car had never left the carriage house. Year by year, in spite of protests, oaths, and prayers, and all their frantic pleading, she had got no use from it herself, and would let no one else use it. No, what is more, she had even refused to sell it later, although a man had made her a good offer. Rather she pursed her lips reflectively, smiled in a bantering fashion, and said evasively: "Well, I'll see now! I'll think it over!—I want to study about it a little—you come back later and I'll let you know! . . . I want to think about it!"—as if, by hanging on to this mass of rusty machinery, she hoped it would increase in value and that she could sell it some day for twice the price she paid for it, if only she "held on" long enough.

And at first they had all wrestled by turns with the octopal convolutions of her terrific character, exhausting all the strength and energy in them against the substance of a will that was like something which always gave and never yielded, which could be grasped, compressed, and throttled in the hard grip of their furious hands, only to bulge out in new shapes and forms and combinations—which flowed, gave, withdrew, receded and advanced, but which remained itself forever, and beat everything before it in the end.

Now, for a moment, as Luke saw the car he was goaded into the old madness of despair. Thrusting his fingers through his hair, and with a look of desperate exasperation in his tortured eyes, he began, "M-m-m-mama—M-m-m-mama—I beg of you, I—wy I entreat you,—w-w-w-wy I *beseech* you either to s-s-s-sell that God-damn thing or—wy—g-g-g-get a little s-s-service out of it."

"Well, now," Eliza said quickly and in a conciliating tone, "we'll see about it!"

"S-s-s-see about it!" he stammered bitterly. "See about it! In G-g-g-God's name, what is there to see about! M-m-m-mama, the car's there—there—there—" he muttered crazily, poking his clumsy finger in a series of jerky and convulsive movements in the direction of the carriage house. "It's *there!*" he croaked madly. "C-c-c-can't you understand that? W-w-w-wy, it's rotting away on its God-damn wheels—M-m-m-mama, will you *please* get it into your head that it's not g-g-g-going to do you or any one else any good unless you take it out and use it?"

"Well, as I say now"—she began hastily, and in a diplomatic tone of voice.

"M-m-m-m-mama"—he began, again thrusting at his hair—"wy, I beg of you—I beseech you to sell it, g-g-g-give it away, or wy-wy-wy try to get a little use out of it!—Let me take it out and drive you round the block in it—w-w-w-wy—just once! Just once! F-f-f-frankly, I'd like to have the satisfaction of knowing you'd had *that* much out of it!" he said. "Wy, I'll p-p-p-pay for the gas, if that's what's worrying you! Wy, I'll do it with pleasure! . . . But just let me take it out of that G-g-g-g-God-damn place if all—if all—wy if all I do is drive you to the corner! Now, *please!*" he begged, with an almost frantic note of entreaty.

"Why, no, boy!" she cried out in a startled tone. "We can't do that!"

"C-c-c-can't do that!" he stuttered bitterly. "Wy, in G-g-g-g-God's name, why can't we?"

"I'd be *afra-a-id!*" she said with a little troubled smile, as she shook her head. "Hm! I'd be *afraid!*"

"Wy-wy-wy-wy *afraid!*" he yelled. "Wy, what's there to be afraid of, in God's name?"

"I'd be afraid you'd *do* something to it," she said with her troubled

smile. "I'd be afraid you'd smash it up or run over some one with it.
No, child," she said gravely, as she shook her head. "I'd be afraid to let
you drive it. You're too nervous."

"Ah-h-h-h-h-h!" he breathed clutching convulsively in his hair as his
eyes flickered madly about in his head. "Ah-h-h-h-h! M-m-m-merciful
God!" he muttered. "M-m-m-m-m-merciful God!"—and then laughed
wildly, frantically, and bitterly.

Now Helen spoke curiously, plucking reflectively at her large chin,
but with weariness and resignation in her accent as if already she knew
the answer:

"Mama, what are you going to do with your car? It seems a shame to
let it rot away back there after you've paid out all that money for it.
Aren't you going to try to get any use out of it at all?"

"Well, now, as I say," Eliza began smugly, pursing her lips with
ruminative relish as she looked into the fire, "I'm just waitin' for the
chance—I'm just waitin' till the first fine day to come along—and then,
I've got a good notion to take that thing out and learn to run it myself."

"Oh, Mama," Helen began quietly and wearily, "good heavens——"

"Why, yes!" Eliza cried nodding her head briskly. "I could do it!
Now, I can do most anything when I make my mind up to it! Now I've
never seen anything yet I couldn't do if I had to! . . . So I'm just waitin'
until spring comes round again, and I'm goin' to take that car out and
drive it all around," she said. "I'm just goin' to sit up there an' enjoy
the scenery an' have a big time," said Eliza with her little tremulous
smile. "That's what I'm goin' to do," she said.

"All right," Helen said wearily. "Have it your own way. Do as you
please: it's your own funeral! Only it seems a shame to let it go to waste
after you've spent all that money on it."

But turning to Eugene, and speaking in a lowered tone, she said to
him, with the faint tracing of hysteria on her big-decent face, and
weariness and resignation in her voice:

"Well, what are you going to do about it? I used to think that you
could change her, but now I know she never will. . . . I've given up
trying. It's no use," she muttered. "It's no use. I worked my fingers to the
bone to help them save a nickel—and you see what comes of it. . . . I
did the work of a nigger in the kitchen from the time I was ten years old
—and you see what comes of it, don't you? I went off and sang my way
around the country in cheap moving-picture shows . . . and came up
here and waited on the tables to help feed a crowd of cheap boarders—

and Luke sold *The Saturday Evening Post,* and peddled hot dogs and toy balloons—and you got up at three o'clock, carried the morning paper —and they let Ben go to hell until his lungs were gone and it was too late—and you see what it all comes to in the end, don't you? . . . It's all given away to real-estate men or thrown away for automobiles they never use. I've given up worrying," she said. "I don't think about it any more. . . . They don't change," she muttered. "I used to think they did but now I know they don't. Uh-uh. They don't change! . . . Well, forget about it," and she turned wearily away.

The year Eliza bought the car, Eugene had been eighteen years old, and was a Junior at the State University. When he came home that year, he asked her if she would let him learn to drive it. It was about the time when every one in town was beginning to own motor cars. When he walked up town, every one he knew would drive by him in an auto- mobile. Every one on earth was beginning to live upon a wheel. Some- how it gave him a naked and desolate feeling, as if he had nowhere to go, and no door to enter. When he asked her if she would let him take the car out and learn to drive it, she had looked at him a moment with her hands clasped loosely at the waist, her head cocked quizzically to one side, and the little tremulous and bantering smile that had always filled him with such choking exasperation and wordless shame, and somehow with a nameless and intolerable pity, too, because behind it he felt always her high white forehead, and her faded, weak, and child- like eyes, the naked intelligence, whiteness, and immortal innocence of the child that was looking straight through the mask of years with all the deathless hope and faith and confidence of her life and character.

Now, for the last time, he asked her again the question he had asked with such an earnest hope so many times before. And instantly, as if he had dreamed her answer, she replied—the same reply that she had always made, the only reply the invincible procrastination of her soul could make.

"Hm!" she said, making the bantering and humming noise in her throat as she looked at him. *"Wha-a-a-t!* Why, you're my *ba-a-a-by!"* she said with jesting earnestness, as she laid her strong worn hand loosely on his shoulder. "No, sir!" she said quickly and quietly, shaking her head in a swift side-ways movement. "I'd be *afra-a-id,* afraid," she whispered.

"Mama, afraid of what?"

"Why, child," she said gravely, "I'd be afraid you'd go and hurt yourself. Uh-uh," she shook her head quickly and shortly. "I'd be afraid to let you try it—well, we'll see," she said, turning it off easily in an evasive and conciliatory tone. "We'll see about it. I'd like to study about it a little first."

After that, there was nothing to do except to curse and beat their fists into the wall. And after that there was nothing to do at all. She had beaten them all, and they knew it. Their curses, prayers, oaths, persuasions and strangled cries availed them nothing. She had beaten them all, and finally they spoke no more to her or to themselves about her motor car: the gigantic folly of that mad wastefulness evoked for them all memories so painful, desolate and tragic—a memory of the fatality of blood and nature which could not be altered, of the done which could be undone never, and of the web of fate in which their lives were meshed—that they knew there was no guilt, no innocence, no victory, and no change. They were what they were, and they had no more to say.

So was it now as she stood planted there before her house. As she had grown older, her body had grown clumsier with the shapeless heaviness of age: as she stood there with her hands clasped in this attitude of ruminant relish, she seemed to be planted solidly on the pavement, and somehow to own, inhabit, and possess the very bricks she walked on. She owned the street, the pavement, and finally her terrific ownership of the house was as apparent as if the house were living and could speak to her. For the rest of them that old bleak house had now so many memories of grief and death and intolerable, incurable regret that in their hearts they hated it; but although she had seen a son strangle to death in one of its bleak rooms, she loved the house as if it were a part of her own life—as it was—and her love for it was greater than her love for any one or anything else on earth.

And yet, for her, even if that house, the whole world, fell in ruins around her, there could be no ruin—her spirit was as everlasting as the earth on which she walked, and could not be touched—no matter what catastrophes of grief, death, tragic loss, and unfulfilment might break the lives of other men—she was triumphant over the ravages of time and accident, and would be triumphant to her death. For there was only the inevitable fulfilment of her own destiny—and ruin, loss, and death availed not—she would be fulfilled. She had lived ten lives, and now she was embarked upon another one, and so it had been ordered in the beginning: this was all that mattered in the end.

But now, Luke, seeing her, as she stood planted there in all-engulfing rumination, thrust his hands distractedly through his shining hair again, and cried to her with exasperated entreaty:

"W-w-w-wy, Mama, if you *please!* I b-b-b-beg of you and *beseech* you, if you *please!*"

"I'm *ready!*" Eliza cried, starting and turning from her powerful contemplation of her house. "This very minute, sir! Come on!"

"Wy, if you p-p-p-*please!*" he muttered, thrusting at his hair.

They walked towards his car, which he had halted in the alley-way beside the house. A few leaves, sere and yellow, from the maples in the yard, were drifting slowly to the ground.

XLI

During all that time, when he was waiting with a desperate hope that rose each day to the frenzy of a madman's certitude, and sank each day to the abyss of his despair, for the magic letter which was coming to him from the city, and which would instantly give him all the fortune, fame, and triumph for which his soul was panting, his family looked at him with troubled question in their eyes. His enthusiastic hopes and assurances of the great success that he would have from writing plays seemed visionary and remote to them. Perhaps they were right about this, although the reason that they had for thinking so was wrong.

Thus, although they said little to Eugene at this time about his plans for the future, and what they did say was meant to hearten him, their doubt and disbelief was evident, and sometimes when he came into the house, he could hear them talking in a troubled way about him:

"Mama," he heard his sister say one day, as she sat talking with his mother in the kitchen, "what does Gene intend to do? Have you heard him say yet?"

"Why, no-o-o!" his mother answered slowly, in a puzzled and meditative tone. "He hasn't said. At least he says he's goin' to write plays,— of course, I reckon he's waiting to hear from those people in New York about that play he's written," she added quickly.

"Well, I know," his sister answered wearily. "That's all very fine—if he can do it. But, good heavens, Mama!" she cried furiously—"you can't live on hope like that! Gene's only one out of a million! Can't you realize that?—Why, they used to think I had some talent as a singer"— here she laughed ironically, a husky high falsetto, "I used to think so, myself—but you don't notice that it ever got me anywhere, do you? No, sir!" she said positively. "There are thousands more just like Gene, who are trying to get ahead and make a name for themselves. Why should he think he's any better than the rest of them? Why, it might be years before he got a play produced—and even then, how can he tell that it would be a success?—What's he going to live on? How's he going to keep going until all this happens? What's he going to do?—You know, Mama, Gene's no little boy any more. Please get that into your head," she said sharply, as if her mother had questioned the accuracy of her remark. "No, sir! No, sir!" she laughed ironically and huskily. "Your baby is a grown man, and it's time he waked up to the fact that he's got to support himself from now on.—Mama, do you realize that it has been over four months since Gene left Harvard and, so far as I can see, he has made no effort yet to get a job. What does he intend to do?" she said angrily. "You know, he just can't mope around like this *all* his days! Sooner or later he's got to find some work to do!"

In all these words, there was apparent not so much hostility and antagonism as the driving fury and unrest of Helen's nervous, exacerbated, dissonant, and unhappy character, which could lavish kindness and affection one moment, and abuse and criticism the next. These were really only signs of the frenzy and unrest in her large, tortured, but immensely generous spirit. Thus, she would rage and storm at her husband at one moment for "moping about the house," telling him, "for heaven's sake am I never to be left alone! Am I never to get a moment's peace or quiet? Must I have you around me every moment of my life? In God's name, Hugh—go! go! go!—Leave me alone for a few minutes, I beg of you!"—and by this time his sister's voice would be cracked and strident, her breath coming hoarsely and almost with a sob of hysteria. And yet, she could be just as violent in her sense of wrong and injustice done to her if she thought he was giving too much time to business, rushing through his meals, reading a book when he should be listening to her tirade, or staying away from home too much.

Poor, tortured, and unhappy spirit, with all the grandeur, valor, and affection that Eugene knew so well, it had found, since her father's death, no medicine for the huge and constant frenzy of its own unrest, no guide or savior to work for it the miracle of salvation it must work itself, and it turned and lashed out at the world, demanding a loneliness which it could not have endured for three days running, a peace and quiet from its own fury, a release from its own injustice. And it was for this reason—because her own unrest and frenzy made her lash out constantly against the world, praising one week, condemning the next, accusing life and people of doing her some injury or wrong that she had done herself—it was for this reason, more than for any other, that Helen now lashed out about Eugene to their mother.

And because Eugene was strung on the same wires, shaped from the same clay, cut from the same kind and plan and quality, he stood there in the hall-way as he heard her, his face convulsed and livid, his limbs trembling with rage, his bowels and his heart sick and trembling with a hideous gray nausea of hopelessness and despair, his throat choking with an intolerable anguish of resentment and wrong, as he heard Helen's voice, and before he rushed back into the kitchen to quarrel with her and his mother.

"Well, now," he heard his mother say in a diplomatic and hopeful tone that somehow only served to increase his feeling of rage and exasperation—"well, now—well, now," she said, "let's wait and see! Let's wait and see what happens with this play. Perhaps he'll hear tomorrow that they have taken it. Maybe it's going to be all right, after all!"

"Going to be all right!" Eugene fairly screamed at this juncture, rushing in upon them in the kitchen. "You're God damned right it's going to be all right. I'll tell you what's all right!" he panted, because his breath was laboring against his ribs as if he had run up a steep hill—"if it was some damned real-estate man, that would be all right! If it's some cheap shyster lawyer, that would be all right! If it was some damned rascal sitting on his tail up here in the bank, cheating you out of all you've got, that would be all right—hey?" he snarled, conscious that his words had no meaning or coherence, but unable to utter any of the things he wished to say and that welled up in that wave of hot and choking resentment. "O yes! The big man! The great man! The big deacon—Mr. Scroop Pegram—the big bank president—that would be all right, wouldn't it?" he cried in a choked and trembling voice. "You'd get down on your hands and knees, and crawl if he spoke to you, wouldn't you?—'O thank you, Mr. Pegram, for letting me put my money in your bank so you can loan it out to a bunch of God-dam real-estate crooks,'" he sneered, in an infuriated parody of whining servility. "'Thank you, sir,'" he said, and in spite of the fact that these words made almost no coherent meaning, his mother began to purse her lips rapidly in an excited fashion, and his sister's big-boned face reddened with anger.

"Now," his mother said sternly, as she levelled her index finger at him, "I want to tell you something! You may sneer all you please, sir, at Scroop Pegram, but he's a man who has worked all his life for everything he has——"

"Yes," Eugene said bitterly, "and for everything *you* have, too—for that's where it's going in the end."

"He has made his *own* way since his childhood," Eliza continued sternly and deliberately—"no one ever did anything for him, for there's one thing sure:—there was no one in his family who was in a position to do it.—What he's done he's done for himself, without assistance and," his mother said in a stern and telling voice, "without education—for he never had three months' schoolin' in his life—and today he's got the respect of the community as much as any man I know."

"Yes! And most of their money, too," Eugene cried.

"You'd better not talk!" Helen said. "If I were you I wouldn't talk! Don't criticize other people until you show you've got it in you to do something for yourself," she said.

"You! You!" Eugene panted. "I'll show you! Talking about me when my back is turned, hey? That's the kind you are! All right! You wait and see! I'll show you!" he said, in a choked and trembling whisper of fury and resentment.

"All right," Helen said in a hard and hostile voice. "I'll wait and see. I hope you do. But you've got to show me that you've got it in you. It's time for you to quit this foolishness and get a job! Don't criticize other people until you show you've got it in you to support yourself," she said.

"No," said Eliza, "for we've done as much for you as we are able to. You've had as good an education as any one could want—and now the rest is up to you," she said sternly. "I've got no more money to pay out on you, so you can make your mind up to it from now on," she said. "You've got to shift for yourself."

And in the warm and living silence of the kitchen, they looked at one another for a moment, all three, breathing heavily, and with hard and bitter eyes.

"Well, Gene," Helen said, "I know. Try to forget about it. You'll change as you grow older," she said wearily. "We've all been like that. We all have these wonderful ambitions to be somebody famous, but that all changes. I had them, too," she said. "I was going to be a great singer, and have a career in opera, but that's all over now, and I know I never

will. You forget about it," she said quietly and wearily. "It all seems
wonderful to you, and you think that you can't live without it, but you
forget about it. Oh, of course you will!" she muttered, "of course! Why
—!" she cried, shaking Eugene furiously, and now her voice had its old
hearty and commanding ring,—"I'm going to beat you if you act like
this! What if they don't take your play! I'll bet that has happened to
plenty of people— Yes, sir!" she cried. "I'll bet that has happened to all
of them when they started out—and then they went on and made a big
success of it later! Why, if those people didn't take my play," she said,
"I'd sit down and write another one so good they'd be ashamed of themselves! Why, you're only a kid yet!" she cried furiously, shaking Eugene, and frowning fiercely but with her tongue stuck out a little and a
kind of grin on her big-boned liberal-looking face. "Don't you know
that! You've got *loads* of time yet! Your life's ahead of you! Of course
you will! Of course you will!" she cried, shaking him. "Don't let a thing
like this get you down! In ten years' time you'll look back on all this
and laugh to think you were ever such a fool! Of course you will!"—
and then as her husband, who had driven up before their mother's
house, now sounded on the horn for her, she said again, in the quiet
and weary tone: "Well, Gene, forget about it! Life's too short! I know,"
she said mysteriously, "I know!"

Then, as she started to go, she added casually, "Honey, come on over
for supper, if you want to.—Now, it's up to you. You can suit yourself!
—You can do exactly as you please," she said in the almost hard, deliberately indifferent tone with which she usually accompanied these invi-
tations:

"What would you like to eat?" she now said meditatively. "How about
a nice thick steak," she said juicily, as she winked at him. "I've got the
whole half of a fried chicken left over from last night, that you can have
if you come over!—Now, it's up to you!" she cried out again in that almost hard challenging tone, as if he had shown signs of unwillingness
or refusal. "I'm not going to urge you, but you're welcome to it if you
want to come.—How about a big dish full of string beans—some mashed
potatoes—some stewed corn, and asparagus! How'd you like some
great big wonderful sliced tomatoes with mayonnaise?—I've got a big
deep peach and apple cobbler in the oven—do you think that'd go good
smoking hot with a piece of butter and a hunk of American cheese?"
she said, winking at him and smacking her lips comically. "Would that
hit the spot? Hey?" she said, prodding him in the ribs with her big

stiff fingers and then saying in a hoarse, burlesque, and nasal tone, in extravagant imitation of a girl they knew who had gone to New York, and had come back talking with the knowing, cock-sure nasal tone of the New Yorker.

"Ah, fine, boys!" Helen said, in this burlesque tone. "Fine! Just like they give you in New York!" she said. Then turning away indifferently, she went down the steps, and across the walk towards her husband's car, calling back in an almost hard and aggressive tone:

"Well, you can do exactly as you like! No one is going to urge you to come if you don't want to!"

Then she got in the car, and they drove swiftly off down hill, turned the corner, and vanished.

The reason, in fact, which argued in Eugene's family's mind against his succeeding in the work he wished to do, was the very thing that should have been all in his favor. But neither he nor his family thought so. It was this: a writer, they thought, should be a wonderful, mysterious, and remote sort of person—some one they had never known, like Irvin S. Cobb. "Now, this boy," they argued in their minds, "our son and brother, is neither wonderful, mysterious, nor remote. We know all about him, we all grew up together here, and there's no use talking—he's the same kind of people that we are. His father was a stone-cutter —a man who was born on a farm and had to work all his life with his hands. And five of his father's brothers were also stone-cutters, and had to earn their living in the same way—by the sweat of their brow. And his mother is a hard-working woman who brought up a big family, runs a boarding house and has had to scrape and save and labor all her life. Every one in this part of the country knows her family: her brothers are respected business men in town here, and there are hundreds of her kins-folk—farmers, storekeepers, carpenters, lumber dealers, and the like— all through this section. Now, they're all good, honest, decent, self-re-specting people—no one can say they're not—but there's never been a writer in the crowd. No—and no doctors or lawyers either. Now there may have been a preacher or two—his Uncle Bascom was a preacher and a highly educated man too, always poking his nose into a book, and went to Harvard, and all,—yes, and now that we remember, always had queer notions like this boy—had to leave the church, you know, for be-ing an agnostic, and was always writing poems, and all such as that. Well, this fellow is one of the same kind—a great book reader but with no practical business sense—and it seems to us he ought to get a job somewhere teaching school, or maybe some newspaper work—which he could do—or, perhaps, he should have studied law."

So did their minds work on this subject. Yet the very argument they made—that he was the same kind of person as the rest of them, and not remote, wonderful, or mysterious—should have been the chief thing in his favor. But none of them could see this. For where they thought there was nothing wonderful or mysterious about them, he thought that there was; and none of them could see that his greatest asset, his greatest advantage, if he had any, was that he was made out of the same earth—the same blood, bone, character, and fury—as the rest of them. For, could they only have known it, the reason he read all the books was not, as they all thought, because he was a bookish person, for he was not, but for the same reason that his mother was mad about property— talked, thought, felt, and dreamed about real estate all the time, and wanted to own the earth just as he wanted to devour it. Again, the fury that had made him read the books was the same thing that drove his brothers and his sisters around incessantly, feeding the huge fury of their own unrest, and making them talk constantly and to every one, until they knew all about the lives of all the butchers, bakers, merchants, lawyers, doctors, Greek restaurant owners, and Italian fruit dealers in the community.

If they had understood this—that he had the same thing in him that they all had in them—they would have understood about his wanting to be a writer, and even the trouble in which presently he would involve himself, and that seemed so catastrophic and disgraceful to him at that time, would not have seemed so bad to them, for his father, one of his brothers, and several of his kinsmen had been in this same trouble —and it had caused no astonishment at all. But now that he had done this thing—now that the one they looked on as the scholar, and the bookish person, had done it—it was as if the leading deacon of the church had been caught in a raid on a bawdy house.

Finally, there was to be some irony for Eugene later in the fact that, had he only known it and grasped it, there was ready to his use in that one conflict all of the substance and energy of the human drama, and that the only thing that was wonderful or important was that they were all full of the passion, stupidity, energy, hope, and folly of living men— fools, angels, guiltless and guilty all together, not to be praised or blamed, but just blood, bone, marrow, passion, feeling—the whole swarming web of life and error in full play and magnificently alive. As for the fancied woes and hardships of the young artist in conflict with the dull and brutal philistines,—that, he saw later, had had nothing to do with it, and was not worth a damn, any more than the plays that had been written in Professor Hatcher's class, and in which a theatrical formula for living was presented in place of life. No; the conflict, the comedy, the tragedy,—the pain, the pride, the folly and the error— might have been just the same had Eugene wanted to be an aviator, a deep-sea diver, a bridge-builder, a professional pall-bearer, or a locomotive engineer. And the stuff of life was there in all its overwhelming richness, was right there in his grasp, but he could not see it, and would not use it. Instead he went snooping and prowling around the sterile old brothels of the stage, mistaking the glib concoctions of a counterfeit emotion for the very flesh and figure of reality. And this also has been true of every youth that ever walked the earth.

The letter came at length one gray day in late October; and instantly, when he had opened it, and read the first words "We regret," his life went gray as that gray day, and he thought that he would never have heart or hope nor know the living joy of work again. His flesh went dead and cold and sick, yet he read the smooth lying phrases in the letter with the stolid face with which people usually receive bad news, and even tried to insinuate a thread of hope, to suck a kind of meagre and hopeless comfort from the hard, yet oily, words, "We are looking forward with great interest to reading your next play, and we hope you will send it to us as soon as it is completed." . . . "Our members were divided in their opinion, four voting to reconsider it, and five for rejection . . . although all were agreed on the freshness and vitality of the writing . . . while the power of some of the scenes is undeniable . . . we must reluctantly. . . . You are one of the young men whose work we are watching with the greatest interest . . ." and so on.

Those on whom the naked weight of shame has rested, who have felt its gray and hideous substance in their entrails, will not smile calmly and with comfort if their memory serves them.

Now a huge, naked, and intolerable shame and horror pressed down on Eugene with a crushing and palpable weight out of the wet, gray skies of autumn. The hideous gray stuff filled him from brain to bowels, was everywhere and in everything about him so that he breathed it out of the air, felt it like a naked stare from walls and houses and the faces of the people, tasted it on his lips, and endured it in the screaming and sickened dissonance of ten thousand writhing nerves so that he could no longer sit, rest, or find oblivion, exhaustion, forgetfulness or repose anywhere he went, or release from the wild unrest that drove him constantly about. He went to bed only to get up and prowl again the wet and barren little streets of night; he ate, and instantly vomited up again all he had eaten, and then, like a dull, distressed and nauseated brute, he would sullenly and wretchedly eat again.

He saw the whole earth with the sick eyes, the sick heart, the sick flesh, and writhing nerves of this gray accursed weight of shame and horror in which his life lay drowned, and from which it seemed he could never more emerge to know the music of health and joy and power again; and from which, likewise, he could not die, but must live hideously and miserably the rest of his days, like a man doomed to live forever in a state of retching and abominable nausea of heart, brain, bowels, flesh and spirit.

It seemed to him that all was lost, that he had been living in a fool's dream for years, and that now he had been brutally wakened and saw himself as he was—a naked fool—who had never had an ounce of talent, and who no longer had an ounce of hope—a madman who had wasted his money and lost precious years when he might have learned some work consonant with his ability and the lives of average men. And it now seemed to him, that his family had been terribly and mercilessly right in everything they had said and felt, and that he had been too great a fool to understand it. His sense of ruin and failure was abysmal, crushing, and complete.

XLII

It was in this temper, after two days of aimless and frenzied wandering about the streets of the town, and over the hills that surrounded it, during which time he was no more conscious of what he did, said, ate, thought or felt than a man in a trance, that Eugene started off suddenly to visit his other married sister, who lived in a little town in South Carolina. He had not seen her since his father's death two years ago, she had written him a few days before asking him to come down, and now, driven more by a fury of flight and movement than by any other impulse, he wired her he was coming, and started out in one of the Public Service motor cars which at that time made the trip across the mountains. Luke had arranged to meet him sixty miles from home at the town of Blackstone, in South Carolina, and drive him the remainder of the distance to his sister's house.

He set out on a day in late October, wild and windy, full of ragged torn clouds of light that came and went from gray to gold and back to gray again. And everything that happened on that savage day he was to remember later with a literal and blazing intensity.

Autumn had come sharp and quick that year. October had been full of frost and nipping days, the hills were glorious that year as Eugene had never seen them before. Now, only a day or two before, there had been, despite the early season, a sudden and heavy fall of snow. It still lay, light but fleecy, in the fields; and on the great bulk of the hills it lay in a pattern of shining white, stark grays and blacks, and the colors of the leaves, which now had fallen thickly and had lost their first sharp vividness, but were still burning with a dull massed molten glow.

An hour away, and twenty-five miles from home, the car had drawn up before the post-office of a mountain village or resort which lay at the crest of the last barrier of the hills, before the road dropped sharply down the mountain-side to South Carolina.

While they were halted here, another car drove up—an open, glittering, and expensive-looking projectile of light gray—and in it were three young men from home, two of whom Eugene knew. This car drew up abreast, stopped, and he saw that its driver was Robert Weaver. And although he had not seen the other youth since a midnight visit Robert had made to his room in Cambridge, the latter peered over towards him owlishly and without a word of greeting and with that abrupt, feverish, and fragmentary speech that was characteristic of him and was constantly becoming more dissonant and broken, he barked out:

"Who's in there? Who's that sitting up there in the front seat? Is that you, Gene?" he called.

When Gene assured him that it was, Robert asked where he was going. When he told him "Blackstone," he demanded at once that he leave the service car, and come with him.

"We're going there, too," he said. Turning to his comrades, he added earnestly:

"Aren't we? Isn't that where we're going, boys?"

The two young men to whom he spoke now laughed boisterously, crying:

"Yeah! That's right! That's where we're going, Robert," and one of them added with a solemn gravity:

"We're going to—Blackstone," here a slight convulsion seemed to scize his throat, he swallowed hard, hiccoughed, and concluded, "to see a football game"—a statement which again set them off into roars of boisterous laughter. Then they all shouted at Eugene:

"Come on! Come on! Get in! We've lots of room."

Eugene got out of the service car, paid the driver, took the small handgrip he had, and got into the other car with Robert and his two companions. They drove off fast, and almost immediately they were dropping down the mountain, along the sinuous curves and turns of the steep road.

Robert's two companions on this journey were young men whom Eugene had not known in boyhood, with whom he had now only a speaking acquaintance, and both of whom were recent comers to the town. The older of these two was a man named Emmet Blake, and he now sat beside Robert on the front seat of the car.

Emmet Blake was a man of twenty-seven years, a frail and almost wasted-looking figure of medium height, straight black hair, black eyes, and a thin, febrile, and corrupted-looking face which, although almost dead-white in its color, was given a kind of dark and feverish vitality by a faint thin smile that seemed always to hover about the edges of his mouth, and the dark unnatural glitter of his black eyes.

He lived a reckless and dissipated life, and drank heavily: time after time, after a hemorrhage of the lungs, he had been taken to a sanitarium in an ambulance, and his death had seemed to be a matter of only a few hours. And time after time, he had come out again, and immediately started on another wild spree of women and corn whiskey with Robert and others of the same breed. He was well-off as to money, and lived expensively, because he was a nephew of George Blake, the great Middle-western manufacturer of cheap motor cars, which in twenty years' time had created twenty thousand jokes, and glutted the highways of the earth in twenty million tinny and glittering repetitions.

The name of the other youth, who was Eugene's own age, and sat beside him on the back seat, was Kitchin. He was a tall, dark, handsome fellow, with agreeable manners and a pleasant voice, the nephew of a retired physician in the town but not native to the place. Eugene had seen him on the streets, but had never talked to him before. It was evident that both Robert and his two friends had been drinking, although not heavily: there was in their manner the subdued yet wild and mounting elation of young men when they begin to drink. They laughed a great deal, rather hilariously, and for no good reason: they insisted frequently that they were going to the town of Blackstone to see a football game, an announcement which would set them off again in roars of laughter.

Almost as soon as Eugene got in the car, and even as they started off again, Blake thrust his thin hand into the leather pocket of the door beside him, produced a bottle that was three quarters full of Scotch whiskey, and turning, gave it to Eugene, saying:

"Take a big one, Gant. We're all ahead of you."

He drank long and deep, gulping the fiery liquor down his throat recklessly, feeling suddenly an almost desperate sense of release from the gray misery of hopelessness which had crushed him down for days now, since the letter had come. When he had finished, he handed the bottle back to Emmet Blake, who took it, looked at it with a thin, evil, speculative smile, and said:

"Well, that's pretty good. What do you say, Robert? Shall we let him pass on that?"

"Hell, no!" cried Robert hoarsely, looking swiftly around at the bottle. "That's no drink! Make him take a good one, Emmet. You've got to do better than that if you keep up with us," he cried, and then he burst out suddenly in his staccato laugh, shaking his head to himself as he bent over the wheel, and crying out: "Lord! Lord!"

Blake handed Eugene the bottle again, and he drank some more. Then Kitchin took the bottle and drank; he handed it back to Emmet Blake, who drank, and Blake handed it to Robert who took it with one hand, his face turned slightly from the wheel, his eyes still fastened on the road, and drank until the bottle was empty. Then he flung it away from him across his arm. The bottle went sailing out across the road and down the gulch or deep ravine that sloped away beside them far down: the bottle struck a rock, exploding brilliantly in a thousand glittering fragments, and they all roared happily, and cheered.

They had finished up that bottle in one round of gulps and swallows, passing it from hand to hand as they rushed down the mountain-side, and almost instantly they were at work on a beverage of a yet more instant and fiery power—raw, white corn-whiskey, in a gallon jug, clear as water, rank and nauseous to an unaccustomed throat, strong and instant as the kick of a mule, fiery, choking, formidable, and savage. They hooked their thumbs into the handle of the jug, and brought the stuff across their shoulders with a free-hand motion, they let the wide neck pour into their tilted throats with a fat thick gurgle, and they gulped that raw stuff down with greedy gulpings like water going down a gully drain.

It was a drink that would have felled an ox, a terrific lightning-blast of alcohol that would have thrown Polyphemus to the earth; and yet it was not drink alone that made them drunk that day. For they were all young men, and they had shouted, sung, and roared with laughter, and pounded one another with affectionate delight as they rushed on—and it was not drink alone that made them drunk.

For they felt that everything on earth was good and glorious, that everything on earth was made for their delight, that they could do no wrong and make no error, and that such invincible strength was in them that trees would fall beneath their stroke, the immortal hills bow down before their stride, and that nothing in the world could stop them.

And for Eugene it seemed that everything had come to life for him at once—that he had emerged instantly and victoriously from the horror of shame, the phantasmal and dreamlike unreality that had held him in its spell. It seemed to him that all the earth had come to life again in shapes of deathless and familiar brightness, that he had gloriously re-entered a life he thought he had lost forever, and that all the plain price-less joy and glory of the earth was his, as it had never been before.

And first of all, and with an almost intolerable relief and happiness, he was conscious of the pangs of hunger: his famished belly and his withered guts which had for days shrunk wearily and with disgust from food, now, under the stimulation of a ravenous hunger, fairly pled for nourishment. He thought of food—food in a hundred glorious shapes and varieties: the literal sensual images of food blazed in his mind like paintings from the brush of a Dutch master, and it seemed to him that no one had ever painted, spoken, or written about food before in a way that would do it justice.

Later, these were the things Eugene would remember from that day with a living joy, for it was as if he had been born again, or discovered the world anew in all its glory. And besides all this—a part, an element in all this whole harmonious design of triumphant joy and rediscovery —was the way the hills had looked that day as they came down the mountain, the smell of the air which was mellow and autumnal, and yet had in it the premonitory breath of frost and sharpness, and the wild joy, power, and ecstasy that had filled their hearts, their throats, their lives—the sense of victory, triumph, and invincible strength, and of some

rare, glorious, and intolerable happiness that was pending for them, and
which seemed to swell the tremendous and exulting music of that magic
day.

Around them, above them, below them—from the living and shining
air of autumn, from the embrowned autumnal earth, from the great
shapes of the hills behind them with their molten mass of color—dull
browns, rich bitter reds, dark bronze, and mellow yellow—from
the raw crude clay of the piedmont earth and the great brown stubble
of the cotton fields—from a thousand impalpable and unutterable things,
there came this glorious breath of triumph and delight. It was late
October, there was a smell of smoke upon the air, an odor of burning
leaves, the barking of a dog, a misty red, a pollenated gold in the rich,
fading, sorrowful, and exultant light of the day,—and far off, a sound of
great wheels pounding on a rail, the wailing whistle, and the tolling
bell of a departing train.

And finally, the immortal visage of the earth itself with the soaring
and limitless undulations of its blue ranges, the great bulk of the autumn
hills, immense and near, the rugged, homely, and familiar trees—the
pines, oaks, chestnuts, maples, locusts—the homely look of the old red
clay—the unforgettable and indescribable naturalness of that earth—
with its rudeness, wildness, richness, rawness, ugliness, fathomless mystery and utter familiarity, and finally the lonely, haunting, and enchanted music that it made—the strange spirit of time and solitude that
hovered above it eternally, and which can never be described, but which
may be evoked by a cow-bell broken by the wind in distant valleys, the
lonely whistle of a departing train, or simply a sinuous gust of wind that
smokes its way across coarse mountain grasses when spring comes—
all this, which Eugene had felt and known in his childhood, and yet
had never had a tongue to utter, he seemed now to know and understand so well that he had himself become its tongue and utterance, the
more its child because he had been so long away from it, the more its
eye because he now saw it again as it must have seemed to the first men
who ever saw it, with the eyes of discovery, love, and recognition.

And yet, for him all these things spoke instantly, intolerably, exultantly, not of home, return, and settlement, but of one image, which now
burned forever in his brain, rose like a triumphant music in his heart.
And that image was the image of the enchanted city, in which, it now
seemed, all the frenzy and unrest of his spirit would find a certain goal

and triumph, and toward which everything on earth, and all the hope and joy now rising in his heart, was tending.

When they got down off the mountain into South Carolina they were very drunk. On a dusty sand-clay road between some cotton fields they stopped the car, and walked out into the fields to piss. The cotton stood stiff and dry and fleecy in its pods, the coarse brown stalks rose up in limitless planted rows, and underneath, he could see the old and homely visage of the red-clay earth.

At one edge of the field, and seeming very far away and lonely-looking, there was a negro shanty, and behind this a desolate wooded stretch of pine. Over all the earth at once, now that the roar of the engine had stopped, there was an immense and brooding quietness, a drowsed autumnal fume and warmth, immensely desolate and mournful, holding somehow a tragic prophecy of winter that must come, and death, and yet touched with the lonely, mournful and exultant mystery of the earth.

Eugene pulled several of the big cotton stalks out of the dry red earth, thrust one through the button-hole of his coat lapel, and tore it through exultantly, although the stalk was two feet long. Then he reeled back toward the car again, holding the other stalks of cotton in his hands, got in the car, and at once began to talk to his companions about the cotton—landing into a passionate oration about the hills, the fields, the cotton and the earth—trying to tell them all about "the South" and making of the stalks of cotton and "the South" a kind of symbol, as young men will, although they all felt and acted just as young men anywhere would do.

But at that moment, all Eugene was trying to say about his years away from home, and his return, and how he had discovered his own land again and was, "by God," one of them—waving the stalks of cotton as he talked, and finding the whole core and kernel of all he wished to say in these stalks of cotton—all of this, although incoherent, drunken, and confused, seemed so eloquent and beautiful to him, so truthful, passionate, and exact—that he began to weep for joy as he talked to them. And they—they were, of course, delighted: they howled with laughter, cheered enthusiastically, slapped him on the back, and shook hands all around, crying—"By God! Listen to him talk! . . . Give 'em hell, son! We're with you! . . . Hot-damn! Thataway, boy! . . . Stay with 'em! . . . Whee!"

Meanwhile, Robert was driving at terrific speed. They had begun to rip and tear along between the cotton fields, and over the dusty sand-clay roads, mistaking the screams of women and the shouts of men, as they swerved by their cars and wagons in a cloud of yellow dust and at a murderous clip, for admiring applause and enthusiastic cheers, an illusion which only spurred them on to greater efforts.

The upshot of it was that they finally tore into town, careening hide-ously along a central street, and with no slackening of their speed whatever. The excited people in that part of the State had been phoning in about them for the last fifteen miles of their mad journey, and now they were halted suddenly at sight of the police who stood lined up across the street in a double row—big, red-faced, country cops—to stop them.

The first brilliant, sparkling and wildly soaring effects of their in-toxication had now worn off and, although they still felt full of power and a savage rending strength, the corn whiskey was now smouldering in their veins more dully and with a sombre and brutal drunkenness. Eugene seemed to see all shapes and figures clearly—the coarse red faces of the country cops and their clumsy lumbering bodies, and the street drowsy and dusty in the warmish autumn afternoon.

The grasses on the lawns of houses were faded, sere and withered-looking, the leaves upon the trees had thinned and hung yellowed, dry and dead, and in the gutters a few dead leaves stirred dryly, a few scampered dryly in the streets before a moment's gust of wind, and then lay still again.

Robert slowed down and stopped before that solid wall of beefy coun-try blue and red: the police surrounded them and clambered heavily over the sides of the car, two standing on the fenders, two on either side of Eugene on the back seat, and one with Robert and Emmet Blake up front.

"All right, boys," said one of them, good-naturedly and casually enough, in the full, sonorous and somewhat howling voice of the coun-try man, "drive on down thar to the station house now."

"Yes, *sir!* Yes, *sir!*" Robert replied at once in a meek and obedient tone, and with a comical drunken alacrity. "How do you get there, Captain?" he said with a cunning and flattering ingratiation.

"Right down this here street to your right," said the policeman in his drawling and countrified tone, "until you come to that 'air second turn-ing where you see that 'air f'ar hydrant. Turn in to the left thar," he said.

"Yes, sir!" said Robert heartily, starting the car again. "We're all strangers here," he lied, as if he hoped this lie might make amends for them. "We don't know our way about yet."

"Well," the policeman drawled with a kind of ugly heartiness, "maybe the next time you come back you'll be better acquainted here," he said, winking at his comrades, and they all guffawed. "We're glad to see you, boys," he continued, still with this ugly falseness of good nature in his tone. "We been hearin' about you," he said, winking at his fellows again, "an' we wanted to git acquainted."

Here the policemen laughed again with sonorous countrified appreciation of their spokesman's wit.

The policemen were all big beefy men, with hearty drawling voices, red countrified faces. They had large square feet, wore dusty-looking black slouch hats with a wide brim, and were dressed in rather gaudy but slovenly-looking uniforms, with stripes of gold braid running up the sides of their baggy trousers, and with the lower brass buttons of their heavy blue coats unbuttoned, exposing areas of soiled shirts and paunchy bellies. Their faces had a look of a slow but powerful energy, a fathomless and mindless animal good nature, and at the same time a fathomless and mindless animal cruelty—instant, volcanic, and murderous—written terribly somehow into their wide, thin and horribly cruel mouths, in which there was legible a vitality that had all the wild and sensual force of nature packed into it, and was therefore beyond nature—almost super-natural—in its savage and mindless qualities.

He had seen them standing idly on the corners of the little towns, huge and slovenly, swinging their thonged clubs in the great muttons of their hands, surveying with their great red faces and their wide thin mouths of fathomless cruelty and good nature the crowds that swarmed around them. He had heard their drawling howling accents of the country, that had all of the moisture and distance of the earth in them, and seen their slow minds wake to a mindless and murderous fury. Once as a child he had seen one of them, a ponderous giant so huge he lurched from side to side when he walked, and seemed to fill the street up with his size, beat a drunken old man—a little howling integument of bone and gristle—to death with his club, smashing the little old man across the skull until the blood rushed out in torrents through his sparse silvery hair, lacing its way in channels of brilliant red across his face and through his beard, until it seemed incredible so small and old a man could have such fountains of bright blood in him.

And these huge creatures evoked for Eugene a whole history of this earth and people, monstrous, savage, and unutterable—a congruent and unspeakable legend which he knew, and all of them knew, down to the roots, and which he could not speak about and had to speak about, somehow, or die. For in these men there was evident not only the savage and mindless energy of the earth itself, with all that was wild, sensual, fecund, cruel and good-natured—the whole weather of life—but there was also evident the fear, the shame, the horror that had crushed them beneath its ocean weight of nameless and cowering dread, and broken or destroyed their souls.

The two policemen who had clambered into the back seat of the car and now sat on each side of Eugene had these mountainous and fleshy figures, heavy, yet with a kind of solid and ugly softness, meaty, and without the muscular and sinewy leanness of young men. The back seat of the car was a narrow one—the car was a new "sports model" designed only for four people—and now the huge fleshy figures of these two policemen, wedged against Eugene, gave him a feeling of disgust and revulsion.

Nevertheless, the feeling of exultant and jubilant power had not yet worn off, and although he had understood at once, when he saw the men lined up across the street, that they were under arrest and would be taken to the city jail, this sordid prospect caused him no uneasiness whatever. Rather, the feeling of drunken joy was still so powerful in him that everything on earth seemed good, and everything that happened wonderful. He hailed the experience of being arrested and taken to jail exultantly as if some fortunate and glorious experience was in store for him, and his exuberant affection for the world was so great that he even liked the policemen.

Eugene howled with laughter, smote them on their broad backs, flung his arms out and around their shoulders, saying, "By God, you're fine fellows, both of you, and you've got to have a drink!"

At this Robert laughed uneasily, saying to the policemen:

"Don't pay any attention to him! We haven't got anything to drink—I swear we haven't."

One of them had been rummaging around, however, and now triumphantly produced the jug from its hiding place beneath Blake's legs.

"Here it is, boys," he cried, as he displayed it. "I've got it."

The glass jug was almost empty, but there was still perhaps an inch of the whiskey at the bottom. Robert's face had a worried look, for the law was such that a capture of this sort might also mean the confiscation of the owner's car.

Blake, meanwhile, had been talking in a low, craftily persuasive tone of drunken insinuation and bribery to the policeman up front, saying: "Now I know you boys don't want to get us into any trouble. We weren't doing anything wrong—just having a drink or two together —and if you fellows will just forget about this thing, we'll fix it up right with you—anything you say," he whispered cunningly, "and get on out of town right now without any one knowing a thing about it. What do you say, now? Come on! You can do it," he said, with a leer of ingratiation.

The policeman to whom he spoke smiled good-naturedly, but said nothing. At this moment they drove up before the station house, a shabby-looking little building of brick, with bars over the window, and which was situated on a side-street.

The shabby street looked warm, faded, sleepy, touched with the ghosts of autumn, but in an instant, as the police got out, opened the doors, and the gay men clambered down drunkenly among them, a rabble-rout of ragged negro boys, grinning, gape-mouthed countrymen with red faces, slouchy-looking barbers in their shirt-sleeves, and wormy-looking loafers, had gathered magically from nowhere, stood in a ring about them and snickered and shuffled about, pressed up to the barred windows and peered in curiously with shaded eyes as the policemen took them into the station.

As they started, Robert held back a little, and said hoarsely, and in a plaintive, troubled voice to the policeman who had him by the arm: "What are you taking us in here for? We weren't doing anything. Honest we weren't. What are you going to do to us?"

The policeman smiled good-humoredly, and then said in a hearty reassuring voice:

"Aw, we're not goin' to do anything to you. We were just afraid you boys might run into something and hurt yourself, that's all. We're just goin' to take you in here, and let you stay here a little while until you feel better," he said, at the same time winking at his fellows.

"Well," said Robert sullenly, casting a troubled and unwilling glance back at his shining car, "—I want to find my car here when I come out. Now if anything happens to that car, there's going to be trouble," he said ominously.

"That car will be right here when you come out the way you left it," the policeman said heartily. "No one is goin' to touch it. No, sir! I'll look after that car myself!" he said, winking again at the others.

"All right, then," said Robert. "That's all I want to know."

Then they marched all of them into the station house.

The room they entered was a large one, and at first, because they had come into it out of the brightness of the sun, and the swimming confusion of drunkenness and arrest, it was so dark Eugene could not distinguish clearly any of its features. Then he saw that it was a square, rather high room with worn wooden floors, wainscoting of a dark varnished brown, and above that rude calcimined walls of white. In the wall along the street, there were, besides the door, two barred windows which were very dirty and not very large, and did not give much light.

At one end of the room, as they came in, there was a row of dull green lockers, probably for the use of the police, and at the other end a high, square, somewhat majestical-looking desk, which was also of a dark maply-brown and which seemed to be built on an elevated rostrum or platform a few inches high. Over this desk a light with a green glass shade was burning, and behind it another large red-faced policeman was sitting. By his look of authority, and the military opulence of his slovenly uniform—for he had epaulets of thick gold braid upon his shoulders that would have glorified the uniform of a general in the Marine Corps—he seemed to be the superior in command.

As for the rest of the room, there was little decoration save for a row of worn and rickety-looking wooden chairs with rounded backs along the wall, and a liberal distribution of large brass spittoons which, to judge from the bare wooden boards around them, were used less frequently as receptacles than as targets, and obviously with uncertain success.

Finally, the whole place had the unforgettable look and smell that police stations everywhere—and particularly those in little towns—have always had. Its stale dark air was impregnated with the odor of cheap cigars and tobacco-juice, of old worn varnished wood, of human sweat and urine and heavy wool, and with the strong tarry odor of a sanitary disinfectant. And somehow, in this stale, dark and weary odor, there was also a quality of terror, menace, and foreboding—as if the huge and dingy chronicle of human tragedy and error which this grim room had witnessed—all the brutal, shabby sinfulness of a little town—that swarming, hideous and tawdry fraternity of poverty, vice and error—dredged from its rat-holes in the dark depths of old brick buildings, hunted out of cheap hotels, pool rooms, greasy little lunch rooms, nigger shacks, and the rickety wooden whore-houses near the railroad tracks, with its vast brotherhood of scarred and battered men and women—chain-gang niggers, drunken country youths and cheap bootleggers, grimy prostitutes and all their furtive bawds and pimps, cutters, sluggers, stabbers, slashers, and brawlers—both those who live by vice and those who are its victims—this whole huge earth of pain and crime and misery had left the terrible imprint of its history so indelibly there that the weary air was impregnated with sorrow and fear, and the wood, walls, floors and ceilings were seasoned and ingrained with the substance of human wretchedness.

When they had come in, the police had lined up Eugene's three companions before the imposing rostrum where the desk officer was sitting, but they had placed him carefully to one side against the wall, like an object too rare and precious for ordinary usage. Now, as the great man behind the desk glowered down gloomily and mistrustfully at them, one of the police spoke to the desk sergeant and, turning toward Eugene with a nod of the head, declared in a full countrified tone:

"This big 'un here's the drunkest of the lot."

And the enthroned law bent his gloomy gaze upon him with a hostile and suspicious look which said as plain as words that it was no more than he had suspected.

Eugene had not realized, in fact, until he felt that wall against his shoulders, how very drunk he was; but he was drunker now than he had ever been in all his life before. He could feel his back slide down along the wall, and then his bending knees would straighten with a jerk, and he would solemnly begin to slide up the wall again. Meanwhile, the room swam and rocked and then was still before his eyes: the shapes of things would melt into a smear, and then resolve into their proper selves once more.

And he was conscious that the police were searching him and his companions, patting their pockets to see if they carried weapons, examining wallets and letters for identifications, taking their watches from them, and arraigning them on a series of formal charges, some of which had no bearing on their case whatever. Drunk, assuredly, they were; disorderly they might have been—although it had not seemed so to them; of driving in a reckless manner they were guilty; but of resisting an officer in the performance of his duty they had been, up to that time, spotlessly innocent.

But such were the charges delivered against them in sonorous and countrified tones. And in the solemn voices of the policemen, the knowing and portentous way in which they searched the young men —as if they were a gang of armed desperadoes, and in a manner that smacked of correspondence-school detective methods—and finally in the solemn countrified tones of the one who had pointed to Eugene, saying: "This big 'un here's the drunkest of the lot," there was something comical and ludicrous.

But in their sense of banded authority, in the stubborn almost conspiratorial way in which they had now hardened in a group against the young men, forsaking the good-humored and jovial manners which had heretofore distinguished them, there was something ugly and revolting—something stupid, provincial, mob-like, and unreasoning, which told the young men plainly that "they had them" now, that they were "foreigners," therefore suspect, and must bow their heads in silence to the obdurate and capricious tyrannies of a local and, for them, impregnable authority.

At length, the sonorous formalities of their arraignment having been completed, the sergeant having scrawled and written in his ledger, the man looked up and ordered sternly:

"All right, boys! Take 'em back and lock 'em up!"

Then the young men were marched back along a corridor into a large two-storied room, which had brick walls and cement floors, two rows of dirty barred windows, a gray and gelid light, and a general feel of raw and clammy dankness. This room, which had a harsh angular steel-and-cement newness that the other did not have, seemed to be of more recent construction, and to have been added on to the front part of the jail. In this room, also, there were several rows of cells, ascending in tiers up to the ceiling. When they entered, the place was quiet, but immediately a drunken negress in one of the cells began to bawl and rave and sob, smashing, hammering, and rattling the bars of her cell like a demented ape. There was everywhere a foul rank odor of undrained fecal matter, tempered with the odor of the tarry disinfectant, and cut more sharply with the acrid smell of some ammoniac fluid.

At the first row of cells they paused, and the police in charge of Robert and Emmet Blake (for Eugene now discovered with a sense of shock that Kitchin was not with them) unlocked the doors of cells two and three and thrust Blake and Robert into them. The last, or end, cell in the row, Eugene now saw was intended for his occupancy and he stood waiting obediently, in the relaxed grip of one of the policemen, until his comrade should unlock the door.

Suddenly, as the door swung open, and Eugene stepped forward into the cell, his vision cleared somewhat, and he saw a young negro standing in the cell, beside the iron bed that projected from the wall, looking toward him with a startled expression on his face that suggested he had been asleep upon the cot, and had been rudely wakened by their entrance. Instantly, one fixed and all-obsessing belief began to burn in Eugene's inflamed and drunken brain. He thought that he was being put here with this negro because the jail was crowded and the cell-space scanty, and further—and this was the thing that maddened him and that he found intolerable—because, as the policeman had said when they arraigned the young men, "this big 'un here's the drunkest of the lot," and they thought he was too drunk to notice or to care about the advantage they were taking of him.

For this reason—and this reason only—he now acted as he did. As far as the negro himself was concerned, Eugene bore no grudge against him, and the feeling of shame and degradation which had swept over him in an overwhelming flood when he saw the cell and knew he was to be locked in it like an animal was so great that he would not have cared with whom he had to share that cell, if it had been the custom of the country so to share it. But the custom of the country was not so, he knew, and the belief that he was being put upon, his drunkenness taken advantage of, and that he was being dealt with less fairly than the others, now so stung his maddened pride that he turned and kicked the iron door back in the faces of the two policemen, just as they were closing it.

Then he started to come out of the cell. When he did, the two big red-faced policemen came running forward with a lumbering, panting, and somehow revolting clumsiness and tried to push him back into the cell. When this happened, something dark, gray, and terrible that he had never known before rose up in his soul—and this thing, which now came to him for the first time, was to return often in the savage years that followed.

As the police came rushing towards Eugene his fury and desperation were so great that he felt little or no fear, but the sensations of horror and disgust were so terrible that they drove him mad, and he seemed to be drowning in them. And the first visible and physical, although perhaps not the basic, causes of these sensations of horror and disgust came from the mountainous figures of the two policemen, and the feel of their huge soft-solid bodies as they jammed against him. For, if they had quelled his rebellion at the outset by smashing him over the head with their clubs, he might have felt a moment's fear before the club crashed on his skull, but he would not have felt horror and disgust.

But the sight, the feel, the smell, the look of these huge soft-solid bodies of mountainous flesh, and the revolting clumsiness of their movements, made the thing horrible. As they rushed towards Eugene and tried to thrust him back into the cell, he grabbed hold of the bars on either side of the door, and began to howl at them and curse them foully, and to butt at them with his head. When this happened the policemen braced themselves together like turn-squat Buddhas, holding on to the bars with their huge muttony hands, that had no leanness in them, and butted back at Eugene with their huge soft-solid stomachs.

They stood, half-squatly, side by side, their muttony hands gripped around the bars, their great red faces moist and panting, their huge buttocks somehow obscenely womanish in their fat breadth, as they butted back clumsily at him with their soft ponderous bellies—all of this, and the revolting contact of their flesh against his own, filled him with such an infinite loathing of horror and disgust that he went mad.

He started to come out of the cell. When he did, the two big policemen came running forward with a lumbering clumsiness and tried to push him back in. One of the men raised his ponderous fist and shouted: "Git back in thar now or I'll hit ye." A huge muttony fist smashed squarely on his nose and mouth: he butted, cursed, amid a pin-wheel aura of exploding rockets: the fist smashed hard again below one eye: the boy screamed like a wounded animal and cursing horribly all the time began to use his head as a battering ram, butting again and again at the fat red faces.

Meanwhile the other one, grunting and puffing, and with his tongue between his teeth, began to thump, tug and wrench at the fingers of one hand, trying to loosen them from the bar, and saying to his fellow: "You git his other hand, Jim, an' try to make him turn a-loose."

During all this time that Eugene had been cursing and butting at these men, he had also been shouting "You God-damned red-faced South Car'-lina bastards, you're not going to lock me up in here with a nigger—no you ain't!"—and now he felt something rough and wooly scraping underneath his arm. It was the frightened negro's head. He went squirming out below Eugene's arm until he was outside peering with white eyeballs over a policeman's shoulder, and when Eugene saw they would not try to keep the negro there with him, he went back into the cell and was locked up. He felt very sick, and everything was swimming nauseously around him: for a while he leaned over the w. c. and vomited into it. Then he sat down on the edge of the cot, and stared ahead, thinking about nothing, but with something hideous, like a great gray smear, inside him.

XLIII

How long he sat there in this way he did not know, for time would pass in a hideous smear of brownish gray while all things reeled, mixed, and were fused drunkenly and shapelessly around him—and then for a moment time would burn in his mind like a small hard light of brilliant color, and he would see everything with an exact and blazing vividness and hear the voices of his comrades in their cells.

The cell Eugene sat in was a little cubicle of space, perhaps eight feet deep, and four or five feet wide. Its only furnishings were a black iron cot or bed which projected from the wall and could be turned up or out, and which had no springs or mattress on it, and a w. c. of dirty white enamel, which had no seat, and was broken and would not flush, so that it had run over and spilled out upon the cement floor. The walls and ceilings of the cell were made of some hard slate-like substance of black-gray, scrawled with the familiar obscenities and pictures of its former occupants. Because of these solid walls, each cell was cut off from its neighbors and for this reason he could not see Emmet Blake, who had the cell next to him, nor Robert, who had the cell on the other side of Emmet, but now, as his mind swam from the stupor of its drunkenness, he could hear their voices, and began to listen to their conversation.

Both were still quite drunk, and for a while they continued a kind of mournful drunken chant, each responding to the other with a repetition of his own misfortune.

"Yes, sir," Robert would say, heaving a sigh and speaking in a hoarse, mournfully drunken voice, "this is certainly a hell of a way to treat a man who's just been admitted to the bar six weeks ago! A hell of a thing!" he said.

And Blake would answer:

"Yes, sir! And I'll tell *you* what *is* a hell of a thing! This is a hell of a way to treat George Blake's nephew! A hell of a way!" he said. "If my uncle knew about this he'd come down here and tear their damned little jail to pieces! He'd *ruin* their town!" he cried. "Yes, sir! He'd wash 'em out and send 'em to the cleaners! Why!" Blake now said in a tone of drunken boastfulness, "there are 70,000 Blake dealers in the United States *alone*—and if they knew that *I* was here," he said, "every damned one of them would be on his way here in five minutes to get us out!"

"Lord! Lord!" said Robert, in a kind of mournful brooding ululation, as if he had not heard Blake's words at all. "Who'd have thought it? A young attorney just admitted to the bar six weeks ago and here he is in jail! The damnedest thing I ever heard of!" he declared.

"Yes, sir," Blake declared, not by way of response, but with the same self-centred concentration on the indignity which had been visited on him. "If you told any Blake dealer in the country that George Blake's nephew was down here in the Blackstone jail, he wouldn't believe you. Uncle George will carry this thing to the Supreme Court when we get out," he said. "It is certainly a hell of a thing to happen to George Blake's nephew!"

"Yes, sir," Robert answered, "a hell of a thing to happen is *right*—and here I've only had my license to practise, for six weeks. Why, it's awful!" he said solemnly.

"Robert!" Blake cried suddenly, getting to his feet.—"Do you guess these damned Blackstone cops know who I am? Do you guess they realize they've got George Blake's nephew here?" Here he went to the door of his cell, rattled it violently, and yelled: "Hey—y! I'm George Blake's nephew! Do you know you've got George Blake's nephew back here? Come and let me out!" he shouted. No one answered.

Then they would be silent for a while, and mournful, brooding drunken time would pass around them.

Then Blake would say:

"Robert?"

"What do you want?" said Robert mournfully.

"What time is it?"

"Hell, how do I know what time it is," said Robert in a sullen and protesting tone. "You know they took my watch." Then there would be silence for a moment more.

"Emmet?" Robert would then say.

"All right. What is it?"

"Did they take your watch, too?"

"Yes!" Blake shouted suddenly in an angry and excited tone. "And that was an eighteen carat, thirty-two jewel platinum-case watch that Uncle George bought for me in Switzerland. That watch is worth $225 and I'd better get it back when I get out of here!" he shouted rattling the door. "Do you hear? If those sons-of-bitches try to steal my watch, my Uncle George will put 'em *all* in jail! I want it back!" he shouted.

No one answered.

Then they were silent for another spell of time, and finally Robert said in a hoarse, brooding, and mournful tone.

"Eugene?"

"Well."

"Are you there?"

"Where the hell do you think I am?" Eugene said bitterly. "You don't see any holes in this place you can crawl out of, do you?"

Robert laughed his hoarse falsetto laugh, and then said with a kind of brooding wonder:

"Lord! Lord! Who'd have thought it? Who'd ever have thought Eugene and I would get put in jail together here in Blackstone, South Carolina. Here I am just out of Yale and admitted to the bar six weeks ago and you boy!" he laughed suddenly his annoying falsetto laugh, and concluded—"Just got back from three years at Harvard and here you are in jail already! Lord! Lord! What are you going to tell your mother when she sees you? What's she going to say when you tell her you've been in jail?"

"Oh, I don't know!" the other said angrily. "Shut up!"

Robert laughed his annoying falsetto laugh again, and said:

"Boy! I'd hate to have to face her! I'm glad I'm not in *your* shoes!"

"Not in *my* shoes!" the other shouted in an exasperated tone. "You damned fool, you are in my shoes!"

Then they were silent for a spell, and gray time ticked wearily around them the slow remorseless sound of its interminable minutes.

Presently Blake spoke, out of a drunken silence, saying:

"Gant?"

"What is it?"

"What time is it now?"

"I don't know. They have my watch," he said.

And gray time ticked around them.

"Robert," Eugene said at length, straightening from his dejected stupor on the cot, "did you see that nigger?"

"What nigger?" Robert said stupidly.

"Why the nigger they tried to put in here with me!" he said.

"Why, I didn't see any nigger, Gene," said Robert in a hoarse and drunken tone of mild and melancholy protest. "When was this?"

"Why, Robert!" the other boy now cried in an excited voice, and with a feeling of hideous dread inside him. "You were right here all the time! Didn't you hear us?"

"Why, no, Eugene," Robert answered in a slow protesting voice that had dull wonder and surprise in it. "I didn't hear anything," he said.

"Why, my God, Robert!" Eugene now cried excitedly, and even with a kind of frenzy in his tone. "You must have heard us! Why, we were fighting here for ten minutes!" he said, for the time of the struggle now seemed at least that long to him.

"Who?" said Robert, dully and stupidly.

"Why, me and those two big cops!" he cried. "Good God, Robert, didn't you see us?—didn't you hear us?—butting and kicking like a goat—hitting me over the head, trying to make me turn a-loose!" he cried in an excited, almost incoherent tone.

"Who did?" Robert stupidly inquired.

"Why—those two big cops, Robert—that's who! Good God, do you mean to tell me that you never heard us when we were cursing and butting away there right in front of you!"

"I didn't hear anything—I thought you said a nigger," he said in a stupid and confused tone.

"Why, Robert, that's what I'm telling you!" Eugene shouted. "They had him in here——"

"Where?"

"Why, in the cell! They were trying to put me in here with him! That's what the trouble was about!" he said.

"Why, Eugene," Robert said with an uneasy and troubled laugh, which yet had a note of good-natured derision in it that was maddening, "I didn't see any nigger. Did you, Emmet? I was right here all the time and I didn't hear any trouble. . . . *You've* been dreaming," Robert now said, with a conviction in his tone that goaded the other boy almost past endurance, and yet struck a knife of cold terror into his heart. And he began to laugh hoarsely his annoying and derisive laugh, as he shook his head, and said: "Lord! *Lord!*—He's in there seeing niggers and policemen and I don't know what-all." And here he laughed hoarsely again, his derisive and falsetto laugh, and said: *"Boy! You've got 'em! You've got 'em bad! You've been seeing things!"*

"Robert, God-damn it!" Eugene now fairly screamed, "I tell you he was here! I tell you I saw him standing in the cell when I came in! I know what I'm talking about, Robert!—there was a nigger here when I came in!"

"Why, hell, Eugene!" Robert said more kindly, but with a hoarse derisive laugh, "you've just been seeing things, son. There was no one there; you just imagined it. I reckon you just passed out and dreamed it happened!"

"Dreamed! Dreamed!" Eugene shouted, "God-damn it, Robert, don't you think I know when I'm dreaming? I'll show you if it was a dream! I'll prove it to you that it really happened! I can prove it by Blake!" he cried. "Ask Blake! . . . Blake! Blake! Blake!" he shouted.

And gray time slid with its slow sanded drop around them.

Blake did not answer: he had not heard their conversation and now they heard him talking softly, slowly, murderously to himself.

"Yes, sir," he was saying, in a low, quiet, drunkenly intent soliloquy. "Yes, sir, I'll kill him! . . . So help me God, I'll kill him dead, as sure as my name is Emmet Blake! . . . I'll pull out my forty-five. . . . I'll get my forty-five out, when I go home . . . and I'll go Ping! Ping! Ping! the minute that I see him. I'll go Ping! Ping! Ping!" cried Blake. "I'll kill him dead, so help me God, if it's the last thing that I ever do!"

"I'll kill him!" Blake continued in a tone of dogged, drunken repetition, still talking to himself. "When I get home I'll kill him if it's the last thing I ever do!"

"And I'll kill *you,* too," Blake muttered in this same brooding and intent oblivion of drunken soliloquy. "You God-damned whore, I'll kill you, too! I'll kill the two of you together! . . . The bitch! The bitch! The dirty bitch!" the man now screamed, starting to his feet, and now really with a tortured note of agony and desperation in his voice. "I know where you are this minute! I know you're with him! I know you'll sleep with him tonight, you—dirty—lowdown——"

"Emmet, you damned fool, shut up!" Robert now said, with a troubled and protesting laugh. "Do you want every one in the whole damned place to hear you?" The dreadful shame and anguish in the man's desperate life had burst nakedly through his drunkenness, and the hideous mutilation of his soul was suddenly stripped bare— "Don't talk like that," said Robert, with a troubled laugh—"you'll be sorry to-morrow for what you said, you know you will: oh, Emmet, shut up!" Robert said again with a protesting and embarrassed laugh.

For Blake was now sobbing horribly in his cell: as Eugene stood leaning against the wall next to him, he could hear him sobbing, and pounding his thin fist savagely into the gray-slate substance of the wall, while he went on:

"The whore! The dirty whore!" he wept. "I know that she's just waiting for me to die! I know that's what she wants! I know that's all she's waiting for! . . . That's what you want, you bitch, isn't it? You'd like that, wouldn't you? That would just suit you, wouldn't it? . . . Ah, I've fooled you! I've fooled you, haven't I?" he panted, with a savage and vindictive triumph in his voice. "You've been waiting for it for the last two years, haven't you? And I've fooled you every time," he gasped. "And I'll fool you yet—you bitch, you dirty bitch!"

And they sat there, saying nothing, listening with desolation in their hearts to the man's naked shame, and now hearing nothing but his gasping sobs, and the slow gray wear and waste of time around them. And then his sobbing breath grew quieter, they could hear him panting feebly like an exhausted runner, and presently he went over and sat down upon his cot, and there was nothing but time and silence all about them.

Finally Blake spoke again, and now in a voice that was quiet, lifeless, and curiously sober, as if this outlet and easance of his grief had also quenched the drunkenness in him.

"Gant?" he said, in a quiet and lifeless tone that penetrated curiously the gray silence all around them.

"Yes," said Eugene.

"I never met you till today," said Blake, "and I want you to know I've got no grudge against you."

"Why, Eugene never did anything to you, Emmet," said Robert at this point, in a tone of protest. "Why should you have anything against him?"

"Now, *wait* a minute!" said Blake pugnaciously. "Eugene," he went on in a maudlin tone of voice, "I'm friends with every one. I haven't got an enemy in the world, . . . There's just one man in this world I hate," he went on sombrely, "and I hate his guts—I hate his life—God-damn him! I hate the air he breathes!" he snarled, and then was silent for a moment. "Eugene," he went on in a moment, in a low voice, and with a tone of brooding drunken insinuation, "you know the man I mean, don't you?"

Eugene made no answer, and in a moment he repeated the question, in a more insistent and pugnacious tone:

"*Don't* you?" he demanded.

And Eugene said, "Yes."

"You're damned right you do," he said in a low, ruminant, and brooding tone. "Everybody knows who I mean. He's a cousin of yours," said Blake, and then began to mutter to himself:

"I'll kill him! So help me God, I'll kill him!" And suddenly, starting from his cot with a scream of baffled misery and anguish, he began to beat his fist into the hard slate wall again, yelling:

"I'll kill you! I'll kill you! . . . You son-of-a-bitch, I'll kill the two of you! . . . I'll send you both to hell where you belong, if it's the last thing that I ever do!"

And he began to sob horribly and curse foully, and pounded his fist into the wall again until he was exhausted, and went back and sat down on his cot again, muttering his drunken and impotent threats.

And Eugene did not try to answer him, for there was nothing he could say. George Pentland was his cousin, and had taken Blake's wife away from him, and got her love; and Blake was dying, and they knew it. And suddenly, it seemed to Eugene that there was in this whole story something dark, and hideously shameful, which he had never clearly seen in life before, which could not be endured, and which yet suspended over every man who ever lived the menace of its intolerable humiliation and dishonor.

For, to see a man—a manly-looking man, strong of body, fearless and bold of glance, deep of voice—physically humiliated and disgraced, slapped and whipped like a cur before his wife, his mistress, or his children, and forced to yield, retreat and slink away, to see his face turn white and the look of the coward shine through his mask of manhood, is not an easy thing to see.

Presently, they heard steps coming along the corridor again, and they were so certain they belonged to a messenger bringing them release that they all arose instinctively, and stood before the barred doors of the cells, waiting to walk out into the air of freedom again. To their astonishment the visitor was Kitchin. They had forgotten him completely, and now as they saw him doing a gleeful caper before their cells, with a grin of triumphant satisfaction written wide across his face, they looked at him with the astounded recognition of men who see a face which they had known years before, but have forgotten—in the lapse of time and memory.

"Where?—" Robert began hoarsely and accusingly, in a tone of astounded stupefaction. "Where have *you* been all this time?"

"Out front!" said Kitchin exultantly. "Sitting in your car!"

"Out front!" cried Robert in a bewildered and resentful tone. "Didn't they lock you up, too?"

"Hell, no!" cried Kitchin, fairly dancing about with gleeful satisfaction. "They never touched me! And I'd had as much to drink as any of you. I've been sittin' out front all afternoon reading the paper! I guess they thought I was the only sober one of the crowd," he said modestly. And this apparently was the reason for his astonishing freedom—this and another, more mercenary reason, which will presently be apparent.

"Why, what do they mean by keeping us locked up back here while you're out front there reading the paper? Darnedest thing I ever heard of!" Robert barked. "Kitchin!" he now said angrily. "You go out there and tell them we want out of here!"

"I told 'em! I told 'em!" Kitchin said virtuously. "That's what I've been telling them all afternoon."

"Well, what do they say?" Robert demanded impatiently.

"Boys," said Kitchin now, shaking his head regretfully, but unable to conceal his own elation and sense of triumph, "I've got news for you—and I'm afraid it's not going to be good news, either. How much money you got?"

"Money!" Robert cried, in an astounded tone, as if the uses of this vile commodity had never occurred to him. "What's money got to do with it? We want out of here!"

"I know you do," said Kitchin coolly, "but you're not going to get out unless you've got money enough to pay your fine."

"Fine?" Robert repeated stupidly.

"Well, that's what they call it anyway. Fine or graft, or whatever the hell it is, you've got to pay it if you want to be let out."

"How much is it?" said Robert. "How much do they want?"

"Boys," said Kitchin, slowly and solemnly, "have you got seventy-three dollars?"

"Seventy-three dollars!" Robert shouted. "Kitchin, what are you talking about?"

"Well, don't shout at me," said Kitchin. "I can't help it! I didn't do it! But if you get out of here that's what you've got to pay."

"Seventy-three dollars!" Robert cried. "Seventy-three dollars for what?"

"Well, Robert," said Kitchin patiently, "you've got to pay fifty dollars fine and one dollar costs. That's because you were driving the car. That's fifty-one. And Emmet and Eugene here have to pay ten dollars apiece and one dollar costs—that's twenty-two dollars more. That figures up to seventy-three dollars. Have you got it?"

"Why, the dirty grafting sons-of-bitches!" Blake now cried. "Telling us that everything would be all right and that they had put us in here so we wouldn't hurt ourselves! . . . All right, you cheap grafting bastards!" he shouted at the top of his lungs, rattling the barred door furiously as he spoke. "We'll give you your dirty graft—but wait till I get out of here!" he cried threateningly. "Just wait till I get out! George Blake will tend to you!" he shouted. "It'll be the worst day's work *you've* ever done!"

But no one answered, although Blake and Robert cursed foully and shouted insults at the men. Meanwhile, Kitchin waited patiently before their cells until the furious tumult should subside a little; when they were calmer he suggested that they pool their resources to see if they had enough to pay the total of the fines. But the sum of their combined funds was only a little more than forty dollars, of which Blake and Robert contributed the greater part, and of which Eugene could contribute less than three dollars, which was all he had.

When it was apparent that their total funds would not be adequate to secure their release Blake, still furiously angry, began to talk in a loud and drunken tone of bravado about his famous uncle, scrawling out a check and instructing Kitchin to go at once to the local agent for his uncle's motor cars and get the necessary money:

"Any Blake dealer in the country will cash my personal check for fifty thousand dollars any time I need it!" he cried with extravagant boast, as if he thought this threat of opulence would strike terror to the hearts of the police. "Yes, sir!" he said. "All you got to do is to walk into any Blake agency in the country and tell them George Blake's nephew needs money—and they'll give you everything they've got!" he cried. "Tell 'em you need ten thousand dollars," he said, coming down in scale somewhat, "and they'll have it for you in five minutes."

"Why, Emmet," said Kitchin quietly, and yet with a trace of mockery and ridicule on his dark, handsome, and rather sly face. "We don't need fifty thousand dollars. You know, we're not trying to buy the whole damned jail. Now, I thought," he went on quietly and ironically, "that all we needed was about thirty or forty—say fifty dollars—to make up the fine and get us out of town."

"Yes," said Robert in a quick excited tone of vigorous agreement. "You're absolutely right! That's all we need, all right!"

"All *right!* All *right!* Go to the Blake dealer! Go to the Blake dealer! That's what I'm telling you," cried Blake with an arrogant impatience. "He'll give you anything you want.—What are you waiting for?" he cried furiously. "Go *on!* Go *on!*"

"But Emmet," said Kitchin quietly and reasonably, in his dark low voice, as he looked at the check which Blake had scrawled out for him. "This check you've given me is for five hundred dollars. Hadn't you better make out another one for fifty? You know, we don't need five hundred dollars, Emmet. And besides," he suggested tactfully, "the man might not have that much on hand. Hadn't you better give me one just made out for what we need?"

"He'll have it! He's got it! He's *got* to have it!" said Blake with a dogmatic and unreasoning arrogance. "Tell him I sent you and you'll get the money right away!"

Kitchin did not answer him: he thrust the check into his pocket and turned to Eugene, saying quietly:

"Didn't you say your brother was waiting to meet you here at a hotel?"

"Yes: he expected to meet me at four o'clock when that service car came in."

"At what hotel?"

"The Blackstone—listen, Kitchin," he reached through the bar and grabbed him by the arm, with a feeling of cold horror in his heart. "For Christ's sake, don't drag my brother into this," he whispered. "Kitchin—listen to me! If you can get this money from the Blake agent here, for God's sake, do it! What's the use of bringing my brother in to it," he pleaded, "when it's all between the four of us, and can stay that way? I don't want my family to know I ever got into any trouble like this. Kitchin, look here—I can get the money for my fine: I've got a little money in the bank, and I'll pay Blake every cent I owe him if you get the money from the agent. Now, promise me you won't go and tell my brother!"

He held him hard in the tension of desperation, and Kitchin promised. Then he went swiftly away, and they were left alone in their cells again. Robert, utterly cast down from his high exaltation, now cursed bitterly and morosely against the police, and the injustice of his luck and destiny.

Meanwhile, Blake, whose final and chief resource, it had now become pitifully evident, was nothing in himself, but just the accident of birth that had made him nephew to a powerful and wealthy man, kept declaring in a loud tone of arrogant bravado that "any Blake agent in the United States will cash my personal check for fifty thousand dollars any time I ask for it! Yes, sir, any of them—I don't give a damn where it is! He's on his way here now! You'll see! We'll be out of here in five minutes now!"—a boastful assurance that was hardly out of his mouth before they heard steps approaching rapidly along the corridor and, even as Blake cried out triumphantly, "What did I tell you?" and as Eugene leaped up and ran to the door of his cell, clutching the bars with both hands, and peering out with bloodshot eyes like a caged gorilla, Kitchin entered the cell-room, followed by a policeman, and—Eugene's brother!

Luke looked at him for a moment with a troubled expression and said: "Why, how did you get in here? What's happened to you?" he said, suddenly noticing his battered face. "Are you hurt, Eugene?"

The boy made no reply but looked at him with sullen desperation and jerked his head towards the cells where his two companions were imprisoned—a gesture that pled savagely for silence. And Luke, instantly reading the meaning of that gesture, turned and called out cheerfully:

"Now you boys just hold on a minute and I'll have you out of here."

Then he came up close to the barred door of the cell where his younger brother stood and, his face stern with care, he said in a low voice: "What happened? Who hit you? Did any of these bastards hit you? I want to know."

A policeman was standing behind him looking at them with narrowed eyes, and the boy said desperately:

"Get us out of here. I'll tell you later."

Then Luke went away with the policeman to pay their fines. When he had gone, Eugene turned bitterly on Kitchin, who had remained with the boys, accusing him of breaking his word by going to Luke. Kitchin's dark evasive eyes shifted nervously in his head as he answered:

"Well, what else could I do? I went to the Blake agent here——"

"Did you get the money?" Blake said. "Did he give it to you?"

"Give!" Kitchin said curtly, with a sneer. "He gave me nothing—not a damned cent! He said he'd never heard of you!"

There was silence for a moment.

"Well, I can't understand that," Blake said at length, feebly, and in a tone of dazed surprise. "That's the first time anything like that has ever happened."

At this moment Eugene's brother returned with two policemen who unlocked the cell doors and let them out. The feeling of coming from the cell into free space again was terrific in its physical intensity: never before had Eugene known the physical sensations of release as he knew them at that moment. The very light and air in the space outside the cell had a soaring buoyancy and freshness which, by comparison, gave to that within the cell a material and oppressive heaviness, a sense of walled and mortared space that had pressed upon his heart and spirit with a crushing weight. Now, suddenly, as if a cord that bound him had been cut, or a brutal hand that held his life in its compelling grip had been removed, the sensations of release and escape filled his body with a sense of aerial buoyancy and the power of wing-like flight.

With a desperate eagerness he had never felt before he wanted to feel the free light and air again: even the shocked solicitude of his companions when they saw his puffed lips and his blackened eye was drearily oppressive. He thrust past them, muttering, striding towards the door.

It was the first time in his life that he had ever been arrested and locked up, and for the first time now, he felt and understood the meaning of an immense and brutal authority in life, which he had seen before, but to which he had always believed himself to be immune. Until that day, he had had all the pride and arrogance a young man knows. Since childhood no one had ever compelled him to do anything by force, and although he had seen the million evidences of force, privilege, and compulsion applied to the lives of people around him, so that like every other native of the land in which he lived, he had in his heart no belief in law whatever, and knew that legal justice, where it was achieved, was achieved by fortuitous accident rather than by intent, he had believed, as every young man believes, that his own life and body were fiercely immune to every indignity of force and compulsion.

Now this feeling was gone forever. And having lost it irrecoverably, he had gained something of more value.

For now, he was conscious, even at the moment he came out of the cell, of a more earthly, common, and familiar union with the lives of other men than he had ever known. And this experience was to have another extraordinary effect upon his spirit and its understanding and love of poetry, which may seem ludicrous, but which certainly dated from these few hours of his first imprisonment. Up to this time in his life, the poet who had stirred him by his power and genius more than any other was the poet Shelley.

But in the years that followed, Shelley's poetry came to have so little meaning for him, that all the magic substance which his lines once had was lost, and Eugene seemed to look indifferently at the hollow shells and ghosts of words, from which all enchantment and belief had vanished. And he felt this way not because the words of this great poet now seemed false to him, but because, more than any other poet he had known, Shelley was the poet of that time of life when men feel most strongly the sense of proud and lonely inviolability, which is legible in everything he wrote, and when their spirits, like his, are also "tameless and swift and proud." And this is a time of life and magic that, once gone, is gone forever, and that may never be recaptured save by memory.

But in the years that followed, just as Eugene's physical body grew coarser and more heavy, and his sensual appetites increased enormously, so also did the energy of his spirit, which in childhood had been wing-like, soaring, and direct in its aerial buoyancy, grow darker, slower, heavier, smouldering and slow in its beginning heat, and densely woven and involved in all its web-like convolutions.

And as all the strength and passion of his life turned more and more away from its childhood thoughts of aerial flight and escape into some magic and unvisited domain, it seemed to him that the magic and unvisited domain was the earth itself, and all the life around him—that he must escape not out of life but into it, looking through walls he never had seen before, exploring the palpable and golden substance of this earth as it had never been explored, finding, somehow, the word, the key, the door, to the glory of a life more fortunate and happy than any man has ever known, and which yet incredibly, palpably, is his, even as the earth beneath his feet is his, if he could only take it.

And as he discovered this, Eugene turned more and more for food and comfort to those poets who have found it, and who have left great pieces of that golden earth behind them in their verse, as deathless evidence that they were there:—those poets who wrote not of the air but of the earth, and in whose verse the gold and glory of the earth is treasured—their names are Shakespeare, Spenser, Chaucer, Herrick, Donne, and Herbert.

Their names are Milton (whom fools have called glacial and austere, and who wrote the most tremendous lines of earthly passion and sensuous magic that have ever yet been written), Wordsworth, Browning, Whitman, Keats, and Heine—their names are Job, Ecclesiastes, Homer, and The Song of Solomon.

These are their names, and if any man should think the glory of the earth has never been, let him live alone with them, as Eugene did, a thousand nights of solitude and wonder, and they will reveal to him again the golden glory of the earth, which is the only earth that is, and is forever, and is the only earth that lives, the only one that will never die.

XLIV

WHEN they got out into the street again, night had almost come. It was about six o'clock, the lights in the streets had gone on, and in the figures of the people that went by, and the motor cars that flashed past sparsely, there was something hurried, mournful, and departing, like the breath of autumn and old leaves stirred by wind and driven on.

Neither spoke for some time, nor dared look at the other: the boy walked with lowered head, his hat pulled down across his eyes. His lips were puffed and swollen, and his left eye was now entirely closed, a blind poached swelling of bruised blue. They passed below a street lamp, paused for a minute in the hard white glare, turned as if impelled by sombre instinct, and regarded each other with the stern defenseless eye of shame and sorrow. Luke looked earnestly at his brother for a second and then said gently:

"How's your eye, Eugene?"

The boy said nothing: sullenly, steadily, with his one good eye he returned his brother's look. Luke stared for a minute at the nauseous, fatted purple where the bad eye was, suddenly cursed bitterly, turned, and walked ahead.

"The d-d-dirty bastards!" he said. "I've always f'ought they were a f-f-fairly decent lot till now, but the nice, damned, d-d-d-dirty South

Car'lina—" he ground his teeth together, paused again, and turned to-wards his younger brother: "What d-d-did they do to you while you were in there? I w-w-w-want to know what happened."

"I guess I got what was coming to me," the boy muttered. "We were all drunk, and we were driving pretty fast. So I want you to know that I'm not making any excuses for that."

"Well," Luke said quietly, "that's all over now, and there's no use to w-w-worry about it. I guess you're not the f-f-f-first one that it's hap-pened to. So let's f-f-forget about that." He was silent for a moment, and then he went on sternly, "But if those b-b-bastards beat you up while you were in there I w-w-w-want to know about it."

"I'm not kicking about it," the boy muttered again, because he was ashamed to tell him of the struggle he had had with the two police-men. "I guess I had it coming—but there was one thing!" he said with a surge of bitter feeling as he remembered it. "They did one thing I don't believe they had any right to do. If it had happened in the North it would have been all right, but, by God, I don't believe they have any right in this State to put a white man in the same cell with a nigger!"

"Did they d-d-d-do that to you?" Luke cried in an excited voice, stop-ping short and half turning as he spoke.

"Yes, they did, they tried to," and then he told him what had hap-pened.

Luke turned completely, and started back towards the station, cursing bitterly.

"C-c-come on!" he said.

"Where are you going?"

"I'm g-g-g-going down there and tell those b-b-b-bastards what I f'ink of them!"

"No, you're not! Listen!" Eugene seized his brother by the arm. "We'll only get locked up again! They've got us and we've got to take it! We're not going! Let's get out of this damned town quick as we can! I never want to see the place again!"

Luke paused and stood, distractedly thrusting his fingers through his hair.

"All right," he said at last. "We'll go. . . . But by G-g-god," his voice rose suddenly and he shook his fist in the direction of the station, "I'll be back. I've done business in this town for years, I've got f-f-f-friends here who are going goddam well to know the reason why a kid is beaten up and locked up with a n-n-nigger by the Blackstone cops. I'll see this f'ing through now if it t-t-t-takes a life-time!" Then, turning to his brother, he said shortly: "All right, Gene. C-c-come on. We're g-g-getting out of town."

Without further speech, they walked on down the street until they came to the place where Luke's car was parked.

"W-w-w-what do you want to d-d-d-do, Gene?" he said quietly. "Do you want to go over to D-d-Daisy's tonight?"

The boy shook his head: "No," he said thickly. "Home. Home. Let's get out of here. Got to go home now."

Luke said nothing for a moment, thrusting his fingers through his hair. "W-w-w-well," he muttered at length, "perhaps you're right."

XLV

THEY left town at once.

Luke drove savagely going out of town. He kept his big clumsy hands gripped hard upon the rim of the steering wheel, his brow knit and furrowed by its ridge of wrinkles, his face taut and drawn from the tension of his nerves. From time to time he would thrust his clumsy fingers strongly through his flashing mass of hair, laugh a wild jeering "whah-whah" of rage and exasperation, and then say in a voice so packed with sneering bitterness and contempt that it was hard to keep from laughing at him:

"S—t! Resisting an officer in the p-p-p-p-performance of his duties! Now ain't that nice?" he said in a voice of mincing refinement and daintiness. "W-w-w-wy the nice neat nigger-Baptist God-damned sons-of-bitches!" he snarled. "The cheap grafting South Car'lina bastards! D-d-d-d-disorderly conduct! S—t!" he snarled with a savage, dainty, mincing bitterness that was somehow wildly and explosively funny.

Meanwhile, they were speeding along through quiet streets that even in the night-time had the worn and faded dustiness of autumn, past withered lawns, by frame houses which had the same faded dusty look, and under trees on which the dry leaves hung and fluttered: the mournful, worn, weary feeling told of departed summer, evoked sadly the memory of a savage heat, and the sorrowful ghosts and omens of the autumn were everywhere about them. October was there with its strange, brooding presences of sorrow and delight—its sense of something lost and vanished, gone forever, its still impending prescience of something grand and wild to come. Above them the ragged cloudy sky had cleared: it was a night of blazing and magnificent stars, set in the limitless velvet substance of the sky, burning with faint brilliance and without light over the immense, mysterious, and mournful-looking earth.

Twice, going out of town, his brother stopped, and both times with a kind of sudden indecisive after-thought. Once, when they had passed a little corner drug-store, he jammed the breaks on suddenly, bringing the car to such an abrupt and jolting halt that Eugene was flung forward violently against the wind-shield. He turned to him with a nervous and distracted air of indecision, saying:

"Do you f-f-f-fink you could go a dope?" (this was the word in common use for Coca Cola) "W-w-w-would you like a drink?" he said, with a comical thrusting movement of the head, a wild look in his eyes, a restless and stammering indecision and earnestness. The boy told him no, and after a worried and restless look of his flickering gray eyes, in the direction of the drug store, he thrust his large flat foot into the clutch and started the car in motion again, with the same violent and jarring movement as when he had halted.

Again, on the very outposts of the town, where there was nothing but the dusty road, a few cheap frame houses, sparely, flimsily, and carelessly built upon the breast of an immense and formless land, which seemed indifferent to them and with which they seemed to have no union, and with nothing but the road, the stars and the huge mysteries of the earth before them, his brother had halted with another jarring jolt, when they had flashed past a filling station where, so read a sign, soft drinks and barbecued sandwiches were for sale.

"How about a b-b-b-barbecued sandwich?" he demanded, looking at Eugene with a wild and glaring suddenness. "C-c-c-could you go one? Huh?"—he said, almost barking at him, with a comical thrusting movement of the head. But even before the boy could answer, and he saw the sullen and exasperated scowl upon his face, he thrust his fingers wildly through his hair, burst into a wild rich "whah-whah" of crazy laughter —a laughter that was all the more strange and astonishing because even as he laughed, the taut and drawn tension of his face and nerves, and the frenzied unrest of his eyes, were terribly apparent—and then started the car in motion again with a jarring, grinding and convulsive jolt. And Luke could not have said why he had halted at these last two outposts of the town—the drug store and the filling station—but certainly the impulse that had made him halt, had little to do with food or drink, for neither of them was hungry, and they had no need or desire for further nourishment.

But the impulse which had made his brother halt belonged to all the dissonance and frenzied unrest of his whole life, and by thousands of actions such as this, the course and pattern of his life was shaped. And finally, his brother had halted because those two small flares of light—pitiful and shabby as they were—had wakened in him a memory of the vast darkness of the huge and lonely earth before them, and because he gave himself into this dark regretfully, and with some misgiving of his soul.

For his spirit was afraid of solitude and darkness and, like all men in this land, his soul was drawn by the small hard blaze of incandescence —even by those barren bulbous clusters of hard light upon the wintry midnight pavements of a little town—which somehow pitifully and terribly suggest the fear and loneliness in men's souls, the small hard assurances of manufactured light which they have gathered as some beacon of comfort and security against a dark too vast and terrible, an earth too savage in its rudeness, space, and emptiness, for the spirit and the strength of men.

And now his brother and he were given to this earth, this dark, this loneliness again. And as they rushed on into the darkness, held, save for the throbbing motor of the little car, in the immutable silence of the earth and darkness, the flickering headlights of the car would suddenly pierce into the huge surrounding mystery of night, lunging for an instant the flashing finger of their light upon some fugitive and secret presence in the vault of night, where all the million lives of men were held. Sometimes, the flashing light would blaze upon the boarding of a little house at the bend of the road, and then the house would flash behind and be engulfed in darkness.

Sometimes, it would reveal the brown and dusty stubble of the cotton fields, a stretch of ragged pine, a lonely little wooden church, a shack, a cabin, the swift and sinuous forking of another road that spoked into their own, flashed past, and curved away—was gone forever—leaving an instant and intolerable pain and memory—a searing recognition and discovery—a road once seen but never followed and now forever lost with all its promises of a life that they had never known or explored, of faces they had never seen.

And again, out of this huge and mournful earth, out of the limitless mystery of this continent of night, the lights upon his brother's car would for an instant pick out faces, shapes, and people, and they, too, would blaze there for a moment in our vision with an intolerable and lonely briefness, and then be lost forever—and in that moment of instant parting and farewell was written the history of man's destiny—his brother's life, and that of all men living on the earth around him.

Once their lights picked out the figure of a country negro: his weary plodding figure loomed up for an instant dustily—a mournful image of bowed back, shapeless garments stained with red field earth, and clumsy brogans coated with the red dust of the road, plodding along against a terrific and desolate landscape of brown cotton fields, clay, and lonely pine, as much a part of it as the earth he walked upon, fixed instantly into it in a vision of labor, sorrow, and destiny, that was eternal.

And again they passed by negroes coming from a country church, and for a moment saw their white eyes and their black and mournful faces staring towards the light, and lost these, too, forever, and passed into a little town and out again, and saw far-off, and at its edges, a pollen of bright light above a little travelling carnival, and heard the sad wheeling music of the carousel, the mixed and woven clamor of the barker's cries, the shouts, the people's voices, and all far-faint and lost and mournful as a dream; and then the earth again—the two back wheels, clay-caked and rattling, of an ancient buggy, the lifting hooves of an old boneyard nag, that slowly turned away from the road's centre to make way for them, the slow, staring, stupid looks of wonder and astonishment of a young country fellow and his girl as they went by them—and finally, always and forever, nothing but the earth—that mournful, desolate, and lonely earth of cotton fields, and raw red clay and lonely pine, wheeling past forever in rude and formless undulations, immemorable, everlasting, and terrific, above which the great stars blazed their imperturbable and inscrutable messages of deathless calm.

And as they rushed ahead into the dark, he thought of the hundreds of times his brother had hurled himself along this road at night alone, going furiously from nowhere into nowhere, rushing ahead with starlight shining on his knit brows and his drawn face, with nothing but the lonely, mournful, and desolate red-clay earth about him, the immense, the merciless emptiness and calm of the imperturbable skies above him. And he wondered if there was anywhere on earth a goal for all his frenzy and unrest, some final dwelling-place of certitude and love for all his wandering, or if he must hurl furiously along in darkness beneath these stars forever—lost, unassuaged, and driven—until the immense and mournful earth should take him once again.

The ride back up into the hills with Luke was cold, dark, bleak, and desolate—the very painting of his own sick soul. Black night had come when they had reached the mountains. The stars were out, and around them the great bulk of the hills was barren, bleak, and wintry-looking, and there was the distant roaring of demented winds upon the hills, the lonely preludes of grim winter among the barren trees. Already, it seemed, the same landscape which only a day or two before had flamed with all the blazing colors of October, and with the enchantment which his hope and joy had given it, had been sorrowfully transformed by the mournful desolation of coming winter. The earth was no longer beautiful and friendly: it had become a waste, a desert, and a prison bleak and bare.

During the ride up the mountain into Old Catawba, the two brothers spoke seldom to each other. Luke, who had made that dark journey up into the hills a thousand times—for whom, in fact, this ceaseless hurtling along dark roads had become the very pattern of the unrest and fury that lashed his own life on forever—drove hard and raggedly, communicating perfectly to the machine he drove the tension and dissonance of his own tormented spirit. This wordless instrument of steel and brass and leather seemed, in fact, to start, halt, jolt, stammer, and lunge fiercely onward as if it had a brain and spirit of its own that was in anguished sympathy with the tortured nerves that governed it. His brother drove, bent forward tensely, his large clumsy hands gripped hard and nervously upon the steering wheel, as he peered out upon the ribbon of road before him, which bent and twisted in a bewildering serpentine that curved constantly upward along the slopes and flanks of the dark mountainside. The boy sat cold and numb and sick at heart, hands thrust in pockets, his hat pulled low across his eyes, his overcoat turned up around his neck. He glanced at his brother once or twice. He could see his face drawn and taut and furrowed in the dim light, but when he tried to speak to him he could not. The sense of ruin, shame, and failure which filled his spirit seemed so abysmal and complete that there was nothing left to say. And he faced the meeting with his mother and his sister with a sick heart of dread.

Once going up the mountainside his brother stopped, jamming his huge flat foot so rudely onto the brake that the car halted with a jarring shuddering thud. They had just passed a road of unpaved clay which led off from the mountain road towards the right, and towards a farm house and a light or two which were clearly visible.

Now, looking nervously and uncertainly toward this house, Luke muttered, almost to himself, thrusting his hand through his hair with a distracted movement as he spoke: "Wy-wy-wy-I f'ink we could g-g-g-get a drink in here wy—if you'd like one. Wy-wy-I know the old fellow who lives there . . . he's a moonshiner—wy-wy-I f'ink—would you like to stop?" he said abruptly and then, getting no answer from the younger one, he gave another worried and uncertain look in the direction of the house, thrust his fingers through his hair, and muttered to himself "W-w-w-well, perhaps you're right—maybe it's j-j-j-just as well if we g-g-g-get home wy-wy-wy I guess that Mama will be waiting up for us."

When they reached town, the hour was late, the streets had a wintry, barren, and deserted look, and the lights burned dim: from time to time another motor car would flash by them speedily, but they saw few people. As they drove across the Square, it seemed almost to have been frozen in a cataleptic silence, the bulbous clusters of the street lamps around the Square burned with a hard and barren radiance—a ghastly mocking of life, of metropolitan gaiety, in a desert scene from which all life had by some pestilence or catastrophe of nature been extinguished. The fountain in the square pulsed with a cold breezeless jet, and behind the greasy windows of a lunch room he could see a man in a dim light, seated on a stool and drinking coffee, and the swart muscular Greek leaned over the counter, his furrowed inch of brow painfully bent upon the columns of a newspaper.

As they turned into the street where stood his mother's house, and sloped swiftly down the hill toward home, his brother, in a tone that tried in vain to be matter-of-fact, and to conceal the concern and pain which his own generous spirit felt because of the feeling of defeat, failure, and desperation which was now legible in every word and gesture of the younger one, began to speak to him in a nervous, almost pleading voice:

"N-n-now I f'ink," he began, thrusting his big hand through his hair, —"I—wy I f'ink when we get home wy—I just wouldn't say anything to Mama about—wy-wy about that trouble—wy—that we had in Blackstone—wy—at all!" he blurted out. "Wy-wy-wy—frankly, I mean it!" he continued earnestly, as he brought the car to a jolting halt before the

house. "Wy-wy—if I were in your p-p-place, John—wy I'd just forget it.
. . . It's all over now—and it would only worry M-m-m-mama if you
t-t-told her about it— Wy-wy—the whole f'ing's over now . . . those—
wy—those cheap Nigger-Baptist South Car'lina sons-of-bitches—wy-wy
—just saw the chance of m-m-making a martyr of you—so I'd j-j-just forget about it— It's all over now— Wy-wy—f-f-f-forget it!" he cried earnestly. "I—I—wy I wouldn't f'ink about it again!"

But the younger one, seeing the light that burned warmly behind the
drawn shades of the parlor, set his sick heart and his grim face desperately towards the light, shook his head silently, and then walked grimly
towards the house.

He found his mother and his sister seated together in the parlor before the fire. In another moment, almost before their first startled
words of greeting were out of their mouths, he was blurting out the
story of his drunkenness, arrest, and imprisonment. As he went on, he
could see his mother's face white, serious, eagerly curious, fixed upon
him, and her powerful, deliberate, and curiously flexible mouth which
she pursed constantly, darting her eyes at him from time to time with
the quick, startled attentiveness of an animal or a bird, as she said
sharply: "Hah? . . . What say? . . . The police, you say? . . . Jail?
. . . Who was with you—hah? Emmet Blake? . . . Weaver? . . .
How much did they fine you—hah?"

Meanwhile his sister sat listening quietly, with an absent yet intent
look in her eyes, stroking her large cleft chin in a reflective manner with
her big hand, smiling a little, and saying from time to time:

"Ah-hah? . . . and what did Blake say then? . . . What did you say
to the nigger when you saw him in the cell? . . . Ah-hah. . . . They
didn't abuse you, did they? . . . Did they hurt you when they hit you?
. . . Ah-hah. . . . And what did Luke say when he saw you looking
through the bars?" She snickered hoarsely, and then taking him by the
hand, turned to her mother and in a kindly yet derisive tone, said:

"Here's your Harvard boy. . . . What do you think of your baby
now?" And seeing the gloomy and miserable look upon his face, she
laughed her high, husky, and derisive falsetto, prodding him in the ribs
with her big finger, saying: "K-k-k-k! . . . This is our Harvard boy!
. . . Hi, hi, hi, hi, hi! . . . Here's your baby son, Miss Eliza!" Then
releasing his hand, and turning to her mother, she said in a good-natured tone, in which yet a kind of melancholy satisfaction was evident:

"Well, you see, don't you? . . . It just goes to show you, doesn't it? . . . I knew it all the time. . . . It just goes to show that we're all the same beneath the skin. . . . We're all alike. . . . We all like the stuff . . . with all his book education and going off to Harvard, he's no different from Papa, when you come down to it," she concluded with a note of sombre brooding satisfaction in her voice.

"Wy-wy-wy—" he could see Luke teetering nervously from one huge flat foot to another, thrusting his huge hand distractedly through his flashing hair as he attempted to stammer out an earnest and excited defense and justification for his disgrace:

"Wy-wy-wy I don't believe that Gene was drunk at all!" he stammered. "Wy I f'ink wy—that he j-j-j-just had the bad luck to wy to f-f-f-fall in with that gang when they were drinking and and and—wy I f'ink those wy those B-B-B-B-Blackstone bastards just saw a chance wy of collecting a wy a little graft and and and wy j-j-just made Gene the goat. Wy f-f-f-frankly I don't believe he was drunk at all. . . . Wy I doubt it very much," he said, thrusting his fingers through his hair. "F-f-f-frankly, I do."

"I was drunk!" the boy muttered sullenly and miserably. "Drunker than any of them. . . . I was the worst of the lot."

"You see, don't you?" his sister said again to her mother in a weary, kindly, yet triumphant tone. "You see what happens, don't you? . . . I've known it. . . . I've known it all the time," she said with sombre satisfaction. ". . . No, sir," she shook her head with a movement of emphatic conviction, as if some one had disputed her argument, "you can't change them! . . . You can't change the leopard's spots. . . . Murder will out. . . . You can't tell me!" she cried again, shaking her head in a movement of denial. "Blood is thicker than water. But you see, don't you?" she said again with this curiously kindly yet triumphant satisfaction; and then added illogically: "This is what comes of going to Harvard."

And his mother, who had been following this broken and almost incoherent discourse of his brother and sister with the quick, startled darting and attentive glances of an animal or a bird, now said nothing. Instead she just stood looking at him, her broad worn hands held at the waist for a moment in a loose strong clasp, her face white and stern, and her mouth pursed in a strong pucker of reproach. For a moment it seemed that she would speak, but suddenly her worn brown eyes were hot with tears, she shook her head at him in a strong, convulsive and almost imperceptible tremor of grief and disappointment, and turning quickly with a rapid awkward movement of her short figure, she went out of the room as fast as she could, slamming the door behind her.

When she had gone, there was silence for a minute, save for the gaseous flare and crumble of the coal-fire in the grate, and the stertorous, nervous and uneasy labor of Luke's breath. Then his sister turned to him, and looking at him with eyes which had grown dead and lustreless, and in a tone that was full of the sombre and weary resignation that was now frequent when she spoke, she said: "Well, forget about it. She'll get over it. . . . You will, too. . . . It's done now, and it can't be helped. . . . So forget it. . . . I know, I know," she said with a sombre, weary, and fatal resignation as she shook her head. "We all have these great dreams and big ambitions when we're twenty. . . . I know. . . . I had them, too. . . . Don't break your heart about it, Gene. . . . Life's not worth it. . . . So forget it. . . . Just forget about it. . . . You'll forget," she muttered, "like I did."

Later that night, when his sister had departed for her home and his brother had gone to bed, he sat with his mother in the parlor looking at the fire. Blundering, stumbling incoherently, he tried desperately to reassure her, to tell her of his resolution to expiate his crime, to retrieve his failure, somehow to justify her in the faith and support she had given him. He spoke wildly, foolishly, desperately, of a dozen plans in progress, promising aptly, swearing eagerly, and sure of nothing. He told her he was ready to go to work at once, to do any work that he could find—like a drowning man he clutched wildly at a dozen straws—he would get a job on the paper as a reporter; he would teach school; there were great sums of money to be made from advertising, he had a friend in that profession, he was sure he would succeed there; he felt sure that Professor Hatcher could get him placed at some small college teaching drama and play-writing courses; some one had told him he could find employment editing the little magazine or "house organ" of a department store in the city; a friend at college had secured employment as librarian of an ocean liner; another made large sums of money selling floor-mops and brushes to the housewives of the Middle West—he blurted out the foolish and futile projects feverishly, clutching at straw after straw, and halted abruptly, baffled by her silence, and by the sudden sickening realization that he no longer had a straw to clutch at—how foolish, futile, feeble all these projects were!

As for his mother, she sat staring straight into the fire, and made no answer. Then, for a long time, he sat there melancholy, saying nothing, while the woman looked straight ahead, hands clasped across her waist, looking into the fire with a fixed stare of her white face and puckered mouth. At length she spoke:

. . . "I have brought them all into the world," she said quietly, "and seen them all grow up . . . and some are dead now . . . and some have done nothing with their lives. . . . You were the youngest, and the last . . . my only hope. . . . Oh, to see them all, all go the same way . . . to hope and pray year after year that there would be one of them who would not fail—and now!" her voice rose strongly, and she shook her head with the old convulsive tremor, "to think that you—the one on whom my hope was set—the one who has had the education and the opportunity that the others never had—should go the way that the others went. . . . It's too bad to bear!" she cried, and suddenly burst into tears. "Too much to ask of me!" she whispered huskily, and suddenly drew the sleeve of the old frayed sweater across her weak wet eyes, with the pathetic gesture of a child—a gesture that tore him with a rending anguish of pity, shame, and inexpiable regret. "Too hard . . . too hard," she whispered. "Surely there's a curse of God upon us if after all the pain and sorrow all are lost."

And he sat there, sick with shame, self-loathing and despair, unable to reply. And then he heard again the remote demented howling of the wind, the creaking of bare boughs, the vast dark prowling of the beast of night about his mother's house. And again he heard, as he had heard a thousand times in childhood, far, faint, and broken by the wind, the wailing whistle of a distant train. It brought to him, as it had brought to him so many times, the old immortal promises of flight and darkness, the golden promises of morning, new lands and a shining city. And to his sick and desperate soul, the cry of the great train now came with a sterner and more desperate hope than he had ever known as a boy. Suddenly he knew that now there was one road, and only one before him—flight from this defeat and failure which his life had come to, redemption by stern labor and grim loneliness, the stern challenge, the sharp peril and the grand reward—the magic and undying image of the city. And suddenly he knew that he would go.

The night before he went away he went out and prowled restlessly about the streets of the town until the hour was very late. A letter from a friend had informed them that there was hope of a teaching appointment at one of the city universities, later, when the spring term began. Meanwhile, a swift exchange of telegrams had promised him temporary employment in New York, soliciting funds from alumni of his university, for a memorial building. And uncertain, specious, and disheartening as this employment seemed to him, he had eagerly seized the offer when it came. He was leaving home the next day.

Now, sick of soul and driven by the unquiet heart, the furious unrest, he prowled the barren night-time streets of his native town. The Square was bleak and lifeless and deserted, with its hard glare of lights: along the main street of the town a few belated citizens hurried past from time to time, faces and voices he remembered from his childhood, driven by like ghosts. Everything he saw and touched was strange and familiar as a dream—a life which he had known utterly and which now vanished from his grasp whenever he approached it—his forever, buried in his blood and memory, never to be made his own again.

When he returned home, it was after midnight, and his mother's old gaunt house was dark. He went quietly up the steps and into the broad front hallway, closing the heavy door quietly behind him. For a minute he stood there in that living dark, the ancient and breathing darkness of that old house which seemed to speak to him with all the thousand voices of its vanished lives—with all the shapes and presences of things and people he had known, who had been there, and who had passed or vanished, or had died.

Then quietly he groped his way along the dark old hallway, and towards the kitchen, and the little room beyond in which his mother slept.

When he got to the kitchen the room was dark, save for the soft flare and crumble of the fading ashes in the old coal range. But the kitchen was still warm, with a curious and recent currency of warmth and silence, as if it were still filled with his mother's life, and as if she had just been there.

He turned on the light and for a minute stood looking at the familiar old table with its sheathing of ragged battered zinc, and at the ironing board with its great stack of freshly ironed and neatly folded linen; and he knew that she had worked there late.

Suddenly, a desperate rush, an overmastering desire to see her, speak to her, awoke in him. He thought that if he could only see her now, he could reveal himself to her, explain the purpose of his failure, the certainty of his success. He was sure that now, if ever, he could speak to

her, and say the things he had always wished to say, but never said—
speak the unspeakable, find a tongue for the unspoken language, make
her understand his life, his purpose, and his heart's desire, as he had
never done before. And filled with this wild hope, this impossible conviction, he strode towards the closed door of her little room to rouse her.

Then abruptly, he paused. Upon an old cupboard, in a glass half-filled
with water, he saw, as he had seen a thousand times, grinning at him
with a prognathous, a strangely human bleakness, the false teeth she had
put there when she went to bed. And suddenly he knew he could not
speak to her. For grotesque, ugly, and absurd as they were, those grinning teeth evolved for him, somehow, as nothing else on earth could do,
the whole image of his mother's life of grief and toil and labor—the intolerable memories of the vanished and the irrevocable years, the strange
and bitter miracle of life. And he knew then that he could not speak,
that there was nothing he could say to her.

He rapped gently at the door, and in a moment heard her voice, quick,
sharp, and startled, roused from sleep, saying: "Hah? . . . what say?
. . . who's there?"

He answered: in a moment she opened the door and stood there, her
face startled, curiously small and white and sunken, somehow like a
child's. When he spoke to her, she answered incoherently: and then she
smiled in an apologetic and embarrassed manner, and covered her mouth
shyly with one hand, while she extended her other for the glass that held
her teeth. He turned his head away: when he looked again her face had
taken on its familiar contour, and she was saying in her usual tone:
"Hah? . . . What is it, son?" "Nothing, Mama," he said awkwardly. "I
—I didn't know you were asleep . . . I—I—just came in to say good-
night, Mama."

"Good-night, son," she said, and turned her white cheek up to him.
He kissed it briefly.

"Now go and get some sleep," she said. "It's late and you've all your
packing to do yet when you get up tomorrow."

"Yes," he said awkwardly. ". . . I guess you're right. . . . Well,
good-night." And he kissed her again.

"Good-night," she said. "Turn out the lights, won't you, before you
go to bed."

And as he turned the kitchen light out, he heard her door close quietly
behind him, and the dark and lonely silence of the old house was all
around him as he went down the hall. And a thousand voices—his

father's, his brothers', and of the child that he himself had been, and all the lives and voices of the hundred others, the lost, the vanished people, were whispering to him as he went down the old dark hall there in his mother's house. And the remote demented wind was howling in the barren trees, as he had heard it do so many times in childhood, and far off, far-faint and broken by the wind, he heard the wailing cry of the great train, bringing to him again its wild and secret promises of flight and darkness, new lands, and a shining city. And there was something wild and dark and sweet in him that he could never utter. The strange and bitter miracle of life had filled him and he could not speak, and all he knew was that he was leaving home forever, that the world, the future of dark time, and of man's destiny lay before him, and that he would never live here in his mother's house again.